We Are Now
Beginning Our Descent

Also by James Meek

The People's Act of Love (2005)
The Museum of Doubt (2000)
Drivetime (1995)
Last Orders (1992)
Mcfarlane Boils the Sea (1989)

We Are Now
Beginning Our Descent

James Meek

HarperCollins*PublishersLtd*

We Are Now Beginning Our Descent
© 2008 by James Meek. All rights reserved.

Published by HarperCollins Publishers Ltd, by arrangement with Canongate
Books Ltd, Edinburgh and New York.

First Canadian edition

HarperCollins books may be purchased for educational, business, or sales
promotional use through our Special Markets Department.

HarperCollins Publishers Ltd
2 Bloor Street East, 20th Floor
Toronto, Ontario, Canada
M4W 1A8

www.harpercollins.ca

Library and Archives Canada Cataloguing in Publication

Meek, James, 1962–
We are now beginning our descent / James Meek.

ISBN 978-0-00-200856-3

I. Title.

PR6063.E445W4 2008   823'.914   C2008-900839-1

RRD 9 8 7 6 5 4 3 2 1

Printed and bound in the United States.
Typeset in Sabon.

October 2001

1

At four a.m., when it was still dark and an hour before the Fajr prayer, Sarina Najafi got up, washed, dressed, ate a hasty breakfast of lavash and cheese and left her family's apartment on the tenth floor of a modern block on the southern outskirts of the Iranian city of Esfehan. Her father, mother and two brothers were still asleep. They were strictly Friday mosque-goers, and fifteen-year-old Sarina was no more devout than that, at best. But the director of her school was trying to make herself look good in the eyes of the basiji, the vigilantes of the Islamic Revolution, and all this week, Sarina and the six hundred other girl students who attended the Liberation of Khorramshahr High School would be praying five times a day. In Sarina's opinion, which she shared loudly and often with her friends, it was too much. Of course, girls had as much right to pray as boys, as the director said. But how would she ever get her class project finished, and study for her English test, with all this praying, all this getting up so early?

Sarina took the lift to the ground floor. Over her favourite lilac manteau she wore a black chador which left only her face showing, and over that, a satchel with her schoolbooks and the borrowed video camera for her class project. She tugged at the top of her chador where her stubborn fringe kept poking out. Whenever Sarina and her friends were a respectable distance away from the mosque, off would come the chador. Five times a day! It was a bore. She didn't like the thought that Faraj, her cousin, would see her in the drab garment, with his way of smiling at her in the street.

Outside it was cold. The harsh streetlights lit the bare earth and concrete. This was a new housing development, built to accommodate engineers and technicians who, like Sarina's parents, worked at the nuclear plant. There were no trees or grass yet, but the apartments were big and bright and the families were delighted with them. A kilometre away, Sarina could see the green neon signs hung on the temporary mosque. It had been converted from a sports hall the previous week. Just beyond, behind a high concrete wall and razor wire, was the nuclear plant. The president had visited a few months earlier, and had said some quite silly things, although Asal had whispered to Sarina that she thought he was good-looking and Sarina had hit her friend's arm.

There was little traffic at this time. Over the sound of the few cars and her own footsteps, Sarina heard a strange noise in the distance, a deep, fast thudding, like the lathes in her uncle's furniture workshop. Or like the sound when the president came. Yes, that was it: a helicopter. More than one, perhaps. Sarina walked on. Gradually other girls, dark ghosts in their chadors, began to fill the street. The sound of the helicopters faded and Sarina heard the giggles and murmurs of her fellow students. An amplified 'click' rang out across the district and the muezzin began their calls to prayer.

A new four-lane highway ran right to the gates of the plant, but the quickest way to the mosque lay across a large empty lot and down a much narrower street, between two rows of comfortable villas where the most senior nuclear engineers and their families lived. For the fourth morning in a row, Sarina found herself in a slowly moving, chattering column of girls dressed in black, sauntering through the pre-dawn darkness in their hundreds, passing under the streetlights like a river.

Sarina saw Asal waiting for her outside her house and greeted her.

'Come on, slowcoach,' said Asal.

'I hate these early starts,' said Sarina. 'Can you see how bad they are for my skin? Did you hear helicopters?'

'Yes!' said Asal, her beautiful eyes widening with fascination. It was the last word Sarina would ever hear her speak.

It all seemed to happen at once. Another sound came from the plant ahead of them, a sort of rattling and scraping, like a ruler dragged along a fence. From the front of the column of girls, they heard the sound of vehicle engines, and screams. Behind them, from the patch of empty ground, was the sound of the helicopters again, now deafeningly loud. Sarina looked back. She saw girls running in panic in different directions and enormous black shapes approaching the ground in clouds of dust. A siren began to moan from the direction of the plant. Sarina turned in time to see a series of blinding white flashes, followed by blasts which made her crouch down and cover her head with her hands. When she next looked, she saw something she could not make sense of. A column of trucks was driving up the street towards her, from the direction of the plant. Soldiers were hanging out of the windows and through holes in the roofs, carrying weapons and screaming in a language she thought she didn't understand but realised, with a shock, was English, although she didn't know all the words. The trucks kept stopping because there were hundreds of shrieking, panic-stricken girls blocking their way.

Without knowing why, she crouched against the wall and took out the borrowed video camera. She began to film. She recorded it all, under the harsh lights. The American soldiers screaming at each other. The stopping and starting of their trucks. The cry: 'Move forward! Move the fucking trucks forward! Any raghead bitch gets in the way, fucking light her up! Move!' The moving of the trucks into the mass of schoolgirls. The screams as their bodies went under the wheels. The shooting. Even when the bullets pierced Sarina's body, the camera continued to record, writing the billions of digits of information that would be found intact in her cold hand, later that morning, among the heaped bodies of the dead.

Adam Kellas halted the free scurry of his pen along the feint of the notebook, read back the last few sentences, crossed out 'raghead' and inserted 'towelhead'. He crossed out 'towelhead' and 'fucking'. *Any bitch gets in the way, light her up!* The extra pejoratives were superfluous. Without it, the sentence was tight, effective craft. Depending on the reader's view, it would provoke anger towards the US troops, or towards him, Kellas, the author. The direction didn't matter; the emotion did. It had the added virtue of distracting attention from the blandness of the petite paragon Sarina, whose only purpose from the off, it might otherwise be clear, was innocence and martyrdom. Six hundred elderly Iranian goatherds slaughtered in their claggy robes wouldn't make such a promising start.

Kellas put the pen down on the rough surface of the desk, locked his hands behind his neck and arched his back as far as it would go. He was surprised at how easy writing the beginning of the novel had turned out to be. He had covered four pages with handwriting in two hours, with not many crossings-out. The acquisition of the desk and chair had helped; he no longer had to write with the notebook resting on his knees, or the floor. Perhaps there'd be time to sand it down and varnish it, if Mohamed could obtain varnish and sandpaper here.

Kellas turned round. Mark was sitting on his mattress, holding his notebook in the crook of his handless right arm, while his good left hand flipped pages and worked his laptop. The room had whitewashed walls and windows on two sides. There was a recessed cupboard, which Mark and his photographer Sheryl had made their own before Kellas moved in; the three roommates each had a cheap tin trunk with brass clasps, along with their rucksacks. The floor was covered in a red fitted carpet and every square foot not covered by their mattresses had cables, power strips and chargers tangled across it. At night, when the main lights went out, and the generator was still on, the room shone with the red and green dots of batteries charging. It was ten p.m. Lately there'd been a great many aircraft overhead, gouging thunder out of the sky. Tonight the generator was the only sound.

Kellas liked Mark, but there were three reasons he disliked him. In fact, liking him – that was a fourth reason. Kellas wanted to know what had happened to Mark's hand, and he couldn't think of an excuse to ask him whether he'd been born that way or whether it had been accidentally severed, or blown off in an explosion, or the subject of a judicial amputation; so he did not ask. He shouldn't have had to. A man with a missing hand had an implied obligation to explain it to his roommates. That was the first reason. Another was that Kellas had overheard Mark yelling at one of the Northern Alliance functionaries, whose job was to shuffle the drivers around among the reporters, that he was an *American* reporter, that he didn't work for 'some bullshit European newspaper'. Kellas was cold with Mark for a while after this until Mark found out what was bothering him and told him not to be offended, that he had never considered Britain to be European. What Kellas most begrudged was how hard Mark worked. Their editors were in different time zones. Kellas's were in London and Mark and Sheryl's were in California. Mark had to work twelve hours of his Afghan day, and then he had to work twelve hours of his Californian day, the whole twenty four, no overlap. Kellas never saw him sleep. It was not that Kellas was lazy, but if a day passed and he wrote nothing, he wouldn't worry. Mark would. He was always interviewing people and trying to find out what was going on. He didn't spend enough time waiting for things to happen.

Kellas asked Mark if he could borrow a couple of AA batteries.

'Borrow?' said Mark.

'I'll get fresh ones back to you by the end of the week.'

'From where? You know the Irish guy? You know the one. The photographer. He came overland from Pakistan, horse and foot. Took him ten days. He's leaving tomorrow because he ran out of AA batteries and nobody'll dip into their stash to help him out.'

'I need a couple.'

'I don't have any. I don't use them. Those are Sheryl's. Ask her.'

'She thinks I've been taking her coffee, but I want her to know I bought my own. The jars look the same.'

'Why don't you tell her?'

'You could tell her when I'm not here.'

'What, are you afraid of losing face?'

'I don't like her.'

'Like her? You don't have to like her.'

Kellas turned his chair round so it was facing into the room. 'You work too hard.'

'So do you. You were out all day, you came back and filed a story, and you've spent the past two hours scribbling in that book.'

Kellas closed the book and put it underneath his laptop.

'What is that, a journal?'

'Yeah.'

Mark laughed and flipped a page in his notebook. He stuck a pencil between his teeth and frowned so that his thick black eyebrows joined together. Kellas could see from the way his shoulders shook that he was still laughing. Shadows moved across the window and indistinct voices came from outside. The compound was crowded. Kellas was lucky to have even a third of a room.

'What's funny?'

Mark shook his head. His eyes were wrinkling up now.

'What?'

Mark spat out the pencil, which bounced off his laptop screen. '"Dear diary! Sheryl wouldn't talk to me today! She is such a bitch! She'll soon find out that two can play at that game! And, oh my God, in Mazar-i-Sharif, six traitors were hanged in front of the shrine! Gross!"' He looked up. 'You know who else has AA batteries? Your friend Astrid Walsh. Right next door.'

'Are we friends?'

'She came across the mountains with you.'

'Some of the way. We parted company after we came over the Anjoman pass.'

'So ask her.'

'I should,' said Kellas, fidgeting with his pen. 'I went up to the hospital with her last night.'

Mark snorted. He was reading the wires. 'Can you believe it?' he said. 'This war's hardly started and they're already talking about the next one.'

Mark and Sheryl had been to their regular hangout that day, the mujahedin house near the front line. The roof had a view. It was more of a stakeout than a reporting opportunity. Sheryl would come back with photographs of explosions on a particular distant ridge where B-52s dropped bombs by the ton. She would spend most of the night editing and transmitting the pictures to her paper in the US. The Californians had an appetite for looking, over coffee, at the exact monumental broccoli shapes their bombs made in the sky after they were dropped. Once, Sheryl showed Kellas a much enlarged detail of one of her photographs on a laptop screen. He could see the bleached fangs of the ridge, the smoke and dust from the explosions wasting away into the blue, and perhaps, under Sheryl's tapping fingernail, something else.

'See him?' said Sheryl. 'See the lil' Taliban man?'

Maybe he could. There could have been a black vertical a few pixels high, and a horizontal. The beige point could have been a face. There could have been a Taliban fighter there, standing up from under his rock, deaf, exultant and choking from the bombs, opening his arms out wide and yelling to America that he was not martyred yet. Kellas couldn't be sure. Maybe it was a gap in the rock. Sheryl had lenses the size of buckets but the ridge was far beyond Alliance front lines. It was halfway to Kabul.

Mark was lost in his work. Kellas slid his notebook out and read through the opening again. He'd decided to write it a year earlier, a novel crafted to sell as many copies as possible in the shortest time, to be made into a movie and video game, to make Kellas enough money to spend the rest of his life writing whatever he liked, which might be nothing. He was thirty-seven. Up to that moment he'd written two novels in the time left over from reporting. He'd wanted them to be great literature, but they were neither great nor bad. Nor were they popular. This had been discouraging, rather than devastating. He reassured himself that each book was an end, and not a means to an end. It would have been difficult to believe if he didn't know that others were telling themselves the same thing. The poet Pat M'Gurgan told him in 1981, when they were about to leave school, that as a writer you could settle for being one year's good harvest from the land, or you could be the land. The characterisation appealed to Kellas. It became one of the expressions he considered wise and original when he was young. Later he might have thought it over, but in the interval, its value as wisdom had been replaced by its value as souvenir, and it didn't occur to him to touch it, particularly since M'Gurgan held to it, until one evening when Kellas, who by then lived in London, called M'Gurgan at his home in Dumfries.

After they'd talked for a while, M'Gurgan announced that he had stopped work on poems and his autobiographical novel. He was halfway through writing a new book, the first volume of a fantasy trilogy for teenagers.

'I don't care what you think,' said M'Gurgan aggressively, before Kellas could speak. 'I'm tired of being poor. The only people I know who read the kind of books I've written till now are my wife and other writers like you. I want to make some money. I want to be popular before I die. You're thinking I've sold my soul. Have you seen my soul recently? It's something the kids kick around the lounge when the telly's bad. Its eyes are hanging out.'

Kellas's skin seemed to stretch and contract over his body. His pulse was elevated. 'How do you know it's going to be a trilogy if they haven't published the first one yet?' he said.

'How do I know? One hundred and fifty thousand of Her Majesty's sweet little pounds, that's how I know.'

Kellas's decision came that night. It came: he didn't make it. It arrived while he was staring through his reflection into the spikes and feathers of his incorrectly thriving garden. It came, and his conscience would have to budge up to make room for it. He was beaten. The great words were not in reach and he would rather be popular than obscurely wise. He didn't delude himself that it would be simple to write a best-seller, to write a novel whose first characteristic was that it would appeal to the largest possible audience. Out there in London were hundreds of writers who believed they could easily write commercial novels if they wished, but chose not to. This false notion was the only barrier standing between them and the rolling floodwaters of despair. Kellas knew it would be hard. It could not be thought of as a lowering, or a coarsening. He would need to learn to be content in the new medium, not merely study it. The next day he bought five fat paperback thrillers with their titles and their authors' names on the front in embossed gold lettering two inches high.

In the September of 2001, after Kellas had made his notes and laid out his plot strands diagrammatically on large sheets of cartridge paper, using different coloured pens for each strand, a group of young men hijacked four airliners and flew them into the Pentagon and the World Trade Center in New York, causing thousands of deaths and great destruction. Kellas hadn't talked about his new book at work and when his colleagues at *The Citizen* saw him that day, staring at the TV monitors, chewing his lip, gripping the back of a chair, teeny fireballs popping in his eyes, they were awed at how hard he seemed to be taking it, as if he knew he had a friend trapped on the high floors. He didn't. He was watching a scenario almost identical to the one he had planned, in the secrecy of his study, as the climax for his novel.

He'd known the thriller market was crowded. He'd allowed for the danger that he might have to compete with a book with the same plot as his. But he had not foreseen the extent to which naïve idealists, with no understanding of human nature, no sympathy with the Other and a childlike faith in the use of violence to produce happy outcomes might persuade real people to act out their lousy plots in the real world. Kellas had worked hard to make his terrorist mastermind a one-sided figure of evil, when the character he had been looking for was a frustrated novelist who did not know he was one. It hadn't occurred to Kellas that men might find it easier to sell their thrilling, unlikely narratives to the masses by asking armies of believers to perform them than to vend their imaginations at airport bookstalls in the accepted fashion.

A few days later, the woman he'd been sleeping with for six months, Melissa Monk-Hopton, a columnist on *The Daily Express*, broke up with him, saying the terrorist attacks on New York and Washington had made her reassess her life choices. Those were the words she used. Kellas asked her how many other men and women she supposed had used the actions of a group of suicidal religious fanatics to rationalise their break-ups that week. She responded in her column next day, proclaiming an end to her 'shameful fraternization with the pusillanimous quislings of the liberal left'. He had desired her on the basest grounds. But even though, while she referred to him as 'my boyfriend', he referred to her out of her hearing as 'a woman I've been seeing', he'd been hurt by the manner of her leaving. It seemed curious to him that he put such a value on knowing women, on understanding women, and boasted to anyone about how much he enjoyed the company of women, yet had never been happy with a woman for more than a few months. He took some days off work and tried to drink but couldn't bring himself to do more than sniff the whisky before he poured it down the drain. He lay on the sofa for hours, cycling his way through the TV channels at two-second intervals, and ordered chicken kormas and calzones from the local takeaways. Salty juices dripped onto his clothes and dried. He studied the faces of the delivery boys, seeking signs of contempt in their eyes, but he saw only fear, or nothing.

When *The Citizen* came to him a few weeks later and asked him to travel to Afghanistan, to relieve a reporter north of Kabul, the editors made the offer in voices brimming with grandeur. They were grave about it, as if they were practising a tone to use for his next of kin, and they were excited. They wanted to be sure he knew he was to be both grateful and solemn. It wasn't the first time they'd asked Kellas to write about a war for the paper, but it was the first time he'd seen his editors so cherishing of each place on the roster. In other wars, fought between dull foreigners, Kellas and his peers would hack out their despatches and fling them homewards, fragmented lumps of narrative that lived and died in a day or two. What Kellas was being offered here was the privilege of slipping with his stories into a greater story, a baton-twirling lit-up marching parade of a story that belonged to a mighty nation of storytellers, myth-makers and newscryers, America, but which other, foreign story-tellers might attach themselves to. The fabulous thing was that it wouldn't matter whether he or anyone else in the great onrushing parade was shouting qualifications, or yelling in a different accent that events were occurring in an altogether other way. America's big loud story would jostle their little stories on together with its own, and his voice would add to the general din, and the general din would give his voice power. He could stay with the parade, or pipe up alone.

Kellas refused to go, and his editors told him they understood, although he didn't give them reasons. They guessed that he was drinking heavily, and the guess became procedure. They gave him the mixture of respect, fear, latitude and contempt that the letters trade gives presumed alcoholics. They knew he was shaken up by events, even if they didn't know that Osama bin Laden had stolen his idea for a book, that his closest friend was confined in an attic room writing about hobgoblins, and that he hadn't expected his lover to leave him. It was true that he didn't like Melissa, but she'd given him to understand that she was fond of him. She responded to his desire with her own, until the day she withheld, and never gave again.

What had changed Kellas's mind about going to Afghanistan, what had made him go back to his editors and persuade them to send him after he'd turned them down, was something he heard in the pub.

'Don't blame you for turning the Afghan gig down, mate,' the reporter said. 'Fucking scare the shit out of me.' He raised and lowered his glass and the lager suds drifted down from the brim. Kellas had nodded slowly, finished his drink and gone to look for the foreign editor. Like many others before him, Kellas found he wasn't brave enough to be thought a coward, and he had flown to the war.

A revised version of his opportunistic thriller had been gestating in him, like a well-loved grudge, ever since he arrived in Jabal os Saraj, until tonight, when it began to unload itself onto the page, with the help of the new furniture. Originally the house had no furniture, only carpets and mattresses: an Afghan house. Meals were served on a plastic sheet laid out on the floor. None of the Americans, Europeans or East Asians staying there had challenged this arrangement until a Spaniard, already marked out by his preference for comfort and his loathing for the eight o'clock rush to the mountains, who spent the morning lying on his back and wiggling his toes, one hand holding a novel above his face and the other supporting his head, who ambled out of the compound for a couple of hours around lunch and, when he came back, would be seen writing something for his newspaper without reference to notes, his thick heavy fingers striking the laptop keyboard as if it were an old typewriter prone to jam – this Spaniard was seen by all one day to have bought himself a deep armchair and a floor lamp, which threw a suburban orange light slantwise across his long rounded body while he sat there, at rest and serene. All he lacked was a television. (Later, he acquired one.)

Up to that moment the foreign journalists living in the house had expressed their defiance of local conditions either by bitching about the Afghans' commercial practices, or by flaunting their gear, their shining multi-tools in hand-stitched pouches, their lightweight trousers of spacesuit fabric or their high-bandwidth antennae, which folded out like altarpieces. The Spaniard's defiance was of a different kind. The sight of him sitting there in his armchair, when till then there had been nothing but red and blue carpet and cushions, affected Kellas. The lack of vertical furnishings hadn't bothered him before. After the journey in the lizard-coloured transport plane from Dushanbe to Faizabad, after the trip here through the mountains with Astrid in Russian cars, the house had delighted him with its plain brightness and its peace. Four walls and a roof, a generator, soft pallets to lie on at night, three meals a day if you wanted them and steel drums in the washrooms which were filled with water and heated by wood furnaces each morning and evening. Kellas didn't bitch about the Afghans. Two hundred bucks a day for a car, a driver and an interpreter was easy to pay. He was glad to be spending *The Citizen*'s money. Every fresh hundred dollar bill rubbed between his thumb and index finger and given to Mohamed – who would glance at it, smile, fold it in half, put it in his pocket and offset it against the thousands of dollars he owed to local small businessmen, each of whom owned an automatic weapon – was a bill less in the pouch Kellas wore around his waist. When he'd left London the pouch contained twelve thousand dollars. It felt as if a paperback was stuffed down the front of his jeans. When he squatted down over the outhouse hole in the morning and lowered his trousers he imagined the money belt breaking and him having to retrieve it from the Marscape of ordure down there, where mice scampered over hills of turds.

What moved Kellas when he saw the Spaniard in his armchair was an imaginative step bolder and more honest than any of the other foreigners in the house had taken. The Spaniard had dared to face the possibility of living among the Afghans for ever. He wouldn't, and knew it. But he had allowed the possibility. Living among the Afghans, that is, not as an Afghan; not growing a beard and buying a shalwar kameez and becoming a Muslim. The Spaniard had allowed the possibility to enter him that he might live among the Afghans not as a colonist, a soldier or an aid worker, but as the man he actually was, a tired, well-read, funny, sexually indulgent, godless, twice-married, wine-loving, seventy-thousand-euro-a-year writer from the rich side of the Mediterranean. By making himself comfortable and ignoring (except for lunchtimes) the war that pattered on just over the horizon, the Spaniard had travelled further into this foreign land than any other *farang* in the guesthouse.

Kellas sent Mohamed to get a desk and two chairs. Mohamed found them in the bazaar. They wobbled, on mixed metal and wooden legs. In this country even the furniture had prostheses. Like all the foreigners in the compound, Kellas was acting, but this time, inspired by the Spaniard, he had decided to change his role. In the clothes they wore, the things they carried and their actions, the journalists were explicitly transient. The Brits played soldier-explorers; the Americans doubled up as missionaries and prospectors. The French were buccaneering scientists, the kind who would kill to get the sarcophagus or bacilli back home before a rival; the Germans cast themselves as students on their study year abroad; the Japanese, astronauts landing on a foreign planet. Some of the British way was partaken of by Kellas, although for him it tended to be less exploratory or military than that of someone sent, with a handsome travelling allowance, to visit a poor relative he had never met and whose address he didn't know. All these roles had in common dealing with life in the hard countries, like Afghanistan or the Congo, but their salient characteristic was the way they helped separate the reporters from their bourgeois contemporaries who stayed safely at home. Such was the Spaniard's genius, and selflessness. There would have been nothing easier for him than to go home and impress his middle-class friends and any number of girls with stories of how he'd survived mines and mortars and Taliban roadblocks. He could ride through the dust clouds in a pakul hat with his teeth clenched and his eyes on the far distance, behind aviator glasses. It would impress nobody in Spain to hear that, in Afghanistan, he'd made himself a comfortable sitting room. For that reason the sitting room was the greater achievement. To take souvenirs of Afghanistan back to the bourgeois European world was trivial. To transport fragments of the bourgeois European world, however briefly, to Afghanistan, was a magnificent gesture. The Spaniard had made a sitting room; Kellas would make an office. He had the desk and the chair. He pinned a map to the wall above the desk. He had the computer. The final prop required was the phone, and although Jabal had neither landlines nor mobile coverage, he had one of them on his desk, too, a satellite phone, a square black object the size and weight of a toasted sandwich maker. It came with a small, square antenna that had to be outdoors, pointed at a satellite over the Indian Ocean, in order to work. Kellas had run the antenna out from the phone on a length of brown cable that stretched from his desk, through a small window and onto the second chair outside. The antenna stood on the seat of the chair, face to the southern stars.

Mark's satphone rang. It was still morning in America. It was the early call from his editors. Kellas was expecting a call of the same sort from London. It was overdue. He tapped one of the buttons on his phone. No bars.

Mark hung up. 'Not getting a signal?' he said.

'No,' said Kellas.

'I don't know if it's related,' said Mark, 'but you know that kid, the little one who guards the gate some nights? He was looking so happy and comfortable in a chair when I came in. It looked like one of yours.'

An emotion dragged at Kellas's insides. The hormones shot first and asked questions later. They fizzed, and notified the brain to step aside while they went about their work. Kellas, under anger's direction, got up and went out into the corridor in his socks. Past the door of the room Astrid shared with the NPR woman and the elderly fellow from Sweden. Had it been open and light and had she been there, cross-legged and the curve of her body over the laptop, eyes looking up through her blonde fringe, anger would have yielded. But not. Through to the broad lobby, past the humps of asleep Koreans, to the door. Boots! Forbidden in the house. Among that park of muddened suede and dust, stiff laces with space fabric, were Kellas's tanky Scottish boots. He had to find two among a hundred still boots before his anger stood down. It was not standing down, however. It was recruiting. Kellas found his boots. He was in too much of a hurry to loosen the laces and push his feet all the way in so he walked out into the darkness with his toes hooked under the tongue of the boots and his heels squashing down the backs. It made his stride jerky and galumphing, like a stop-motion animated monster from a 1960s B-movie. The cold night settled round him and the line of trees along the compound wall spread a dim net of twigs across the sky. Kellas came to the corner of the building and saw that the chair had been taken from underneath his window and the antenna left on the ground, facing the wrong way. The same thing had happened the night before. He had been angry then, but now it was more wonderful and intoxicating, a gush of rage that made him refreshed, clean and free. He was astonished to find so much of something in him that he hardly knew he even had a little of. He stalked over to the gate of the compound. The guard stood up quickly from the chair. He was a boy of fifteen or sixteen, a head shorter than Kellas, in a frayed shalwar kameez with an old v-necked woollen jumper on top. He wore plastic slippers on his bare feet. His Kalashnikov hung diagonally across his chest, held there by a filthy canvas sling over his shoulder. The varnish was almost worn off the stock, like a piece of driftwood, and each raised edge of pressed gunmetal was worn silver with age. It was probably the family gun, the only thing worth money he and his kin owned apart from sheep and daughters. The boy's broad face told Kellas how angry Kellas looked. The boy's head was uncovered and his hair was short and almost fair and he narrowed his eyes and pinched his mouth. He trembled a little and looked red and defiant. Kellas saw that this was how the boy's face would front up to a beating or a humiliation from an elder and that now he, Kellas, was the elder. The anger still poured through him, undammed, with the terrible quality of a flood, concealing or simplifying all boundaries. Kellas was both the flood and the body being carried along by it. Kellas grabbed the chair with his left hand and lifted it.

'I told you!' he yelled. 'That's my fucking chair!' The night seemed to record the words in a deep, adamantine groove, and play them back to Kellas many times. The part of him being carried away by the flood couldn't speak. The flood surged again and Kellas shouted the same words to the boy, who didn't move, and didn't utter a word. He didn't know English. Kellas's words were a mad roar.

With his left hand, Kellas shoved the boy in the chest. His palm came into contact with the teenager's hard warm little body for an instant before the boy teetered back a step. He recovered, compressed his mouth more tightly and stared into Kellas's eyes. Kellas turned and stomped to the house with the chair. The rage had ebbed and he felt calm. The shame came on behind. He placed the antenna back on the chair.

A sound came from the darkness overhead, as if the sky had turned to stone, and a slab was being dragged across it. Sometimes the engines of an American aircraft would hush or roar out suddenly. Kellas looked south. In the far distance he caught a faint flash. He heard the sentry boy murmuring behind him. He wondered if it was a prayer, or a curse. Kellas had fallen back on the striking and the screaming. Language was the obstacle, of course, but since the break with Melissa, Kellas had come to distrust words and his skill in their use even when he shared the language. Even in their moments of greatest apparent unity he and Melissa, and his ex-wife Fiona, and Katerina in Prague, had remained impermeably single.

Shoving the sentry boy was the closest he'd come to feeling the warmth of another human body since he'd put his hand on Melissa's bare shoulder to wake her up on the morning she left him. No, this wasn't true. For some reason he'd found himself holding Astrid's hand in the bus to the hospital the night before. They'd talked. They'd looked into each other's eyes. It was too bad that he no longer put faith in talking, or seeing. There'd been a time when Kellas thought the meeting of eyes, with its infinite regression of looking, him looking at her looking at him looking at her, and so on for ever, was the purest form of intimacy, when souls come close to meeting, like two birds flying down to drink from the same deep, narrow pool. Now he wondered if the meeting of eyes, even lovers' eyes, was nothing but a more refined form of blindness.

From many miles away, the slightest of thuds came from the direction of the flash. Strange that it should carry so far; a trick of the atmosphere. The sound of America prodding the surface of the night side of the world.

He intended to keep away from Astrid. He'd given up on an old hope that two people might form a whole. He remembered thinking once that two people could experience together a communion with the world that the solitary soul achieves easily. He could imagine. He had done that. The first time he'd fallen in love, as a boy, it had been with a girl he never spoke to. He achieved what he couldn't have if they'd been together: he shared the ecstasy of solitude. For that reason, and because it was the first time, it acted on him like a toxin, like not-fatal cancer. He recovered, but he was changed. Damaged, perhaps. Where love was concerned, it was impossible to distinguish between damage and mere change.

On the way to his room he passed Astrid walking in the other direction carrying an open laptop. She had on her too-big anorak. They smiled at each other.

'Hey,' said Astrid. Through her fringe her grey eyes looked at him with curiosity and doubt. She passed him and stopped and said over her shoulder: 'Did you get your chair back?'

Kellas turned round. 'The shouting wasn't cool,' he said.

'Yeah,' said Astrid. 'Young boys with guns. That's as proud as it gets.'

In Virginia she was a hunter.

'He wasn't going to use it on me.'

'That's what makes you a bully.'

'Was I being a bully?'

'Yeah. When unarmed men shove armed boys around because they know they can. What does it sound like to you?'

'I didn't see you at the bomb village today,' said Kellas.

'I got up early. I was out there and back by ten. The guy, Jalaluddin. He was so bereft. Fuck.'

Kellas had forgotten the name of the husband, although he had written it down. He did remember the man's bereftness when the reporters left him sitting on the ruins of his house.

'I gave him money,' said Astrid, looking past Kellas into space. 'Kinda wish I hadn't. Like I was trying to buy something. A hundred bucks.'

'It wasn't your bomb.'

'Oh, it was my bomb,' said Astrid absently. 'They're all my bombs.' She looked at him. 'Did you give him something?'

'Yeah. Same amount.'

'Here,' said Astrid. She closed the laptop, tucked it under her arm and put her free hand into one of her anorak pockets. She took out a couple of Duracells and held them out to him. 'Mark said you needed some.'

Kellas thanked her and lifted the batteries from her hand. His fingertips touched her palm. He felt the trace of damp in the lines that crossed it and the warmth that the heat of the computer had left there.

'Thanks. I don't know when I can give these back,' he said. Astrid was opening her laptop again. The cuffs of the anorak rustled against it.

'But you will, right?' she said.

'As soon as I can.'

'Don't forget!' she said over her shoulder. She was smiling when she said it. Kellas called after her to see if she wanted to take a walk later, but she didn't answer.

December 2002

2

When the express to Heathrow left Paddington, Kellas's mobile phone vibrated in his pocket. Although he had no intention of answering, he took it out and looked at the display each time he felt the buzz. It was his voicemail. He had eighteen new messages. He had twenty text messages, and forty missed calls.

If he'd had the kind of mobile in Afghanistan that could take pictures, a year ago, Kellas would have a photo of Astrid now. Perhaps it was best that he hadn't. She wouldn't have aged. She was thirty-four then. But a person's nature shows in motion and change, and this made the stillness of every portrait photograph a kind of lie. Memory was more plastic. The gap between how you remembered a friend and how they were when you met again could be pinched, joined and smoothed over by memory when there was no photograph in the way. Now that Kellas had a camera phone, he knew the game, where you kept taking pictures of each other until you were left with a single image that pleased you both. If months passed without meeting again, the agreed truth of the moment became its possessor's holy image. You either stopped believing it, or you began to give it your faith.

The phone buzzed with an SMS from Liam Cunnery. *Psychotherapist says Tara showing signs of post-traumatic stress. Well done Adam.*

The train had left the station at nine a.m.; Kellas was catching a flight to New York at eleven. Was it possible that Cunnery had got Tara in to see a psychiatrist able to diagnose post-traumatic stress in a ten-year-old child in the nine hours since midnight? He could have. He had a confident private school voice and an alert, sly, bright-eyed 'Follow me!' look, promising London mind-healers that they, too, could be part of the international struggle for the rights of the oppressed in which Cunnery acted as invigilator. Alternatively, there was patronage. A thousand-word opinion piece in the weekly Cunnery edited, *Left Side*, was still a prize for an ambitious shrink. The claim of post-traumatic stress was more dubious. Didn't you have to wait for the trauma to be at least a day old before the post-stage kicked in? Cunnery's use of 'psychotherapist' in full, in a text message, struck Kellas. Cunnery tended to the brisk and cheery in his personal communication and to the apocalyptic and enraged in his magazine. Tall, sallow and well-dressed, slightly hunched, he moved between restaurants and offices in Clerkenwell, Bloomsbury and Westminster with a set smile on his face and a permanent furrow of concentration in his brow, like a surgeon in the soaps. Women told each other they were ready to be seduced by him, but he wasn't interested in that direction. As a lover, he stayed close to his wife Margot. An ectoplasm of higher purpose lingered in his wake. Even indoors, he seemed to be cutting through slipstream, as if the wind of change couldn't resist playing with his soft fair hair wherever he was. When you caught him in a good mood it meant that some atrocity had been committed in a country far away for which the British government, the American government, capitalism, the IMF, the World Bank, multinational corporations and the Vatican must be held responsible, regardless of the identity of the victims and perpetrators. The only time Kellas had seen him gloomy was when the Soviet Union fell in. Cunnery's depression lasted for a day or two before he realised that the end of the communist superpower meant the last constraint to blaming everything atrocious on Washington and capitalism had been removed. It gratified Kellas that now, when Cunnery considered his own young daughter had been involved in an atrocity, he didn't blame the White House or the World Bank. He blamed Adam Kellas.

The train gathered speed through west London. The December sky showed in turquoise wedges between ramps and pillars and the sun seared white patches on nettles and hawthorns and two-litre cider bottles by the trackside. Kellas heard Afghanistan mentioned on the BBC news bulletin being played back inside the carriage. The screen opposite showed a still picture of Hamid Karzai. A new moment of inaccuracy by the United States Air Force was being reported. Kellas hadn't been back to Afghanistan since he bought a place on a helicopter out of the Panjshir valley a few months after arriving. With the helicopter roaring and bouncing off the ground and the co-pilot looking back over his shoulder to check everyone had paid up, with the loadmaster in corduroy trousers and a leather jacket shaking a fist stuffed with dollars at Kellas and Astrid and shrieking 'Six hundred! Six hundred!' over the noise of the engine, with the twenty other foreigners and Afghans wedged into place over luggage and fuel tanks and looking robbed and nervous and impatient, Kellas had given his money to the load-master and Astrid had put hers back in the pocket of her jeans. She'd shouted in Kellas's ear: 'I'm not coming. Don't call me', grabbed her rucksack and jumped out of the open door. Kellas made it to the edge after her, with the loadmaster's hand squeezing his upper arm and yelling in Dari, and saw her already fifty feet, sixty feet away on the flattened grass below the rising helicopter, sprawled where she'd fallen, getting up, hoisting her rucksack on her shoulders and walking to the cluster of drivers and officials without looking back, the tails of her headscarf writhing in the last of the helicopter's downdraft. Then they were atoms of colour on the sliver of green and mulberry groves by the tilted blade of the river, and the mountains pressed in around the gasping aircraft like the hands of blind giants seeking a dragonfly by its hum, and the loadmaster half-flung Kellas to a place away from the door. That was the last time he'd seen or heard from Astrid, until a few hours ago, when he'd picked up her email begging him to come to see her immediately.

She'd been strong for a skinny-armed, thin-shanked woman, the way she toted that rucksack. It would sit upright on the ground, sagging at the top, and she would bend at the waist to hoist it. Her wrists would poke out thin and white from the sleeves of her too-big anorak, her fringe would hang down and her jaw would come forward a little way. A sound would come from her lungs as she held the strap of the rucksack and took its weight and swung it onto her back. One time he had offered to help and she shook her head. She would notice him watching her. Sometimes she would smile and sometimes she would not, but she would never look him in the eyes until the rucksack was up on her back and the straps were tight. More than once in Afghanistan Kellas had caught himself thinking about the sound, the exhalation with voice, which came from her involuntarily as the weight pressed on her. He thought of the air in her breast, and the rush of it in her larynx, and the bones containing them, and the flesh around them. He'd recognised the thing of which this tiny sound was the centre: a fascination. A fascination was what came about when a single life wasn't enough to contain the presence of someone else inside him. He needed to be running two or three lives at once. Not even words had made the fascination, just the flex of her limbs and the tiny sound as she took the strain of her pack. Just those things had crossed into him, and faint as the chances were, he wanted to follow them back to their source.

On the train Kellas's skin prickled. He had no idea where his bag was. He began to get up from his seat, then remembered he had no luggage, only his passport, wallet and mobile and the clothes he was wearing, a black linen suit, a white shirt with a blood-stained right sleeve, and a pair of black leather boots, city boots, with smooth soles and side zips. He'd abandoned his coat at the Cunnerys' and spent the night at a hotel because he'd been afraid to go home. If he'd gone back to his flat in Bow and picked up Astrid's message there he would have packed a bag of some kind but still, flying across the Atlantic without anything to carry was something he'd never done. He'd imagined it like this, that he'd be travelling alone, answering an urgent call, discarding all burdens, walking away from things he should attend to if duty were the only consideration. He'd imagined that he wouldn't have to worry about money on the journey, and this, too, had come about. A publisher was offering him an advance of a hundred thousand pounds for world rights to *Rogue Eagle Rising*, the thriller he'd begun in Afghanistan. The book was finished.

Just before going to Central Asia Kellas had been to stay for a few days with M'Gurgan and his wife Sophie in Dumfries. They had a two-storey Victorian terraced house faced in red stone in the middle of town. Kellas had grown up in one like it on the mirror side of Scotland, on the north-east. It must have seemed to adult visitors then like the M'Gurgan place seemed to him now, with the same unbalanced, clashing, comfortable slew of furniture, home-painted sticks from the auctions and the one good sofa, scuffed walls with crayon marks, the fortune in derelict toys and electronics stacked in dusty piles on wardrobe tops. There was a working light bulb in every room, but not always a lampshade around it. Clothes of all ages and sizes were drying in at least two rooms and any place not immediately accessible to a simple vacuum cleaner had a miniature rockfall of bran flakes and plastic soldiers uncleared against it. Kellas and M'Gurgan had been at school together for six years before they left Duncairn and M'Gurgan, who'd lived in an almost bookless bungalow in one of the new estates by the Aberdeen road, envied the Kellas bookshelves, spread along hallways, hung under ceilings and crammed between chimney breasts. He ran his hand back and forth against the spines of an old set of Dickens that had belonged to Kellas's grandfather, swore when he saw how Kellas's mother had repaired with insulating tape a first edition of *Deaths and Entrances* from the same collection, and pressed his nose against the pages of an early *Alice in Wonderland*. He ran his nostril up the margin and inhaled, lifted his face, big and rosy already at fourteen years old, grinned till

29

his cheeks dimpled and said to Kellas: 'I feel like I just sniffed the Reverend Charles Dodgson's stash of young girls' knickers.' This was beyond Kellas at the time. After M'Gurgan had gone, he took the book to his room and sniffed the pages till he sneezed but couldn't and didn't want to believe that girls' underwear smelled of damp basements. In Dumfries, M'Gurgan the patriarch, by his own boast, wanted to emulate and surpass the Kellas family home library and had done so. Every hallway was narrowed by book-shelves, books ran along the tops of doorways, books advanced in steps up the wall beside the staircase, lined the windowsills and occupied the flat tops of toilet cisterns. M'Gurgan wrote in the half-converted attic, in a tiny cell walled-in by books and lit by a well of sky from a roughly glassed-over hole punched in the roof.

Dinner was unlike the Kellas dinners of his childhood. The television didn't stand at the head of the table, it was absent from the kitchen where the M'Gurgans ate. The table was loud, busy and brawly, illuminated by fights between the two M'Gurgan daughters from his first marriage and the son and by decent wine. M'Gurgan insisted that the children, who were aged from eleven to sixteen, drank wine. He poured them each full glasses, topped off with a finger of tap water. Sophie watched without saying anything, waiting for her husband's folly to meet its natural punishment. M'Gurgan proposed a toast to Kellas and raised his glass. Kellas and Sophie raised theirs and the children, as if by prior agreement, sat with their arms crossed, staring at their father.

'Children, I'd really appreciate it if you'd raise your glasses and drink a toast to our friend Adam, who's come all the way from London to see us, and who's going to Afghanistan next week,' said M'Gurgan.

'He hasn't come to see us, he's come to see you and Sophie,' said Angela. 'What would he be coming to see me for? I'm a fourteen-year-old schoolgirl and he's a forty-year-old man.'

'Thirty-seven,' said Kellas.

'Like there's a difference,' said Angela, looking steadfastly and dangerously at her father. 'I'm going to tell at school that you're getting me drunk and pimping me out to old men.' Carrie, the older girl, glanced at Kellas and giggled.

'Angela, I don't want you using that gangster language,' said Sophie.

'What's pimping?' said the boy, Fergus.

M'Gurgan said: 'I would like you all to show a little respect to me, your father, to my friend Adam, and to this 1996 Bordeaux, which I paid fifteen pounds for at Haddows.'

'It smells like bus shelters,' said Angela.

'You shouldn't be encouraging us. We're not old enough for binge drinking,' said Carrie.

'It's not binge drinking!' shouted M'Gurgan, banging his fist on the table. 'It's civilised – European – French – Jean-Paul fucking Sartre culture.'

'Oh, I feel dead civilised now,' murmured Angela. 'If you're wanting us to drink alcohol, how come I can't have a blue Margarita?'

M'Gurgan's face darkened and he stretched his arm out at Kellas. 'Do you realise that by this time next week, Adam could be blown to pieces by a landmine? Sorry, Adam.'

'It's OK,' said Kellas. 'Hope I won't, though.' He grinned. 'Cheers,' he said, raised his glass and took a drink.

'Aye, cheers,' said M'Gurgan. The prospect of Kellas's violent death soothed everyone and the daughters took prim sips of wine. Angela wrinkled her nose and stuck out her tongue and Fergus, who'd already emptied his glass, held it out for more.

As the meal drew to its end, with the second bottle almost empty and the children gone, Kellas began to feel the fright before his confession hopping in his stomach. He wanted to receive the same kind of shallow loving anger M'Gurgan had shown Carrie and Angela. True disappointment would be tolerable. The worst would be understanding, the absence of surprise. He feared M'Gurgan had expected him to sell out all along. He was about to ask M'Gurgan how his fantasy trilogy was coming along. Sophie spoke before he could open his mouth, to ask if he was still seeing Melissa.

'It was a mistake,' said Kellas.

'Who's that? Did I meet her?' said M'Gurgan.

'You know you did,' said Sophie. 'The posh one.'

'Oh, I remember her,' said M'Gurgan, smiling. He twirled his empty glass by the stem and tapped the rim against his upper lip. He regarded Kellas. 'I remember you explaining that.'

'Do you?' said Kellas.

'You said you'd always had an ambition to sleep with a right-wing woman,' said M'Gurgan. 'You felt they'd be less encumbered by guilt than the left-wing ones. They'd assume they were entitled to pleasure. You hoped they might share some of their selfishness with you.'

'I don't remember saying any of that,' said Kellas. A smile worked at the edge of his mouth.

'Did she not meet up with your hopes?' said Sophie. She was looking hard at Kellas, with curiosity, her very dark brown eyes intent under her cropped chestnut hair. The three of them had attended the same school in Duncairn, although M'Gurgan's timetable had been such that he did not meet her until years later.

'Liam Cunnery knows her,' said Kellas. He realised he was blushing and looking down at his hands as he fidgeted with the pepper mill. He looked from M'Gurgan to Sophie and back, grinned and looked down at his hands again. 'He gave her a job as a TV researcher once. He does a nice job of separating the person from their ideas. He can pick out Melissa's ideologies and get on with Melissa, like a vegetarian picking out the scraps of bacon from a salad and leaving them on the side of his plate. But she is a snob, and she does think rich folks' kids are born brighter. And the last thing she said when she was leaving was: "You know, Adam, if your cock could have been just half an inch bigger." She held her fingers up, like that. The precision of it, like some kind of scientific instrument. I think she might have closed one eye when she did it.'

Their laughing was in the downswing a short time later and M'Gurgan went to fetch another bottle. Upstairs, they heard one of the girls scream, a door slam, and Fergus singing the chorus from *Hotel Yorba*. When he got to 'I'll be glad to see ya later', there was a series of thuds and a moan.

'I'll go,' said Sophie. She went upstairs making anxious threats.

'Your boy's drunk,' said Kellas.

'We got drunk when we were boys.'

'We're drunk now.'

'Come on,' said M'Gurgan. 'Walk.'

Fergus's head injury wasn't serious. Kellas and M'Gurgan walked through the streets of Dumfries. It was Tuesday night and the pubs had long since closed. Cars rounded corners in ones and twos, somehow hunched in the darkness and furtive. A stout old man tautly zipped into a synthetic fleece walked slowly behind a panting black Labrador. His belly swung slightly as he walked, like a side of pork nudged in the chill room. A drunken girl yelped and swore a few streets away. Passing a darkened pub, they thought they heard the clack of two pool balls inside and M'Gurgan hammered on the door, suspecting a lock-in. No one came. They arrived at the square. The clocktower said midnight. They leaned against the plinth under the Robert Burns statue and M'Gurgan passed Kellas a plastic bottle of Grouse.

'He was our age when he died,' said Kellas, nodding up at the poet.

M'Gurgan said: 'His wife had their last kid on the day they buried him.' He was slurring his words a little. 'He was such a fecund bugger and I think half the boys round here have his genes. You'd think condoms had never been invented. I hate to be the untrusting father but when you see the carry on like tonight with Angela and Carrie, you think are they just winding me up with the not-drinking or is one of them pregnant? Children are like books. Once you've finished making them, they're not yours any more.'

Kellas knew the time was coming when he would have to tell M'Gurgan what he was writing. He asked M'Gurgan if he'd finished the first book of his fantasy trilogy.

'I changed my mind,' said M'Gurgan.

Kellas's arms pimpled and he shivered. 'What do you mean?' he said.

'I changed my mind.' He shrugged and screwed the cap back on the bottle. 'I gave the money back. I'm not doing it.' He looked at Kellas, widened his eyes and made a single high-pitched note of laughter. 'I haven't told Sophie. She might leave me. She's been planning a holiday in Egypt for us.'

'She won't leave you.'

'Yeah. Maybe. Ah, I couldn't do it. It was ridiculous. I was sitting there one night and I realised I'd spent two days coming up with names for elves. I was saying to myself should it be Balinur, or should it be Balemar? Or Balagun? And I realised I'd turned into this raving fool. I wanted to sell out so we could live better but I couldn't look at Fergus in a Versace suit if I knew it'd been bought by a man sitting in an attic inventing names for non-existent creatures with pointy ears. Maybe there's another way. I'm back onto *The Book of Form* now.'

Kellas made approving sounds. He knew *The Book of Form*. M'Gurgan was a poet and it was a poet's novel. He'd been working on it for fifteen years. It was dazzling, lovely, like exquisitely tooled, streamlined, burnished parts of a flying machine that hadn't been put together because they'd never been designed to be, couldn't fit, and would never fly.

M'Gurgan asked Kellas what he was writing. Kellas began to answer him slowly by referring to a novel. While he spoke, his mind was scouring the void for a way to justify to a socialist Scottish poet he had known since childhood – who, despite having learned *To Brooklyn Bridge* by heart at the age of nineteen and

34

being able to pick out a good part of the American folk song cata-
logue on his twelve-stringed guitar, would refer to Americans as
'fucking Yanks' – the writing of a commercial thriller designed
from the first page to appeal to audiences in multiplex cinemas in
the mid-western states of the US and to young male aficionados
of shoot-'em-up computer games. He could only think about Robert
Burns, and how M'Gurgan the father was vexed by the promis-
cuity of Burns' young descendants, and how M'Gurgan the remnant
boy, as a known Dumfries poet, was not certain to be loyal to
Sophie, and how time forgave poets any degree of infidelity, not
only to their wives but to their ideals, so long as they were passion-
ately, lyrically sung at the moment they were sung. Burns the
Scottish patriot and the British patriot, Burns the monarchist-
revolutionary. Burns who sang in joy at the French Revolution, and
sang in joy at the American Revolution. What song would he have
written if the French had tried to make the American Revolution
for the Americans before the Americans were ready? A gust of air
blew through Kellas's brain, clearing the fat spirals of wine and
whisky twirling there. Kellas began to explain his new book to
M'Gurgan as if he'd always intended it to be this way, but it came
to him then and there, as he spoke it. He explained to the poet
how he intended to write a best-selling novel pitched at the militaristic market. It would subvert the genre by making America the
enemy – not a group within America, but the American government, the American majority and the American way. American
characters would be portrayed as clichéd, humourless, two-dimen-
sional, degenerate, ignorant caricatures, while their European counterparts, the heroes and heroines, would be wisecracking, genuine,
loving, courageous, salt-of-the-earth types. The book would play on
the reservoir of anti-Americanism and European patriotism that went
so deep and was so seldom tapped. Readers would be made to
believe in a limited war to save civilization, with a motley group of
British, French, German and perhaps even Spanish, Italian and
Russian warriors defeating a perfidious American plot to thwart

international justice. Europeans would love it. It would be denounced in pulpits and on talk radio in the States, and Americans would hate it and would buy it in enormous quantities to find out what was so worth denouncing. Kellas hadn't plotted the whole thing out, he said, but it would surely include a scene in which the Europeans would storm a US airfield in East Anglia using a collection of iconic old vehicles.

'I think there'll be an Austin Allegro,' said Kellas. 'A British woman pilot at the wheel and a veteran of the Foreign Legion shooting down an American bomber with a missile poked out of the sun roof.'

M'Gurgan didn't say anything while Kellas was talking, and didn't look at him, just stood there with his back against the plinth, frowning and blinking, head slightly bowed. After Kellas had finished there was silence for a time. A police car slowed down opposite them, then speeded up and disappeared.

'What's it called?' said M'Gurgan.

'I haven't got a title.'

'How about *The Antichrist Strikes Back*?'

Kellas smiled. M'Gurgan asked if it was satire. Kellas was about to say yes and hesitated because it would not be the truth. He shook his head. The book would only work if it appeared sincerely shallow. If he was going to do it, lying to the readers wouldn't be necessary; all that mattered would be lying to himself and believing himself when he made the world a simpler, sillier place than he thought it was. Although he hadn't spent much time with prostitutes, and had until now avoided becoming one himself, he understood what made some more popular than others. It was the opposite of satire. They entranced themselves into an appearance of sincerity so perfect that it was indistinguishable from sincerity.

'You know I meant it when I said I liked your last one,' said M'Gurgan. 'I loved *The Maintenance of Fury*. I think you were onto something there.'

'I never saw it in a bookshop.'

'You look miserable. Do you think I'm going to give you a hard time over this?'

'Maybe I'll change my mind, like you.'

'I don't think so. But you'll never sell a book like that now. Everybody reckons America's the wounded puppy after the Twin Towers went down.'

'What do you mean, you don't think so?'

'You're closer to soldiers than I am to elves. You're going to Afghanistan next week. I'm not going to the enchanted forest to make magic with some bunch of goblins.' M'Gurgan flung out his hand in irritation, as if he was shooing a wasp out of a room. 'Everybody compromises. It's hard to be pure.'

Kellas took the train back to London the next day. He'd already obtained his Russian visa. He'd flown to Moscow, got a visa for Tajikistan, bribed his way to a ticket on Tajikistan Airlines, flown to Dushanbe, acquired an Afghan visa and flown in the lizard-coloured plane to Faizabad. M'Gurgan had been wrong. By the time Kellas returned from Afghanistan, the US prison camp at Guantánamo Bay had opened and Kellas and others like him had begun sending off for maps of Iraq. In London, Frankfurt and Paris they heard the rising note of puppy snarl. His book had not been hard to sell.

The Heathrow train was in the tunnel beneath the airport, slowing down. Kellas stretched and folded his arms. A stickiness in there. He would have to buy a fresh bandage before getting on the plane. He watched the business people line up their briefcases on wheels in the aisle.

There was one message he would reply to. His thumb worked the keypad, telling his agent to fax the final contract for the book to his publishers' office in New York. He'd sign it there. He stepped out of the train into the contrived shadows of the station's south aisle. He was the only one not hurrying. Suits and briefcases on wheels flowed around him. He read M'Gurgan's single contribution to the morning's flow of text messages. It said: 'Adam. More blood and darkness than you or we deserve. Call me.'

He switched off the phone and walked towards the escalators.

3

Kellas bought a first-class, one-way ticket to New York at one of the airline counters. He'd never flown first class. The saleswoman was friendly. Perhaps they were more friendly after you paid four thousand pounds for a first-class seat. It was a lot to pay for an extra square yard of space, free champagne and metal cutlery. He was going to spend like a lottery winner for a few days. He might turn out to be good at being rich. He'd been watching them. He noticed that they made luxury seem like something that had been imposed on them regardless of their wishes. It was impossible to tell whether they enjoyed champagne or not. It was what was provided, like water in the tap, and they bore it.

'You've been in the wars,' said the saleswoman when she handed him his documents. She had a Sinhalese name. She wore dark, heavy lipstick and had a constellation of tiny moles, like freckles, on her cheekbones. She was looking at his grubby bandage, which looped out from under his cuff over the base of his thumb and back inside the sleeve.

'Yes, I have,' said Kellas. He smiled. 'It's a war wound.'

The woman's mouth turned down at the corners and her eyes became rounder. 'From where?' she asked.

'From Camden last night,' he said.

'You should get it seen to before you board. Have a nice flight.' She smiled widely and he thanked her and walked away. She'd been checking on him, that he might not behave in an inappropriate way, bleed like the underclass on the starched napery of a 747's royal enclosure. He looked round and at the same moment she looked up from her screen and caught his eye. This time she didn't smile. She looked anxious. He should have stayed away from the war wound fuckwittedness, the being cute. The ticket clerk's family was probably from Sri Lanka some generations back. Who knew what real war wounds flexed sinuous and pink here, crimped by healed-up thread holes, under nice jeans and skirts and T-shirts.

Once through check-in and security, Kellas went to Boots. He bought a pack of AA batteries and asked if they had bandages. It turned out that they did, a clinical range and variety, as if regiments of the wounded regularly stopped to change their dressings in transit through Heathrow. Four laden shelves barked the legacy of sawbones past, with layers of boast like the multidecker ads in old newspapers. Advanced First Aid – Stops Bleeding Fast – Dressings – For Larger Cuts And Grazes – Absorbs Blood – Hypoallergenic, said one box. Faster Healing – Skin Closure Kit – For Deeper Cuts. Kellas took two of these, and two stretch bandages (High Quality – Non-fray – Bandages To Hold Dressings Firmly In Place). He would use one of each, and the remainder would constitute his goods for the voyage to America. He didn't want to enter the first-class saloon with frayed bandages. By the time he reached the washroom, a luxurious bead of fresh blood was stroking its way towards the saddle of his hand. Kellas yanked a wad of paper towels from the dispenser but still a drop fell onto the floor tiles before he could blot it up. A cleaner in a green polyester suit set down his bucket some distance away.

'You can't do that in here,' he said, as if a place elsewhere in the airport had been set aside for that purpose, with its own pictogram. The bleeding man, black on yellow.

'Sorry,' said Kellas, ducking down and removing the spot with a dab and a smear. 'I need a fresh bandage.'

He took off his jacket, laid it next to the washbasin, rolled up his bloodied sleeve and ran the bandaged arm under a stream of cold water. He'd made a mess of it, and he was going to make a mess of it again, because it was hard to dress a wound on your own forearm. He took off the ragged cloth he'd bound the cut with, using teeth as a third hand, a few hours earlier. Now the cloth looked a hundred years old. Washed, the cut was long, not deep, a sticky channel where the clot had split down the middle and begun to bleed again. A doctor might counsel stitches, but he could get by without. It was still difficult to understand how he'd done it, although he had filled the Cunnerys' with sharp, jagged edges in a short time. He'd been efficient enough in that way and only when all the women, Melissa, Lucy, Sophie, Margot and Tara, were screaming and yelling at once had he grown tired and careless. All the men, too; a seamless bellowing and barking, like cattle and wolves in the pen together, disturbed from their struggle with each other by a more terrible common enemy from the plain beyond. It was perhaps the sight of the blood that had stopped them laying hands on him for long enough for him to run out of the house.

He took the skin closure kit and bandage out of the Boots plastic bag, out of their boxes and out of their clear plastic wrapping and laid them on either side of the tap. The men coming and going from the washbasins on either side all glanced at his medical supplies. Nobody asked, and the question marks were hidden in the sound of flushing and banging cubicle doors and zips and hot air dryers. Kellas picked up the kit and prepared to use his teeth. He felt a hand on his shoulder and the cleaner took the kit from him. Without speaking, without looking at Kellas's face until the end, the cleaner took charge of Kellas's wound. He had warm, gentle hands, slightly rough, and treated Kellas with the fatherly, sceptical firmness of a cheap barber. He had grey curly hair and a grey moustache and North African features. He must have been in his fifties. A smell of cologne came from the warmth of his head and neck. Kellas was grateful for the help and more grateful still that the cleaner neither spoke nor expected him to speak. He had intended to ask his name, and where he was from, but when the cleaner finished his swift, neat work, stood back, grasped the haft of his mop and nodded at Kellas,

Kellas only said 'Shukran', one of the cluster of words he'd memorised since beginning to learn Arabic a few months earlier in anticipation of the invasion of Iraq.

The cleaner smiled. 'You're welcome,' he said. 'Have a nice flight.'

When he came back out into the lurid mall of departures Kellas felt an unpleasant tang at the back of his mouth and began to blink. The cleaner had been kind; kindness was not good for Kellas now. It would have been better if the cleaner had punched him in the face. Kindness was fine by itself, but shame was always tagging along behind it, wanting to join in. When you saw kindness, you knew shame was around the corner, with all its snivels, whimpers and regrets. Where are you flying to today, sir? New York? That's lovely. And could I just ask, what are you flying from? Your enemies? That's not what it says here, sir. Look, it says 'Friends'.

What he needed was to see the aircraft, the broad, heavy, thick-winged, four-engined ones, quaking along the runway and floating free of the ground like mercy, like a miracle, towards the ocean. When he saw them move and take off, he would be all right. One of them would carry him away into the clouds and out to the blue west. He was not a fugitive, although others could think it. He had gone back before dawn and pushed a blank cheque through Cunnery's letterbox, with 'Whatever it takes' written on the back, in capitals, for some reason. They could think that he was on the run from them but that was because they did not know he was running towards someone else. He had wanted to see her for a year and now she had asked to see him, and he was coming. Kellas started to walk towards the departure gate.

He passed a woman in low-cut jeans and a cropped green woollen cardigan which showed her belly and her shoulders. She had her hair in lacquered ringlets and scarlet lipstick over a deep tan and a gold stud in her belly-button and she went by on heels, hauling a carry-on bag behind her. She glanced at him and looked away. He would like to have been sure he wasn't crossing the Atlantic for sex. People did this. Men and women flew tens of thousands of miles, expending hundreds of pounds and thousands of litres of jet fuel, in order to have sex, and not only middle-aged, rich-world sex tourists in Bangkok or Zanzibar, but fit, attractive young men and women from London or Brisbane or Buenos Aires who'd got tangled up with somebody who lived on the other side of the world and who, even though they were not fond enough of each other for either to settle closer at hand, found it easier to cross the oceans every six months to touch their counterpart's naked body than to find somebody new to share their bed in their own towns. It wasn't that. Part of the idea of travelling so light was his hope that, when he arrived, the woman he'd travelled to see would need less weight to hold him there. He didn't want to lose his nerve. Of course she was pretty, but an awful lot of people were, and they were no good to be around; they were only curators of their own beauty. They could show you it, but once the tour was over, there was nothing left. Astrid was one of those other ones, who inhabited her looks. They were hers and she lived there.

He'd met her after dark, in the gardens of the Northern Alliance guesthouse in Faizabad, in the October of 2001. The generators were down and all he could see of her to begin with was her silhouette against the stars. The stars were thickly sown and distinct and the river roared where it bent around the rocks at the foot of the outcrop the guesthouse stood on. To Kellas it seemed that he and the other foreigners spread out among the bushes and trees, murmuring into their satellite phones, were sitting on the shore of the cosmos, listening to the roar of time. He was crouching on the grass with his head back, gawping at the Milky Way, when he heard her moving, and she stood over him.

Astrid's satphone batteries were all used up. She asked if she could call her editor and her father on Kellas's phone. He'd already made the same sort of calls in the same sort of order, and told her she could talk for as long as she liked. He stood a little distance away. There was a green glow from the phone display. It touched her face but he couldn't see her. It had just been her dark shape moving like a wing across the starfield and her voice asking to use his phone. So in those first minutes he only knew her by her voice. She sounded preoccupied with herself, but when she spoke there was a hesitancy and an opening-up, a kind of respecting shyness, as if to her everyone was wise until proven a fool, and she didn't want to risk missing the thoughtful ones.

When Astrid finished her calls, they stood and talked in the gardens. They'd both arrived that day, Kellas by plane from Tajikistan, Astrid overland in one of the convoys from Dushanbe, across the Aru Darya river, then east by truck. Neither had been to Afghanistan before.

'They have a way of looking at us here. At us, the foreigners,' said Astrid. 'They make me feel less real than they are. They make me feel recorded and projected, like I can be switched off and not exist, while they go on existing. I'm going to sit down. I'm not feeling so good.'

They sat on the dirt. Kellas was starting to be able to see by the starlight and he saw that Astrid had a narrow face, with high cheek-bones and a wide, finely delineated mouth. When she frowned, which she did often when she spoke, as if to reassure others and herself that she was thinking seriously, a dense pattern of four horizontal lines appeared on her forehead – they made her look older, and carried pain; when she smiled, the lines vanished and her face shone with more happiness than she could possibly use for herself. There was enough there for everyone.

He could see by the tired, impatient way she moved that she was sick and uncomfortable. His transition had been sharper than Astrid's. He hadn't known that morning if he would fly or not and until the lizard-coloured transport plane had taken off from Dushanbe airport, he doubted. He and the other foreign journalists and Alliance Afghans sat on canvas seats against the fuselage. In between them, occupying most of the aircraft's cargo space, sat two tons of bottled water for CNN. Forty minutes after they took off they landed on a stretch of roughly flattened earth and stones

44

surfaced with the steel strips put down by military engineers when they're in a hurry. They walked out of the plane off the back ramp into a cloud of dust from the aircraft's propellers and when it cleared they could see a line of Afghans waiting and watching, letting the dust settle on them. For the children the arrival of the plane was the final grand, ridiculous piece of stage machinery in the play of the day, and they jumped, singing in English, 'How are you? How are you?' Most of the others were drivers, but not importuning. They held back and waited for the foreigners to come to them. One of the Afghans waiting seemed to have no reason to be there other than to watch the plane come in. He looked at Kellas with blank intensity, with his hands behind his back. It was a look Kellas hadn't seen before, and would see again in Afghanistan, the look of clever, curious and uneducated men, lusting for a messenger. They would fight and die for their religion here but a bold man could write his own religion in eyes like that, if he dared and the religion was bright enough.

Kellas put his gear into a Uazik and for twenty-five dollars was driven into town along a cratered highway. On either side of the road, traders were lighting kerosene lamps in their wooden booths. There was a smell of cooking fires. The country was rich in darkness and its lights and fires shone against it correspondingly, like gems in fur. Kellas's doubts in London belonged to someone else. He was glad that he had been sent to this other world to carry out tasks, to report back. There were duties and some were his.

'I might stay here a long time,' said Astrid. 'It clears my head. Kinda . . . exalted. Can you excuse me for a moment?' She moved to the edge of the garden. Kellas heard her retching and coughing. He heard a limb slipping through grass, a cry and the sound of a branch breaking. He ran over and caught Astrid's wrists as she slid down a steep embankment towards the sheer rocks above the river. He helped her scramble up and she thanked him. Her wrists were cold and clammy and she was trembling slightly. He put his hand on her forehead. It was cool and damp.

45

'That was so clumsy,' said Astrid, laughing in relief. 'I shouldn't have tried to throw up in the river.'

'That's what they drink here, too,' said Kellas.

'Yeah,' said Astrid. 'I don't think I've got any of it on me.'

'You need to be warm,' said Kellas. They went back to the guest-house as the generator started up and the lights came on. He made sure the Poles she was sharing a room with got her, shivering, into her sleeping bag and he came back later with some mutton and rice the Afghans had cooked, a glass of tea and a couple of ibuprofen tablets. Astrid consumed it all. A group of Swiss was taking two Uaziks to Jabal os Saraj the day after tomorrow, she said, they could both go with them. Kellas said she should rest more.

'This'll be gone by tomorrow night,' said Astrid quickly. She shuddered with nausea, turned on her side and closed her eyes. Strands of her hair were stuck to her forehead.

Next morning Kellas called for her. His room was at the other end of the building's single corridor. It was seven and barely light. The Poles said she had gone out. She'd left her things behind. Kellas walked down into Faizabad, the smoky clench of mud brick, crooked timbers and dark, narrow openings that sat fast on the valley floor and mountainsides like burned scrapings in a stewpot. He exchanged dollars for a greasy wad of Afghan money and found the town baths, where he stripped to his pants before the eyes of laughing men in sodden bloomers and dipped his body in a steaming font. Later he walked through the alleys, by ways of straw and dung and mud marked by foot- and hoof-prints. There weren't many vehicles. Every time a Uazik or a Kamaz or an old Toyota drove through it came like a tiger on a leash, roaring and honking, parting boys and elders and women in pale blue burqas as if they had never heard an engine. It occurred to Kellas that if he spoke Dari, he'd be able to find Astrid easily. She was the only skinny white one in jeans and a too-big black anorak and blonde hair coming out from under a pakul hat. They would all have seen her. He felt like a fool without the language.

He came to a marketplace, where old men who looked as if they had heard the crying of their children fade and turn to silence too many times led donkeys carrying panniers of gnarled, sawed-up tree roots, drawn like wisdom teeth from the back jaws of deforested hills, to sell as firewood. He found Astrid with her head bent towards a cage that held a plump, exquisite grey bird.

'Bet they'd cook it for you,' said Kellas, who was hungry.

'Bet they wouldn't,' said Astrid. 'It's a fighting partridge. The fight's tomorrow, though. We've got to be out of here. I'd have put money on this fella to take down any partridge in this city. See the eyes? This one's a killer. What d'you think? Could I take it with me to Jabal?'

'Why not?' said Kellas. There was no fever left in her. She looked younger. She still had faint lines under her eyes. It made her look wise. She tried to get Kellas to buy another partridge, so they could stage fights when they crossed the mountains.

'If you like,' said Kellas. One of the two would end up in the pan that way.

Astrid looked at him in a manner he cared for, intense and curious. 'No, you're right,' she said quietly. 'It was a dumb idea.'

'I said yes.'

'It wasn't what you were thinking, was it.' said Astrid.

At dawn next morning they found places in the two Uaziks hired by a Swiss TV crew to make the three-day journey through the mountains to Jabal os Saraj, where Alliance troops had been preparing a last stand against the Taliban until the Americans began to hammer from the air at their new common enemy, there on the Shomali plain, at the portals of Kabul. With the Swiss reporter and cameraman and his Slovenian producer, their Tajik interpreter from Dushanbe, an Afghan escort and two drivers, they were nine with their gear in the cars when they drove up the valley. The escort was a former bodyguard of Ahmed Shah Massoud, proud without scale of his acquaintance with the hero of the Hindu Kush, a pride not dented by his failure to prevent Massoud being assassinated by al-Qaida a

47

few days before the attacks on New York and Washington. The bodyguard was a handy cocky talker through each of the checkpoints they passed, always three young men with old guns and a piece of rope stretched across the road. Before setting out the westerners wrapped their equipment in clingfilm and wound scarves around their faces. The Swiss reporter invited Astrid to ride with him, the cameraman and the bodyguard, while Kellas rode with the interpreter and the producer.

'The old Swiss guy, he's going to fuck her,' said the interpreter, Rustum, after half an hour's travelling. He said it without emphasis, as if he were talking about the past, rather than the future.

'What if she doesn't want to?' said Kellas. He was mistrustful of the producer, a tanned and moody individual looking for an opportunity to turn into Werner Herzog once he had a good day of wilderness on either side of them.

'Where's she going to go?' asked the interpreter, but less confidently, startled and then made gloomy by Kellas's assertion that Astrid was capable of independent action. He was twenty five. He'd already made one profitable trip to and from Afghanistan since the big western TV networks rediscovered the country. He smoothed his moustache and rested his chin on the shoulder of the Slovenian producer in the front seat.

'What do you think, Alex?' he said.

'Is fifty old?' said Alex. 'Not for a Swiss guy.'

At first the road was a swathe of small, half-loose rocks embedded in soil that had become dust as fine as talcum powder. Once a second, the old Soviet army car jolted and lifted the passengers in their seats. The dust splashed off the tyres of the Uazik in front as fluid as milk before spreading high and wide around them so that the day turned yellow and they bound their scarves tight across their mouths and nostrils. It was mid-October, and they were thousands of feet above sea level, and climbing, yet the sun shone. It was warm. In the heights the dust lessened and the stones of the road became coarser still, rounded boulders the size of cow heads,

48

with gaps between. However high they climbed there was always a swoop of red rock and scree on either side looming over them, a hard gradient up to a ridge implausibly close to the sky. They passed ammunition trucks, boxes marked 'Grenades' shifting in their open trailers with each bump, and CNN's water, and convoys of brutalised donkeys carrying panniers of dried dung. They drove round lakes where the water was the colour of blood and lakes where the water was the colour of grass. At the first crossing of a river, they stopped, and everyone got out except the drivers. The bridge was a row of crooked, spindly tree trunks laid from one bank to another without being fixed to either bank, or to each other. The drivers crossed with swift bravado and the others walked across. When they got back into the cars, Astrid switched. She sat in the middle of the back seat, between Rustum and Kellas. Kellas noticed that she sat down warily.

'Wait,' she said, holding up her hand when he tried to get in beside her. She reached into the waistband of her jeans, under her anorak, and took out a pistol.

'Never seen a reporter with one of those before,' said Kellas.

'I bought it just now from the bodyguard. He wanted five hundred for it but I beat him down to one-twenty. Don't worry, the clip's not in. Here. Move to one side a second.'

She held the chunky L-shape by the grip, ran the action back and forth, squinted down the bore, held the gun up with both hands, pointed it out of the open door at the rockface, closed an eye, sighted and pulled the trigger till the hammer fell with a sharp tap that rang in the empty chamber. 'What a crummy piece of Soviet crap,' she said. 'They must've pressed these out like tin kettles back in the day.' She unzipped a pocket, took out a pair of ski gloves, put the gun inside and stuffed the gloves back on top. 'Get in, Adam, let's get moving. Don't look at me that way. You can guess what kind of sanctimonious garbage I was getting from the Swiss guys. More of it now because they know they can't be taking advantage of me. What you see in that car up ahead is Nietzsche in action. "Truly

I've laughed at those who think they're virtuous 'cause their claws are blunt."'

'I told you!' said Rustum, slapping his knee with one hand and pinching his moustache with the other.

'There's no law here,' said Astrid. 'Single girl needs protection.'

'I'm tired of guns,' said Kellas. 'There are too many in this country.'

'That's one out of circulation.' She grinned at him and patted her pocket. She was energised by the purchase. Kellas's conscience impelled him to tell her that he disapproved, while some other force within him made him dizzy and blinking, as if he'd come out into the bright light of the present after a long time in a dark room. He believed it was foolish for a journalist to carry a gun. Guns attracted guns. But he had no righteous indignation left. He didn't care. He asked Astrid if she'd be able to claim it on expenses.

'They paid for a helmet and a flak jacket, which I left behind,' she said. 'They must be dropping a thousand a week on the insurance. They can pony up a hundred and twenty bucks for one of the Kremlin's Saturday night specials.'

'It makes you a combatant,' said Kellas.

'Oh, and you're not a combatant?' Astrid laughed. 'What do you think you're doing here? You're looking for where the war's at. You're selling it. That's enough. You're in it. You've joined.'

'You gun nuts, you're bad comedians,' said Alex, the Slovenian producer. He didn't turn round. He lifted his head and they saw the blurred trace of his eyes in the rear-view mirror as the road of boulders shook the Uazik.

'I'm not a gun nut,' said Astrid.

'Maybe,' said Alex. He was shouting over the noise of their travelling. 'You're not a man. Maybe that makes a difference. I used to think men loved guns because they made them seem serious. It's death in a tube, and death's serious, right? Carrying death around, it makes you a serious person. I saw what happened to friends of mine who joined up and went into elite units, you know, the special forces bullshit. I saw what happened. These were the guys who really wanted to be able to make people laugh, but they were so dumb, they couldn't tell a joke. They couldn't even tell a funny story. And all jokes in the world are variations on one joke: man walks along the street, slips on a banana skin, falls over, looks like a fool. That's the only thing that the gun nut understands about comedy. They understand that death's the greatest banana skin joke of all. It's the most ridiculous thing that happens to anybody. One moment you're walking along, hey hey hey, king of the world, the proud guy, centre of the universe. Then bang! The comedian pulls the trigger and the proud guy's eighty kilos of meat. Much funnier than a pie in the face. The gun nuts are terrible comedians, and they're always itching to tell the one joke they know. It's a deadly, final, no-comeback joke, they're longing to tell it, and they know they can't.'

'That's good. You go with that when the Indians come over the ridge there,' said Astrid. 'You go with that philosophy of yours because I am not coming to your aid.'

The next day, after spending the night in a village where men reached inside the folds of their clothes and brought out lumps of lapis lazuli to sell, the convoy took a noon break in a marketplace outside the walls of a warlord's fortress. They ate kebabs tasting of petrol. Cloud cut off the peaks of the mountains and the air was dank. It smelled of winter. The grazing was thin and muddy. The traders, and men who were not traders but squatted and watched, looked at them as if reckoning the worth of their valuables, and their party's strength. The walls of the fortress were twenty feet high, flush with the sheer rock they rose off, and pierced with slits.

While they were eating, a convoy of three cars arrived, heading back towards Faizabad. They halted close to the Swiss team's Uaziks and the occupants got out. Kellas recognised Miriam Hersh from Reuters. She came over to him and Astrid. Kellas kissed her on both cheeks and Miriam told them how squalid it was down in Jabal os

Saraj, how overcrowded, how little was happening. She was going home. Kellas asked where she was based now and she looked at him with tired, watery eyes.

'That's it, finished,' she said. 'When I say home, I mean home. London. Reuters is bringing me back for good.' The wind blew her wispy brown hair across her face and she tossed it away and pulled the cuffs of her fleece down over her hands. She was beginning to shiver. 'It's time. I've been abroad long enough.' She sniffed and shifted her weight from foot to foot. 'I don't want to be a professional expat when I'm fifty.'

'Miriam and I met when I was based in Warsaw,' said Kellas to Astrid.

'Based?' Miriam laughed. 'When were you ever based anywhere?'

Kellas blushed. 'I was,' he said.

Miriam smiled at Kellas, although her shoulders were shaking with the cold, and turned to Astrid. 'Adam was famous in eastern Europe in the 1990s for never living in one city for more than six months. And he was there for – how long? Ten years?'

'Nine,' said Kellas. 'Two of them in Prague.'

'They weren't consecutive years in Prague, though, were they?' said Miriam. 'It was like a king rotating his residency through his dominions. Six months in Budapest, four months in Kiev . . .'

'I think it sounds like a good life,' said Astrid.

'You know how it is,' said Kellas, looking from face to face. 'You stay in one country for more than a few months, you start to know so much about it that the editors aren't sure what you're talking about any more. They want you to get some of your ignorance back. You've moved too far from the readers.'

'What he means is that he was never satisfied,' said Miriam to Astrid.

Kellas laughed and denied it.

'You're a good reporter, but you were short of staying power,' said Miriam. 'You were the opposite of those TV reporters who think that because they're somewhere, that place must be where the story is. Wherever you were, you were sure that place wasn't *it*. Whatever *it* was, it was somewhere else.'

'And a woman in every port?' said Astrid.

'Those were landlocked countries,' said Kellas.

Miriam was jumping up and down. She'd thrown a bag on the wrong truck when she was leaving Jabal and lost her winter gear.

'I've got an extra pair of gloves,' said Astrid. 'I don't need them.'

'If you're sure. It might save my fingers.'

Astrid unzipped the pocket. A finger of one glove had caught in the trigger of her pistol and when she took the gloves out the gun followed. It thumped onto the grass. Astrid handed the gloves to Miriam and picked the pistol up and put it back in her pocket. Miriam followed the gun with her eyes.

'I thought you were a journo,' she said, pulling the gloves on.

'Is there something about me that makes you think different?'

'The gun? Who are you with, *Stars and Stripes?*'

'I hope those gloves help you with the cold,' said Astrid, looking into Miriam's eyes. 'You need to be more careful with your gear.'

'Appreciate it,' said Miriam faintly, held by Astrid's gaze. 'I'll send them on when I get back.'

'Don't,' said Astrid. She walked across to the Uazik she'd been travelling in and reached into the back for her rucksack. Kellas listened for the tiny sound from her lungs as she lifted it but at the same moment Miriam's travelling companions called to her and their engines started.

'I have to go,' said Miriam. 'Are you travelling with her?'

'Astrid. Astrid Walsh. She works for *DC Monthly.*'

'You do understand what a liability she is.'

'Do you know her?'

'She just dropped a fucking gun out of her pocket. That's a sackable offence in any outfit I know. You can tell she's a flake. A military groupie. I know her type. She's one of those women who doesn't have any women friends. You should wait here for another convoy.'

'She's OK,' said Kellas. 'Eccentric.'

Miriam pressed her lips together and stared at Kellas, holding her breath. She let it out. 'I see. I would say keep your distance, but – I see.' They wished each other good luck and Miriam went back to her convoy.

That afternoon Kellas and Astrid's cars crossed the Anjoman pass. The road was a looping trail of black rocks and compacted snow. On either side the snow cover lay a few inches thick. As they traversed the highest point a blizzard came in and twice they had to get out to help push the Uaziks through. Kellas and Astrid stood next to each other, Alex and Rustum on either side, with their hands pressed against the Uazik's rear door, and put their weight against it. Their lungs hurt and their heads spun with the altitude. The drivers said that, within a week, only horses would be able to make it across. On the way down Astrid tried to rest her head on Kellas's shoulder and doze, but the jolt of the road kicked her awake each time. When they were in their sleeping bags at nightfall in a guesthouse at the top of the Panjshir valley, Kellas watched Astrid asleep, and saw how the four frown lines on her forehead sharpened into being, then were smoothed away, then returned.

The next morning, as they were packing up to leave, Astrid's mood changed. Her face closed and she told him curtly that she was staying behind. She'd come to Jabal later.

Kellas kneeled there over the maw of his rucksack, his things spread around him, the winter clothes, the bottle of whisky for the *Citizen* correspondent he was relieving, the books. He felt a strange dryness on his tongue and realised that his mouth was hanging open. He cleared his throat and asked her what the matter was. Astrid looked at him like a beast of prey for whom he was not prey, cold, distant, proud in herself, without the faintest glow of human social need. She didn't answer him and turned away.

Kellas got into the Uazik without her and they drove off. The ride shook him hard with two instead of three in the back of the car, without Astrid's body to brace him. He wasn't troubled by the sharp shift in her temperament, but he was surprised. He spent the morning thinking about Astrid, and why she meant so little to him. Rattling down the Panjshir his thoughts darkened. The mountains were closer and steeper and cast more persistent shadows. By the afternoon he was full of the sense of lonely cheatedness that comes when all the favourite characters in a drama are dead, yet the drama continues. When he tried to remember Astrid's face, to try to understand why he didn't care, he wasn't sure that he was remembering it well. It would be easier if she were there. The only thing he was sure he was remembering right was the tiny sound that came from inside her as she hoisted a load onto her back. He listened to his memory of the sound of the life in her until it got dark and the Uaziks' headlights swept at last onto a metalled road.

4

An automated voice at Heathrow called the boarding of Kellas's flight. He passed the last cluster of shops before the walk to the gate. There was a bookshop, and he had nothing to read. He stood a few feet from the entrance, staring at the first table, which was stacked with copies of an American revelatory liberal tract called *From Plato to Nato*. If he went any closer there was a risk he might see copies of a book with a green-and-red cover that he had been avoiding since it was published, although he had read it twice. He'd seen it last night, at the Cunnerys'. It'd been brought out; it'd been signed. Conversations had followed and events had occurred, the memory of which snapped at and menaced his footsteps. He turned away from the bookshop and walked to the departure gate, empty-handed, injured and eager for champagne.

He walked down the gangway into the electric smell of the aircraft and the whine of the generator. For a moment he was part of the tired shuffling in the plane's porch, a procession fenced-in toughly by the bared teeth of the crew, until they found him to be one of the privileged, and directed him left into the first class cabin. The passengers already boarded there lolled in bloated loungers, sunk in the pleated folds of dyed cowhide like child kings. He found his place by the window. In the aisle seat next to him was a tall, heavily-built woman in her twenties wearing pearls and an expensively tailored suit the colour and texture of white water-lily petals. Here in the nose of the 747 there was so much space that she didn't need to move her feet, let alone stand up, as he came past her. She looked up from the book she was reading. He could see it was Chinese or Japanese. She smiled at him and they said 'Hi' to each other. Kellas fastened his seatbelt. He fidgeted with the buckle and bit his nails and sweated. He was not a bad flyer. It was the ground that was making him ill. The longer the aircraft stood at the gate, the more rituals, the hot towels – why did people wipe their faces with them? Did they have dirty faces? – the more calm drivel from the pilot, the more unlikely it seemed that this lumbering, thin-skinned metal crucifix stuffed with travellers could fly him off the island and across the ocean and away from the shame that was growing in him. Like prayer beads through his fingers, he felt and counted the things he had done and said at the Cunnerys'. It was still possible that – if a Mr Kellas was on board, could he make himself known? He anticipated the cold of the handcuffs against the skin of his wrists, and their weight. He looked over his shoulder. There were fast feet down the aisle, almost running, and dark cloth. It was one of the cabin attendants. He looked at Kellas, put his hand to his mouth, bent his knees, reached out and touched him on the shoulder. 'Did I frighten you? Oh, I'm ever so sorry. I'm in such a hurry today! Everything all right?'

'It's OK, I'm fine,' said Kellas, feeling he'd spilled something on himself. He was placing the eight guests around the Cunnerys' table. Cunnery to his left. Sophie M'Gurgan on his right. Lucy Flagg facing him, Pat M'Gurgan next to her, Joe Betchcott in the too-tight sweater and Margot and Melissa at the far end. Your own mind was a hard thing to manipulate: it had so many automatic processes. Where he wanted to tab it was the question about Afghanistan to which he'd given such a plain answer. He would rather hold that as the start point of this sagging weight of guilt, heavy on his stomach. He would have preferred to keep the other details as another class of remembered things, moated from the rest. But the mind was demo-cratic, a synthesiser. It connected. He remembered, for instance, that Sophie had watched how he looked at Lucy's cleavage, sharp and young in the deep bare scoop at the front of her small dress. That everyone, and not only Lucy, had heard him tell her that she looked sexy. That he'd called Joe Betchcott 'a fucking fascist wanker' long before the war question had occurred, when he only had one drink in him. The hardest thing was that he hadn't been drunk at any time. He needed to drink now, to quell the inertia of the organising mind. He needed to be controlled. He needed to put it out of himself that his answer to the war question had anything to do with him coming into the dining room and seeing the pounds of bright cutlery there, the multiple forks, and him picking up one and putting it down and remarking to Cunnery about the surprising lack of silver snail tongs in a way that sounded sarcastic, envious and sly. Could he fairly malign the only child Cunnery for putting his deceased parents' silver out for dinner guests? Was it that, as an avowed socialist, he was supposed to have sold the silver and donated the proceeds to the struggle? Perhaps. Yet as long as Cunnery had the tableware, Kellas would have taken greater offence if the places had been set with pressed steel knives and forks. Kellas's soul hadn't been pinched in the same way at other feasts. It had been a kind of lavish show when Rab Balgillo held his wedding reception at his father-in-law's farm in Orkney a few years back, and this had seemed no worse than generous. Balgillo had spent, and his family had spent, and the bride's family had spent; everyone had spent, including Kellas, and the whole long weekend in Orkney had been nothing but joy. The M'Gurgans were profoundly in debt at the time, and Kellas had been earning well as a freelance. It had taken him days of persuasion to get Pat and Sophie to agree to take his money to cover their expenses on the trip and then to promise that they would never try to pay him back, or mention it again. The feast days had flowed out to gather them; Kellas and Katerina had flown from Prague to Edinburgh, hired a car and driven to Duncairn to stay with Kellas's parents. Pat and Sophie had joined them and they'd driven up to Thurso together and taken the ferry to Stromness from there.

It'd been midsummer in the north and the sun scarcely set. They'd spent their nights suffused in red and gold. Although Katerina was by some way the most beautiful person at the wedding, this was not meaningful in the evening light; in the radiance all human shapes and skins seemed to realise a dearly-held intention implicit in their being. Pat, Sophie, Kellas, Katerina, Rab, his bride Leslie and the artist Hephzibah Cooper lay in the long grass by the standing stones, listening to the insects, tickling each other with sedge and talking nonsense about the universe and the islands. When the wind blew it was warm and carried the smell of peat and salt water. Kellas spent a long time gazing at the thin gold chain on the back of Katerina's neck while Hephzibah talked about how the stones went three yards underground, and somebody asked her how she knew, and she said Rab had told her, and Rab denied it. The voices and laughter came to Kellas through the waving seed heads and he listened, waiting for the next dart of wind to move Katerina's hair and for her to put it back in place.

The party was held in and around a barn, decorated with the farmer father-in-law's real hay and with the father-in-law's ponies saddled and haltered for the guests to ride. The guests had been instructed to dress Western. Kellas and Katerina wore jeans and checked shirts, with cowboy hats and sheriff's stars from a toy shop in Kirkwall. Sophie had found hand-stitched boots, an embroidered shirt, a bootlace tie and a real Stetson; Pat glowered as Pancho Villa, with bandoliers and a sombrero and a plastic moustache six inches wide. The band played till two and Katerina danced with a guest dressed as a cactus. Only his face showed, the costume was entirely rigid, and halfway through the Gay Gordons, he fell over and rolled around the floor, kicking his feet like an overturned beetle.

By four a.m. the sun was well above the horizon and Kellas, Katerina, M'Gurgan, Sophie, Hephzibah, Rab and Leslie were drinking on the floor in the front room of Leslie's house. Somebody had asked M'Gurgan what Kellas's parents' place was like and

M'Gurgan had asked whether they'd heard about the cat. He had the storyteller's beckoning smile on him as he said it and when he said to Kellas 'You tell the story', Kellas said 'No, you do it.'

'We've come back from the pub,' said M'Gurgan, 'and we're sitting in the kitchen. All the women have already gone upstairs and Adam's dad comes in all ready for bed, which is quite an operation. He spends an hour patrolling the house making sure everything's switched off, the doors are double locked, the heating's turned up to tropical. The lasers are primed. You know, stakes coming out of the walls to impale intruders. So he's done his rounds, and he's standing there in an Albanian dressing gown and a tasselled cap from Uzbekistan, which he only wears when Adam's there 'cause that's what Adam gives him for presents when he comes back from one of his assignments to shitholes. And Adam's dad says to us: "Can you make sure, if the cat comes in, you don't let it out again?" And he shows us how to lock the cat door, and off he goes to bed. The allotted task seems simple enough, and we go on talking. Couple of whiskies. After a while there's this sound from the back door. Now I've heard cats come through cat doors before. I have experience, and I know, they're very lithe creatures. It doesn't matter how big they look; they slip through that little opening with just a wee clatter, and they're in. But this sound is different. It isn't a clatter. We hear the "clat", and we're waiting . . . and there's no "ter". So we go and take a look. The cat is gigantic! It's the size of a sheep. And it's stuck halfway through the cat door, with its head and front legs through, and its hind legs and arse hanging out the back. It looks like a lion that's tried to jump through a quoit. So I ask Adam what the hell this Gargantua is and he says his parents have only just got the animal, this is the first time he's seen it. So we open the door, and the cat just moves with it, like this. Then Adam goes outside, and we close the door, and he puts his hands on the cat's arse and pushes, and I take the cat's front legs in my hands and start to pull. And Adam keeps saying "Don't hurt him!" and I'm trying to pull delicately, and the cat looks at me very calmly and sinks its claws into my hands. Deep. I jump back and bang my head and start cursing the cat and Adam says "Not so loud, my dad's a light sleeper." I'm trying to staunch the blood from my wounds and then I see it's looking bad with the cat. It's making these little panting sounds, like two voles fucking. I imagine. Meanwhile Adam's getting really agitated and I have an idea: we'll use some butter to grease the cat. Adam starts rooting around and all he can find is a bottle of extra virgin olive oil. And this is when I know the kind of lifestyle he has because he starts drizzling the olive oil over the cat. You know – like it's a rocket salad. I'm waiting for him to start shaving the Parmesan. So I massage the oil into the cat's skin and we take our positions again, he pushes, I pull, the cat screams blue murder and it just shoots out of the cat door and into the kitchen. The next thing is Adam's father comes storming in, in his Lebanese night attire, shouting at us for all the noise we're making. We explain that the cat got stuck in the cat door. Adam's dad looks down at this enormous mutant cat, panting on the floor, its paws covered in my blood and its belly all smeared in extra virgin olive oil like some avant garde north London starter, and he says: "I've never seen this animal before in my life!"'

On the plane, Kellas laughed out loud. McGurgan had still been wearing the false moustache when he was telling the story. A cold hard bolt shot into Kellas's laughter and he felt the muscles around his mouth flatten and his lips closed. After what had happened, after what he had done, it didn't seem possible he could ever be in a room with the M'Gurgans again.

The Boeing rolled back off the stand. From where Kellas was sitting, so close to the front, the moan of the engines when the crew spun them up sounded far away. Once the aircraft was turned round and began to move forward under its own power, Kellas felt the shame start to melt inside him. They joined the queue of aircraft waiting to use the runway. Tall tailfins moved across each other like sails crowding a harbour, and the narrow strips of cockpit window darkened and twinkled in the sun like the frowns of racing beings before the charge to speed. When the 747 carrying Kellas swung into the compass degrees at the start of the runway, and the sound of a sudden rush of burning kerosene into engines the size of blast furnaces reached his ears remote and muffled, like thunder in the next county, his shame at what he had done was almost gone. When the aircraft accelerated and he was pressed into his seat and the frame of the 747 shook a little and glasses in the galley chattered together like crystal teeth, the shame vanished, and when the aircraft parted from the ground, the faces and sounds of the night before in Camden stayed there. The old island had shed him to the mercies of the air like a gnarled tree shedding a dot of blossom and although he was still as doomed as anyone his doom had a vector and a velocity taking him away from the witnesses to what he had done.

The aircraft banked as it climbed. Kellas looked through the window and back to the wings. He liked to watch them bend, flap a little at the wingtips as they took the strain of turning the big ugly jumbo through the thick air, and streaks of vapour like smoke shoot from the leading edge. The sky was crowded, the pilot told them, and they would level out low over the West Country for a while before they climbed to the high cold of the transatlantic jetway.

On the lands below there were shawls of frost on the rises, and lines of snow in the shadows unmelted from a week ago. Britain held a baseline greenness even in midwinter. Distance conferred mystery on the place, on any place. From here you couldn't tell it was an island; it had a scale to it, a rumpled, hazy majesty. One thing that happened from ten thousand feet was that people only existed on the ground if you imagined them. Kellas could make out the half-legible Braille of villages and farms down there, but he couldn't imagine the people in them. From this height, it was easier to place King Arthur in the mist lapping at the Welsh Marches, and Titania and Oberon bowered by those fluffy copses, than to populate the market towns with the real millions, one by one. The best you could hope for from a stranger looking down, an American or Arab or African who'd never visited the island, was that they'd take it for more than Airstrip One; more than the lounge where Elvis meets Tintin when each is on his way to somewhere else. That they'd construct some decent facsimile of life below in the grass, brick and grey stone, perceive the human grain making up the fabric of the view. Otherwise what could the eye see as it looked down on a strange land from so high, except history instead of yesterday, prophecy instead of tomorrow, and a today that was either a view, or a target.

It was from about this height that the F-18 pilots would have looked down on the Shomali plain, between Kabul and Jabal os Saraj at the mouth of the Panjshir. Ten thousand feet was as high as a Stinger could rise to shoot them down, and none ever had been shot down. The pilots had left the air-conditioned cabins of their aircraft carriers, flown over Pakistan into Afghanistan and tattooed the earth with bombs, then flown home for a meal and a shower. They were still doing it. Hitting was also a kind of touching. But if hitting was the only kind of touching you did, you would damage the one you touched so badly that, by the time you came to embrace them, they would recoil from you.

The pilots had seen what they did from afar. They could not land. There had always been the distance. America reached out for thousands of miles and its sense of touch stopped three miles short. It threw the bombs, and pulled away again. It wasn't entirely a matter of retribution, strong as the passion of vengeance was then. There was curiosity in that reach, and a kind of regret. In any act of hurting there remained the ghost of intimacy. Like the nineteen martyrs whose suicide had summoned them to Afghanistan, the American pilots showed that the power they represented was great and their cause irresistible. They were not afraid to kill or die. Yet no fulfilment lay in the destruction without a moment of understanding, an instant when all the bomber imagined about those he bombed, all his spite and defiance towards his imagined victims, converged with their forced embrace of death. When the bomber understood whom he was killing and the bombed understood whom they were being killed by, and they became one. In Afghanistan Kellas had wondered when this moment of union and consummation came. Was it the instant the hijackers saw the glass of the towers fill the cockpit windows, and the office workers saw a rush of darkness eat the light? The moment their bodies were vapourised together in an incandescent bloom of jet fuel, and their consciousnesses lingered just long enough to understand? When the Taliban tasted the dust kicked up by the American bombs falling around them, or when America and America's pilots saw the explosions of those bombs on their screens?

Kellas had watched the jets jinking over the mud walls, irrigation channels and mulberry groves at the northern end of the plain. Once he had almost trod on a mine, following the sharky twists of the plane against the blue and not looking where he was walking. The sound of the F-18's engines had drowned out the shouts of his colleagues, warning him that he was straying from the marked path. The F-18s were pretty accurate, on the whole. They killed and maimed the Taliban, as they were intended to. Every so often, though, they fucked up.

There'd been a night when they'd heard that the Americans had bombed an Alliance village by mistake. The reporters and photographers in Jabal were bored and tetchy because the war was everywhere and nowhere, like God; they were telling their editors that they believed in it but they seldom heard it, let alone saw it, apart from the sound of the planes and the columns of smoke on the horizon. It was late October. All of them expected a stalemate on through Ramadan, Hanukah and Christmas, to the very Year of the Horse. The rumour of deaths in a friendly village nearby, with the wounded taken to an Italian charity hospital in the Panjshir, gave them hope for a story.

Kellas glanced at the seatbelt sign. It was still lit. They were climbing again, over the Irish Sea. If he couldn't remember every

64

word and look of Astrid's, what value did this journey to Virginia have now? He'd written to her, but she had not written to him, or called. A year had passed. He knew that he wanted to see her but to know what it was in her he wanted to see he could only delve back into the weeks in Afghanistan and sort through the jumble of her humours. They had fucked together and they had killed together and he did not know her.

On the night after the bombing he'd seen the sudden joy of leadership in her. The kind of leader that hopeless local rebellions threw up, or partisan bands, or complicated games of children, quick, eager and right. The journalists' regular drivers had knocked off with the lateness of the hour and it was Astrid who organised a Toyota minibus to take them up to the hospital in the Panjshir before midnight. She'd turned to Kellas, who wasn't sure where he stood, and said: 'Want to come?' She cocked her head to one side and raised her eyebrows and smiled and Kellas nodded. He remembered what she wore: the red woollen jumper, a little frayed at the hem, with the black scarf and too-big black anorak and jeans, and the black suede boots with toes that were almost pointed. When it was awkward for her to have her head uncovered she wore the scarf over it, or tucked her hair into a pakul hat. It flopped out.

Kellas and Astrid sat at the back of the minibus. In front of them two photographers were talking in French. The moon was bright enough for the silhouette of the mountains to be clear against the sky. There were no artificial lights on the plain or in the streets of the town. The mud buildings reflected the moon. Their walls seemed to glow with a faint phosphorescence, as if they were made of lunar material, and their glassless windows were dark as cavemouths. The Toyota hammered past the silent unpowered houses like the eyes of an atheist skimming the Koran.

'My newspaper doesn't give me the space to write that it's beautiful here,' said Kellas.

'The people who read it wouldn't be happy if it did,' said Astrid.

'They'd think they were awful sinners if they went looking for the truth about war in one of your articles and they found you'd slipped some beauty into it.'

'They ought to know war isn't something that oozes out of the ground in this country. No more than it does in our own.'

The four furrows appeared on Astrid's forehead as she thought over each word she spoke. 'You can write poetry another day,' she said, leaning forward, talking into the seat in front of her. She turned and looked at him. 'You can have the beauty, but that's your prize, Adam Kellas, it's what *you* see. What your paper needs is what the Afghans see. I don't know that it looks so pretty to them. It just looks like being poor.'

'I never wanted to come here,' said Kellas.

'Why did you?'

'Habit.'

Astrid smiled. Her forehead smoothed over. Kellas wondered if she'd seen through him. She asked: 'What made you think you ought to break the habit?'

'A country sends its travellers abroad like words spoken from one person to another,' said Kellas. 'Like me talking to you now. The country sees its travellers leave and I hear the words as they leave my mouth and enter you. But the country doesn't see what happens to its traveller when he arrives in that foreign place and I can't know how you take the words I speak.'

'I'll tell you, if you want,' said Astrid, smiling and fiddling with her ear.

'I'll never know what happened to the words,' said Kellas. 'And the traveller never comes back. He becomes another man, who belongs a little to the place he travels to. He belongs more to that place every day he stays there. And that's the very part, the belonging, that I never find out how to pass to the people at home. Maybe because I can't get it right. Maybe because they don't want to know.'

'You want too much,' said Astrid. 'The best of us is still a small messenger, with a short quiet message. One of us can't make one

66

country understand another. It takes the whole chorus and a million messages just to make a tiny connection.'

'What do you see when you look out through that glass?' said Kellas.

'Oh, darkness is another country,' said Astrid. 'The night's another world. Not so much the hider of secrets, more like the maker of mysteries. I can't help believing there are things out there that don't exist in the daylight. You can always set yourself up with something to chase when the moon's out.'

'So you're here for you.'

'I'll write what I write. I send my messages back. But that's duty. It's not the reward. I figure you'd be a lot happier, too, if you kept your duty and your rewards separate.' She stopped and bent her head forward and picked at a loose thread on the knee of her jeans. 'When I was a teenager I had a thing about Artemis the hunter. I owned a picture book with stories about the old gods. There was this one page I kept on looking at, which was Artemis running through the forest at night with one hand carrying her bow and the other stretched out towards me, the girl looking at the picture. The deer's point of view. But I didn't feel like a deer. I felt like Artemis was chasing me because she wanted to be with me, and I wanted to be with her, but I wanted her to chase me first.'

She told Kellas about the place she lived, on the island of Chincoteague at the southern, Virginian tip of the Delmarva peninsula. Her mother had been a history teacher who'd jumped to her death from the roof of the high school where she worked in Washington DC, just after setting her eighth-grade class an assignment on Manifest Destiny. On several occasions afterwards the principal told the family that he was sure the nature of the assignment had nothing to do with their mother's suicidal intentions. Knowing her mother, from whom hope and peace drained each evening and each autumn with the certainty of tides, Astrid reckoned this was probably true, but it twisted her up inside that the principal said it

67

not because he was trying to protect the family but because he was trying to protect History. They left Washington; Astrid's brother Tom moved to Seattle and Astrid moved with her father, who'd retired from academia, to a house in the peninsular pinewoods. She still lived with him, and joked about being Daddy's girl, but she wasn't often there. After college, film school, a few years managing a band, a few years making short films and a few years running a gallery, she'd gone to Yugoslavia and Rwanda and made a name in magazine journalism.

She told Kellas how once, one April night, kept awake by hay fever, she'd gone into the kitchen and looked out into the moonlit garden to see a doe, tearing at the young leaves of a pear tree. She watched the animal for a while in peace but there was some urge in her on the warm spring night, with the full moon on the deer's white throat. She thought about her rifle, but she might bring out the neighbours, and anyway it was well past the end of the hunting season, and she'd already killed her quota. With her cheeks burning and her heart beating she went to her room, dressed and went back to the kitchen. The deer was still there. She left the house on the other side and began to move as slowly and as quietly as she could around the building. When she was just past the first corner, she could hear the branches of the pear tree shaking as the deer tore at the leaves with its lips and teeth. The sound stopped. Astrid guessed the deer had smelled her out. She took several deep breaths, then ran out in time to see the deer's white rear end and her neat hooves flick powerfully into the bushes at the far side of the garden. Astrid chased after the beast, tripped on a root and fell onto the pine needles. She heard the doe crashing through the trees ahead of her, already hundreds of yards away.

'I remember the smell of the resin from the needles,' said Astrid. 'I could smell everything. I even thought I could smell the deer, the heat of it and the musk. I was a wild human for a second. I don't know what I would have done if I'd caught her. Rip her throat out

68

with my teeth?' She laughed. 'Glad I didn't have it in me. She might've been pregnant. I wanted to put my hand on her but I didn't want to scare her.'

The minibus jumped and shook on the bad road up the valley, at times a tight space, only the gorge and the river, at times opening out to green meadows, orchards and fields where in daytime peasants steered rough ploughs behind oxen, like European villeins in a book of hours. Some of the bumps were the remnant tracks of Soviet tanks, destroyed by Massoud's men twenty years before and gradually digested into the tissue of the road. The river was good for trout. From the window of the Toyota, Kellas could see flickers of silver where the moon caught the rough fast water. He looked round. Astrid was watching him.

'I've seen Afghans fishing down there,' she said.

'There's a place further up the valley,' said Kellas. 'They sell fried fish and potatoes.'

'Fish and chips,' said Astrid. She leaned in against Kellas and lowered her voice. 'I wonder if any Afghans are out in the dark now, here in the valley, fucking. What do you think?'

'They could be, I know, in among the mulberry trees. The leaves and the darkness to hide them, and the sound of the river covering the noise.'

'The houses are crowded, and all the prohibitions,' said Astrid.

'If you can be killed for doing it, and nobody does catch you, it must make it intense.'

'You'd have to choose your time, and choose your place, and plan,' said Astrid. 'I guess all the lovers are like partisans here.'

'Some of the lovers are married to each other,' said Kellas.

'That's true,' said Astrid. 'But I was thinking of those that aren't and can't be.'

'I asked Mohamed about it,' said Kellas. 'He was shy and he was giggly. A European man can't know. They meet you at the edge of their villages and you can't know what's happening inside. You could, perhaps. Veil up and enter their houses.' He took Astrid's hand on her lap, so it couldn't be seen, and she clasped it. He looked at Astrid and he could hardly see her in the darkness. He could see her eyes only when they moved.

One of the French photographers turned round. His name was Louis-Bernard. He was growing a beard for the first time in his life and it was growing out in some places and not in others. Astrid and Kellas slipped their hands apart.

'That's why the Muslims get so angry,' Louis-Bernard said. 'They have nowhere to go to masturbate in peace.'

The other photographer, Zac, turned and said: 'He was brought up in a boarding school run by Jesuits, so he knows.'

At the hospital, with its lights on generator power and the charity name painted in four-foot-high capital letters on the wall, they were turned away, although they were persistent in their questions. The English woman running the place lost her temper, and the journalists made the hour's journey back to Jabal empty-handed. Kellas and Astrid went to their sleeping places alone. In the morning, Kellas went to see what had happened in the bombed village.

The bomb site was on the plain between Jabal and Bagram airfield. It was several miles from the closest Taliban positions, among fussily divided portions of loamy fields that were themselves divided by duckponds, irrigation channels, clusters of poplar and willow and narrow mud dykes. The houses were big and roomy and solid, but humble between the trees, with their outlines made by the quick weathering of untreated mud-bricks. The journalists from Jabal had to park their cars half a mile from the place where the bomb had fallen and take a zigzag course on foot between the channels, with their interpreters stopping often to ask for fresh directions. The lines of cars badly parked and jammed together where the road ran out made Kellas think of a country wedding rather than a funeral. As Kellas and Mohamed walked between the trees, they could see other journalists and interpreters behind and in front of them, converging on the site along parallel dykes, carrying notebooks and cameras and bags like guests bearing gifts.

The sky was the same rude clear blue as every morning, and it was the most comfortable hour, when the night chill had gone and the midday sun hadn't begun to burn. The sound of water flowing from channel to channel and the touch of willow branches on Kellas's shoulder took away his awareness of past and future and he felt contented. Crowns of sharp yellow mulberry leaves, cruel and fine like victory, bit the sky.

A barefooted Afghan man in grimy grey clothes and a gold cap squatted in the dirt in front of the bombed house. It was his house. The explosion had killed his wife while she was sewing clothes for a wedding, and wounded his two children, his mother and his brother. He squatted near the ruins, with his long clay-stained red hands resting on his knees, and reporters came to ask him questions. He answered, although he could not meet their eyes. For hours he had a changing little group of people standing awkwardly in front of him in western clothes, taking his picture, writing down his words and filming him. The same set of questions would be asked, and the Afghan man, whose name was Jalaluddin, would answer, and when that group of journalists was halfway through, another set would arrive and get him to start again from the beginning.

Most of the reporters, including Kellas, asked him how he felt towards the Americans. Perhaps he'd say something unexpected. Come up with a theory that they had done it on purpose, or shrug and scratch his nose and say: 'It's better that the Taliban should be beaten than that my wife should live and my children not be hurt by shrapnel. I'm sorry about my family, but that's war. It's all for the greater good, in the end.' But Jalaluddin didn't say anything unexpected. Kellas could have written that the Afghans do quiet dignity awfully well but it would not have been true. They did not do it. It was what was there. All Jalaluddin said, as Mohamed translated it, was: 'My wife is dead. The Americans destroyed our family. What should I do? They should bomb the enemy. Not us.'

71

He'd been watching his sheep the previous afternoon when he heard the explosion. He ran back and with the other villagers began pulling his family out of the rubble with his bare hands. There was no doubt that it was an American bomb. Kellas could still see bits of it, jagged tearings of thin steel painted dark green, and the swivelling tail-fins that were supposed to steer it. It had numbers painted on it in white. You could see it had been a neat and well-made thing. The fragments were embedded in the rubble the bomb had made. Because of the nature of the material, it didn't look like rubble, or ruins. It looked as if the ground had spontaneously shaped itself into lumps with some straight edges and belched into the air. A man from the BBC was standing halfway up the slope of fragmented clay, doing a piece to camera. Kellas climbed up to where one of the family rooms stood opened up to the world, cross-sectioned, half-intact. The inner walls of the surviving part were whitewashed. A narrow, lumpy bed was carefully made, with the edges of the counterpane quite straight and no wrinkles. Pink and green plastic vessels which had been used many times were still stacked on a dresser. The small wall clock with arrowhead hands had stopped at half past four. On the wall was a photograph of a young man wearing an American sports top and grinning, with modern Middle Eastern buildings in the background. Kellas found out from a neighbour that the picture was of a cousin of the dead wife's in Iran, and from Mark that the cousin was wearing a San Francisco 49ers shirt. He wrote it down. Jalaluddin's wife had already been buried in the overgrown village plot, under a short oblong of raised earth. Villagers had dragged thorny branches over the top to stop livestock walking on it or dogs and jackals digging the body out. Half an hour after Kellas arrived a memorial service began. One of the elders spoke a sermon. He stood just inside a circle the men formed. The women of the village stood further back, in a body, under the shade of the trees, and the foreigners formed a loose outer perimeter, the writers leaning in to listen to their interpreters, the photographers roaming to and fro for good shots. The one who preached had a white beard and a haj cap and a string of beads swinging from his hands clasped in front of him. He spoke with his eyes closed. His clothes weren't ragged or dirty, but they weren't expensive. He was older than many in the gathering, but he wasn't old. Some of the elders there were bent and shaking. Surely he was the preacher, the one who led the prayers, the one who best knew the Book and the writings of the scholars who had subjected it to thirteen and a half centuries of exegesis. He was like the others; that was what gave him authority, not his learning. For a preacher, he lacked vanity. He stood there speaking like a man who didn't believe he had a special self and it was his ordinariness that could give his words the tune of revelation, if his words were good enough. Kellas relied on Mohamed to tell him what the preacher was saying. It was hard for Mohamed to do that. He wasn't up to simultaneous translation. He could manage just about every second sentence, or clumps of sentences. It was like looking at a flip-book cartoon of the sermon. It moved and jerked and the action became clear in fifty flickering stills. The preacher said: 'A woman has been killed. She had wishes in life, but we must think of God, and how we are subordinate to his will.' Later, he said: 'The Americans come here, drop their bombs on Afghanistan and kill innocent people. We do not condone this. Still, is it not our fault? We invited them here. Nothing breathes without God. God is using America to hurt the guilty among us by punishing those of us who have done no wrong.' The villagers stood and listened without words or expectations and then went back to work.

Kellas asked a reporter he knew from the Prague years if he'd seen Astrid.

'She was here earlier,' the reporter said. 'She asked about you. She wanted to know about your wandering days. She seemed disappointed when I told her you'd moved back to London to settle down.'

'Disappointed,' repeated Kellas. He watched Jalaluddin drift away from the burial place, his shoulders bent and his body racked with trembling.

'I've had enough,' said the reporter. 'I've been to too many strangers' funerals in places like this. I want stories where I can be home for supper. I want stories I can wear cardigans to. I miss my children.'

They saw Jalaluddin talking to a group of village men, who shook his hand and left him. Jalaluddin looked up at the ruins of his house, where his neighbours were starting to sort good bricks from the rubble. He climbed a little way up the heap, slowly and doubtfully parted some earthen shapes, then stopped, dropped the lumps he was holding, and sat down. He bent his head a little. Kellas went over to him, followed by Mohamed. Kellas asked Mohamed if he should give him money. Mohamed said it'd be a good thing. Kellas took a million in the local currency out of his pocket, about twenty-five dollars, and gave it to Mohamed to give to Jalaluddin. He shook Jalaluddin's hand and told Mohamed to tell him that he hoped life would become good again. Mohamed said something and gave Jalaluddin the money and Jalaluddin took it without looking at it or them and murmured something.

'He says God be praised for your kindness,' said Mohamed.

'Did he really say "God be praised for your kindness?"' said Kellas as they walked away. 'Did he mean it?' He trusted Mohamed least when he was translating the small courtesies of the poor. Mohamed tended to snobbery when he was bored, which he often was. His view, Kellas suspected, was that the poor could not afford to depart from stock platitudes, and if they did, he would correct them by translating what they should have said. Kellas and Mohamed began to walk back to the car. Kellas looked round once and saw that Jalaluddin hadn't moved. He sat still with his head bowed, looking at nothing, the money in his hand, while his neighbours threw bricks on their pile with exaggerated energy.

Kellas leaned forward, pulled out the airline's entertainment guide and leafed through the films on offer. He took a glass of champagne from the tray offered by the attendant. *Sweet Home Alabama*. That had been kindly reviewed, Reese Witherspoon revealing a talent for mainstream romantic comedy. It'd been that night, the night after he'd gone to the village and met Jalaluddin, that he had lost his temper with the sentry boy and shoved him in the chest and screamed at him that it was his fucking chair. One of those moments of rage that seemed to come from nowhere, but couldn't, since Kellas experienced them so seldom. He could still replay his shout exactly as it had sounded in the darkness, so loud as to be distorted in his ears, and remember how it felt when his palm touched the boy's warm bony chest. If he'd taken up *The Citizen*'s speculative offer of psychiatric counselling, shyly suggested by the managing editor like a father slipping a drugs counselling service brochure under his son's door, he could have made it sound neat and sympathetic. Sensitive, liberal Kellas goes to the village where the careless executioner of war has carried out his fatal warrant. Kellas's heart begins to bleed. His conscience swells to enormous size, pokes into his brain and turns it to poisoned mush. I had a breakdown, doctor. War is so cruel and my noggin is so fragile. I don't know what came over me. I lost control. A cheap doctor nods and understands. A smart doctor would tell Kellas he was lying. How come, smart doctor asks, you didn't lose control when the Taliban let three rockets off into the market in Charikar when you were there and there were body parts everywhere? If you were so frazzled that afternoon, what's with you being fly enough to lie to Astrid about how much money you gave to Jalaluddin? If you were all cut up by the cruelty of war, what's with sitting down that evening at your crippled desk to write your bullshit novel? Smart doctor sees into Kellas. Smart doctor says: I know you. You know I do. I don't see you made berserk by bombing. The way you went for that Afghan boy was something else. Like a man in a mask and helmet and goggles looking down through a Perspex canopy at something far away

75

he doesn't understand, and the only way he can try to understand it is to hit it.

Kellas had finished his champagne. He looked around for a refill. The woman next to him was coming back to her seat after applying a fresh layer of crimson lipstick, which contrasted appealingly with her pale skin and the perfect white of her suit. She smiled at Kellas as she sat down and picked up her book.

'Don't move,' said Kellas.

'What?' The woman smiled again, less easily.

'I remember,' said Kellas carefully, 'that when I was a child I used to play with my mother's lipstick – don't move! – not to put it on, I mean, only to make the stick come in and out of the tube, it looked like a robot's tongue, and sometimes tiny flakes of it would fall off. I'm surprised now, thirty years later, that they haven't got around to making lipstick that doesn't flake – keep still, I'm nearly finished – there's a piece on the lapel of your jacket. Don't brush it off! You'll smear it.'

'I can use my fingernail.' She had an American accent, and Chinese features.

'No. I know a better way. This is how the vacuum cleaner was invented.'

'You brought a vacuum cleaner on the plane?'

'Wait.' Kellas took a paper napkin from his table, peeled off a single sheet of the two-ply tissue, exhaled till his lungs were almost empty, and placed the tissue over his slightly open mouth. He began to inhale gently and lowered his mouth to the woman's lapel where the crimson mote lay. With the tissue paper fluttering against the stiff cloth he sucked in sharply, pulled away and folded the cloth in his right hand. He picked apart the folds with his fingers and pointed to the minute speck of lipstick. The woman looked down at her lapel. There was no mark. She laughed and clapped her hands a couple of times.

'Well, thank *you*, sir,' she said. 'That was smooth. Do you always put a tissue over your mouth when you do that?' They both laughed and blushed.

'An old girlfriend taught me,' said Kellas. 'The only other time I tried it, I made a terrible mess.'

'Either way, it's an introduction, right?' Her name was Elizabeth Chang. She was from Shanghai – 'CBC,' she said, 'Chinese-born Chinese' – her family lived in Boston, she was studying art history at Oxford. It was her second degree. She was on her way to visit a friend in New York. There were diamonds set in the gold of her earstuds. She was big, not fat but tall and broad and strong. She had a deep, hearty laugh, like an older woman's, which made Kellas feel comfortable, and she laughed readily, at the slightest hint of a joke.

'Oh, my God, my friend's a writer!' said Elizabeth after she asked what he did, and he told her. 'She's just got an amazing deal with Karpaty Knox for her first novel.'

'That's my American publisher,' said Kellas. 'I'm signing the contract for my book there this afternoon.'

Elizabeth congratulated him.

'Thanks. Karpaty Knox, you know, and my British publishers, they're owned by this old French publishing house, Éditions Perombelon. The guy who runs the operation, Didier, he made his Anglo-Saxons buy it. He liked the plot. He had me go over to Paris to meet him. How much is your friend's deal worth, if you don't mind me asking?'

'A million dollars.'

'That's a lot of money,' Kellas said, after a moment. 'How old's your friend?'

Patricia Lee Heung, the friend, was the same age as Elizabeth, and, like her, had been born in Shanghai and emigrated to America with her family as a teenager. Her novel was called *Red Hearth, White Crane*. It was a multi-generational saga about a young woman whose Chinese mother dies in childbirth, is persuaded by her communist lover to help assassinate her American father, suffers persecution by Red Guards in the Cultural Revolution, escapes to America, rises to wealth as a luxury Chinese cookware manufacturer, gets romanced by a handsome young American who marries her and tricks her out of her fortune, returns to China as capitalism becomes legal, and meets her former communist lover, now a recently widowed software billionaire. He begs her forgiveness, and they marry, with a glamorous wedding. The book ends with the children from their previous marriages graduating top of their class at Harvard together.

'That being tricked out of your fortune, it's a bitch,' said Kellas.

'Listen to you, Mr First Class Traveller! You don't like that kind of book, do you?'

'Is it a kind of book?'

'Yeah, the kind of book where brave good-looking people overcome their problems, get rich, fall in love, get married, have children and live happily ever after. That's the kind of book American and Chinese people want to read.'

'That's one and a half billion bookmarks. Better alert the trade.'

'Maybe they should be reading yours. What's it about?' She'd become a little aggressive on her friend's behalf. She was enjoying herself. Kellas looked out of the window. An unbroken plain of biscuity cloud spread to the horizon. The champagne was getting warm, but he kept on drinking it.

'It's a thriller,' he said.

'Uh-huh.'

'It's set in the present. It's about a war between Europe and America.'

'That'll never happen!' Elizabeth looked as if he'd uttered something profane. Her expression made Kellas feel better about the book than at any time since he'd finished it.

'Probably it won't,' said Kellas. 'It's a novel. It's a work of the imagination. Mind you, America is a work of the imagination, too. It's real now. But it was imagined first.'

'So what happens? The Americans start bombing London?'

'No,' said Kellas. As she said it, the words had that strange potency of the literally possible combined with the fantastic – the first characteristics of pornography – that had made him begin to fidget with the idea in the first place. 'An American army unit gets into trouble when it intervenes in the Middle East and commits a horrible atrocity trying to escape. The troops arrive in Europe on their way back to America and the Europeans decide that they have to try to arrest them and put them on trial. The American government says the Europeans have to let them go.'

Elizabeth asked what it was called. When he told her, she laughed. 'It sounds like one of those big fat paperbacks with huge metallic letters on the cover and an explosion on the front. They always have something like *Rogue Eagle* in the title. *Ultimate* this and *Final* that.'

'It is. It is one of those. And that is how you make the title. I drew a grid. Adjectives on the left, nouns on the right.'

'Why did you want to write a book like that?'

'To make money. To be read.'

'Oh.'

'You look disappointed.'

'What I said about the kind of book people want to read,' said Elizabeth. 'I mean, despite what I said. I like to think there are people out there writing books that I can only read by working hard at it, even if I never do read them. Even if I never do the work. I like to think that there are writers left who don't give a fuck, you know? "Here's my book. You don't like it, you can go fuck your-self, I don't care." I'm like my dad, I suppose. He'd run a mile if he saw some tough guy coming after him with a club. But he likes to think they're out there. He watches *The Sopranos*. He wants to think there are tough guys. He wants them to be real. That's me with difficult books. I'm probably never going to read them and the guys who write them probably know that most people are like me and the way they still keep on writing those difficult books is sort of touching, you know?'

'I don't know why you thought I was that kind of writer.'

'You don't dress like I imagine a thriller writer would dress.

You don't have any carry-on. I'm not being rude, but you look as if you slept in your clothes. And there's blood on your shirt cuff.'

The cuffs had slipped out of the sleeves of Kellas's jacket. He told Elizabeth he'd had a kind of accident the night before and she asked him to tell her what had happened.

'I'm not good at telling stories out loud,' said Kellas.

'You're a writer!'

'Why am I supposed to be able to talk as well? I'll try and tell you what happened. But I'll hesitate, I'll repeat myself. I'll tell you too much about some of the people and use the names of others I forgot to tell you about. I'll begin in the middle, go to the end, and then go back to the beginning, and end in the middle. Everything is middle.'

Elizabeth leaned forward, put her hand on his forearm and said: 'This is all you telling me that the reason you became a writer is you can't talk too well. And yet you've been yakking away at me about your book and your life ever since we took off.' Kellas laughed. 'If you're going to tell me a story, tell it. Otherwise you might as well shut up. I'm right, right?'

'Right,' said Kellas. He was still laughing.

The moving map in front of him showed the northern tip of Ireland and the Western Isles nudging off the edge of the screen. Words of ink and words of air. Forty lifetimes and all the ink from Bibles to Google hadn't chased it out of them, the hour the Celts learned that there was an art called writing, and an art called reading. Still they harboured it there in the west, still they had bards and druids in the inmost bulb of their onion hearts. In the way of their speaking, like the sound of a blast of melted rock and ash still circling the world long after the crater is cold, he could still hear the far whisper of the anger at the deed of writing words down, soaking their words of air in ink till they were sodden and sank. They'd learned and overmastered the art, sure, but in their pubs and beds and at their wakes and wooing they still resisted. Even that they weren't all Behans and Thomases and M'Gurgans to be known so surely. Or even Celts. Just to cleave to the idea that speech could be a song, that speech might be a song.

'I was at a dinner party,' said Kellas. 'Last night. I lost my temper and some things got broken. One of the guests was this guy, Pat M'Gurgan, an old friend of mine. I was at school with him. His parents were Irish. They moved to the east coast of Scotland when he was small. He could tell you the story better than I could. He's a writer too. He started out as a poet and he's just written a novel which is doing well. It's called *The Book of Form*. It won prizes.'

'But he's not here, so . . .'

'What you need to know about Pat M'Gurgan is that he's a bard. The thing is – what I'm saying is – there's two kinds of writers, bards and priests. It hasn't changed since it began. The bard is the one who talks. He talks so well that everyone thinks he must be a beautiful writer, and sometimes he is. But the words come out of his mouth with this great love of speech and skill. He entertains. He tells stories. He knows jokes. He draws a crowd in a bar, he exaggerates, he lies so beautifully that even people who know they're being lied to love it. He laughs at himself. He can cry as well, and talk about love all night. He turns the dead into heroes and the living into villains and clowns. He remembers the people he meets and makes history out of things that have only just happened. You know what I mean? You know that bard, don't you – you were there! You saw the same things! But to you, it was just daily moments, and to him, he can make a story out of it. He loves small crowds. He loves attention. He's an agent of instant glory for anyone he likes. He charms the ones he desires and when he leaves, the whole room misses him. When he's alone, he feels miserable, and thinks everyone hates him, and wonders if he's shallow. He's weak. He drinks.'

'I like bards.'

'The priest, on the other hand, isn't there to tell stories, and he's no good at jokes. He's trying to sell you ideas. The way the priest sees it, truth is more important than happiness, the past and future is more important than the present, and big ideas are more important than you or me or next Monday. People take the priest seriously, but find it hard to concentrate on what he's saying. He's rude and awkward in company and can only cope with intense, long drawn-out, painful personal relationships. He's more comfortable addressing a million people than ten but he doesn't often get the chance.'

'That's you, is it?'

'The sad thing is, most priests are longing to be bards, and most bards really want to be treated as priests.'

'You're not telling me this story very well. Maybe you've had too much champagne.'

'Maybe.' It was his third glass. 'Let me think about it a little more.' He was finding it difficult to concentrate. He wanted to put words to the events of the night before and put the words into the head of a stranger he would never see again, to bury the story, not to spread it. He was trying to make the story clean and spare and confined, but each moment and each character opened up into a forking path through time and space into other stories, and each path led to another fork, and though he would always find his way back, there were so many forks. On the way in his head from a dinner party in Camden to the dawn of literacy in Roman Britain he'd passed M'Gurgan, a memory of the man when they were seventeen. M'Gurgan standing at the bus stop talking to a girl, talking in her ear softly, insistently, incessantly, while she stared directly ahead, not moving. She'd looked sad, proud and hurt. Kellas hadn't heard about her and saw the two of them had already been through a small life together. M'Gurgan could have been telling her why he loved her, why he didn't love her, why she should leave, why she should stay, why he was going to Oxford, why she should have an abortion, why she should keep the baby, or why Pound was better than Eliot. Kellas never asked him because he didn't want to harm his wonder at the way M'Gurgan talked and talked, and the girl listened, when Kellas couldn't talk to the girl he thought he loved. He wrote her letters.

5

Kellas was half an hour late for dinner at the Cunnerys', and five minutes' walk away, when Margot phoned. He was carrying an expensive bottle of Bordeaux from a shop in Paris. Margot told him that they'd invited Melissa.

'We blanked,' said Margot. 'I'm so sorry. I called you to – I'm in the street. She's here already. We forgot the two of you had a history. We can't ask her to leave. She knows you're coming and she doesn't seem to mind. She smiled when I told her. I'm not an expert Melissologist so I don't know what kind of a smile it was. Anyway I wanted to warn you and give you a chance to pull out. But we really want you to come, of course. It's your call.'

Kellas asked if Melissa had come alone. She had. Kellas gripped the bottle in its plastic bag by the neck and walked down the Cunnerys' street. The night spat rain. The houses in the street lacked curtains. The people who lived here did not mind passers-by looking into their kitchens and sitting rooms, which were light and dressed in wood and primary colours, with pianos, bookshelves and paintings.

The Cunnerys had the whole of a Georgian four-storey terraced house, with the front door reached up a short flight of steps. That floor was mostly taken up by an open plan living room running the length of the house, with a window at one end looking onto the street and a window at the other onto the garden. The kitchen and the dining table, and the door to the garden, were below in the basement.

When Kellas arrived he kissed Margot on both cheeks, gave her the wine and hung his coat on the line of hooks on the wall inside the door. He should have brought flowers. Margot wore a close-fitting dress of sheeny material, with a pattern of pink, cerise, brown and white squares. She had dark skin and didn't need the make-up she was wearing. A smell of roasting meat came from downstairs and small within it was Margot's fussy perfume. Although she was entirely English there was a stillness, a languor and a grace about her that made her seem as if she had grown up strolling along the boulevards of a country with warm nights.

'Nice dress,' said Kellas. 'Is it silk?'

'Yes, it is. And look at you in your handsome suit. We're all dressed up, aren't we? And there are only going to be eight people. Are you sure you're going to be OK about this? I am so sorry, it was stupid of us.'

Margot was wiser than her husband, more knowledgeable about the social human and more kind. She lacked Cunnery's political instinct and his ego. Sometimes, while her husband was talking, she had the eyes of a witness. She was loyal and faithful, as he was to her. Yet she was like one of those trusted counsellors of the powerful who succeed in making supplicants forget that they are not on the same side. People who wanted something from Cunnery would seek Margot out with the intention of sending Cunnery a message, and, finding her so sympathetic, would start telling her what it was about her husband that they didn't like. They couldn't stop themselves, even though they knew Margot would tell Cunnery everything. Perhaps that was why such people so often got what they wanted, that it satisfied Cunnery to hear so clearly the specifics of other people's dislike. And perhaps their real intention was not so much to receive Cunnery's patronage as to have him listen to them. The sentence Margot heard most often was: 'Why doesn't Liam like me?'

Kellas was doing it. He couldn't stop himself. He and Margot were keeping their voices low in the hall. 'To tell you the truth, I was surprised to be invited,' he said. 'I don't know Liam all that well.'

Margot looked at him for a moment with widened eyes. She shook her head, took his hand and led him into the living room, saying: 'Now you're being silly.'

As Margot opened the door into the living room, somebody began to play the piano. The music stopped, went back to the beginning and started again. At the far end of the room, side-on to the door, the Cunnerys' daughter Tara sat next to Melissa on the piano stool. Tara was playing. Melissa had her hands pressed between her legs and was watching Tara's fingers on the keys. She looked up at Kellas as he came in and bent her head over the keyboard again, whispering to Tara. Sophie and Pat M'Gurgan were sitting together on a sofa near the empty fireplace, watching the recital. They were leaning forward, slowly turning the stems of their wineglasses in their hands, their mouths stretched out in similar desperate smiles.

Cunnery was standing next to a side table with drinks bottles on it. He turned and moved towards Kellas and shook his hand. His face reminded Kellas of the mask of Greek comedy, the pallor and the demonic smile, and inside the mask, the glint of real eyes. Cunnery offered Kellas a drink in the sort of hushed murmur ushers use for latecomers. Kellas took a full glass of red wine from him. Tara was not to be stopped, although she did keep stopping. Melissa was twenty-five years older than the girl, yet the two of them looked like sisters. Kellas's eyes strayed from the piano. He saw a copy of *The Book of Form* on a low table near the M'Gurgans. The red and green of it. Even the cover was a work made with craft and soul. Above the fireplace was a bust of Lenin. M'Gurgan had acquired it on a trip to Hungary in 1981, when he was a student at Oxford. Two years later, when he and Cunnery graduated, they won grants from the East German government to work in theatres in East Berlin for a year. M'Gurgan went; at the last minute, Cunnery changed his mind and went to New York instead. He'd explained to M'Gurgan in M'Gurgan's digs, with a strong smell coming off him as his donkey jacket dried by the two-bar electric fire, that socialism, however compromised, was secure in East Germany for at least two generations. The furrow in his forehead had deepened as he reached his conclusion. New York was where all the lines of force intersected – class, capitalism, race, art. He'd stood up, taken the bust of Lenin, and said to M'Gurgan: 'I'm taking this with me.' M'Gurgan didn't stop him. After nine months in East Germany, M'Gurgan felt differently about Lenin and didn't want it back. Cunnery had spent a year in New York, writing for radical weeklies, dancing and living off party food, before heading to Nicaragua to write despatches for *Left Side*.

Tara ended her performance with an athletic discord, using all ten fingers and thumbs to cover twelve keys. Everyone applauded, including Tara, who clapped her hands over her head, like a substituted footballer saluting the fans. Pat and Sophie got up and hugged Kellas.

'That was good, wasn't it?' said Sophie. 'What was it?'

'I think it was Mozart,' said M'Gurgan. 'Either that or Van Halen.'

The doorbell went. Cunnery left to answer it and Melissa came over with Tara. Margot introduced the girl to Kellas and they shook hands.

'It was Nick Cave,' said Tara to M'Gurgan.

'Of course it was,' said M'Gurgan. 'I loved it.'

Margot set a CD going quietly in the stereo, The Charlatans, and took Tara off to bed. Kellas and Melissa were left looking at each other.

In winter she was dressed for summer, in a white dress with a loose roll collar. She was tanned. She was stroking her neck with her right hand. Her hand was not free for shaking his. Kellas's eyes went to her fingers for a second, rubbing the tendons across her throat. The last time they'd been in bed together they'd been without a condom and he had come on her, at her urging, and it had landed there, across her neck. Now he was forbidden to kiss her. He felt he had treated her badly and that if he had treated her worse they might still be together.

'You look well. As if you've been on holiday,' said Kellas. Gold shone from her ears between the dark brown coils of hair. She lifted up her other hand. More gold.

'Seychelles with my fiancé,' she said. 'Separate chalets. No nookie till the nuptials and then flat-out for kids. I'm going to have five.'

'I know,' said Kellas. 'I saw what you wrote. That's the thing about having a columnist for an ex. I can read your mind.' On the anniversary of the 9/11 attacks, the *Express* had given Melissa a double-page spread to announce her babymaking resolution. She compared the aircraft suicide crews to activists who campaigned against restrictions on abortion. 'Let those of us who do not want to see Britain turned into an Islamic terror state remember this,' she had written. 'Like the IRA of old, the Islamic terrorists have two strategies to overwhelm us – the Kalashnikov and the cradle. Whether they bomb us into submission, or outbreed us, the result will be the same. As a woman, a patriot, and a Christian, I know where my duty lies. I shall, I hope, be a mother not just for myself, my husband and my children, but for Britain.'

'He used to claim he never read the papers,' said Melissa to the M'Gurgans. 'That's the trouble with journalists, he used to say, they spend all their time reading each other.'

'Are you in love with him?' said Kellas. 'This man, the fiancé.'

'Love. Oh, Adam.' Melissa put her hand on his arm. 'You're just not qualified to use the word, my dear.'

'Don't call me "my dear". I'm older than you. Not as old as your new squeeze. What is he, fifty-five?'

'He's forty-nine,' said Melissa. 'It's going to be a terrible problem getting you an invitation for the wedding. The château can only take two hundred. Anyway, Pat, I wanted to say, your book is fantastic.' She took him by the wrist and faced Kellas. 'This is a man who's qualified to talk about love. This is a man who knows life. A poet *and* a husband *and* a father.'

'Thanks,' said M'Gurgan. 'Did you like the scene with the crows?'

'It was brilliant. Do you get jealous of him, Adam? None of your books has been as successful as Pat's, has it? You haven't published anything for ages.'

'Adam's last was a great novel,' said Pat. 'It's not our job to shift units.'

'I got as far as the fourth page, I remember,' said Melissa. 'Still, keep trying, eh?'

'I'm glad you care,' said Kellas.

'That's why he reads my column! He wants to see if he gets a mention. Adam, you weren't that important.'

'I'm sure I saw a bowl of crisps around here earlier,' said M'Gurgan.

Margot put her head around the door. Tara was calling for Melissa. She left to read Tara a story.

'Permission to use the word "bitch",' said M'Gurgan.

'Granted,' said Sophie. 'What's Tara's bedtime story, *Dangerous Liaisons*?'

'I read your book twice,' said Kellas, 'and I don't remember any crow scene.'

'She hasn't read it.'

Cunnery came in with Joe Betchcott and Lucy Flagg. Lucy was a 26-year-old nuclear physicist who earned a high salary at Goldman Sachs casting a net made of numbers over the dark waters of the financial markets. When her computers hauled the net in, it was filled with profits from the deeps. Nobody else could understand where they came from, but the money was as real as any other kind. She had smooth white skin, short black hair, a black dress and glasses with black oblong frames. The only thing about her that wasn't black or white was her scarlet lips and her blue eyes. In the shaking of the hands Kellas heard himself saying to Lucy, whom he'd only met once before, that she looked sexy. Everyone was surprised. They all felt it and they all hid it. Lucy smiled a pinched little smile and frowned and Cunnery laughed and Sophie said quietly 'Adam', and that was all. But everybody's ears went back and the hairs on their necks rose. Kellas was surprised that he had said the words aloud. It was like finding that the rock between you and the lava below was infinitely thinner than you had thought, inches thin. A delicate crust was all that lay between him and uncontrollable activities incompatible with peace. The room configured and Kellas sat on a sofa with Sophie at the other end and Lucy between them.

'I shouldn't have said that,' said Kellas. 'Although it is true.'

Lucy drank a sip of white wine in a way that he saw her mouth was dry and he was making her nervous. 'It's good to hear what people are thinking,' she said.

'Not always,' said Sophie. 'There are too many people who can't tell the difference between thoughts and hormones. Adam.'

Kellas looked across at Sophie. She was looking at him. She'd been watching him while she talked to Lucy, while Kellas was regarding Lucy's body, for what he'd thought was a moment, but became more than one.

'You must be so happy about your husband's book,' said Lucy to Sophie. Kellas got up and went over to Betchcott, who was standing by himself at the drinks table while M'Gurgan wrote a dedication in the Cunnerys' copy of his book. Betchcott was a photographer doing a series for Cunnery, snatching pictures of the world's paparazzi while they went about their work. He dressed as if he believed he was a younger, fitter man, in a tight black sweater that clung to his sagging torso. He wore Ray-Bans and had eczema. He was always moving, making jerky little movements of his head, shifting from foot to foot, swinging his body from side to side, like a bird waiting for grain to fall. He had no gum, but his jaw worked as if he did. Kellas asked if the paparazzi minded having their pictures taken.

'Fucking love it,' said Betchcott. 'Had to get Mel Bouzad to stop winking at me the other day on Sunset when was staking Russell Crowe. Take the piss about the money but don't like it when I get the stars on my side. Leicester Square, couple of weeks ago, big premiere, guy comes up to me: 'Jennifer wants to help you show what these monkeys look like from her side.' Next thing know, I'm in J-Lo's limo shooting across her tits at the goatfuck on the window,

screaming and the flashing and fifty grand's worth of Nikon banging
on the glass, and she's just sitting there in her diamonds, smiling.
Went for a drink and she said to drop in on her in LA but I've been
so fucking busy, know.'

Kellas was listening and watching Lucy while Betchcott talked.
She wasn't wearing jewellery. Her hands rested on her knees. She
had black tights and she was nodding and smiling at what Sophie
told her.

'Are you . . . are you and Lucy seeing each other?' said Kellas.

Betchcott puffed and clicked denial. He looked over his shoulder
and shifted his weight and looked into his drink. 'I've got a girlfriend. Lucy's this incredibly obedient, willing thing. She'll do
anything. She'll suck your cock, if you ask her. She's pathetic. It's
embarrassing.'

'I don't believe you.'

'I'll show you.' Betchcott turned round and began snapping his
fingers at Lucy. 'Hey. C'mon. C'mere a sec.'

Lucy got up quickly and came over. She left her wineglass on the
floor, she looked up into Betchcott's face. 'Mmm?' she said.

'Tell Adam what you said last night.' Lucy looked confused,
glanced at Adam. 'You know what I mean.' Lucy was about to speak
when Sophie came over with Lucy's glass. Lucy took it and held it
with both hands, looking down into it. Then she put one of her
hands around Betchcott's arm and moved closer to him. Her way
of moving altered. Her eyes became bigger and her shoulders hunched
slightly. Betchcott started to talk again, looking at Kellas and Sophie
as if Lucy wasn't there, and after a few moments he shook his arm
and Lucy let her hand fall by her side.

'Series should've run in the *Sunday Times* magazine, but all the
Iraq stuff bumped it,' he was saying. 'Big piece of crap about the
fucking Kurds. Was some nice shots by starlight. I could've done it
better for them but I don't do the foreign shit, know?'

Sophie laughed.

'What's funny?' said Kellas.

'Boys.'

'I don't see what's funny. Is "foreign shit" funny?'

'He's not talking about you, Adam.'

'I know, he's talking about foreigners.'

'Don't have a problem with foreigners,' said Betchcott. 'It's the fucking losers and timewasters and slackers and toerags in this country. All the meetings and debates and protests and votes.'

'Votes?'

'Yeah, I don't see the point. We should have a dictatorship. Let the successful people get on with it.'

'I hate to hear people talk that way,' said Kellas. He noticed that his voice was rising and that there was nothing he could do to stop it. 'You stand there in your dark glasses and your black sweater in a living room in Camden Town and you're spitting on your ancestors' graves, you fucking prick.' These last words were very clear and sincere and loud enough so that the whole room went quiet. Betchcott's face changed colour and he turned round and went out, with Lucy following a few steps behind. Cunnery came over and put his hand on Kellas's shoulder. He was grinning.

'I'm sure Joe said something obnoxious that I wouldn't agree with either,' he said, 'but I'd rather you didn't have a stand-up fight about it in our house today. This is no man's land. There has to be one of those so we aren't killing each other and screaming at each other all the time.'

'We never do kill each other. And who's "we"?'

'Who do you want to kill? Joe?'

'No. But he is a fascist.'

'He's not a fascist, he's a photographer. He's got views. The furthest he's ever gone with political thought is to tell me once that not allowing a government which would abolish human rights was a breach of his human rights. You know I believe in resistance. But organised. It doesn't start just because you lose your temper.'

'And in the meantime the socialists and the fascists sit down to dinner together in the socialist's nice big house in Camden.'

The Greek comedy mask of Cunnery's face didn't change. His eyes behind the mask seemed to become darker and fiercer, as if the actor in the mask had heard something he didn't like and was frustrated at not being able to express it with his face.

'There aren't any real fascists in London in 2002, Adam,' said Cunnery. 'It would be so much easier if there were. I think the food's ready, so let's go and eat.' He led the way out. Cunnery didn't like references to his property. It was true that he couldn't be blamed for having well-off parents, or that a house he'd bought for £200,000 in the 1980s was now probably worth one and a half million. London was full of embarrassed millionaires. Socialists with mortgages: the whole history of Europe since the Second World War was contained in those three words.

The M'Gurgans went ahead of Kellas and stopped in the doorway before Kellas could follow Cunnery downstairs. M'Gurgan was rosy. He had already filled and emptied his wineglass a few times. For a moment, the sources of M'Gurgan became invisible to Kellas. He saw him as he might appear to someone who hadn't known him for thirty years, wise, funny, powerful, dangerous and vulnerable. The bulk and the scepticism, the silver hair on his crown, the new black jacket and Paul Smith shirt Sophie had made him buy with some prize money. The man who had explored deep inside himself and who had found the words to describe what he had seen. The unselfconscious bard of self. The big bad Celt in London. His lack of interest in exploiting it magnified his allure.

'How are you feeling?' asked Sophie.

'Less than the sum of my experiences,' said Kellas.

'Wish I'd sworn at Betchcott,' said M'Gurgan.

'I know,' said Sophie. 'But Adam, maybe you should go home.'

'Miss my dinner.'

'Melissa being here, and then you raving with Captain Unpleasant. Don't you think, Pat?'

'Everybody's full of darkness,' said M'Gurgan. 'Like everybody's full of blood. You need it and it needs to stay on the inside. You try to keep your skin away from sharp blades and you try to keep your soul away from the kinds of cutting that could make you bleed your darkness over other people's carpets.' He laughed. ''Member that time you did bleed for a certain girl? Pricked your thumb in English, went over to her desk, smudged your blood on her paper, drew a heart around it with an arrow through it and walked out.'

Sophie said quickly: 'I know you like that girl, Lucy, but don't get predatory, Adam. She's stunningly bright but there's something wounded about her. Since it looks as if you're staying.'

'Yes,' said Kellas. 'It's OK. I decided when I got up this morning that I was going to be nice to everyone today. Listen, Pat, I know I've told you this in email and on the phone but I wanted to say it again to you now, your book is a marvel. A wonder. Everything is deserved. I'm proud to know you.'

M'Gurgan laughed and went even redder than usual and mumbled a thank you, fiddling with his fingers and looking down at them. Sophie asked him to go downstairs and tell the others that they'd be a moment and M'Gurgan went. She turned back to Kellas.

'You think I'm trying to organise you,' she said. 'You think I'm being one of those ordinary women who gets things done.'

'I said that ten years ago,' said Kellas. 'You're still making me pay a duty for it. I didn't want you ever to hear me saying that about you. The language you use about people behind their back is a different language from the one you use to their face. Words don't mean the same thing. You know that.'

'How does it sound when you say it to my face again?'

'Like this: "Sophie, you're one of those extraordinary women who makes things happen."'

Sophie started to laugh and stopped. 'Thanks for not being jealous of Pat. You'll be where he is soon.'

Kellas swallowed. 'His work's been an inspiration for the book I've just written,' he said. 'Did Pat tell you what it was?'

'No, the two of you have been very secretive about it. We should go. You know everybody loves Pat's book, it's so peculiar and tragic and funny about his life. It's all in there. You're in there. Everything and everyone's in there, except me. There's no trace of a wife in there and no trace of me.'

'Nobody should marry a writer,' said Kellas. 'They'll always imagine someone better.' Sophie bit her lips shut and began to blink and clumsily stroked a knuckle along the edge of one eye. Kellas put his arms around her and gave her a squeeze.

'What about you?' asked Sophie. She took a step away, clasped her hands together in front of her and looked up at him. She sniffed. 'Are you seeing anyone? What about the woman you met in Afghanistan?'

'She didn't write back.'

'And you wanted her to.'

'I shouldn't have mentioned her,' said Kellas. 'We have to go down to dinner.'

The basement was floored in slate and the kitchen had granite surfaces and copper pans of all sizes. From the area where the oak dining table stood Kellas could see that there was another woman in the kitchen helping Margot. The table shone with silver and glass. On the mantelpiece over the granite fireplace stood family photographs in hardwood frames, some small sports trophies, a few of Cunnery's prizes and some white lilies in a tall square-sided glass vase. The green stalks of the lilies gave the thick irregular glass their colour. The walls were hung with grainy A3 black-and-white photographs by Margot of white working-class life in England in the 1990s. Two floor lamps, translucent glass globes on slender chrome stalks, lit the table. Kellas took his place beneath a photograph of a young girl bending over, trying to rouse another girl who was lying in the gutter with her eyes closed. Kellas sat between Cunnery, at the head of the table, and Sophie on his right. Lucy and M'Gurgan were opposite. He had been well fenced-off from Melissa and Betchcott at the far end of the table.

M'Gurgan was talking to Lucy too quietly for Kellas to hear. M'Gurgan's eyes widened and narrowed, his smile came and went, his hands gripped and opened. Lucy kept nodding and starting to laugh and then stopping and nodding again. He had all her attention. Sophie was talking to Betchcott and Melissa. Margot and her helper, who wore a plain black dress and looked as if she might be from South America, handed out bowls of chestnut soup. The helper's face had a curious, detached expression, as if she was actually somewhere else, as if she was dreaming the dinner party while she slept in a bed on the other side of the world. Kellas had hoped to taste the wine he had brought from France but the Cunnerys seemed to have bought a case of some Chilean red and they were having that. Kellas took a glug and gazed at Melissa in profile. That full mouth turned up at the corners. Sometimes it had been good to listen and sometimes he had kissed her just to try to stop her clever, fast, needling talk. She had been so insistent and sharp and cruel in her characterisations of everyone around her that he had come to feel more and more exposed in his own immunity. Sure enough, it ended.

Melissa had excellent peripheral vision. He'd forgotten that. She noticed he was staring at her and looked over. She turned away, leaned forward on the table on her forearms and began speaking to Betchcott.

'Great soup,' said Kellas to Cunnery.

'Thanks. Someone said they saw you learning how to put on a chemical warfare suit at a country house in Surrey a few weeks ago.'

'I learned how the last time,' said Kellas. '*The Citizen* wanted me to take the course again. That way they get a discount on the war insurance. It's a week of sitting there being talked to by ex-squaddies about indirect fire and, you know, arterial bleeding.'

M'Gurgan turned from Lucy and leaned in towards Kellas and Cunnery. 'Adam was telling me about the squaddies,' he said to Cunnery. 'Apparently they'll stand there and say: "Right. Now. You've just realised you've walked into a minefield. What's the first thing you're going to do? Anyone?" And at the end of the day they go home to single rooms and neatly made beds and letters from daughters they see once a fortnight and you wonder if maybe they need a course themselves. "Right. Now. You've just realised you've walked into a relationship with a woman. What's the first thing you're going to do? Anyone?"'

'It hasn't been easy for you in that way either,' said Cunnery to Kellas.

'I'm not trying to teach anyone,' said Kellas.

'Sorry about inviting Melissa.'

'Are you?'

'Because of you, I mean.' Cunnery asked him if he thought Iraq had chemical weapons.

'I don't know,' said Kellas. 'But if I thought there was any chance of Saddam using them, I'd never have agreed to go. It's academic now, I'm not going. I've left *The Citizen*.'

Kellas didn't intend to say this loudly or clearly yet the words travelled the length of the table at once. In the silence after the questions cleared he said that he'd sold a book for a decent amount of money and that he'd resigned from *The Citizen*. Cunnery raised his glass and proposed a toast.

'Please don't,' said Kellas.

'False modesty!' shouted Melissa, and raised her glass and drank. 'Sorry, I meant accurate modesty.'

Sophie rubbed his shoulder and was saying well done, well done. Lucy was looking at him and smiling and he tipped the glass to her and smiled and drank.

'Is that the one I think it is?' said M'Gurgan. He looked as if he hoped it wasn't.

'Have you read it?' said Lucy to M'Gurgan, resting her left hand on the edge of her chair and leaning into him. 'What's it about?'

M'Gurgan didn't say anything. He just nodded at Kellas and raised his eyebrows.

'It's a thriller,' said Kellas. 'About an imaginary war between Europe and America.'

'Which side are we on?' asked Cunnery.

'Europe's.'

'That's rubbish!' called Melissa from the far end of the table. 'PC *and* selling out!'

'I'm intrigued,' said Cunnery. 'We should do a piece on it. Your last one was more literary, wasn't it?'

'Yes,' said Kellas, looking at M'Gurgan. 'But the only people I know who read the books I've written till now are my girlfriends and other writers like Pat. I want to make some money. I want to be popular before I die. You're thinking I've sold my soul. Have you seen my soul recently?'

'I've never seen his soul,' shouted Melissa, grinning. 'Sell-out!'

'If it's popular, it doesn't mean it's poor work,' said Cunnery, tearing a piece of bread in half and making precise gestures with the pieces. His frown deepened, and so did his voice. 'Pat's book's selling well and he wasn't trying to follow the money, were you? It's still a great work of literature.'

'I don't know about great,' said M'Gurgan.

'Oh, take the praise, for God's sake,' said Kellas.

'You can't follow the money,' said M'Gurgan. 'It'll always run ahead faster than you can catch it. You just have to go where you want to go, and if you hear the money rustling behind you, don't look round. Wait for it to catch up.'

'That's your philosophy now, is it?' said Kellas. 'That wasn't what you said a year ago.' He became aware of a hand on his forearm and that everyone was looking at him. He probably had raised his voice a little. It was becoming hard to tell. It would be best to stop with the booze. The strange thing was that he hadn't drunk much.

'Adam,' said Sophie, whose hand was on his arm. Why'd she been so upset to be described as ordinary? Getting things done, that was a compliment. As a radio producer, she held her station together. Lucy was staring at him with a dislike that astonished him. Margot called down to Cunnery to help her clear the soup bowls. Cunnery got up. Then M'Gurgan got up.

'Do I have time for a fag outside before the next course?' he said.

'I might join you,' said Lucy. The two of them headed off for the garden, carrrying their wineglasses with them. Melissa asked Sophie something and Sophie turned away from Kellas. Left by himself, Kellas picked up his side plate and weighed it in his hands and turned it over. The crockery was an attractive set of white china glazed with black line drawings by a post-Soviet caricaturist. Kellas clicked out a tune with the tip of his tongue on his palate. *There was an old man called Michael Finnegan/ He grew whiskers on his chinnegan.* Cunnery had bought the crockery from a famous Soviet kitsch restaurant in Moscow in the late 1990s. The collapse of the Soviet Union had made it possible for the cartoonist to celebrate the Soviet Union's existence, and also to make money. Kellas had been to the restaurant: the crockery was expensive. He got up and went to the kitchen, asking if he could help, but the soup bowls were in the dish-washer already and Margot and the helper were starting to ladle stew onto dinner plates from a cast-iron casserole.

'I'll call the smokers,' said Kellas. The stew smelled rich and fertile, like somebody's happy ending. Kellas opened the back door and found himself in a small porch, made mainly of glass, darker than the kitchen and lighter than the night. He could see the shapes of Lucy and M'Gurgan on the patio, in their smokers' poses, M'Gurgan holding the metal of the fire escape with one hand and his cigarette tip moving wide from side to side as he told his story, Lucy standing a few feet away, left arm across her chest and tucked in under her right elbow, taking her weight on one leg, head dropped back to blow a gust of smoke into the air.

'Hey, tobacco lobby,' called Kellas. 'It's time to eat.' He waited until Lucy and M'Gurgan had put their cigarettes out and walked past him into the house before he went inside himself, closing the door behind him.

Kellas heard Betchcott and Melissa praising the stew to Margot. It was venison. The only reason Kellas had wanted to join the Iraq enterprise was in the hope of meeting Astrid there. He'd called *DC Monthly* to see if they were sending her, and where was the best chance of bumping into her, in Baghdad, Kurdistan or Kuwait, but all they told him was that she didn't work for them any more.

'I did a fashion shoot deerstalking in Scotland a couple of years ago,' said Betchcott. 'Lots of fucking tweed. Gave all the models loaded shotguns. Look in their eyes, it was worse than giving cocaine, know? Plenty of that too. One of shot a fucking dog in the leg. Good shoot. The fucking spike heels on the carcass, it was classic. One of gave me a blowjob in the back of a Range Rover on the way down the mountain.' Margot, Melissa and Sophie burst out laughing. 'Did!' M'Gurgan and Lucy turned away from their conversations and looked over. Sophie, Melissa and Margot were groaning and laughing and shaking their heads and demanding Betchcott name the woman, and he sat there with their faces reflected in his dark glasses, with his bold risking grin.

'Worst thing was, could feel this little nose butting against my thigh when was down on me,' said Betchcott. 'Could tell had no septum left, about to collapse. Didn't tell her. Shame, nice soft mouth.'

'I can't believe that you just said that,' said Sophie.

'Oh, Soph,' said Melissa, through her laughing. Margot and Sophie had stopped. 'It's only a bit of ripe badinage. It's what made English strong back in the Boswell and Johnson day, before the rot set in.'

'Is that your next column?' said Kellas. 'Sanctity of family life and the lighter side of casual celebrity sex?'

'What? I can't hear you, Adam. You don't speak very clearly.'

'I didn't realise we'd moved back to the eighteenth century already. That's three centuries in two courses. We'll be in the Dark Ages by the time the coffee comes round.'

'You don't like it when people are inconsistent, do you? That's why you're stuck in the middle of the middle class. You want to iron out all the peaks and troughs and flatten everyone to your level.'

'Kids,' said Cunnery.

Melissa ignored him. 'It just breaks you up, doesn't it, that I'm here at Liam Cunnery's table and I'm enjoying myself. You can't bear it that I get on with working-class poets like Pat, and men's men like Joe, and Marxists like Margot and Liam, and rich toffs like my fiancé's family. Character transcends class, Adam. The only people I can't tolerate are chippy, sanctimonious, bourgeois compy boys like you.'

'Kids!' said Cunnery, raising his voice and his hands. 'Please.'

'There's more venison, if anybody would like some,' said Margot.

Smiling broadly, Melissa got up and left the room towards the stairs, passing Kellas. As she passed, Kellas said, without turning round: 'Bring your fucking demons to my door. I'll wrestle them all.' Melissa didn't speak and they heard her feet going upstairs.

Kellas glanced at M'Gurgan and Lucy. Now Lucy was talking quietly to Pat while he ate, looking down at his food.

'I do wonder,' said Kellas to Cunnery. Cunnery raised his eyebrows. 'About you having Melissa here. And Joe.'

'They're friends. It's—'

'Yeah, I know. I know. Only what it is – it makes me think about being a young reporter in magistrates' courts. There's the guy in the dock, the accused, with his hands behind his back, flexing his knees, with the scars on his cheek and the tattoos on his neck, looking straight ahead. And in front of him there's two lawyers. There's his guy, the lawyer who's supposed to be defending him. And there's the Crown Prosecution Service guy, the one who wants to have him banged up, wants to see he doesn't get bail. They're supposed to be on two opposite sides. One of them's on his side, and the other is his enemy. And they're all standing there, waiting for the magistrates to come in. And the guy in the dock sees the two lawyers, the one who's against him and the one who's for him, talking to each other. He sees they know each other pretty well. Then he sees they're making jokes. They're laughing. They're friends. They don't mean anything they say to the magistrates when they ask for bail or for bail to be refused. They don't give a fuck about whether he gets bail or not. They don't care about him. It's only a game.'

'You're not in the dock, Adam,' said Cunnery.

'It's your readers. They read you in *Left Side* and they read Melissa in the *Express*, or at least they've heard about her, and it sounds as if you really believe, as if it matters, as if there must be some outcome. A struggle between right and wrong, good and evil, and you're on different sides. They don't know you're sitting down to dinner together at your table. As if it's a game. Two teams in the same club.'

'You went out with her, didn't you? You shared a bed?'

'Yes.'

'And you don't agree with what she writes?'

'It's foul.'

'So who's the hypocrite?'

Kellas blushed. 'I couldn't help it. The right-wing ones are so dirty.' Melissa came back into the room and sat down, not looking in Kellas's direction. Sophie leaned across Kellas and asked Cunnery about Tara's school. Kellas looked at Lucy and M'Gurgan. Both were sitting without saying anything now, looking down at their plates while they lifted food to their mouths, like an old couple in a restaurant who had no more to say to each other. Kellas was about to ask Lucy about her work when he realised that Lucy and M'Gurgan's silence was single, shared silence, a shaking, dangerous one. Lucy put down her knife and fork quite suddenly as if she had remembered something and asked Cunnery where the bathroom was. She was a little out of breath. He said there was one on the first floor, but could she use the one at the top of the house instead so as not to wake Tara. Lucy went out and after a moment M'Gurgan got a text message to call his agent and apologised and went out into the garden.

Kellas declared a wish to switch to white wine, and said he could go to the kitchen to look for a clean glass. He said hello to the helper as he passed her. She was cleaning up. She didn't say anything back. Kellas went into the porch. He could just see M'Gurgan climbing the fire escape to the first floor. Kellas went back to the dining room, walked past the table and out and began climbing the stairs. When he got to the first-floor landing he stopped and listened.

He heard what could have been a plastic cup of toothbrushes falling over and M'Gurgan snorting and giggling. He heard feet on a creaking floor. Tara's bedroom doorway lay dark and open a couple of yards away. There was an alien smell of other people's cleaning products. Kellas climbed the last flight of stairs to the top of the house. All the doors were open except one. Trying to move quietly, he walked towards it. He heard a tiny sound, which could have been a sound Lucy made at M'Gurgan kissing her while he touched her. Then he heard Lucy say, in a slow murmur: 'Your wife could be listening at the door right now.'

'Look at me,' came M'Gurgan's voice. 'Just put your hand there. D'you like that?'

'Hate it,' said Lucy and laughed.

'You're not wanting me to stop, are you?'

Lucy drew in breath. 'No.'

'Did you grow up in the country?'

'In Hampshire. Oh. Mm. Why?'

'I was thinking about what the lassie says in a bit of Burns.' They were both speaking very quietly.

Something made Lucy gasp and she said: 'It's a bit late for poetry now.'

'It's where the lassie says nine inch will please a lady. And then she says: "But for a koontrie cunt like mine, in sooth, we're nae sae gentle; We'll tak tway thumb-bread to the nine, and that's a sonsy pintle."'

Kellas walked away from the bathroom door, went downstairs and used the bathroom there. When he came out, Tara was standing in front of him, blinking in her nightie.

'I'm sorry. I woke you up,' he said.

'It wasn't you,' said Tara grumpily. 'It was that lady screaming upstairs.'

'Oh, really? I didn't hear anything.'

'There was a lady and she screamed. Did you like my piano playing?'

'Yes, it was lovely.'

'Melissa thinks I should have my own band.'

'How old are you again?'

'I'm ten.'

'All you need is to practise more.'

Tara's face folded into itself like paper and she let loose an unfettered wail.

'You see?' said Kellas, squatting down and putting his hands on her shoulders. 'You see what happens when people tell the truth? It's nasty medicine. Come on.' He stood up and took her hand. 'Let's go downstairs. All the grown-ups are telling the truth down there and I feel just like you.' He heard the bathroom door open upstairs and he led the weeping Tara away and down.

'I'm sorry,' he said when they reached the basement. 'Lucy was in the bathroom at the top and I had to go.' Tara ran down the table into the arms of Margot. Kellas sat down just as Lucy came in.

'He said he hated my piano playing!' wailed Tara.

'Not in so many words,' said Kellas. 'I'm really sorry I woke her up.'

'It wasn't him! It was the lady screaming upstairs.'

Sophie looked at Kellas, and at Lucy, who seemed confused and out of breath, and not so pale as she had been. Sophie leaned close to Adam and whispered: 'You could at least have come back a few minutes apart.'

'I'll take her, darling,' called Cunnery to Margot. 'You go and get the pudding.'

M'Gurgan came in from the garden and sat down.

'Everything OK?' said Sophie. 'That was a long call.'

'I thought he was quick,' said Kellas.

'Long enough for you,' said Sophie. She looked angry.

'Was he saying something about me?' said Lucy to Sophie, nodding at Kellas.

'The agent was on about the film deal,' said M'Gurgan.

'Is there a film deal?' said Kellas. Too many people were talking and some difficult, rare cocktail of emotions was shifting inside him. His soul was being driven down, into some deeper place than he had known of, while his body tingled and felt strong and light and cold.

'Some Hollywood big-shot has optioned it, but you know how it is, it'll probably never get made,' said M'Gurgan.

'It bothers me about you that you didn't have the patience to take her home and do it there, out of a child's earshot,' whispered Sophie in Kellas's ear.

'Did you have to tell Tara what you thought about her piano playing?' said Margot, as she laid a piece of chocolate cake in front of Kellas. 'She's only ten.' She sounded tired, long-tired, as if she'd been acting not-tired all evening and had just given up.

'What did you say to her about me?' said Lucy to Kellas. She was trembling slightly. Perhaps she was about to cry.

'Nothing,' said Kellas. M'Gurgan was excavating forkfuls of cake and shovelling them into his mouth.

Melissa came down the table, leading Tara by the hand. Tara climbed onto Cunnery's lap and curled up there. He put his arms round her. Melissa looked at Kellas, opened and closed her mouth, shook her head and said: 'God forbid that you should ever have children.'

Kellas looked down the table at Betchcott. Betchcott stared back, grinning. It occurred to Kellas that he hadn't seen Betchcott smile until now. Betchcott wasn't grinning at him, but grinning with him. You are just like me. Kellas put down his hand to pick up a spoon. A curious thing happened. Both his hands acted, and instead of lifting the spoon, they lifted the plate with the cake. Only by a couple of inches, before he put it down and rested his fists on the table. His senses dimmed and he began to follow a willed sort of dream where he got up and walked through the house and, in a small far room, came across Astrid, working, and she turned from her work and looked at him and smiled.

Kellas was distracted by a voice. He realised Cunnery was talking to him, jigging Tara up and down on his lap, about whether America and Britain would invade Iraq, and what would happen if they did. He talked about oil, and imperialism, and Israel, and how cruelly Britain had behaved when it was master in Mesopotamia. He talked with confidence, knowledge and accuracy about the history of the region. After a while, when Kellas didn't say anything, Cunnery asked Kellas what he thought.

Kellas shrugged. 'I don't know,' he said.

'Oh, come on,' said Cunnery. 'You're a reporter. You were in Afghanistan. You must have an opinion.'

'I'm trying not to have opinions,' said Kellas. 'It gets in the way of the "is" of the "is".'

'The what?'

'The "is" of the "is". As in "Something real *is* happening and I am not doing anything real about it."'

'You mean the truth?'

'That's not what I said.' Kellas was listening to his own voice. It had developed a tone he didn't like. 'You care about the Iraqis, don't you? And the Palestinians, and the Afghans, and all the rest? You've got Arab friends, at least that's what you call them when you write about them in your magazine. You don't want the Americans and the Brits and the Israelis to drop bombs on them. That's good. It makes you a good man. It shows you care.'

'I don't know about good, but there's nothing wrong with caring, is there? I'm not sure what you're saying. Are you saying you're in favour of dropping bombs on people?'

'I might as well be,' said Kellas. 'I pay my taxes. I went to a press conference with the prime minister a few months ago and I didn't lunge at him and try to kick him in the face.'

'Nobody expects you to do that.'

'That's because the price of caring is set so low. You just have to say you care and you've paid. You don't have to give anything up.'

'I give a voice to people who do. In the magazine. On the Internet.'

'But it's you. It's you. You can talk as radical as you like here on the island and you can live such a, such a comfortable life and people'll still call you a Marxist. When you're so safe. Your house is safe, your money is safe, your family is safe. Your reputation is safe, and so's your sanity. Your British passport's safe. Even your spare time is safe. How can you write about so many jeopardised people so self-importantly when you're so unjeopardised yourself? When did it happen that people who stand up for the losers began to be so afraid of losing anything at all? You hung out with the Sandinistas for a while but you never were one. You came home. You don't speak Arabic. You don't live in Baghdad. You've never lived underground. You've never tried to live as an honest, secular, left-wing, property-owning, intellectual journalist with a young daughter and a working feminist wife in an authoritarian Islamic country. You could, but you never have.'

Cunnery looked down at Tara, asleep in his lap. He stroked her hair. He raised his eyes to Kellas. His voice was cool. 'Is this what you learned in Afghanistan?' he said.

'I didn't learn anything in Afghanistan. I made an office there.'

'I suppose it is difficult,' said Cunnery slowly, 'to know, really know, what it's like for them. For people like the Afghans. I mean, those pieces you wrote for me from there – they weren't able to convey the reality, were they? Perhaps it's impossible to know.'

'You're wrong. It's very simple. But I don't think you want to know. That's what I've been saying.' Kellas's heart was beating very hard and he was having some trouble breathing regularly.

'No, I do want to know.'

'Are you sure? What it's like?'

'Yes.'

'OK.' Kellas stood up, pushing his chair back. The people in the room were very indistinct. He could see that they were different from each other but there was a shimmer to them that made it hard to look at them directly. The objects, the furnishings in the room were clearer. Their position, and their destructibility. First, his plate. He picked it up, raised it to shoulder level and dropped it onto the slate floor, where it broke into several pieces, which went skittering over the tiles. He grabbed the plates in front of Sophie and Cunnery, put them together, and hurled them onto the floor, harder this time. The wineglasses! They went with a sweep of his forearm and in what must have been a very short time his feet stood in the kind of crunchiness that occurs after an explosion or an accident. The people around him were engaged in forms of recoiling and retreating, but their voices were beginning to be loud. Kellas took the vase off the mantelpiece, threw the flowers away and smashed it on the fireplace. One of the fragments somehow ricocheted off the floor and stroked his left arm. It was a comforting feeling, but it may have caused him to bleed. The sound of breaking glass and crockery encouraged him but there was a part of him which was embarrassed that he couldn't think of anything to say while he was doing so much damage. He shoved the rest of the tat off the mantelpiece, noting that the glass on the family group picture fractured but didn't break, then yanked the nearest of Margot's photographs off the wall and brought it down with a crack on the edge of the table. It would have broken in half, but the frame only bent. He felt hands pawing at him and it was becoming impossible to ignore the fact that his name was being shouted. Blood on the floor. For an instant he hesitated, having run out of proximate objects to destroy. Was he really so weak, and these two-hundred-year-old walls so strong, that he couldn't kick them through like plasterboard or dried mud? He drew in breath and heaved at the edge of the table. Now he was finding a voice of his own. With a roar and a stabbing sensation in all his muscles he pushed the table over, sending the remaining glass and crockery to its doom. He pulled at and smashed one more of Margot's pictures. In front of him, a face acquired definite lines and sounds. A small child was bawling. He wanted to say something, something temperate and measured, but when he formed the words the only register he found was shrill.

'THAT'S WHAT IT'S LIKE!' he shrieked into Tara's face. Everyone was shouting, except the helper, who had come out from the kitchen to watch. She was looking at Kellas with her mouth set. He walked away, ran up the stairs, grabbed Lenin, left the house and lobbed the Great Leader through the Cunnerys' front window. After the windowglass had lain down in pieces, its own curt chimes complete, Kellas could hear the faint sound of a child sobbing from inside the house. He looked down at his wrist. His sleeve was sticky with blood. He started running down the street. On the corner, he passed a pillar box. He stopped and took out his wallet. There were first class stamps in there, and a receipt for a bookcase. He found a pen in his pocket, squatted down, smoothed the blank side of the receipt onto his thigh and wrote: 'Dear Sophie, it was Pat who had sex with Lucy at the Cunnerys' house. He went up the fire escape. Regards, Adam.' He folded the receipt in half, stuck the halves shut with a stamp, put another stamp on the front, squeezed Sophie's name and the M'Gurgan address on between the printed characters, and posted the piece of paper into the dark mouth of the box. Then he ran again, and vanished like a stone into the deep well of London's night.

6

The sound of cutlery delicately touching glazed pottery woke Kellas. Elizabeth was cutting a steak into small pieces. She put her knife and fork down, picked up a spear of asparagus, dipped it in hollandaise sauce and bit off the end. She looked at Kellas.

'You just closed your eyes and stopped,' she said, chewing while she spoke. She put the rest of the asparagus spear into her mouth. 'Like somebody cut your strings.'

Kellas's table had been set with a wineglass, a folded linen napkin, a menu and a pink flower in a thumb-sized vase. In this class the table was twice the size and swivelled to one side. He looked out of the window. Seven miles below, a mosaic of ice lay on the ocean like congealed fat on last night's stew. He turned to ask Elizabeth what time it was. The screen she had swung out from her armrest showed the paused image of *Spiderman*.

'I'm sorry,' he said. 'Watch your film.'

'I like Toby Maguire,' said Elizabeth. 'I guess I gave up hoping to hear your story.' She looked at Kellas with a casual affection he'd seen before, a distant sort of concern, between a mother's mocking patience with a slacker son and a daughter's amused but short moments of affection with her misanthropic father. She smiled, put her headphones on and made Toby Maguire move again.

With luck, one of the engines would fail, and they'd have to divert to Greenland or Goose Bay. A night in the Arctic, stolen from events. Only luck could steal time like that. Otherwise it was avoidance. The appearance of sea ice meant that they were approaching the

Canadian coast. He would land in New York in two hours, and events would begin again. Kellas put his hand in his jacket pocket and took out a piece of ruled paper, folded into four. It had the Cunnerys' address, and in a different colour, written with the hotel pen, the text of the email from Astrid he had copied off the TV Internet screen, lying on the heavy dung-coloured corporate counterpane, smearing the remote keyboard with blood. *Adam Kellas*, it began. On a line by itself, no punctuation. The fact that she had used both his names was strange. Perhaps she was emphasising her seriousness. The message was short. *I want to see you now. I want you to come to me, it doesn't matter how late it is, and tell me exactly what you want from me.* He wondered about the 'doesn't matter how late' part. It was as if she thought he was in America already. The final phrase also puzzled him. It seemed to refer to a conversation the two of them had been having recently, yet they hadn't exchanged a word since the day in December 2001 when she jumped out of the helicopter in the Panjshir. The three 'wants' in the message aroused and encouraged him. If, instead of the first 'want to', she had written 'wish I could', he wouldn't have taken a plane. He counted the words. Only twenty-nine! With twenty-nine words she'd picked him up and hurled him from one side of the Atlantic to the other at five hundred miles an hour. The dispiriting word was the 'exactly'. Astrid surely meant what she said: an oral test on love. On the evening of this day, because he could make it to Chincoteague by then, he'd be ringing a doorbell and seeing the woman who'd been in his mind all year, and there would not be any evasion. She wouldn't tolerate him telling her what he wanted simply by the act of taking it. He wouldn't be able to touch her, or sleep with her, or walk with her, or even be around her, until by spoken word alone he was able to convince her he'd found there really was a state of being which refused to be called anything except love. This when love was a word neither of them should utter until each was sure it coded for the same condition. It was an unreasonable set of terms and surprising so many people signed up. It was like begging an executioner for your life without knowing which language the executioner spoke, and without any way of finding out, until she lifted off the hood and embraced you, or the trap door opened under your feet.

He unfolded the piece of paper. It was a page torn from one of the notebooks in which he'd written *Rogue Eagle Rising* in longhand before transferring it to his laptop. The lines were badly broken up by crossings-out and insertions. It was one of the passages he had found most difficult. The task, at that stage of the book, had seemed both clear and straightforward: to commit an act of deliberate misimagining. To take a real, complicated country, in this case, the United States, and to simplify it to a set of caricatures so blatant, and so crude, that few readers would doubt his sincerity. A naïve entertainer, but sincere. The simplified country was an elementary exercise. It was populated by a homogenous mass of deluded, toiling dopes, decent but easily swayed, and a handful of crooks and thugs who'd led them astray and had them in thrall. What the thugs and the dopes had in common was their language and their lack of a sense of humour. The defining quality of the misimagined country was that it did not contain within it the possibility of its own salvation.

> The secretary of defense – *don't give the thugs in the simplified country names, only positions* – was a tall, tough old man who'd seen ten presidents come and go and served half of them. It wasn't the first time he'd ~~did~~ done what he did now, take a pile of black folders out of an attaché case and ~~deal them~~ toss them to the eight other people sitting around the table, ~~like a dealer~~ as if he was dealing the cards for a hand of poker. It wasn't the first time he'd astonished experienced men and women at the heights of power, whose careers had taught them not to be astonished by anything, with the reach of the Pentagon's foresight. But he knew that ~~this time~~ on this occasion astonishment would be too mild a word. This would be shock. He sat back in his chair and listened to the sound of turning pages.
>   The secretary of state was first to speak. 'You mean to tell me you actually had a plan ready to attack Germany?'

Defense chuckled. ~~'We've got a lot of plans.'~~ *Too* human!

~~'Is there a plan to attack the State Department in there?'~~ *Too much humour! Too democratic!*

Defense placed his fingertips together on the table in front of him. ~~The thick glass and frames of his spectacles hid his eyes.~~ *Too real!* 'That is correct,' he said. 'This contingency was foreseen by our planners. We can be ready to move in 24 hours.'

~~'Bottom line?' asked the president.~~

'Summarize the likely success of this operation,' said the president.

'We have the capability to immobilize the tactical and satellite communications of all our Nato allies, apart from the French,' said Defense. 'This is a low-casualty, surgical operation. We'll ~~have our boys out of there~~ return our forces to the Continental US ~~before you can say New World Order~~ before any European politician or general knows ~~what's hit them~~ what has happened.'

~~'We can't afford to lose this one,~~ gentlemen We cannot afford to lose face!' said the vice president.

~~'We got the Brits on board?' asked the president.~~

~~'I take it those patsies in Downing Street are playing ball,' said the president.~~

'Are the British on our side?' asked the president.

'Their government has learned that their foreign policy has only one dimension – ours.'

Kellas heard villainous laughter around the table in the film of the book. He would have to process the karmic consequences of this 110,000-word lie for the rest of his life. He put the paper back in his pocket. The cabin attendant came to offer food and more champagne. Kellas shook his head, which was hurting. Even if all four engines failed now, they would be able to glide to a safe landing in Canada. He could fly to DC, hire a car and drive to Chincoteague from there. His guts hopped with anxiety. He was close.

It was Astrid who had imprinted him in Afghanistan, yet if proximity, dependency and time were the components of intimacy, Kellas might have married Mohamed. Each day for weeks the interpreter had called for Kellas after breakfast in the compound in Jabal os Saraj. They'd driven around Parvan province and parted in the evening, when Kellas went into the compound for supper and to write, and Mohamed went to the lodgings he rented in town. The residences of the Afghan generals and men of power were scattered and they seldom answered their satellite phones. Kellas and Mohamed visited in the hope they would find them, in the hope they would be treated as guests. Lunches lasted for hours around the platter of mutton-hidden-in-rice. The generals and ministers grinned and guessed the future as if they had no way to affect it. The public lie was not a lie. Around them, rising up over white buildings and autumn tanks sheathed in barkish rust, and tiny skinny Alliance soldiers in half-buttoned new uniforms and blistering new European boots such as they'd never worn, some of them wearing eyeliner and some of them smoking dope, were the bare red mountains. They overwhelmed human action with their size, age and stillness, like a physical manifestation of fate. The white chalkstripe drawn across the always blue sky by the B-52s seemed to belong to that world of fate. There were no humans up there at the tip of the chalk. They could not see you or know you. The stripe of white in the blue and the red peaks belonged to eternity, for which flesh was as transient and insubstantial as light. Kellas found himself no longer looking up as he roamed with Mohamed on the Alliance's stubs of roads. He studied the yellow mulberry leaves, and the brass kettles, the steam curling off the glass and the leaves turning in the amber tea, the tensing of fishing rods over the river, the women on the road covering their faces as they passed, and the men taking the ends of their shawls in their mouths when the wind blew. Sometimes he met their eyes. He smelled woodsmoke, cardamom, kerosene, sheep dung and cooking oil. He and Mohamed sat on the veranda of the teahouse in Gulbahar and in the kebab restaurant at the Charikar crossroads, a cavernous empty place whose trade had died with the war, and span out lunches. They sought interviews from refugees and bandits and people smugglers and heroin dealers and doctors. Kellas had brought no music. He became used to the riffs of the different muezzin. Once he'd asked Mohamed to find him musicians and one afternoon sat like an impresario in the garden of the Charikar police station while four bands played for him, one after the other, on lutes and pipes and wooden boxes containing pegs and strings. They took it in turns to curse the Taliban for taking away their wedding business. While they were packing up afterwards a shrieking sound pointed at them from the sky and they bent and hobbled for cover like felons running the gauntlet. When the Taliban rockets exploded in the marketplace half a mile away the police chief took Kellas's elbow, grinning, and led him into his office to feed him sugared almonds while he listened to casualty reports on his walkie-talkie. Kellas and Mohamed went to the market and saw the chickens walking free with human blood on their feathers and the dark stains on broken melons and the dead wrapped in rags. They marvelled at the redundancy of those who had died. That night Kellas filed a long story about the musicians and the next day his editors asked if he'd heard about a rocket attack on Charikar, which was in the rival papers that morning.

When the days were a drive up the Panjshir, through the gorge where cars scraped each other passing rather than fall off the edge or yield, past Yunus Qanuni's residence, refugee camps, the unfinished monument to Massoud, to the high green pastures where the Panjshiris farmed and hid long-range rockets and where their big broken Soviet helicopter gunships sat in the mulberry groves like worn-out old hounds slumped in the shade; these days ended on the road between Gulbahar and Jabal, at dusk. The road looked down thousands of feet over the Shomali plain and the evening sun was attenuated three times, once as it dipped behind the mountains at the rim of the plain, by the atmosphere, and by the dust rising from the roads and fields. The plain was rich with trees and crops, but mainly trees; from up on the road at sunset, it looked like a forest. The crinkled surface made by the tops of the trees seemed to swell in the hazy gold light, and to vanish into the promising yellow distance.

Mohamed was a man of curves and circles, like a happy pagan idol, with a long, bulbous nose, a round face and a tranquil, comforting belly. He had a thick black beard and eyebrows and moved around the Alliance towns and valleys in a black leather jacket over a brown shalwar kameez. He tried to make his five prayers a day. He often forgot. During Ramadan the communal sense of imminent fast-breaking that built up in the late afternoon, when the food stalls were cooking full pelt, the air was rich with hot fat and the Afghans clenched their jaws to stop themselves drooling, affected Mohamed badly. He would buy bags of dough-nuts fresh fried at the roadside and stow them on the back seat, sit in silence, jiggling his foot, muscles twitching in his face, till the appointed moment for the fast ending, when he would reach back with a poor attempt at nonchalance and begin chewing. He had no authority, land or money, just a house in the Salang pass and a house in Kabul he hadn't seen since the Taliban came, but the local generals and men of power knew him, and seemed to Kellas to respect him. He had his debts; money debts. It wasn't as if he was owed a great many favours. The smoothness with which he navigated the social terrain of Parvan was a consequence of the way he had moved through a generation of civil war without partaking of the disgrace, shame and dishonour that was as much a parasitic attendant on it as buzzards and scrap metal merchants. Mohamed appeared at first to be so amiable in his slyness, to be so recklessly optimistic about every project, so fallible and jolly in the matters of dollars and eating, that Kellas had mistaken him for a clown. He was not, and he had been required to compromise. He had served the Soviet occupiers as an artillery instructor for Afghan troops, then served Massoud. In the Jabal marketplace his eyes saw all the layers of collaboration and resistance piled one on top of each other in each face, and others saw it in him. Here it was almost impossible to distinguish between constancy to a cause and madness. If you wanted to be virtuous, you had to accept that virtue would have a crooked shape. What Mohamed had done was to change uniforms and to change sides.

He had been there while comrades in arms turned homes and schools and mosques from places of life, light and voices to broken piles of dirt with human meat in rags laid out beside them. Perhaps he'd even helped, but not directly. For those who commit atrocities, atrocities are just business, but they do know what they have done, and with men like Mohamed there, who find a rare point between condemning them and joining in, those who commit atrocities are in a dilemma. They want the Mohameds to be implicated. They want the Mohameds to dip their fingers in the blood and smear it on themselves, to spread the blame more thinly over more consciences. But they also want the Mohameds to be clean. Whether they take pride in their wickedness, or still believe there is a route to redemption, they need to carry a stock of virtue among their supplies, as a reference point to how far they have travelled from goodness, and how far back the journey might be. Still, it had been difficult for Mohamed, after all those years moving through war without it entirely corrupting him, to remain a good man without acquiring, if only as a screen, some of the characteristics of a buffoon. He never looked comfortable in the shalwar kameez, like a Scotsman wearing a wedding kilt to the office on Monday. When Mazar-i-Sharif unexpectedly fell to the Alliance in November, and it became clear that the Taliban's time in Kabul was numbered in days, Mohamed asked for time off to visit a tailor and ordered two new suits for his return to the big city. As soon as they were ready, he began to wear them. They were made of thick brown corduroy; the jacket came in at the waist, cinched tight like a British soldier's battledress of the 1940s, and had epaulettes, and two rows of huge buttons down the front. It was tight over his belly and his beard spread over the little collar. He looked like an extra-large stuffed toy.

Mohamed introduced Kellas to the generals, told him in secret which of them were illiterate, explained to him how he could tell the difference between a T-54 and a T-55 tank and sat with him on the roof of a forward outpost one night with the lights of the Taliban pick-ups a mile away, the ripped-fabric sound of American fighters shooting across the sky and the occasional fireball on the horizon, and the shrieking of the jackals from the Shomali groves around them, like a mob of drunken teenagers. Once they drove up to the mouth of the Salang tunnel, at the top of the valley, on the road to Mazar. They passed Mohamed's house along the way, embedded in an agglomeration of mud buildings behind grey stone dykes, and Mohamed went inside for half an hour and then came out. He didn't invite Kellas in to meet his wife and children. He had two sons and three daughters. He was the same age as Kellas. Kellas knew enough now not to be surprised or offended. He was disappointed. Mohamed's Kabul liberation elephant cords had seemed like a vote for modernity, a vote for the party of coming down from the hills and embracing the big post-Taliban city, electricity and yellow taxis and free women. From the roof of the farmhouse on the plain that night they'd seen the grey glow of Kabul's streetlights, thirty miles to the south. The news of the fall of Mazar had come over the radio and the Alliance trenches had started singing, the soldiers' voices merging with the shrieking of the jackals. The teeth of Mohamed's grin had shown in the light from Kellas's laptop and he had been hearty and happy and Kellas had believed he could ask him for help in a matter concerning Astrid. Kellas wanted Mohamed to arrange a place where he and Astrid could be alone together, undisturbed for a night, with a roof and something resembling a bed. Before the beginnings of the Taliban collapse the small-town morals of Parvan province had made it seem a hard thing to ask Mohamed for. When the sense of the imminent opening of Kabul gushed into the hearts of the Alliance and the foreign journalists quartered with them, it was as if the way lay open not only to the reunification of Afghanistan but the unblocking of channels that connected Afghanistan with the shining light-bubbles of Islamabad, Tehran, Beijing, and beyond to Paris, New York, London, LA. For a short while Kellas allowed himself to imagine that the true Mohamed was one who had tasted and enjoyed the liberal facet of communist Kabul and Soviet

Uzbekistan, where he'd once been stationed; more than the vodka and the miniskirts, that he'd seen a bigger, brighter world in the faces of the girl and boy students talking in the cafés, on street corners with bundles of books under their arms, unveiled and rebellious. When Kellas saw Mohamed strolling away from his Salang village that afternoon with a serene smile, looking sated and paternal, moving slowly towards the car as if Kellas and the driver were working for him, Kellas understood that the mountain road, with its guns and old feuds and sequestered women, was as much his home as the city, and that his awkward observance and shalwar kameez were more a sincere sign of wanting to belong in the village than the camouflage of a liberal yearning to escape it. The corduroy suits were sincere, too. Mohamed wanted to belong in Kabul. But of the two worlds, he was less himself in the metropolis, and he knew it.

Kellas hesitated to say or do anything which might turn on him the expression that must have passed across Mohamed's face when he'd been present at the wicked deeds of his companions. Kellas hadn't seen the expression, but it had to exist, and he didn't want to witness it directed at him. Of course, Kellas wasn't going to be responsible for a massacre. But there was a possibility that by asking Mohamed to help in the arrangement of an act of fornication – Kellas hoped, several acts of fornication – by two infidel foreigners in a Muslim country, in a war zone, Kellas would see that expression. If not when he first raised the subject, then when he raised it a second time, or when it was time for it to happen, or after it had happened. The jollier and kinder Mohamed was, the more Kellas dreaded the moment of his seriousness, when he would distance himself from the foreigner. In spite of this, Kellas had to bring it up. It was a commission of a sort. 'Listen,' said Astrid one night. She spoke with a gentleness, clarity and directness that made his hide tingle. 'What you and I need is a place where we can sleep together. You arrange it, and I'll come.'

The declaration hadn't come out of nowhere. It came at the end of days when Kellas was distracted by thoughts of Astrid. He never dreamed about her. Yet because he thought about her when he was awake, he twisted the interpretation of what dreams he had onto the Astrid path; it affirmed his care and deepened his fascination. In one dream, he was in a small café in a narrow street in an Italian city. He sat inside because the tables outside were covered with a seething mass of sparrows. A waitress came to him, a short, stocky, buxom, dark-haired girl who looked nothing like Astrid, and told him he would have to leave, because of the sparrows. Kellas said that he wasn't afraid. The woman said: 'The sparrows are just holding the tables till the eagles arrive.' Kellas, who believed dreams to be the chaotic by-product of thoughts and impressions, leftovers passing out of the mind like other material surplus to life's requirements, nonetheless put this down as a dream about Astrid. That he had been waiting for her without knowing it; that he'd patiently sit out the tiresome chatter and squirm of the world in the hope of the arrival of something dangerous but magnificent. In the dream, there were no eagles, and he turned into the waitress, but he ignored that part.

Kellas couldn't remember when the sight of Astrid began to trigger such a strong reaction in him. He tried to think about chemicals and signals, to hide from himself his joy at the return of a state he'd believed he could no longer reach.

Even before the terrible question of what she felt for him, he tried the nature of his attraction to her. He had time while the war stuttered, and *The Citizen,* which had flooded south Asia with correspondents, spurned the nuanced inconclusiveness of his despatches in favour of the punchy certainties of unattributable sources in London and Washington. No matter who they sent to Jabal, the editors enjoyed the decisive reports of journalists who wanted to be there more than the uncertainties of the journalist who actually was. For weeks on end in the October and November of 2001 the marketable truth in Afghanistan lacked narrative or familiar reference points. Since Astrid refused to work alongside him, pointing out that he had to file most days, whereas she was only there to write one or two long articles – 'My drum beats once a quarter,' she said – there was time for glimpsing, glancing, paths crossing first and last thing, awkward courtesies at the doors to the wash-rooms, and for Kellas to wonder what he was doing. He tried matching Astrid to the template of old attachments. None fitted, although he couldn't be sure he was remembering them right. Love belonged to that class of experiences that couldn't be remembered. Only its symptoms and proximate causes could.

He had found that it was hard to turn adoration into sex, but easy to turn sex into dangerous, short-lived adoration. This discovery was made early in the course of his premature marriage to Fiona. She had been so fascinatingly curly and petite and wide-eyed and had a way of blushing rapidly and deeply whenever she was in the grip of any strong emotion. One night when the two of them were in the company of another journalist in Edinburgh who was blind to any human relations outside the sphere of politics and who could talk for ever in a steady, insistent monotone, Kellas tuned out his words into an insect hum for half an hour while, first, he thought about how much he wanted to touch Fiona, and then looked at her, and knew she was thinking the same thing. Their soft, sweaty young palms and fingers locked and squeezed under the table. For a while, sensing that their heartbeats and desires were in synch, they sat watching the other journalist's lips forming words, and remained aware of the undulating whine coming from his vocal chords. Then they made their excuses and ran into a taxi, out of the darkness of the pub, one of those places in the gullies of the old town where the smells of damp, old wood and stale alcohol merge and thicken, and into the warm pulses and scented skin of each other's necks. Kellas had passed the subsequent few days in a state of such bliss, such delight in her endearing shrieks, in the freeness with which Fiona gave her body and the pleasure she seemed to take from him, that he forgot how much his happiness was sharpened by the period of sexual famine preceding it. The long silences that punctuated their lovemaking, when they lay breathing, skin to skin, in each other's beds, seemed at the time like evidence of telepathic understanding, rather than evidence that they had nothing to say to each other, which is what they turned out to be. Kellas noticed the fanatical neatness of Fiona's flat. How could he not? All the surfaces shone, nothing old or worn survived, the furniture was arranged at Pythagorean angles. The flat was a declaration of the need for order made at well above conversational level. But he chose to believe that the quick, careless, eager way Fiona undressed, the way that to begin with there was no part of each other's bodies they couldn't touch, was likely to transmit itself to a more relaxed attitude to house-cleaning, instead of the other way round, which was what happened. A few months after they were married, Fiona began asking him to wear a second condom on top of the first.

Kellas hadn't made that mistake again. He'd made different mistakes. He marvelled at the variety of his errors, which came disguised as success. Katerina in Prague had been so beautiful that it had seemed to compensate for her love of dancing to German techno music in the clubs four nights a week, and for her reluctance to take a paid job, and for the hours she spent sitting hunched on a hard chair on the balcony in a shawl, one knee up, smoking, watching the steeples and biting her nails. But it hadn't compensated. She'd boarded the train to Beauty at thirteen and when a few years later she arrived, instead of getting off, she decided to stay on and see if there were more, better stops on that line. By the time Kellas met her, when she was twenty-six, she believed she was old. She confessed it to Kellas like a secret, weeping on his shoulder.

There was an area of ground in front of the Jabal house, inside the walls of the compound and partly overlooked by trees, where the Afghans had tried to make a lawn. The grass hadn't taken and it grew in patches and single tough blades out of the dirt. In the mornings an ex-special forces reporter from Australia would do press-ups there, and talk to his wife in loud, fluent Thai on his satellite phone, while correspondents wearing flip-flops walked across the grass to the outhouse in the far corner, trailing toilet paper, like disaffected campers. In the evenings, photographers would set up their transmitters on the failed lawn, spaced out and all aligned by compass towards the same artificial star in space above the Indian Ocean. They sat there with their backs to the house, silhouetted against the glow of their screens, watching the byte-count bars track from left to right, absorbed, cultic, elsewhere. One night Kellas was on the near-grass with Mark and Rafael from *The New York Times*. Rafael's interpreter was dialling the satellite phone number of one of the generals in the north over and over again, to break through the busy signal. Rafael was in a hurry. He was one of those who believed the war was faltering, like a slow line of goods. It needed promotion. Mark, who usually worked at this time – at all times – was waiting for his editors in California to wake up. He'd brought his red plastic fly swatter out with him. His only recreation was to sit upright in his sleeping bag in the early morning and kill as many flies as were within reach.

'Where do the flies go at night?' he asked. 'Do they go home to their fly-homes with their fly-wives and their 2.2 million fly-children?'

Kellas was watching Astrid, who he could see in the dimness at the far edge of the lawn, where the light from the house was faint. She was talking to the reporter from *The Guardian*, who lodged in another street. Astrid was half-smiling as she looked down, her hand stopped in the middle of a gesture while she thought about what she wanted to say.

'Why'd you get your translator to ask me about my arm?' asked Mark.

'I didn't,' said Kellas.

'I don't mind. I just don't understand why you couldn't ask me yourself.'

'He wanted to know. He was curious.'

'You were too embarrassed to ask me yourself so you got your translator to do it.'

'I didn't!' Kellas laughed. They wouldn't see him go red in the dark.

'My guys think you had it cut off for stealing,' said Rafael. 'Did you get through?' His interpreter shook his head. 'Keep trying.'

'I've been dialling the same number for two hours. My finger is hurting.'

'Keep trying. I pay you to get sore fingers.'

'In Somalia,' said Mark, 'they said "He makes love to women using his stump."'

'So what happened?' asked Rafael.

'I was born with it.'

'No shit. Did you get through?' The interpreter began yelling into the phone. 'Ask if he can get the American special forces guys on the phone. Ask if I can speak to an American!'

'I suppose you'll put me in some cheap British novel,' said Mark to Kellas.

'They're not that cheap.'

'I'll sue, you know.' Mark was speaking to the side of Kellas's head. Rafael and his interpreter were shouting over each other in English and Dari. Mark said: 'She's like a cat.'

'Who?' said Kellas.

'Astrid. The cat who walks by herself. She never travels with anyone.'

'She's trying to get an interview with Massoud's widow.'

'You never travel with anyone either,' said Mark.

'Mohamed. Drivers. People we pick up on the road.'

'Anyone not Afghan.'

Kellas asked him if he knew anything about Astrid. Mark said he'd read a couple of her articles, one about Bosnia and one about Kosovo. They'd been good, unusually good, memorable. She'd got deep inside a Serb family getting ready to leave Pristina. They'd made space for her in the truck that took them to Serbia, with their family tombstones stacked in the back and their ancestors' remains bagged up in builder's sacks. Mark mentioned the name of a famous photographer she'd been going out with in those days.

'I say "going out". They slept in the same hotel bed, I heard, the same cowshed or cave or whatever, when the things they wanted to do happened to take them to the same area. They were living in different cities at the time, one in Rome and one in Zagreb or Budapest, I don't remember. It wasn't like they ever really dated. They relied on coincidence to get together. But coincidence can be pretty reliable in this line of work, can't it? There are only so many places giving off the smell of that sort of death at any one time.'

'It doesn't say much about what she's like.'

'You think? I heard "wild".'

'What the fuck's "wild" supposed to mean?'

'Steady. That's all I remember, and I don't know who said it. Wild, I don't know. Party animal? Wild in bed? Feral, raised by wolves?'

Kellas's eyes were red with early starts and the dust of the day. He pressed them tight shut and opened them. No moisture, like the tenth squeeze of a lemon. Mark was too kind a man to be anything but married and content and he'd forgotten how immense the gap was between two people who hadn't decided to be together. He'd forgotten what a journey that was to make. How easy it was now to travel thousands of miles to be within touching distance of somebody, and how hard to travel those last few inches from their head to their heart. In the early Afghan mornings Mark would be on the phone to his desk in San Diego, where it was still the evening of the previous day. He'd be trying to sell his article to the front page, and he'd be selling Sheryl's pictures. 'Art,' he always called them. 'The art's great.' The art was always great. Sheryl wasn't his wife, she was a colleague, but it must have made her feel good to over-hear it. It was a kind thing. Mark was boosting his own chance of a front-page shot, and Sheryl was talented, but it was still kind, the way Kellas supposed a good married couple would be, supporting.

'Would you go for Astrid?' Kellas asked Mark.

'No.'

'Why not? Don't you think she's good-looking?'

'Yeah, I guess she is.'

'She's clever.'

'Yup, she's smart. Good at what she does.'

'So why wouldn't you go for her?'

'Why do you care?'

'I don't. Just tell me.'

'I told you at the start. She's a cat. She hunts by herself. She always goes after what she wants and you have to follow her or let her go and neither is what I'd like to be doing all the time.'

'What if what she wants is you?'

'I don't want to be hunted.'

'You don't know her.'

'I never pretended to. I'm just telling you what I see.'

Kellas looked over at Astrid again. He felt the gut-bite of jealousy. Was Mark so virtuous, or was it that he was too busy to cheat? The man from *The Guardian* was getting up and leaving Astrid. He was a small pale man with delicate hands, gingerish hair, round glasses and a slightly lopsided smile. On his way across the lawn his foot caught in one of the photographer's leads and he stumbled, shook the cable off, and walked on. Kellas wondered if Astrid was carrying the pistol. He wondered how many other people in the compound knew she was armed. It would hurt her if it came out. Still, knowing the gun was around was something they shared.

He got up and went over to where she was sitting. She'd opened her laptop and was typing. She looked up and moved her fringe to one side.

'Hi,' she said. She smiled.

'You look busy.'

'It's OK. The guy from *The Guardian* was trying to get some contacts for Massoud's widow off me. Sit down. We never get time to catch up, huh?'

Kellas sat cross-legged on the grass opposite her and Astrid closed her laptop and laid it to one side. She clasped her hands in front of her and looked at him. Kellas had become so convinced of the disorder and carelessness of the universe that the possibility of harmony staggered him. He trembled. His desire was accompanied by a fear that she would lose interest in him quickly. It was the old, just, women's suspicion about the wants of men, and now he faced it from Astrid. Her care for him had become precious and he did not want to lose it afterwards. His novelty could go stale in a night. One night! All this time he watched her, her eyes on him, and saw the freckles on the bridge of her nose and a single strand of one eyebrow making what little gold was to be gleaned in the dimness. Once, in London, he'd spent evening after evening listening, with real interest and partial concentration, to a woman whose account of her life was like Borges's fabulous 1:1 map of a country. Every story she told lasted at least as long as the events she described, often longer. One night they did go to bed together and afterwards saw each other for exactly enough time for Kellas to understand how hurt she was that he no longer wanted to listen to her. What made it worse was that she tried to hide it. She was tough, laughing, making out that she was as bent on gratification as him. That this was what grown-up men and women did. She didn't think it, and she was hurt. Kellas could see and he promised himself he would never do it again. Then he did it again.

He wanted Astrid, and some other state inside him was trying to stop it, hold it back, would rather be like the satellite to Astrid's Indian Ocean world, eternally descending towards her at exactly the same speed as she was moving away, so they would always be face to face, but never collide, never merge, never know.

'I don't want to break the silence,' said Kellas, 'but I can't deal with it.'

'I'm just checking you out,' said Astrid.

Kellas asked her where she'd gone that day.

'I watched,' said Astrid, starting slowly, then picking up speed, 'I watched a bride being dressed for her wedding. One of Massoud's distant relatives. She was sixteen. She stood in the middle of the carpet and she didn't know which part of her she should cover with her hands. Her nipples were the colour of rainclouds. The women from her family made her step into a tub and they washed her with water from jugs they brought from a room next door. They shaved her all over with an old cut-throat razor, and washed her again. After that they dried her, and sprinkled her body with cologne, and gave her a pair of silk bloomers to put on, and a white petticoat without sleeves. They put her in a red dress, a bright red, like poppy petals.' Astrid stopped, smiled at Kellas, and went on. 'It was tight over her arms and her waist and it had gold coins sewn to it that clinked together when she moved. I asked her if she'd met her husband and she shook her head. I asked her if she wanted to get married and she nodded and started to cry and turned around and I could see her shoulders shaking. She shook her arms a little to make the coins clink to hide the sound of her crying, but all the coins on her back were shaking anyway . . . Are you jealous of me, Adam, seeing that today?'

'No.'

'You're lying! Did it turn you on?'

'Yes.'

Astrid gave Kellas a light punch on the shoulder. 'She was only sixteen!'

'You titillated me! That's entrapment.'

'If that's titillation for you, does that make you easy to please, or hard to please?'

'I didn't ask to be pleased.'

Astrid stopped smiling and widened her eyes. 'That's not you. Being tough and hardboiled.'

'I'm tougher than you think.'

'Out there, maybe.' She jerked her thumb over her shoulder at the wall of the compound. 'Not with women. I can believe you being a bastard where women are concerned, but not being tough.'

'I'm going to start being tough.'

'No,' said Astrid seriously, with certainty. 'People can't change. You do know that, don't you? People can't change, except by becoming more like they are.'

'Do you know how you are?'

'I'm the same woman I was in America. I haven't changed. I've just put myself in a place here where some of the afflictions don't flourish. I'm like one of those alien species which thrives in a strange climate. I'm like the rabbits in Australia, the kudzu in Mississippi. No natural enemies.'

'Your afflictions don't flourish here,' said Kellas. 'What about your desires?'

Astrid laughed, looked at him from under her fringe, then lowered her head and plucked grass stems from the soil, one by one. They broke with a snap. 'A man is flirting with me in a war. Is this a good time, I wonder.'

'It's the best time. The worst thing is that the Taliban and the Alliance are such slackers that neither of us can pretend we might be killed tomorrow.'

Astrid laughed. 'We can pretend.'

'If I'm not tough, you're not coy.'

Astrid looked at him, reached out her hand and placed her palm against the side of his face for a second. 'No, I'm not coy,' she said. 'Tell me what it is that you want from me.'

Kellas thought, looking at her, that he would have to lie, or rather tell a part of a greater truth. He'd have to fool Astrid into thinking he was tougher. Part of that for sure was the thing he was going to ask her for, and not a minor part. He did want to make love to her. How many times with women had he half-deceptively, half-earnestly hidden that desire in promises of cohabitation and shared futures, felt the need to fog the lust in a spray of twitters about intimacy and friendship and taking time to get to know? And how often had he been seen through? Often. With Astrid he'd be going the other way, one hundred and eighty degrees. Concealing from her, so that not a flash of it showed, his wish to adore her and be adored by her; and show her only the other thing, as if it was the main thing. The only way he could see to hide his real desire was to choose words rough and coarse enough that they'd have the appearance of truth by their directness. Astrid might be susceptible to the notion that lies do not sound naïve. Besides, what he was going to say was true; it was a lie only in that it was a false answer to her question.

'What do I want from you?' said Kellas. He swallowed. 'I want to fuck you.'

He expected her to laugh, or raise her eyebrows, or turn cold, or, at best, reward his dishonesty with the words: 'At least you're honest.' But Astrid's expression didn't change at all. She blinked a couple of times. Her smile didn't harden or tighten. 'What you and I need is a place where we can sleep together,' she said. 'You arrange it, and I'll come.'

7

A cabin attendant handed Kellas a visa waiver form. The American immigration authorities wanted to know the address of his first night's stay. He wrote in the number of an apartment on Prince Street where he'd stayed sixteen years ago, on his first visit to America. Out of the window now, through gaps in shabby sheets of cloud, he could see the white and black of Canada cranking by. What still acres of larch down there, what pullings-up of pick-up trucks at crossroad coffee stops; and random points of snow darting against them, to roll and settle in the coat-folds of family men with necessary chores, and plain destinations? Kellas felt the winter wind blow through the holes in his ragged plans. His confidence astonished him. Perhaps he would really go to the apartment on Prince Street, find some lonely New Yorker in residence, charm them with his accent and his story of sleeping in the place during the San Gennaro Festival of 1986. Yes, he could do that. There was nothing wrong with his imagination. He could come up with stories and do more than write them down: he could put himself in them. He could turn up for real in any story. He'd drafted a story in the hotel room after the Cunnerys'. A man on the run from a fight gets a cry for help from an old lover on the far side of the ocean and straight away flies off to meet her. They embrace. No words. They know. The end. The beginning. That was his story. He didn't know what story Astrid had written to meet it. The story he'd set in Bagram a year ago had been simpler. Man meets woman. They hit it off. They make love. The beginning. The end. It should have played out that way. Even if he'd written it as tragedy, he wouldn't have written it so that those who died were strangers.

The notion of Bagram as the trysting place had come to him almost at once, the morning after talking to Astrid on the lawn of the Jabal compound. Mohamed knew a small-time commander who ran a group of local Alliance mujahedin close to the runway, which at the time was about a mile from the nearest Taliban positions. Kellas had spent a few hours there one afternoon and had intended to ask Mohamed if he could stay for a whole night, to witness and describe for *Citizen* readers the American bombing of the Taliban at close range. The commander's outpost was set among a group of high, roofless, horseshoe-shaped shelters built two decades earlier to protect Soviet aircraft from attack, the same aircraft whose wrecks now lay scattered across the airfield. Behind these walls the mujahedin and their old weapons, which included a single broken-down tank, were almost invulnerable to the Taliban, who anyway seldom shot at them once the US bombing began. The men slept and ate in safe buildings below the level of the fortifications' parapet. They watched the opposing side from a wooden watchtower, a roofed-over platform on stilts, which rose, exposed, fifteen feet above the aircraft shelters. The platform was a pleasant, shady place in the heat of the afternoon, and the mujahedin would spread out a cloth on the wooden floor to eat lunch. Blankets could deal with the cold of the night. The commander would want to keep a man on sentry duty there during the hours of darkness. But the sentry could be Mohamed; and it wasn't necessary for the sentry to be on the platform. He could keep watch almost as well from the foot of the ladder that gave access to it.

Kellas raised it with Mohamed the same day, in the late afternoon, after they'd failed to make it in time to a press conference being held by the Alliance foreign minister, high in the Panjshir. Instead, in Gulbahar, he and Mohamed found a table on the balcony of the teahouse on the river. They sat in the sun with glasses of cardamom-flavoured tea while the driver, by choice, sat at another table inside. Two women in filthy white burqas came to stand under the balcony and raised their open hands. Kellas could hear them calling but their faces were invisible behind the mesh of the burqas' face screens. Mohamed dropped into their hands some of the small-denomination notes he kept for mendicants. The women moved on and the narrow street brimmed with a clatter of old, well-tended engines. On the other side of the balcony, the gluey river ran shallow around flat stones and piles of rubbish which had been picked clean of anything recyclable. Mohamed began talking about one of his projects to become rich. He and some friends were going to rent a shipping container and stuff it full of raisins when the seasonal market was overflowing with raisins and the price was low. The following year, before the new season's raisins were on sale and the price was high, Mohamed and his partners would open the doors of their shipping container and sell their raisins at a giddy profit. Kellas was sure there was something wrong with the idea, but he didn't know anything about the raisin market. Perhaps Mohamed had hit on something. Perhaps Kellas could settle down in Gulbahar and open a raisin futures exchange. To sit in the sunshine, slowly drinking tea and discussing raisins for the next few hours would be easier than asking Mohamed to facilitate Kellas's sexual liaison at the front. He would ask, though. The thought of the encounter had taken hold of him. It would be awkward if *The Citizen* found out, but the aim gave his being there a significance and sense of purpose that writing reports for readers in Britain didn't. The very intention made him more in Afghanistan than he had been before. Fools and lunatics were exiles at home; they found it easier to be at home in exile. A little madness oiled the journey.

Neither man paid attention to the sound of a propeller-driven aircraft high overhead, until shouting began in the street, first children, then men, then the few women outdoors. For a minute it snowed paper. Boys and girls shot back and forward gathering the small squares up. The people of the alleyway snatched at them. There was jostling until they realised it wasn't money. Kellas saw the two beggar women fighting over them, holding them up to their faces and ripping them to pieces.

Mohamed picked up one of the squares that had landed on the balcony. It was an American propaganda leaflet, meant for the inhabitants of Taliban territory. It showed a fuzzy picture of a Taliban militiaman beating women with what looked like a piece of thick black electrical cable. The caption asked whether this was a just way to treat women.

'What do you think?' asked Mohamed.

'I don't think women should be beaten.'

'No, but about women.'

'Women should be free,' said Kellas.

Mohamed laughed. 'You always say that! But I don't know what it means. In English, a "free woman" means a woman who is not in prison . . . yes?'

'That's one meaning.'

'And a woman who is not claimed by a man.'

'Unattached. Yes.'

'And a woman who is not busy.'

'OK.'

'And a woman who does not cost any money to buy.'

'No. It doesn't mean that.'

'You say, for example, "medicine should be free". It's the same. "Women should be free."'

'No, it's not the same. That's bad English. Don't go on or I'll have to pay you less.'

'Pay me less? Why not pay me nothing? "Interpreters should be free."'

'You missed out the important meaning. Women should be free as in "not dependent", able to choose how they want to live, where they want to live, who they want to live with.'

'But, Adam, you cannot be changing your mind all the time, and once you make your choice, you are not free.'

'You can choose again.'

'Tell me, is it just women who should be free, or men too?'

'Men, of course.'

'Am I free?'

'More free than the women.'

'Can I move to America?'

'No.'

'Can I move to France?'

'No.'

'Can I move to London?'

'No.'

'Can I buy a new house?'

'I don't think so. Maybe, if your raisins pan out.'

'Can I leave my wife and children?'

'Yes.'

'Yes. And will my children be free then? Free from me, yes? Freedom in English means loneliness, does it not? And to be free is to be . . . what is the word, the word is . . . greedy! Greedy and lonely.'

'No, no, no.'

'I must be a terrorist, Adam. I hate freedom. I like being married.'

Kellas laughed, and Mohamed with him, and Mohamed went on. 'What about the woman in your house, the American, the blonde one? She has a black coat with zips.'

'Astrid? What about her?'

'Is she a free woman?'

Kellas hesitated. Although Mohamed had out-talked him, Astrid had entered the conversation. 'She's one of the freest,' he said. 'She does what she chooses.'

'Freest! Hm! Free, freer, freest. You can say that? Free, freer, freest. Like cold, colder, coldest.'

'That's right.'

'Dead, deader, deadest.'

'No, you can't say that. You can only be dead or alive. Everybody who's dead has exactly the same amount of deadness.'

'But everybody free is free in a different way.'

'You're beginning to talk like a Russian philosopher.'

'The Russians came here.'

'I know.'

'We beat them.'

'Listen, Mohamed, you talked about Astrid. She's a friend of mine. A friend, a close friend. There's something, a thing, I wanted to ask you. If you could help me, and her, with a private matter.'

'Of course.' Mohamed started to laugh, and the laugh turned into a giggle, and he carried on giggling and nodding, biting his tongue, while Kellas made his request. Kellas tried to find euphemisms Mohamed would understand. He talked about him and Astrid 'wanting to spend the night alone together. Alone, not to be disturbed.'

'Adam,' said Mohamed, 'as soon as you said "close friend", I understood everything.'

'And the tower's a good place?'

'I'll ask the commander.'

Kellas sat back in his chair, put a sugar-lump in his mouth and looked down at the river. The sweetness fell to ruins on his tongue and he felt a whisper of sadness that Mohamed cared so little for his mortal soul. To be an unbeliever was to be outside the walls of Mohamed's city of religious morality. Mohamed leaned down from the ramparts, watching the atheists and apostates yelp and burrow and mount each other in the dust. Pointing them out to his curious, well-behaved children. It wasn't that Mohamed was to be assumed virtuous. He might be arranging such liaisons for himself. The city of religious morality was full of sinners. But Astrid and Kellas were outside the outer circle of sinners, freaks in search of a circus. In Kellas, Mohamed had a pet. Now he'd have a show.

'Mohamed, nobody gets to watch,' said Kellas.

Mohamed giggled.

'I mean it. No spying.'

'Of course. Of course.' Mohamed cleared his throat and tried to swallow his fit. 'Mm. Do you love Astrid?'

'It's not your business.'

'Does she love you?'

'She loves freedom.' Kellas closed his eyes and rubbed his forehead with his left hand and marvelled at the idiotic phrases Mohamed trapped him into saying. Mohamed's tactic was to lure Kellas's vanity into the open and see it die in the light. Ask him naïve questions. Steer him into the role of teacher, knowing he had nothing to teach.

'If she does not love you, why—'

'Stop,' said Kellas. 'Stop. No more questions. This is your country. I ask you the questions.'

'Ask me any question. Any question, Adam, and I will answer, even if it is the most secret thing in my heart.'

'Why don't you introduce me to your wife?'

Mohamed looked down and cocked his head to one side. 'It's not what we do,' he said. He looked up and laughed. 'If I introduce you, what then? Do you have something to say to her? To ask her to drink Scotch with you in Jabal in the evening?'

'I don't think you would translate that for me.'

'No.' Mohamed's laugh eased slowly to a smile and that unstretched to small straight red lips in his beard. 'No. Anyway, you eat too much.' He began giggling again.

Kellas and Astrid arrived at Bagram a few days later in separate cars, an hour apart. It was before sunset when the driver dropped Kellas and Mohamed off at the aircraft shelters. To get there they drove through the villages on the edge of Bagram, down a pocked highway lined with stalls selling roughly cast, greaseproof paper-wrapped iron tools from factories in Pakistan, Chinese toys fey with flashing coloured lights, uncountable varieties of cheap contrivance to beat out the seconds of life with the businesses of fixing, hanging, cutting, binding and stowing, steel pots with the heft to boil a whole sheep, charcoal, cauliflowers, carrots the colour of beetroot, apples and flyblown lumps of mutton sagging on ropes of fat. Kellas got Mohamed to buy two live chickens and Mohamed sat with them in the back, holding them upside down by their feet, serene amid a rage of beaks, wings and floating chickendown. There was a back road to the east side of the airfield, protected by three men and a length of string hung between two posts. They knew Mohamed and waved the car through onto the airfield taxiways. The car turned onto the runway and sped along it, as no aircraft had done for five years, past the bony struts of bombed-out fighter planes. The evening sun put a scarlet gleam on the tailless, wingless fuselages of broken Antonovs, a brilliance that mocked their own dead lights, like the ghost of a failed science. All that was left of the thundering airborne troop-carriers from Soviet Kiev were notched fingers pointed at the mountains from where their doom had walked in cheap, hard plastic shoes. Kellas and Mohamed left the car and cast the chickens onto the tarmac, where they righted themselves, shook off the indignity and sought pickings.

The local mujahedin fought in shifts, if waiting was fighting. This was the time when the night levies walked and cycled in. The commander had a dozen men at any one time. He, Mohamed, Kellas and a clean-shaven man in a boiler suit climbed to the platform. Kellas was the last to climb up. The three Afghans stood grinning at him like three good uncles. A double pallet had been laid out on the floor and covered with sheets, a blanket and an embroidered bedspread. The bedspread was cream-coloured, sewn with a pattern of green leaves and flowers like foxgloves and like bolls of ochre cotton. On a child's classroom chair by the bed was a green plastic basin and in it a blue plastic jug of water. A small towel hung over the rim of the basin. Above the bed, from a nail projecting out of the chest-high wooden parapet of the platform, was a posy of plastic violets and red roses with a poem written in silver Roman letters, in a Turkic language, on a pink plastic heart. The whole arrangement had a strong whiff of betrothal. Kellas nodded his head slowly as he looked around, put his hands on his hips and made himself smile back at the Afghans. He knew Mohamed was the only one who spoke English.

'Did you tell them that Astrid and I were married?' he said.

'Adam,' said Mohamed. 'It was the best way. I told them that you shared a room in Jabal, but that it was very crowded, with very thin walls. They have wives. They understand.'

'Tell them I'm very grateful. Tell them my heart is full. Tell them that I feel like the prince in a Dari love poem.'

From the open edge of the platform, between the parapet and the roof, Kellas could see the bumps of Taliban positions, an expanse of gently sloping desert behind them, and the mountains beyond that. The Taliban held the ground to the east and the south, straddling the plain, blocking the way to Kabul. To the west, a mile away, the shell of the aircraft control tower poked up into the dusk. All of its glass was smashed and the steel and concrete remainder was eaten away by old cannon fire. After dark, so everyone believed, Americans set up equipment there to shoot beams at targets in the Taliban lines, guiding their bombs and missiles in when they were released from the heavens, like the mechanisation of cursing.

Kellas heard a car pull up below, the doors open, the sound of a diesel engine running and voices. Astrid had come. The engine must have been a Uazik, but it sounded like a London cab. Kellas had a moment of vertigo. He told Mohamed to ask the commander to get his cook to kill and prepare the chickens, and said he hoped they could all eat together.

He looked down from the platform to see her smiling up at him and his voice shook a little when he said: 'Apparently we're married.'

They ate together, Kellas, Astrid, Mohamed, the commander and four of his men, in a room built into the side of one of the shelters. The mujahedin sleeping quarters were in a like space in another shelter. The eight of them sat around a cloth laid on a floor of worn linoleum, by the light of a kerosene lamp, and helped themselves to rice and bread and radishes and fresh green herbs and pieces of boiled chicken in broth. The commander sat at the head, to Kellas's left. Astrid was opposite Kellas, with Mohamed next to her. Astrid hadn't brought her interpreter. The Afghans talked among themselves in Dari. Once in a while Mohamed translated a fragment. The nights could be silent, or there could be bombing. There was no telling. It was like weather. Kellas and Astrid ate and watched each other. She had been careful to tuck her hair inside a headscarf which she wore tight against her forehead and round her neck in the Persian way, like a wimple, so that only her face was showing. She wore no make-up. A grain of rice stuck to the corner of her mouth, and she lifted it on the end of her fore-finger and licked it off. She met Kellas's eyes and they both smiled and he raised his tea glass to drink, thinking that if he didn't, he would laugh out loud. He had it bad. Each time she blinked, moved her head or reached for another piece of food, his body quivered like a bell.

'The commander is asking why you wear no rings,' said Mohamed to Kellas.

'It's not our way,' said Astrid.

The commander made a short speech and Mohamed said: 'I don't know how to translate his question. He asks what your way is. Your way . . . what your rules are.'

Kellas looked at the commander, who was watching him with his head held back a little and his eyes widened, the questioner. He had a curly grey beard and was short, broad, inquisitive and jolly. Kellas turned to Astrid.

'You're the husband,' she said.

'You're the wife. What are our rules?'

'Do we have any rules? Ask him what he means. Marriage customs?'

'Not only that,' said Mohammed. 'The communists came and they had a way to do everything. A way of living, and death rules, marriage, business. They told us all the time what to do.' The commander began speaking, and another man from the corner, a man in his thirties in a ragged grey shalwar kameez, talked at the same time. The Afghans laughed. Kellas asked Mohamed what the man had said and Mohamed said it was very rude and wouldn't repeat it. Kellas told him he had to.

'He said the Russians like Afghan girls, and the Taliban like Afghan boys, but the Americans and Europeans only like each other.'

Kellas's eyes were on Astrid's knees in her jeans. He wondered how smooth they were to the touch when she was naked and whether if he put his hand on them they would be warm, or cool. The commander spoke again. 'The commander says the Americans are different from the other people who came here. They are here and they are not here. They watch from up there, and they bomb, but they're not here. They are not like the communists or the Taliban. They do not visit the houses of the poor people. They do not have a way. The commander says he is waiting to hear the voice of the Americans.'

'I'm American,' said Astrid. 'This is what it sounds like.'

Mohamed translated and the Afghans laughed and the commander spoke. 'He says, he still wants to know, what is your way? When are you going to tell us what we should do to make everything all right?'

Astrid put down her bread, frowned, smiled, and held her right knee in her clasped hands. She looked at the commander. 'Do you want to be told how to live by foreigners?'

Mohamed translated, and the commander replied. 'He says of course not. He says we will kill any foreigner who tells us how to live.'

Astrid bent her head, then raised it. 'That's the American plan. If we don't have a plan, you won't kill us.'

'He says they might kill you anyway.'

The ragged man in the corner spoke for a time. It was hard to see his face in the dimness, but his expression was so familiar that Kellas felt he knew him. It was the man in an audience whose question was never answered, and who did not expect it to be, but who asked it nonetheless; the man who had no trace of either deference or rebellion, and was condemned to neither accept the world as it was, nor act to change it. Mohamed translated. 'Zulmai says how can we know the Americans if they do not visit the houses of the poor people and talk to us? We see them from a distance. We hear the planes and the explosions. They should come to the houses of poor people, on foot, and tell us who they are and what they want, and what they will give us.'

There was silence for a while. Then Astrid said: 'Two chickens.'

Everybody laughed and the Afghans agreed that Astrid was cleverer than her husband. Sardar, the man in the boiler suit, began telling a story. Every time Kellas asked Mohamed to translate, Mohamed told him to wait until it was finished. When Sardar stopped speaking, Mohamed told them what he had said.

'Sardar was talking about his uncle, who had a partridge. It was a very hard partridge, a strong fighter. The partridge was called Shahrukh Khan.' When Mohamed said the words 'Shahrukh Khan' among his English words all the Afghans looked up and grinned, and some echoed the name. 'Sardar's uncle trained him for years, and when Shahrukh Khan began to fight, he beat all the other birds. So Sardar's uncle won a lot of money in Kabul, in Jalalabad, and in Peshawar. And Shahrukh Khan could not be beaten. Sardar's uncle kept him in a cage shaped like a bell and when the cage opened and Shahrukh Khan came out into the ring, he went to fight straight away, he used his beak, he used his feet, he used his wings for balancing. Shahrukh Khan could fight several times in one day and not get tired. His wing was broken and he even lost one eye and still he fought better than the other partridges. Once a dog got into the ring, and Shahrukh Khan attacked the dog, and hurt the dog on the nose with its beak, and the dog ran away. One day, Sardar's uncle was trying to get to Kabul from Charikar with Shahrukh Khan. He was bargaining with a truck driver to take him and Shahrukh Khan there. The truck driver didn't want to take him. He had a truck full of live chickens in the back. So Sardar's uncle and the truck driver were arguing, and Sardar's uncle got up on the step to shout at the driver, and put Shahrukh Khan, in his cage, on the roof of the truck. The driver got very angry and began to drive the truck. The truck moved forward like that! – and Sardar's uncle let go of Shahrukh Khan's cage to stop from falling. Shahrukh Khan's cage fell back from the top of the truck into the chickens. The chickens were very close together. When they found Shahrukh Khan later, the cage was broken, and this hard, strong bird was dead.'

'From the fall,' said Kellas.

'No! Not from the fall. Shahrukh Khan was still alive when he got out of the cage. The chickens. Sardar said his uncle found him covered in wounds from claws and beaks. There were so many of them. They made – panic. Shahrukh Khan was lost. He could have killed them all but he didn't even fight them. He lived always only in the cage, and in the ring. That was where he was a fighter. Never in the world. He was lost there.'

Astrid asked Mohamed to tell Sardar that she liked his story, and Sardar grinned and a quieter laugh ran around the room.

Later Kellas set up his satellite phone in the space at the base of the tower and called London to say he might send a report the following day about spending twenty-four hours on the front line. Distracted, they thanked him. He called his parents in Duncairn. They were out. He left a message saying he would call tomorrow. One of the commander's men asked if he could call his brother in Hamburg and Kellas dialled the number for him and put him on. The man was excited to make the call, and shouted into the receiver, but he didn't speak for long. It was practical stuff, plainly. Birth, marriages, deaths and the movement of money. The man thanked Kellas and moved away into the darkness. Mohamed stood at the edge of the patch of ground, watching the headlights of Taliban vehicles moving on the far side of their lines. Did it ever occur to them to switch the lights off, and be unseen? Mohamed had been lent a short, fat Kalashnikov which he held in his fist at his waist, casually, like an architect with a rolled-up plan. The stars were opulent and heavy. Kellas felt a touch on his shoulder and Astrid was beside him. 'Shall we go up?' she said.

'Look at the stars,' said Kellas.

'I know what they look like,' said Astrid. She took his hand and led him in the darkness to the foot of the ladder. She let go his hand and began climbing up. It was getting cold. The night was silent. He could hear every creak of the wood as Astrid's boots stepped on the rungs, then the clunk of each boot on the floor of the platform as she discarded them.

Kellas glanced at the dark, still bulk of Mohamed. He asked if he would be warm and Mohamed told him not to worry. Kellas climbed up to the platform. He took off his boots, laid them carefully side by side close to the top of the ladder, and went over to where Astrid was standing, leaning over the parapet on her folded arms. He put his arm around her waist, and let his hand slip down. The feel of the soft curve under his fingers, ending in the blunt point of bone on her hip, made him glad. Astrid shivered. She'd taken off her coat and was wearing just a sweater and a T-shirt. He asked if she was cold and she said: 'That's not the only reason I'm shivering.' She turned towards him and they kissed for a long time. He put his hand down the front of her jeans and his fingertips traced the line where her belly curved into hair. She gently pulled at his wrist till he took it out.

'Wait a little,' she said. 'Not so eager. We've got time.'

'I know,' said Kellas, although he was eager. They leaned together on the parapet, shoulder to shoulder, hip to hip. Kellas took Astrid's hand and pressed it against the hard place in his jeans. She stroked it a few times and took her hand away and let her head rest on his shoulder.

'Look at the headlights of those Taliban cars out there,' said Astrid. 'Can you figure out why these guys don't just blast them?'

'I know,' said Kellas. One of the stars overhead moved away from its constellation and swept a slow arc across the sky, flashing as it went. The skies were crowded up there, and nobody in Afghanistan owned anything able to shoot so high.

'What was all that about visiting the houses of the poor?' said Kellas.

'They wonder when our guys . . .'

'Your guys.'

'. . . my guys are going to go looking for converts. That's all they reckon America can try to get worth having here, the inside of their heads.'

'Christianity.'

'I think they mean Americanity.'

'I used to think there was that. That America had a way.'

'Yeah, me too, but if there is one, you have to emigrate there to find it. You can't convert to Americanity and not go to America. Maybe they won't let you in. But you have to at least *want* to go.'

'When did you last have sex?'

'Too long ago,' said Astrid, and she pushed her tongue into his mouth and started undoing his belt. They fell onto the bed, fighting with their clothes to put skin against skin. The smell of the bedding surrounded them, old and clean and musty, like the smell of the bedlinen in a country cottage that is seldom slept in. In the darkness where touch was vision Kellas beheld a kaleidoscope of hot skin, cold air and rough cotton. Astrid was slick and wet when he touched her there. They began to praise each other and named the particulars of what pleased them. They tasted each other and when he went into her he knew he'd always want to get back to what he felt when he heard the silly, forgettable utterances she made then. It was not the words but the shape of them, like a key of the cheapest metal that opened the heaviest, greatest lock. He or she, or both of them, it didn't matter, grabbed the covers and made them fly up and open out like a parachute and settle down big, square and warm over their nakedness, keeping out the cold and the world while they made love.

When Kellas woke later it was still dark and he was comfortable and strange in a bed. He had been spending his nights in a sleeping bag for almost a month. He was alone. There wasn't the bare hot body next to him he'd hoped for. He raised himself on two elbows and sought her out. Astrid was standing at the parapet, looking towards where the Taliban were. She had dressed and put her coat on over her shoulders. Kellas got out of bed and went naked over to her. The cold stung now. He took one side of the coat off her shoulder and squeezed inside it. He asked what time it was.

'Not even midnight,' she said.

'Why did you get dressed?'

'I couldn't sleep. Maybe I'll go down and talk to Mohamed.'

'Was there any bombing?'

'No. Nothing. Just the headlights. And the mystery.'

'The hell with the mystery. I went out on a limb to get this bed for us tonight and you and I are going to stay in it together till the sun comes up.'

Astrid took his face between her hands and shook his head gently. 'I like you, with your eyes all full of the world and your dumb little rages,' she said. She went to the hatch and began descending the ladder. Before he could ask her where she was going, she was gone. He heard her talking to Mohamed below and couldn't make out what she said. It took Kellas minutes to put on his clothes and boots and when he tried to follow Astrid his first foot on the ladder skidded off into space. For a moment he was hanging by his hands. He recovered and shinned down. Mohamed came towards him, asking what the matter was. Kellas was looking round and he saw Astrid walking towards the runway. He went after her, with Mohamed telling him to be watchful. A stillness that could not be divined hung over the commander's outpost; sleep or wakefulness, neither admitted the shouting of English words. In the starlight, reflected off the concrete panels of the runway and the taxiways, Kellas could see Astrid walking ahead of him. She reached the runway and began to walk along it, back the way they had arrived. She had a lead of about thirty yards. A man squatted at the edge of the runway, his Kalashnikov resting

in the circle of his arms like a shepherd's crook. His head followed
Astrid past, then Kellas.

Kellas began to run. The concrete was pitted with the pox of time
and Astrid heard the scratch of his boots on the grit that accumu-
lated there. She turned round once, saw him, stretched her legs and
ran forward with a good stride. They ran for two hundred yards in
this way, keeping the same distance from each other, like competi-
tors in a marathon, hanging off each other, waiting for their moment.
The cold thinned the air. The stars brushed against Kellas's skin and
prickled. He thought that if he looked up he might see that they
were crushing dark tracks through the stars, like children running
through a cornfield. He could not think what he would say to Astrid
now. He had stopped thinking. There was the rush of cold air, the
beat of his feet on the ground, his heart, the stars, the darkness and
the runner ahead of him. He did not know if he was pursuing or
being led.

Astrid cut a turn off the runway towards where one of the ruined
aircraft lay. Kellas put on a sprint. Astrid looked round again but
did not, or could not, run faster, and he caught up with her. They
stopped and stood face to face, a few feet apart. They were both
breathing hard. Kellas's whole being was violently flushed through
with a desire to have Astrid, not merely to have her but to take
her, and he would not know until he tried whether she wished to
be taken. He could not stop this. He stepped towards her and she
began to run again, with Kellas after her. She ran into a dead end,
another one of the aircraft shelters, open to the sky, but this one
empty. She backed up against the far wall. He could see in the
faint light that she was watching his face as he approached her.
Her face said to him: I want to see what you will do with me.
Kellas went up to her and took hold of the waistband of her jeans
with both hands. He unfastened them and pulled them and her
panties down a few inches and put his thumb inside her. The skin
of her navel was cold as he brushed against it and the heat inside
her spread to him through his skin. He felt her press her clitoris

against the saddle of his hand and she pushed herself off the wall and began to ride his thumb. They kissed, more ravenous than before. Astrid was very wet and Kellas took his mouth away from hers and crouched down, holding his arm out stiff for Astrid to fuck his thumb, adding a finger as she twisted and her breathing grew louder, adding a second finger, before Astrid pulled him out and he bared his cock and they lay down on the bare concrete and fucked till they came.

'That was new,' he said later.

'That was something new,' said Astrid.

They walked back to the watchtower, climbed the ladder and went to sleep together, breast to breast, his knee between her thighs, his head muffled between the pillow and Astrid's hair.

He woke suddenly, alone, not knowing if the gunshot receding in his head was dreamed or real. It was morning. He sat up. The light outside burned his retina. It was still cold in the shade of the platform. He heard the sound again, the dismal, consequential sound of a gunshot, and a wave of human voices, a moan, or a cheer. He pulled on his jeans and shirt and went to the parapet. He couldn't see anyone. Mohamed was gone. He finished dressing. While he was descending the ladder he heard the gun being fired again.

He found them at ground level, in the old taxiway between the aircraft shelters. Astrid was standing with her back to him. Next to her was Sardar, in his boiler suit, taking aim with Astrid's pistol at a pair of large-calibre shell cases set up on a rusted barrel about thirty yards away. A group of the commander's fighters, and the commander, stood on either side of them. They heard Kellas coming and looked around. They grinned and laughed and bent their heads a little as if they expected him to be angry. As if they expected him to bring order to a scene they did not understand themselves.

Sardar squeezed twice and the gun went off and rocked against his wrists. The second shot hit one of the shell cases. It jumped in the air, fell back onto the surface of the drum and rolled against the rim. Astrid called out 'That's one with two, man.' Sardar lowered the pistol. Astrid turned and saw Kellas and grinned, shaking her head. She looked round at the fighters, holding her arms out and nodding. 'I win, right? Right? I got two with two.' She hadn't put her scarf back on and her fringe swung bright in the heavenish light of morning.

The fighters laughed and shuffled and looked at each other, not sure what to do next and not sure where to put their hands. Astrid took the gun from Sardar, stuck it in her anorak pocket and extended her right hand towards him. Smiling and blushing, slowly and afraid, he moved his right hand to meet hers. Astrid took it and shook it and Sardar withdrew it and let it hang limp from his wrist, as if it no longer belonged to him. The other fighters were laughing.

They roused Mohamed, a motionless hump in the dark, warm-sweat smell of one of the shelter buildings, and sat around the cloth, as the night before, to eat breakfast. Astrid avoided meeting Kellas's eyes. She talked only to Mohamed and through him to Sardar. She was excited and talkative. Her voice was fast and unsteady. Apart from Sardar, who had gained confidence, who was anxious to persuade Astrid of something and kept interrupting her and Mohamed, the commander and his fighters were no longer smiling so much. There were frowns and they looked more into their tea and at each other than at Kellas or Astrid.

Astrid stopped talking and looked at Kellas. 'You're quiet,' she said.

'I ran out of things to say.'

Astrid rocked her head from side to side, looked down, folded a piece of bread and jam and put it in her mouth. She spoke loudly to him with her mouth full. 'You don't like to see me with the gun, huh?'

'I like you better without it. "Don't ever mess with guns."'

'If it's Johnny Cash you're thinking of, "Don't ever play with guns" was the line. My mother did tell me that. She was right. But this isn't playing. Where do you think you are? You can't pretend that you're not here. That you have nothing to do with all this.'

'I'm trying to be neutral.'

'There's only two ways to be neutral in a war. One is not to know about it, and the other is not to care.' Astrid got up abruptly, brushing her hands. She beckoned to Sardar to follow her and leaned down to Kellas on the way out. She patted the pocket where the gun was and said: 'Being professionally friendly.'

Kellas looked after her, then looked at the commander and put his hand on his heart.

'I'm sorry,' he said. The commander waved at him that he shouldn't worry, spoke a few words of benediction and ran his hands over his face. The meal was over, and the company stood up and went out. The cook and his boy came, climbed up to the platform and began with great care to remove the bedding. Kellas watched them for a while, soothed by their diligence and trouble. It took them ten minutes to lower the pallets down the ladder.

Astrid was on the other side of the taxiway between the shelters, sitting on the back of the tank while Sardar stood half out of the turret, a spanner in each hand, gesturing to her. There was an oil stain on his forehead. Kellas walked over.

'Hey,' said Astrid.

'Hey. Do you speak Dari now?'

'Sardar spent a year at college in Belgrade. We both speak about the same amount of Serbian.'

The cars wouldn't come to pick them up for another six hours. Kellas climbed the platform and waited for the bombing to begin. He spent time looking through an old pair of Soviet field glasses at the Taliban positions. They had a reticle painted on the lenses for an artilleryman to reckon distance. He studied the desert behind the Taliban lines. He saw trucks, grinding through the dust.

Kellas turned the binoculars to look at the tank. He twisted the focus knob until Astrid's laughing mouth could be seen clear and sharp, and Sardar listing points with gestures of a spanner. He seemed eloquent in Serbian.

When Mohamed and the commander came up to the platform, Kellas asked about the trucks. Mohamed said they were Taliban trucks. Kellas asked the commander why he didn't fire at them; why none of the Alliance troops fired at them. Mohamed translated the question, and the commander smiled unhappily, turned from side to side and looked out over the parapet. He had a broad pakul hat and wore a fawn blanket over his dark grey shalwar kameez. He moved with impatience, like a small-time builder forced to take on a mean, tiring, low-margin job. Through the binoculars, Kellas could make out the flapping canvas over the backs of the trucks, and the bounce of the cabins as they bucked through the desert. Without the magnification, they crawled across the ground like lice.

The commander spoke, looking at Kellas only once he'd finished speaking. Mohamed translated.

'If we hit and destroy ten trucks, the Taliban will still have enough,' he said.

Kellas put the binoculars down and glanced at the tank. Sardar was beckoning to Astrid. He disappeared inside the turret and Astrid clambered over, picked up an oil-stained canvas bag and stood looking down into the hatch. She reached into the bag and passed a tool to the red hand that came out.

'That's not much of an argument, surely,' murmured Kellas to the commander, picking up the binoculars again. 'You have to start somewhere.'

The commander rolled a little and stepped in and out of his flip-flops when Mohamed translated.

'If we fire at them, they fire back,' said the commander. 'Why should I risk my men, and you, and Mohamed, when the Americans are going to win the war for us anyway?'

The day was getting bright. The light off the sandy ground had turned harsh. Kellas wondered if it was too early to call Duncairn.

His parents were early risers. It looked as if he'd picked a non-bombing day. Perhaps there was a way to get the cars to come earlier. There was no need for Astrid to be loitering around Sardar and his broken-down tank.

The commander spoke in a voice Kellas hadn't heard before, the raised voice of a man with responsibilities, offended by foolish subordinates. Kellas was interested to know who he was talking to and looked round and saw that it was him. He blushed and waited for Mohamed to translate, but the commander spoke for a minute, his eyes fixed and wide and his mouth snapping, and Mohamed only looked at the ground, pinching his left thumb with his right thumb and index finger.

'The commander is saying he doesn't have good links with the artillery,' said Mohamed in the end. 'They often miss. He says it would be a waste of ammunition.'

'Tell the commander it's OK,' said Kellas. 'I didn't mean to offend him.'

'He is angry with you,' said Mohamed. 'He thinks you are criticising him.'

'Tell him I'm sorry,' said Kellas.

Before Mohamed could say anything the commander began talking angrily again. By the end he was shouting and Mohamed tried to interrupt him, gently touching his sleeve. 'The commander says those trucks over there, the ones you call Taliban trucks, they're carrying goods for the Taliban now, but maybe tomorrow or the next day they'll be carrying goods for us. They're only drivers.'

Kellas and Mohamed tried to soothe the commander. He stopped shouting and began taking short steps back and forward along the edge of the parapet, fidgeting with the controls of the walkie-talkie he carried and muttering. Kellas left the platform. At the bottom of the ladder he looked over and saw that Astrid and Sardar were squatting in the weeds on top of the aircraft shelter where the tank was parked. Sardar was pointing out something in the distance and Astrid was leaning in to look along his arm. She turned, saw Kellas and beckoned to him. He walked across and found the path up to where the two were crouched.

'See that tree trunk over there?' said Astrid. She pointed to a broad swelling in the ground about a thousand yards to the east, of sand scaled with stones and scrub, where a squat, branchless wooden vertical poked out of the crest.

'I see it,' said Kellas.

'Sardar reckons he can hit it with one shot. I say he can't.'

Kellas looked down at the tank. The open turret hatch was encircled by stained tools. The entire machine looked as if it had been dug up, passed through fire, then water, then left to rust for decades.

'The tank works?' he said.

'Of course.'

'Don't fuck about with it, Astrid. Leave it alone.'

Astrid was not listening to him. 'He needs the commander's permission before he can fire the gun. Can you ask him? The commander won't listen to me. The commander thinks you're the commander of me.'

'I can't do that. What if you hit someone?'

'It's nowhere near us, or the Taliban. It's no man's land.'

'It's not right.'

'Treat your wife the way you should,' said Astrid, looking hard into his eyes. 'Stop pretending you aren't here.'

Kellas looked at Sardar, who grinned at him and nodded.

'Are you jealous?' said Astrid.

'No,' said Kellas. He left them and went to the room where he had put his satphone. He lifted the case and climbed with it up to the platform. When he got there the commander hailed him too loudly, with an edge to his voice, as if he had something to say, but when he asked Mohamed for a translation, Mohamed shrugged and said the commander had only greeted him. Kellas set up the phone on the floor, took out the aerial and propped it on one corner of the platform parapet, where the ledge was broad enough to support it. He squatted by the phone, switched it on and waited for it to find the satellite. After a few minutes it came up: four bars. He took the handset and stood up. The flex was long enough for him to be able to use it while resting comfortably with his forearms on the parapet.

The commander asked how much the phone cost and Kellas said that he didn't know, that it belonged to his newspaper. He offered the commander the use of it and the commander laughed and asked who he would call. Kellas's finger rested on the dialling buttons on the back of the handset but he did not dial. He looked at the commander, who had been watching him.

'Mohamed,' he said. 'Can you ask the commander if he would mind Sardar firing a couple of shots to show my colleague – my wife – how the tank gun works?'

Mohamed translated. The commander laughed and said a few words to Mohamed, then lifted his walkie-talkie and spoke into it. The walkie-talkie beeped and a reply came.

A mile away, to the south-east, two more trucks were making their painful traverse of the desert behind Taliban lines.

The commander spoke and Mohamed said that he was asking Kellas who he was calling. Was he making a report? Kellas said he was calling his family but before Mohamed could translate, the commander spoke again.

'The commander says: "We're only ordinary soldiers",' said Mohamed. 'He says that they do what they're told. He says he'll do what you ask.'

Kellas dialled his parents' number and after a few seconds heard the British ringtone. He watched the trucks in the distance. They were dogged. Whatever it was they were carrying, it would get through.

Somebody picked up.

'Hello?' said Kellas.

'Is that Adam?'

'Hi!'

'How nice of you to call. I was just thinking of you,' said his mother.

The commander spoke into his walkie-talkie again and a frying voice answered in Dari.

'Hope I'm not calling too early.'

'No, we've just had breakfast.'

'Is it still dark there?'

'No, the sun's up. It looks as if it's going to be a beautiful day.'

Kellas saw Astrid and Sardar hurrying down from the top of the shelter, kicking pebbles and dust as they descended.

'I didn't hear from you after that last email so I thought I'd give you a call.'

'I thought I'd replied.'

'It doesn't matter. How are you?'

'We're fine.' The reception was good. Kellas could hear the faint exertion in his mother's voice as she sat down. Perhaps he could hear the creak of the wicker chair in the hall. It could have been static. At that time of day the light would be shining through the coloured glass around the door. It would be brighter if they had cut back the ivy.

'I can't speak for long,' he said. He saw Sardar shout to someone, then slither down the turret hatch and, after a moment, Astrid lower herself in after him.

'I know,' said his mother. 'But I must say I was a little bit cross with you the last time you called and you hung up suddenly.'

'I'm sorry,' said Kellas. 'I had to go.'

'Please don't do it this time. How are you?'

'I'm fine. It's very quiet here.'

A youngster, a boy, darted out of the corner of Kellas's vision, leaped onto the front of the tank and slid into another hatch.

'We had our peace vigil yesterday evening,' said Kellas's mother. 'There were about a dozen of us on the square, with candles.'

'Good for you,' said Kellas.

'A lot of people stopped to ask questions, so that was good.'

'Great.'

A roar from powerful machinery stirred the air. The tank farted

155

black smoke and lurched backwards a foot, then forwards. One of the reasons Kellas had written it off was the way it was parked, its gun facing the wall, wedged in between slabs of concrete, with no way to get itself pointed at the Taliban without many slow manoeuvres. But the tank was not a limousine. It was a Russian tank, ancient and nimble. It jerked backwards out of its bay, coughing fumes and squealing with every wheel and every link of track. The driver's head poked up from a hatch by the front. He looked calm and focused. He aligned the tank with a slope of earth that ran up from the aircraft shelters at a forty-five degree angle.

'What was that noise?' asked Kellas's mother.

'A tank moving.'

'A tank! Where are you?'

Kellas laughed. 'Don't worry. They're just practising.' He beckoned to Mohamed to hand him the binoculars. The commander was looking at him and grinning and nodding his head. He made the thumbs-up sign to Kellas and Kellas made the gesture back and took the binoculars from Mohamed's hand.

'How's the garden looking?' asked Kellas. He settled the binoculars on the bridge of his nose and watched the tree trunk. With the magnification he could see that the rest of the original tree had been torn off by a past explosion.

'Well, it's November. Not the best time of year for the garden, you know. It's raking up leaves. That's it. Compost. You get a better view of the firth in winter, of course.'

The tank driver made the rusted hulk turn with the heavy gliding grace of a curling stone, then hurled it at the slope. The tank hit the bottom of the slope, reared up, showed a foot of air, bounced back, slipped, roared with heightened frenzy, gripped the dirt, shot up the ramp of earth and stopped with its turret above the top of the shelters.

'Listen, Mum, there might be a couple of bangs,' said Kellas. 'Don't worry, it's just target practice.'

'Oh, God,' said his mother, affecting a nervous laugh that really was nervous. 'Where did you say you were, exactly?'

'Hang on,' said Kellas. He tightened the focus on the tree trunk. The commander's walkie-talkie crackled and the commander spoke a few words into it.

With a deep crack that shook their breastbones, the tank's big gun fired.

'Hear that?' said Kellas in the still second while the shell flew.

'Yes!'

'At an airfield,' said Kellas.

'An airfield?'

'That's strange.'

'What's happening?'

'He missed by miles.' Through the binoculars Kellas could see for more than a hundred yards on either side of the tree and there was no sign of a shell landing. Yet he heard the far-off thud that signified an impact, and cheering from the commander's fighters below. He took the binoculars away from his eyes and saw the smoke from the explosion drifting black into the air a mile away, halfway between the two trucks.

'Mohamed, what the fuck?' shouted Kellas.

'Don't worry, he's going to fire again!' said Mohamed.

'What's happening?' said Kellas's mother. Kellas's mouth was entirely dry. There was too broad a span to take in. The tank, the smoke, the trucks, the tree trunk, the commander, Mohamed.

'There are people in those fucking trucks!' shouted Kellas. 'He was supposed to fire over there.'

'What's happening?' said Kellas's mother.

'I'm going to have to go,' said Kellas.

'Adam, it was what you wanted,' said Mohamed. 'You wanted the commander to fire at the Taliban trucks. You asked for the tank to fire.'

The commander said something quickly. He looked confident. 'The commander said: this time he'll hit one.'

'Tell him to stop!' shouted Kellas.

'Why? They are the enemy. You asked for this.'

'Adam, I want to know what's going on. I'm very worried,' said his mother.

'It's OK,' said Kellas.

'You sound worried.'

'It's OK. The tank driver made a mistake but he missed.'

'I heard you say there were people in the trucks.'

'He missed, Mum, it's fine. Everything's fine. I'm sorry but I have to go.'

Before he could put the receiver back the tank fired again. Kellas saw it rock on its suspension. His mother was saying something and when the shell landed the mujahedin cheered again and Mohamed and the commander cried out something like the Arabic praise for God. This time the smoke did not blow away. Some source that kept gushing black smoke had appeared in the desert. Kellas counted the trucks. One was still moving. The other was not there. The shell had struck one of the trucks and set it on fire. Kellas swore. He saw the turret hatch of the tank open and Astrid haul herself slowly out. All her energy had left her and her face was bloodless white. She glanced up at the platform and began to walk towards it with her head hanging down.

The commander shouted and laughed and said something to Mohamed while his eyes flicked towards Kellas.

'Adam!' said Mohamed. 'The commander says: two for one! Look!'

'Adam, tell me what's happening,' said Kellas's mother. 'I heard another bang. Is everyone OK? What happened to the people in the truck?'

'Wait,' said Kellas. The burning truck, like a gash through which darkness was pouring out into the sunlight, was broadening. Two dots detached themselves from it and moved away.

'It's OK,' said Kellas. 'There was an accident but it's OK, they got out.'

He lifted the binoculars. Now he could see that the two dots were burning. They were men on fire, burning like candles. One of the men was lying on the ground, no longer moving. It looked as if he had already burned to death. The other was still running, strands of smoke coming off him twisted together with licks of flame. Kellas couldn't make out features, only the black lengths of his body and limbs and head. The survivor fought for a while, then fell to his knees, then collapsed and didn't move again. The two of them must surely have screamed as they ran in flames out of the burning truck and their skin was burned away but at this distance there was no way to hear them. It played out clearly and silently and quickly. Kellas heard the binoculars drop onto the floor of the platform after they slid out of his wet hand.

'Adam?'

'I'm still here, Mum.'

'Are you all right?'

'Yes, I'm all right. It's not me.'

'Who? Who's not all right?'

'There was a mistake.'

'Not a mistake!' shouted Mohamed. 'Taliban!'

'Adam, please tell me what's happening. I know you don't want to.'

'The men in the truck.'

'Are they going to be OK?'

'No. They're not going to be OK.'

'Are they dead?'

'I'm sorry, Mum. They were Taliban.'

'Not while we were talking? Did you know them?'

'Adam! Two with one!'

'I'm sorry, Mum.'

One of the bodies was still burning. A man's fat was his own wick.

'Were they people you knew?' His mother's voice was trembling.

'No. They were just people, poor people, Taliban, Mum, people who just died just now, unfortunately.'

There was a rustle over the PA and all the movies froze. 'Ladies and gentlemen,' announced the chief of the cabin crew. 'We are now beginning our descent into New York.'

8

The immigration officer found the old Afghan visa in Kellas's passport and asked why he'd been there. Kellas said he'd been covering the war for his newspaper.

'What war?' asked the immigration officer.

'Your war,' said Kellas.

'My war?'

'Not you personally. America's war. After, you know. The . . . ' He held his left hand up vertically, side-on to the immigration officer, and softly drove his horizontal right hand into it.

The immigration officer's eyes narrowed. He closed the passport. Instead of handing it back, he stood up and flapped it rapidly to and fro, like a wet print, looking around the booths and queues in the hall, as if he would see something there to help him. He shook his head, laid the passport down, stamped it and gave it to Kellas. He held up his left hand vertically, side-on to Kellas, and softly drove his horizontal right hand into it.

'I wouldn't do that again while you're here,' he said. 'Enjoy your visit.'

Kellas walked into the United States. He withdrew three hundred dollars from an ATM, bought a copy of the *New York Times* and went outside to the taxi rank. The cold air frisked him and he closed the jacket and turned the collar up and hugged the bulk of the *Times* to his chest. He needed winter clothes. Good that he'd arrived rich and not like a poor immigrant. Good that the people in Europe were paying him the best part of two years' salary for his work imagining a future war between this side of the Atlantic and theirs. He got into a cab and asked for 19th Street and Park Avenue South.

It was overheated in the car, and gloomy in the low, deep, black seats, the partition up against his face. The sky was a fathomless grey. They were fast on the expressways through Queens and hit traffic on the approach to the bridge. The grimy painted wooden slats on the walls of the small houses backing onto the road, the screen doors, the scruffy verges, the brake light in front brightening scarlet under a silver sign that read 'Cadillac', triggered in Kellas unmixable sensations of the alien and the familiar. He was undergoing the only experience an American born in the USA could never have. Their movies and TV and songs were a fake version of the real thing to them, and they knew this. They grew up with both. For foreigners arriving here, America was a marvel harder to believe, infinitely more wondrous: a real version of a notorious fake. It was a visitation of the legend played across their eyes in two electric, high-contrast dimensions, of the myth lining their ears note by note, since before they could remember. What a sound! What a sight! Like a long-lens paparazzi shot of Jesus on the beach, paler, flabbier, shorter, with less holy eyes than the icons had it, staggeringly real. Here it was, known, recognisable, and so much lumpier, grainier and messier than the exported songs and stories, and impossible to simply hate or love; with its unfinished parts, and its wide streaks of dullness, and its immense tracts of quietly getting on with things, and parts with a savagery or beauty or down-to-the-atom peculiarity that could not be National Geographicised and sold abroad. That first minute in America is the minute of the European shiver, when America's smells are first smelled, and the realisation breaks that America is no exception to the iron rule that every country, seen from outside, seems to know itself, and that no country, seen from inside, ever does.

'This time of day, it's usually clear,' said the driver. They were stationary. 'It's never like this.'

'Maybe somebody broke down.'

'What's that?'

'I said maybe somebody broke down!'

'Yeah, maybe. I think maybe it's to do with the sales. Everybody's here for the shopping.'

'I need a coat.'

'You need one here, mister. Is that the reason what for you're here, shopping?'

'I'm visiting someone.'

'A female acquaintance?'

'Yeah, a female acquaintance.'

'Where d'you live, if you don't mind me asking? London?'

'Yes.' Kellas looked at the driver's badge. His name was Vitaly Morgunov.

'She must be special for you to have come so far.' When Kellas didn't reply, the driver looked in the rear-view mirror at him and spoke again. 'Did you meet her on the Internet?'

'No.'

'Because these Internet dating agencies, they're a big scam. This friend of mine, he paid thirty bucks for letters in English from a beautiful girl in Czech Republic. It was her picture on the Internet. Then he finds out she's sent the same letters to thousands of guys all over America and Europe. And she didn't write them, either, and she's not beautiful. I don't even know as that she was a girl.'

A horn sounded behind and the driver moved the car forward. Kellas picked up the *Times* and began working through the sections. Murders in New York were down in 2002 compared to 2001. To be precise, 503 people had been murdered, as of mid-November. The deaths in the World Trade Center weren't being counted in last year's total. Something different, that must have been counted as, of a more noble category, not regular joe murder. Six people had been murdered over the weekend, one shot dead in the Bronx after refusing to hand over his leather jacket. United Nations inspectors in Iraq suspected that the US and Britain weren't telling them all they knew about Iraq's secret weapons projects. The *Times* quoted a story in its London namesake claiming that Saddam Hussein had ordered hundreds of Iraqi VIPs to hide parts of weapons of mass destruction in their homes. In Australia, the prime minister said he was in favour of attacking countries that harboured terrorists before the terrorists showed their hand. In Kuwait, the foreign minister said there needed to be regime change in Iraq in order to pull Iraq back together. In Israel, at the funeral of two boys killed in a suicide bomb attack on a hotel in Kenya, one of the mourners said: 'It's better to have a war. Better war than a drop here, a drop there. Better for them, too. What we have now is worse.' The *Times* had chosen it as its quotation of the day. A shopper coming out of the Rockefeller Center was quoted as feeling let down because the cashmere sweaters at J. Crew weren't reduced in the sales; but there were good deals to be had at Banana Republic. Sharper Image's top seller was an air purifier at $249.95, with a second at half price, and a free third one for the bathroom.

The parents of the bus driver Robert Mickens were interviewed. They said they'd warned him before about his Taliban jokes. Mickens had driven a Greyhound bus for five years between Philadelphia and New York. Before that, he'd worked for the parks department in Brooklyn. On Saturday he'd been taking thirty passengers to New York when he'd hit heavy traffic on the New Jersey Turnpike and tried to get around it by taking a short cut near Hightstown. He didn't tell the passengers what he was doing and, as he drove through the unfamiliar small towns of Manapalan and Freehold, the passengers began to voice their anxiety. As they drove into Marlboro, with the passengers demanding to know where he was going, Mickens lost his temper and called out: 'We're going to the Taliban, don't worry about it.' The passengers used their mobiles to call the police. A few minutes later, the bus was hemmed in and forced to stop by a dozen police cars. Mickens was taken from the bus at gunpoint, handcuffed and charged with disorderly conduct.

Kellas looked through the glass at the questing face of a girl in a red scarf, stepping past the green neon cross in a pharmacy window, and a fat man in a beret with two chihuahuas on leads. He read snatches of songs in the junctions, in white letters printed on green signs where Delancey Street met Clinton Street. His mind snapped at lives it couldn't reach. He would rather even have been in the Leonard Cohen song, where there was music on Clinton Street, all through the evening. It was cold in New York, Cohen sang, but he liked where he was living. There was warmth in that song. The hero had lost his wife to junk and a friend, and he forgave the friend, and he forgave the wife. The song was full of friendship, regret and craving. Of all the characters in the song, Kellas most envied the heroin. To be craved! Craving was the sort of breach in Astrid's singleness large enough for him to pass through and in his bloody hotel den the night before he'd seen the breach open up on the screen of his netmail, when he'd been most longing to believe he was craved. That'd been the madness of injury and broken glass and darkness and the longing to escape. The first gust of freezing American wind at the sliding open of the terminal doors had uncovered the frailty of his hopes.

They were a few blocks away from the publishers', he reckoned. He would take refuge in the deal. There was solace in money. He had Astrid's postal address. He would hire a car and drive there. Buy himself some nice clothes, so she could see he was doing well. A black sheepskin coat and some good Italian boots. It would show her that he had nothing to worry about except her. He'd tell her what had happened at the Cunnerys'. It could be made to sound like an episode in the biography of a famous dead writer, one of those monstrous acts of selfishness and savagery that come to seem an ingredient in their genius, comforting the consumers of biographies simultaneously in their own timid virtue and their own squalid, secret transgressions. Kellas could afford to arrive in Chincoteague bloody, but not ragged. He took out the pen and the page of his manuscript and sketched little sums in a blank space. He had no money now; in fact, he was overdrawn, and since he'd resigned from *The Citizen*, there would be no more salary. Once he signed the contract for *Rogue Eagle Rising*, he'd get two-thirds of the advance, about £66,000. Minus the agent's percentage, minus tax, he'd probably be left with £35,000. Minus the five thousand he'd just spent on a six-hour trip across the Atlantic. If Liam Cunnery cashed his blank cheque, he could be down another five. How easy it had been to spend ten thousand pounds in twenty four hours, smashing things, shouting, drinking champagne, pursuing women and sleeping. He would make a fine rich man.

Kellas paid Vitaly Morgunov off with a showy tip and pushed through a stiff revolving door, its heavy glass panels framed with thick strips of tarnished brass, into the lobby of the building where Karpaty Knox occupied three floors. The lobby was warm and light and faced with pale stone. As he walked towards the lifts, Kellas began to smile. The comfort of associating with book people; an organisation waited for him. Even though he despised the book he had written, he was succoured by the prospect of receiving the compliments they were obliged to pay.

A sharp voice cut through the quiet and the pleasant smell of the lobby, calling 'Sir!' The man called again, and Kellas looked round. He saw that a security guard in a coffee-and-chocolate coloured uniform, with a tin eagle pinned to the front of his hat, had got up from his desk and was coming towards him. He was carrying a clipboard. He asked Kellas what his name was. Kellas told him. The security guard ran his forefinger down the list of names on the clipboard, didn't find Kellas, flipped a page, and found him halfway down.

'Kellas, Adam?' he said, looking into Kellas's face.

'Yes.'

'You're down to see Madeleine Baker-Koontz.'

'She's one of the editors, yes.'

'Can you come with me, sir?' The security guard crossed Kellas's name off the list and led him back towards the desk. Instead of stopping, he put the clipboard down, and went on through to the street. He looked round to make sure Kellas was following him. He stood on the pavement with his hands on his hips and waited while Kellas came out. Kellas put the collar of his jacket back up. He'd left the newspaper in the cab. He began to shake with cold. The deep horn of a truck sounded from a block away and a medley of car horns answered. Two men in overalls, gloves and hats were hefting crates of beer bottles from a parked van and stacking them outside a restaurant next door to the Karpaty Knox building. The guard leaned forward and put his hand on Kellas's shoulder and raised his voice to make himself heard over the din of crashing bottles. 'If you'd like to go across the road to the diner opposite, right over there –' he pointed to a red illuminated sign '—grab yourself a coffee and wait, Mrs Baker-Koontz will join you shortly.'

Before Kellas had finished uttering the first word of his first question, the guard had his hands held out and his chin up, stopping him. 'Sir – sir – sir – please. Those are the instructions we've been given. I don't have any more information, and I can't let you wait in the lobby. No, Mrs Baker-Koontz is not inside the building. Please. Sir. Please.' His hand on the shoulder; a little pressure, now. 'If you'd just like to go over to the diner and have a coffee, or a tea, whatever, and Mrs Baker-Koontz will be with you. That's all I'm authorised to say. It's fine. Everything's fine. Please go, sir.'

Kellas crossed the road to the diner, found an empty booth and ordered a coffee. He clasped his hands around the glossy white sides of the thick china mug. He needed the heat more than the drink.

Something landed on Kellas's table with a heavy slap. It was a padded yellow envelope. A woman in her forties, wide, big-bosomed and agile, had dropped it there. She was taking off her handbag, coat and scarf, and while she did so, she was staring down at Kellas, as if he knew very well what was going on and she was interested to hear from him how it might be his fault. There was pity in her eyes, and anger. She checked his name, introduced herself as Madeleine Baker-Koontz and shook his hand when he got up. They sat down facing each other. It seemed to be an effort for her to fashion a screen of gentility over her face. She forced a smile, picked up the menu, opened it, closed it and put it down.

'You're not in a hurry, are you?' she asked.

'No. Are you?'

'No!' She laughed. The information that she wasn't in a hurry filled Kellas with senseless fear, the kind that rises out of banal, harmless words in the last nightmares before sunrise.

'We haven't met,' said Baker-Koontz. 'We exchanged emails.'

'About a promotional trip next year.'

'Right.' She nodded, and laughed again. It wasn't only that she found this funny; to her it was hilarious, too, that things she'd taken seriously before had turned into jokes. She was high on irony. 'Well, I'm here to tell you that it's not going to happen.'

'The trip.'

'Not just the trip. We're not publishing your book. I should be—'

'In America?'

'Anywhere. France, Britain, America – we're not publishing your book, period. I should be saying "they", not "we". I don't work for Karpaty Knox any more. I quit a few hours ago. So I shouldn't really be doing this, meeting you, giving you the bad news. It's not my job. But I thought, poor guy, he's flying into New York City from London, he's going to step off the plane, get to the office and nobody's going to tell him anything.'

'Thanks for the pity.'

Baker-Koontz laughed again. Kellas realised that he had just used his teeth to pull a strip of skin off his lower lip, where it had puffed up and hardened in the cold of the street. 'They said "Sure, go ahead, but take it outside." They made me clear out my desk first.' She looked with curiosity at Kellas. 'You're taking this pretty well. You're not a weeper.' Kellas shook his head. 'You know, this would all have been much easier if you'd seen your emails today, or answered your phone. I've been calling you for the last couple of hours. What do you have a cellphone for, if you don't switch it on?'

'I'm still—' Kellas cleared his throat and started again. 'I'm still in this world without it.'

'Don't blame me, Adam. You don't mind if I call you Adam? I had a long talk with your agent. She was pretty upset. She was worried about you. She didn't understand why you were coming here.'

'Did she say anything about a dinner last night?'

Baker-Koontz shook her head and told Kellas that she'd been called at two-thirty a.m. by a friend at Éditions Perombelon in Paris, saying that the company, with all its foreign subsidiaries, including Karpaty Knox, had been taken over by a French industrial conglomerate called DDG. 'I've never heard of them before, have you?' she said. 'Apparently they're huge. They make nuclear reactors and yoghurt. They saw a synergy.' The chief executive of DDG, Luc Vichinsqij, a graduate of one of the grandes écoles and of Harvard, had held a press conference in Paris at eight a.m., looked in on the Perombelon offices, got on a plane and flown to New York. At noon, chin smooth and eyes clear, without a crease in his black suit, with a sapphire tie pin in a metallic pink tie and smelling of sandalwood, he'd turned up at Karpaty Knox to meet the staff, and personally fire three of them.

'Including you,' said Kellas.

'No, I told you, I quit. I quit when Luc told us the company wasn't going to sign the contract with you. I could have kept my job. In fact, I probably would've got a promotion. But I asked. I said "What about the Kellas book?" – because I was going to be your English-language editor, and I knew he'd already got rid of the guy in Paris who was so keen for us to buy it, you know, the old chief, Didier. And Luc said "We don't need another piece of anti-American bullshit now." And that was when I knew I was going to have to quit. Because I really, really hated your book, and I never had the guts to say so. I'm a liberal, and I don't like a lot of what this country does, but when I read your novel, that was exactly what I thought. Another piece of anti-American bullshit.' Baker-Koontz paused and looked at Kellas closely, as if waiting for him to respond. Kellas had too many ways to go. He couldn't choose, and he couldn't speak. He felt weightless, cut loose from the certainty gravity provides, and at the same time his chest was filled with a pulsing and a thrumming, waves of numbing force, like the first seconds of a general anaesthetic. Baker-Koontz began speaking again. 'When I heard this French guy say out loud what I'd been too afraid to say, I started to despise myself. I was ashamed. It's Monday today. If you'd come here on Friday, you would have signed the contract, and got your advance, and I would have taken you out to lunch and I would have lied to your face. I would have said how excited I was, how excited we all were, what an honour, what a privilege, the whole phoney spiel. It's just loathsome to contemplate. I had to get out and clear my head.'

'It must have been tough for you.'

Baker-Koontz laughed again. 'I mean, what were you thinking? The ashes at Ground Zero are barely cold and you're bringing a sick fairy tale to Manhattan about Americans butchering Arabs and having gunfights with bobbies in English country lanes?'

'Iranians, not Arabs.'

'Whatever. Jesus. Anyway, it's over. Here, I brought along my copy of the manuscript. Got to try and recycle. *Rogue Eagle Rising*—' she did air quotes, rocked her head and put on a British accent '—is trash. If you'd put in even one sympathetic American character! One character with more depth and substance than a Post-it note. You thought you were dumbing it down for the masses, but the masses are smarter than you. One or two of the Europeans have a trace of reality about them, but with the American characters, it's like you deliberately pinched out any flame of humanity or sympathy you saw. Even the good ones are dolts. Obnoxious, pompous, humourless clods. I read it through again, just to check this, because I couldn't believe it, but it's true. There's not a single humorous word out of the mouths of an American character in your book. Not one funny word. Americans aren't like that, Adam. We're funny!' She laughed, meeting his eyes for a second then turning them away and down, as if she was sharing her laughter with another person who wasn't there. 'Write what you like about us but you mustn't ever forget our wry sense of humour. You can't go charging around the world, expecting to sell your shallow cultural stereotypes to the same people you're stereotyping. It won't wash. You've no right.'

'Will you find another job?' said Kellas. An anxiousness came into him that Baker-Koontz would get up and leave. He wanted her to stay. He would rather be abused than be alone.

Baker-Koontz shrugged and folded her arms tightly across her bosom. 'I was talking to Corriman before all this happened,' she said. 'There could be openings there.'

'Corriman. They're doing a book by a friend of mine. *The Book of Form*.'

'My God, you *know* Patrick M'Gurgan?' Baker-Koontz pressed her hands on the edge of the table and leaned forward as if she was about to spring at Kellas and bite his chin. Her eyes were big.

'He's my closest friend. We were at school together.'

'I so loved that book.' Baker-Koontz pressed her hand to her heart and shook her head from side to side. 'Oh. God. It transported me.' She seemed to be having trouble breathing.

'I saw him last night at dinner. That's when I got this.' Kellas held up his left arm. The jacket cuff slipped back, exposing the bandage. The cleaner at Heathrow had done an excellent job. The dressing was still firmly in place and there was no sign that any blood had leaked through.

'You had a fight with Patrick M'Gurgan?' said Baker-Koontz.

'That's right,' said Kellas. 'I was denouncing America at an elitist dinner party and he stood up and said he couldn't bear to hear the land of the free being insulted any longer.'

Baker-Koontz watched him without moving for a moment. She said: 'Do you really think I don't know you're kidding? You do, don't you? You don't think we know what kidding is. Mr Kellas, we invented kidding.'

'He gave me a sound thrashing.'

She was buttoned up, bag hoisted. 'All I have to say is, try to learn from this.' She held out her hand for him to shake. It was cool and dry, the bones in it like keys in a half-filled purse.

'I suppose you have to go,' said Kellas. His eyes and the inside of his nose itched and he swallowed.

'Switch your phone on,' said Baker-Koontz. 'Talk to your agent. Talk to your friends. Ciao.' She left.

Kellas asked the waitress for more coffee and ordered a steak and fries. The warmth of the diner was grand and generous now that he had less than no money. He did not feel poor. That would come on the road. The certainty of being poor next week made him feel richer now, with two hundred dollars in his wallet and a plate of hot food on the way, than he had shooting the breeze with Elizabeth Chang and the rest of the high-rollers up in the jet stream.

Didier would be fine, Kellas supposed. He should never have pretended to go along with the old French patriot's enthusiasm for his fictional Europe, united in a just, bloody war against America. Kellas had taken a workmanlike satisfaction in engineering the book but hadn't expected it to be taken by an eminent publisher like Didier as anything other than entertainment. Not that Didier had mistaken it for literature; more as a necessary exercise in dreaming, to inspire the young. Such a courteous, paternalistic man, he'd set his enthusiasm at a low level of intensity, the slightest of smiles, shifts of the eyebrow and inclinations of the head to indicate approval, as if modelling himself on some imaginary mode of English gentle-manly restraint that had long since ceased to exist but in his expres-sion of it could not avoid, like an Italian in tweeds, being more elegant than the original. All this, and so titillated by thoughts of war. Kellas had felt like a child who'd poked a stuffed lion in a museum and seen its eyes open.

In Paris he'd been taken straight from the station to a pristine arrondissement and a temple of gastronomy where the waiters, like Didier, were in their mid-sixties, and quivered with the effort of keeping their instincts of deference and contempt in equilibrium. Didier, tall and thin and slightly stooped, with a nose like a fin, had risen to shake his hand. He'd watched Kellas drinking, rather than sipping, the wine; had ordered another bottle; had listened carefully while Kellas, slightly drunk, began explaining, then defending, then apologising for, his book, completely losing his way in the process and, without noticing until afterwards, using the side of his hand to shepherd a tiny flock of breadcrumbs across the tablecloth so that they formed a precise circular pattern halfway between two yellow spots of soup he'd spilled earlier; only then had Didier explained, over coffee, why he wanted *Rogue Eagle Rising* to be published. Kellas had forgotten the details. He remembered Didier saying 'We need this, and we need more like it', and Kellas saying he wasn't sure what Didier meant by 'we', and Didier saying 'Europe.' Kellas should have declared that he cared much less about Europe than about euros, and had cynically couched his commercialism in terms of European patriotism in order not to alienate his friends. Yet Didier had looked so noble in his well-fitting grey suit, and a hundred thousand pounds was so much money, that Kellas had held his tongue.

Now he'd been sacked. Kellas found it hard to imagine the life of a wealthy, patrician, elderly Frenchman in retirement. What confidence Kellas had brought to imagining the lives and deaths of young Iranian girls, when he'd never been to Iran. And with Didier his imagination kept getting stuck on Fernando Rey in the films of Luis Buñuel; discreet charms and obscure objects. When it was hard to live that life any more, outside the restaurants with old career waiters, all of them dying off and not being replaced. In Europe, as in America, there was no longer either deference or contempt, only hourly billing.

It must have been that the food in that restaurant in Paris was of the finest quality. Something extraordinary. Yet Kellas could not remember what he'd eaten. The ten-dollar steak on the plate in front of him had a seam of gristle shining along its length, the fries were chewy and the coffee was stewed and bitter, and despite that, the

173

meal was giving him a sweet sense of refuge such as he hadn't known for a long time.

The sense of well-being, which Kellas made stretch to another coffee, began to subside. He was overwhelmed by his own lack of involvement in the great business of this city. There was only Astrid left. He paid, asked for directions to the bus terminal, and left the diner. It was already almost dark.

He walked quickly to get some heat into his body. A decent coat wouldn't leave him with much change out of a hundred dollars and the subway was only a few blocks away. It was frosty, all right. The paving was beginning to sparkle and the steam was boiling up from the vents in good thick columns. Shoppers walked by him, sealed in brightly dyed wool and Gore-Tex, with a prancing, anticipatory gait; the colder it got, the more they earned hot treats just by breathing. He would skip the coat purchase. The subway was heated, the bus was heated, the south was warm, and he didn't know how much the ticket would cost. He'd taken the book with him, intending to sling it into a trash can in the street, but the 400-page manu-script, packed in a padded envelope, made excellent insulation, slipped inside his buttoned-up jacket and held in place by his tightly folded arms. He caught the eye of a homeless man squatting like an owl next to a heating vent, half obscured by vapour. The man was holding a paper cup, begging out loud. When he saw Kellas, he quickly looked away. As a rule homeless people, like dogs and small children, saw Kellas as a mark from a long way off. That Kellas was inadequately dressed for the season, was not trying to hail a cab and hadn't shaved since the previous morning must have tagged him as a loser. The suit and shoes were plain enough warning in themselves that here was someone in the midst of their descent from security to insecurity, a man yet to settle in his new location on the bottom. The bandage wouldn't help. Another reason not to buy a coat was that he might need to pay a doctor to look at his arm. He had no insurance.

When Kellas tried to buy a ticket to Chincoteague at the

Greyhound counter, nobody had heard of it. The clerk spent time searching in her computer before she told him that, if such a town existed, no bus went there. Kellas went out into the cold again, into the fever of Times Square, where it seemed impossible there could be so much light and power and no heat, yet it was so. In a branch of one of the big book chains he found the travel section and worked out, after picking up and putting back several guides, that the closest bus stop to Chincoteague was ten miles away from the town, in a place called Oak Hall, on the highway to Norfolk.

Before leaving the book store, he went to the section where they kept militaristic thrillers on display. He took out the envelope containing his manuscript and buried it carefully in a stack of Tom Clancys. He began walking to the door and was almost out when a security guard caught him and gave the manuscript back. Kellas thanked him. The security guard opened the door for him and closed it behind him and stood there with his arms folded while Kellas walked away.

The ticket for the eight-forty-five bus to Norfolk cost seventy-five dollars. Kellas joined a queue of passengers waiting in a chicane of blue nylon ropes in the departure hall in the bus station basement. It was eight-thirty. Somebody had written in small, shy letters in marker pen on the wall 'OSAMA IS A BUSH'. There were no seats in the line. There were no seats anywhere. The passengers, all of them black except Kellas and a young man with prominent cheekbones and a shaved head, looked tired and used to waiting. An old man with bad knees, who walked with a stick, hobbled away and came back dragging a plastic milk crate, which he upended and sat down on. Further up the queue a younger man had already found his crate and was sleeping on it, his back against the wall, the hood of his top stretched over his head to keep out the light. There was a stoicism, a quietness and a gentility about the line, which resembled the true face of some much admired founder generation whose reality had been obliterated by the earnestness of the modern actors hired to portray it. Kellas sensed that his fellow passengers would have considered it ridiculous to make this journey in any other way than straight from work and at any other time than the hours allotted for rest.

Boarding depended on a tall, paunchy man in a dark blue uniform, with a synthetic blue fur hat, who guarded the glass doors that led to the buses. Eight-forty-five came and went. At nine, Kellas stepped out of the queue and asked the hat about the bus.

'It's gone,' said the hat. 'The driver was here. He's gone.' He looked at Kellas's ticket, held it further away from his eyes, then up to his face. 'You should have been here on time. I just put fifty-five passengers on that bus.'

'I was here!'

'You should have waited in line like everybody else. Like these folks here.'

'I did!'

'Sir. Sir. Don't touch me.'

'I'm not being aggressive. I just—'

'You touched me.'

'I just—'

'If you want to get on the bus, wait in the line.'

'I did.'

'Tell me this. Are you in the line now?'

'I—'

'Are you in the line now?'

'No.'

'Then how you going to catch the bus?'

'I didn't. I missed it.'

'Exactly. Exactly. That's what I've been saying. So if you go back in the line now, you won't miss the next one. There's a bus to Norfolk at ten. The driver'll let you off at Oak Hall.'

Kellas went back to his place in the line. Robert Mickens, the arrested bus driver, had, it was to be assumed, been joking about driving his passengers to the Taliban. It would be tough to get a Greyhound bus there, together with those on board. You'd have to ship the bus and passengers onto a freighter somewhere on the east coast, sail across the Atlantic, through the Mediterranean, down the Suez Canal, down the Red Sea, across the Arabian Sea to Karachi. That would take several weeks. Once in Karachi, it would be a straightforward enough drive north to the areas close to the Afghan frontier, where the Taliban were the strongest. No scheduled stops. The Pakistani police would probably prevent them crossing into the tribal regions, of course, so the journey would in all likelihood be a wasted one. It was too bad. These people ought to have met each other.

Astrid had been upset after the deaths of the truck drivers at Bagram. Sitting in the tight, dark humming space inside the tank, she had helped Sardar load the shells into the breech of the gun. She'd only realised after the truck was hit that her friend wasn't shooting at the tree trunk. That was about all she told Kellas, after he'd told her what had happened to him. Her car came and took her away, and it was a long time before Kellas saw her again. She had been upset. She made a show of being tough about it. Some shaky words about responsibility, and not pretending to be detached, and her eyes glistening with tears that never quite fell, and her face white. Just before they parted at Bagram, he remembered, a different look had come over her, as the colour came back and her eyes dried. A look of acceptance, almost comfort, as if the corrosiveness of the shock had been familiar, as well as painful.

Soon afterwards, with Astrid's whereabouts unknown to anyone at the Jabal guesthouse, Kellas had driven to Kabul with Mohamed, walked into the city on the morning of its liberation, found it busy with yellow cabs and bicycles as if the war had been a fable of country folk. They'd sat down to a late breakfast of chicken and chips in a restaurant where, the waiters informed them, Arab jihadis fighting for the Taliban had eaten the previous night, unaware that their Afghan allies had already fled. Here and there about the city crowds of laughing Afghan flâneurs milled around Taliban corpses. A couple of such fatalities lay bloated on the pavement not far from the restaurant, their clothes half scorched off, their skin already spoiled blue-grey. Small boys hopped around them, grinning, entranced by the notion of men who had lost the ability to respond to any abuse or humiliation, since they were dead. Witnesses said the men had been delicately killed in the middle of the night by an American helicopter that had picked off their Toyota pick-up in the middle of the street without damaging anything else around it. Sure enough, the remains of the Toyota lay where it had been struck, the tyres partly fused to the road, the twin barrels of the cannon on the back blackened and lumpy like burned-out sparklers.

For three weeks, Kellas was busy filing reports for *The Citizen*, as the UN arrived in Kabul, western ambassadors returned and fighting moved first to the north, then the mountains in the south. Four journalists were murdered on the road from Pakistan. Kellas asked after Astrid, and worried about her.

Was she right? Was there really no good reason why the Bagram killings should trouble him more than, for instance, the deaths of two Taliban fighters in Kabul? He marched with the Alliance, and thus, with the Americans; he took their hospitality. He was not a guerrilla for peace, sneaking out at night and sabotaging weaponry. He'd never tried to persuade an Afghan that killing was wrong. He observed, he reported, he did not intervene, and as far as that, he was culpable in the project. Without his words and Astrid's actions, it was true, those men would not have died that day; yet neither he nor Astrid had intended harm. It was not even that he was tormented by the memory of tiny stick figures burning to death in silence. No post-traumatic stress, he didn't dream about it; the only times he had dreamed about Afghanistan since the fall of Kabul it had been a twee, foppish, comfortable alternative Afghanistan of cake stands and Shaker furniture. And yet, as more *Citizen* correspondents arrived in Kabul, and he had more time on his hands, he found it gnawing at him.

There was a distance, a modern distance of things, a terrible modern distance where the warriors and their camp followers were neither close enough for the intimate killing of blades and teeth, when you would see the enemy's face, smell his sweat and hear him panting, nor as far away as the home fires used to be from the front lines. Close enough to see, but not close enough to know. The cleverer wars and the world became, the more bitter the struggle to preserve ignorance. The fuller and the closer the world, the more desperate the struggle to keep the distance. Now that the world could be spanned in a day, now that anyone could learn any language and speak to anyone anywhere at any time, the battle for distance, on which war depended, had taken on a shameless, frantic character. There was a cult of seeing without knowing and watching without touching. The generic foreign faces on television: you knew them, because you could see them, you could hear the foreign sounds they made. But you had to avoid knowing enough about them to prevent your imagination making them out to be what you wanted them to be. You had to turn away from the knowledge that you could reach them on the phone. That they had phones. That they could call you. The horror of the labour required if these truths were accepted drove people to celebrate the distance and nurture it, to turn their wills towards preserving the difference between a *here* and a *there*, in a world where there was no *there* any more, where everyone was already *here*. Citizens conspired with rulers to give the far-off Other qualities of evil or innocence they did not know they had been given, and could not own. It made no difference whether the fantasy was that the far-off Other was quite unlike us, or that the far-off Other was just the same as us; the dearly cherished fantasy was that the Other was far off. The certainty of members of all the world's overlapping Ummahs was that they would never have to justify, in person, without an intermediary, in language each could understand, that which was being done in their name to those who lived out the consequences.

Ever since the day at Bagram, Mohamed had been less sincere with him. The smile had been contrived and Mohamed had been more wary, not, Kellas suspected, because he had been troubled by the deed in itself, but because he was sick of war, had seen Kellas as a minor harbinger of its end, and now saw him as part of its perpetuation. He was tainted. Mohamed had been happy on the day he returned to Kabul but after that it became harder and harder to find him. He was busy seeing old friends and fixing up jobs against the day Kellas would leave. When Kellas did track him down one day and asked him to look for the families of the truck drivers who had been killed, Mohamed was reluctant. He didn't ask why; he wasn't interested. He explained how difficult it would be to find them, how they could be anywhere, not only in Afghanistan or Pakistan but in Saudi Arabia, Algeria. Where would you start? Kellas dragged him down to the old state truck depot and to the places on the edge of town where the truckers congregated and made him ask. They got nowhere. In the end, on the promise of double pay, Mohamed spent two days with him, trying to find the remains of the burned out truck. Towards the end of the second day they found it, or what they decided must be it, on a gently undulating field of dust, speckled with small stones. A soupy grey sky hung low above their heads. It looked as if it was about to snow. In the distance, at Bagram, they could see the commander's tower, and cranes moving where the Americans were building a new base. Tubby American transport planes, painted a grey which matched the snowclouds, trundled along the taxiways. The howl of their engines was borne on the cold wind.

Mohamed kicked the rusty, blackened chassis of the truck. There was no sign of what it might have been carrying. If there had been number plates, they had been taken away. Kellas looked around to see if there was any trace of the victims' remains but there was nothing, not a bone. There wasn't a habitation for miles. Perhaps the Taliban came out and took them for burial. There were jackals; there were buzzards. Kellas caught Mohamed's eye and felt foolish.

'I'm sorry to have brought you all this way,' he said.

'Why sorry?' said Mohamed. 'For you, I would go to the ends of the earth.' Kellas knew that they wouldn't work together again.

'Don't think about the men who were in this truck,' said Mohamed. The wind tugged at his shalwar kameez, pressing it against his ankles. 'They were bad men, foreigners. Pakistanis, Arabs, Chechens. They were the enemies of America and Britain. They deserved to die. Anyway, men are killed here often. What if you found their wives and children? What would you say to them? Would you give them money?'

'No. I don't know what I would say to them. Tell them what happened, perhaps, and listen to what they told me.'

'It wouldn't help them,' said Mohamed. He shifted his feet and with his right hand fingered the edge of the fawn blanket slung over his shoulder. His eyes flicked away, then returned to Kellas. 'And, if they lived here, they would know you, and they would know me. But you would leave, and I would stay. It would be trouble.'

'Did you find them?' asked Kellas.

'You must believe me. The families of the men who died here only want money or revenge. They do not want to shake your hand or to see your tears. It is not enough.'

'Did you find them?'

'Adam,' said Mohamed. 'Adam Kellas. When you were a boy, were you beaten?'

'By the teachers.'

'Was it always justice, that they beat you?'

'No.'

'Do you want to see the teachers again, to talk about it with them?'

'It's not the same!'

'Take it like a beating, Adam Kellas. Sorrys are not always of use. Not all things can be closed and put away. If everything could be forgiven and made right, what would stop men doing more and more terrible things? When you're in London, you'll remember that we're here.'

'It's cold,' said Kellas. 'You found them, didn't you?'

In the car on the way back Kellas told Mohamed that he was

leaving. Mohamed said that he should come back and visit him, that he would always be glad to see him.

'What will you do in London?' asked Mohamed.

'I'm writing a book.'

9

Soon after ten o'clock the bus, with Kellas aboard, crossed the Hudson and entered New Jersey. For a short while the lights of Manhattan blazed to starboard before an embankment gulped them down. At Newark, a score of passengers pressed around the door of the bus, waiting to be let in. They looked cold. Several other buses arrived at the same time and passengers ran backwards and forwards trying to find the right one. Their overfilled suitcases on wheels would twist like reluctantly led beasts on the end of their thin handles, tip and roll over, and in their hurry the passengers wouldn't heed and would scrape them upside down along the ground. A man in a plastic Stetson who spoke in Spanish heaved a cardboard box longer than he was into the luggage compartment, climbed on board, found a seat, got up, got off, dragged the box out again and loped away for another bus. They set out once more. Kellas tried to sleep, but he was thirsty, and hot air was pouring from a vent under the window by his seat. He took off his jacket. He began to sweat. The veins around his head pulsed and what moisture was left in his mouth felt sticky, stringy. The man next to him had a small, half-full bottle of water in his hands. Kellas said: 'May I have some of your water?'

The man turned to him, smiled, and said: 'It's OK.'

Kellas said again: 'May I have some of your water?'

The man said: 'It's OK.'

Kellas leaned his head back on the seat and closed his eyes. The heat and thirst writhed in him like a second body coterminous with his own, making him shiver awake every time his thoughts wandered to the edge of sleep. Each time he opened his eyes he would see similar fast-food joints and gas stations at similar crossroads, identical traffic lights hanging from the same cables, yet all the time, they were moving south. Little changed except for the illuminated slogans outside the churches. They passed a sign reading 'A Friend Of God Is A Stranger To The World'.

Some time after midnight they reached Wilmington. There was a smaller crowd waiting to board. Among them, hanging back, eyes glittering with hope, were the homeless. The bus terminal had been chained shut. Kellas could see there was a Pepsi machine in there. He got off the bus and banged on the chained door. One of the homeless men said there was a door on the other side. Kellas and another passenger, a man with a conical head and sideburns and an enormous torso, with a T-shirt that read 'Little Italy' on the front and 'Home of The Sopranos' on the back, marched to this other door. It was sealed from the inside. It didn't have a handle. Kellas tapped on the window and attracted the attention of a man in a khaki raincoat, who let them in. Kellas fed a five-dollar bill into the machine and it laid a cold plastic bottle of Pepsi in the groove, and no change. While Kellas wrenched off the cap and emptied the bottle into himself, the bus station attendant began yelling at their saviour. 'Why'd you let them in?' she shouted.

'I was wondering, sirs, if you could possibly help me out,' said the homeless man, inclining his cup towards the Little Italy patriot. 'Here's my ID. I was in Vietnam.'

'I had to let them in! You can't have people standing around in the cold.'

'A little spare change, sirs, would go a long way towards putting one former Marine back on the right course. Semper fidelis.'

'I want to get home tonight. You don't have any business opening that fucking door.'

'Don't speak to me like that,' said the man in the raincoat. 'I don't care who you are, I deserve respect.'

The Little Italy patriot dropped coins into the ex-Marine's cup, his large, meaty fingers showing delicacy. 'You made your choice when you joined the Marines, my friend. Nobody forced you.'

'Are you kidding? You never heard of conscription?'

'You've got no right to speak to me that way,' said the man in the raincoat.

They boarded a few minutes before the bus set off again. Kellas dozed until they reached Dover. The immigrant with the water had gone. Kellas's neighbour now was a man of about his age, portlier, with a black woollen jacket buttoned up to his throat and an expression – eyes staring ahead, a little too wide, braced – of waiting for the next bad thing to happen. As the bus moved off again, Kellas saw dark tyre-stripes drawn through a lacy layer of white on the blacktop. Snow grains swarmed around the lamps.

Kellas asked his neighbour if he knew how far it was to Oak Hall. The man said he'd never heard of it. He was going to Raleigh. His name was Lloyd, and he worked as a medical biller. They shook hands.

'I've never met a medical biller before,' said Kellas. 'We have a different system.'

'You done the right thing,' said Lloyd. 'What we have is a mess. We'd be better off with socialised medicine. I always said that. Where you from? Yeah? How come you're travelling on the bus?'

'It's cheap.'

Lloyd laughed. 'Yeah. It's cheap.'

'What happens in America if you get cancer and you don't have insurance?'

'You die.'

'Come on, that's not true.'

'You want to know what's true? I'll tell you what's true. I'm going down to see my sister in Raleigh, OK? She's got no insurance, and she needs thirty thousand dollars' worth of drugs every year just to stay alive. She's got a shitty part-time job in a grocery store, and as long as she hardly earns enough to feed her kid, the state of North

185

Carolina pays for her medication. She could get a better job. She's had offers. But the moment she earns anything more than a poverty wage, the state stops paying for the drugs. Either way they make sure the poor die quicker.'

'What's wrong with her?'

'It's personal. D'you mind if I ask what your profession is?'

'I'm unemployed.'

Lloyd laughed sceptically. 'Come to America to look for a job? You should have stayed at home. I hope you've got insurance.'

'No. In fact, I've got this arm, this injury on my arm. I don't suppose you'd take a look?' He pulled back his jacket sleeve and held the bandaged wrist out towards Lloyd.

'Whoa! I said I was a medical biller. I'm not qualified to treat injuries. I don't even know first aid.'

'I know you can't treat it. I thought you might be able to tell me how much it would cost for a doctor to do it.'

'Oh, the cost?' Lloyd raised his eyebrows, held the wrist between thumb and forefinger and moved it warily up and down. 'I don't know, probably an 881 oh two code, or an 881 twelve. Can't imagine it would cost more than five hundred bucks, as long as they didn't have to do any tests.'

'Five hundred?'

Lloyd laughed. 'You'll have to get your British health service to send you a plane to pick you up and fly you to England.' He shook his head. 'How'd you get here, anyway? You get such good social security over there you can afford to fly here from Europe?'

'I thought they were going to publish my book. I thought they were going to give me lots of money. It was a mistake.'

'What you write?'

'Novels. Do you read?'

Lloyd breathed in, tucked his chin into his chest, turned, held his two forefingers up to Kellas and said gravely, as if repeating a rehearsed confession: 'I have to tell you that I am not a great reader. I will try to read *Time* magazine once a week. If I go into the coffee shop and there's a newspaper there, I'll pick it up. I like the sports section, sometimes the Op-Ed. My wife reads a lot, and my kids . . . they're into Harry Potter. I dipped into that. That was fun. I love that magic shit. The last proper grown-up novel I read was . . . what was it called . . .? *The Killing of . . . To Kill A Mockingbird*. We read that at school. I loved that book, but . . . it's time, you with me? There's no time. Sometimes when I'm on the road and I'm staying in a hotel I'll take the Bible out of the drawer and start to read that. I'll go through the TV channels first, and when there's nothing on . . . No, you know what? It's when there's really great shit on several channels, and I watch it all, I watch maybe like a whole movie, and then some chat shows, and then a couple of cartoons, with all the commercials, and I start to feel strange, know what I mean? Like I've drunk too much soda. That's when I get to opening the drawer. A couple of months ago I read the whole of the Book of Genesis before I turned off the light. Now that, for me, is a story. A lot of people I know are always talking about Revelation, and the Rapture, and Jesus is coming, you'd better be ready, but Genesis, that's the one I prefer. I prefer the beginning to the end, know what I'm saying? So what's your book about?'

'It's a thriller. It's about a war between Europe and America.'

'Europe and America?' Lloyd laughed. 'Right, you're going to take us on.'

'It's not about how there *will* be a war between Europe and America, or how there *should* be a war between Europe and America. It's about how there *could* be.'

'No way. That'll never happen. America's too strong and you Europeans, you're a bunch of pussies. Look at what's happening with Iraq. We saved your asses in World War Two and the French and the Germans are too yellow to help us out now when we ask. Not that we need the help, but it'd be nice.' Lloyd had stopped smiling. His forehead was twisted and he stared at the seat in front of him. 'Anyway, you're British, right? You're on our side. What you talking about?'

'It's a book about an imaginary future,' said Kellas. 'It's a thriller. It's fiction. It's entertainment.'

'My sister's best friend is in Kuwait right now with the Marines. That ain't much of an entertainment.'

Lloyd and Kellas were silent for a little while, although Lloyd had acquired some indignation; he sat in the seat with his arms folded, looking straight ahead or down the aisle. He was ticking over. A couple of times he made a 'hm!' sound. Eventually he turned to Kellas and said: 'What I want to know is, where do you get off imagining that kind of future?'

'It's no big deal,' said Kellas. 'People do it all the time. Books. Movies. Politicians.'

'What I'm saying, you can imagine your future, go ahead, but you ain't got no business imagining ours.'

'Here,' said Kellas, reaching into the envelope and taking out the manuscript. 'Take it. It's not going to be published anyway. You might as well have it. Read it, see what you think.'

'No,' said Lloyd. The gesture appeased him and he smiled. 'You're OK.' He leaned back and closed his eyes.

Kellas switched on the light above his seat and began to read his book. The bus stopped at Salisbury. The snow had been replaced by heavy rain, driven by a strong, gusting wind. Waves of air and water wriggled across the empty white rectangles marked on the tarmac of the parking lot. The boarding passengers smelled of wet wool as they processed up the aisle. They had the expression of survivors just winched off the roofs of a flooded village. Lloyd opened his eyes. Once the bus was back on the highway, he asked Kellas if he was reading his own book; then, if he ever read his books out loud.

'I'll read you some now, if you like,' said Kellas.

'Yeah, go ahead.'

'From the beginning?'

'Read me what you got right there,' said Lloyd. Kellas began to read aloud. He'd reached the part where Tom de Peyer of Special

Branch was about to set out for a decisive secret meeting with his European counterparts, concealing his trip from American intelligence by travelling in the middle of the night, inside a shipping container, aboard a cross-Channel freight train. His mysterious boarding of the train was observed by two young Londoners, Waz and Franky, spraying tags on a bridge.

'You nearly done?' said Waz.
'Done the white, got to put the red in.'
'Get a fuckin' move on, man. Those geezers look well dodgy.'
'You're paranoid, bruv. It's the mersh. That was bad shit, bruv.'

'What's 'mersh'?' said Lloyd.
'London slang for cannabis.'
'And what's with the accent?'
'It's a London accent.'
Lloyd smiled with half his mouth. 'I mean how come you do the accent for one of them, and not the other?'
'They're different.'
Lloyd laughed. 'Is Franky by any chance a young man of colour?'
'Is it a problem?'
Lloyd laughed. 'Doing the accents.'
'Shall I go on?'
'Sure. Hope you're going to give me some action soon.'
Kellas read on through the part where he described, in great detail, the route the train took through Europe on its way to a secret cavern hidden off the Sophiaspoor Tunnel in the Netherlands. The passage took several minutes to read and he was aware of a restlessness in the seat next to him.
'You said it was a thriller,' said Lloyd. 'I hate to say it, but all this shit about trains, it's boring.'
'It's the slow build-up.'
'You got the slow part.'

'It's a trick. You think one thing is the main thing and the other is the background, but it's actually the other way round.'

'OK, professor, read on.'

Tom de Peyer, deputy head of Special Branch's Manchester section,

'That your hero?'

'Yeah. This a new section starting now. There's a space.'

'OK.'

Tom de Peyer, deputy head of Special Branch's Manchester section, felt the shipping container sway as the crane lifted it off its bogey. After a few moments, there was a gentle thud as the steel box was deposited on the ground. He released the safety harness holding him into the aircraft seat that had been quickly and crudely welded to the floor of the container, went to the door, opened it and stepped out. His feet crunched on stone chips and he held up his hand to shield his eyes from a harsh white light.

'No baggage, as ever,' said a familiar voice. 'Sorry it wasn't exactly club class.'

'Casp!' said de Peyer, stepping forward to shake the hand of Casp Haverkort, the lean, tanned, Dutch intelligence officer he'd worked with a decade earlier to smash a Croatian arms-smuggling ring.

'What is this place?' asked de Peyer, looking round at the cavernous space off the tunnel's main railway tracks, lit by arc lights mounted on masts. Shipping containers with open doors lay scattered around the chamber like discarded cardboard boxes outside a grocer's. Small huddles of men and women, some in uniform, stood talking and smoking.

Haverkort grinned and his piercing blue eyes twinkled.

Kellas glanced at Lloyd, but there was no reaction.

'We underspent our budget one year,' he said. 'Somebody thought it might be useful to have a piece of underground real estate nobody else knew about. Not even our friends across the Atlantic. It's pretty much snoop-proof. You heard the Pentagon moved another satellite to watch western Europe.'

'Just a minute,' said Lloyd. 'Who are the good guys here?'
'You have to read on to find out.'
'But the Pentagon is the *bad* guys.'
'In this book, definitely.'
'Everybody in the Pentagon?'
'The whole institution.'
'What, like America got taken over by some kind of evil dictator?'
'No, they just had a normal election.'
Lloyd exhaled. 'This is such bullshit. OK, go on.'

De Peyer nodded. 'I take it this meeting isn't happening.'
  'We're absolutely not here, my friend. No records, no minutes. You must rely on your excellent memory.'
  'Who turned up?'
  'Everybody. Except the Canadians. They sent the most encrypted good luck message in history. The French are trying to take charge, of course. The Germans were terrified that one of the Americans at Ramstein might be Jewish. But they have a convicted hacker working out of his prison cell who managed to get into the Pentagon's personnel files. No Jews in that unit. The Spanish are surprisingly gung-ho.'

'Wait, the Germans are Nazis again?'
'No, they don't want to be Nazis, that's why the thing about the Jews.'

'This is very confusing. Go on.'

'*What about your people?*'
'*Us? We're ready to draw a line. I was at Srebrenica.*'

'What's that?'
'Srebrenica. A town in Bosnia where a bunch of Muslims got massacred after a Dutch UN battalion let the Serbs in.'
'OK. That actually happened? OK.'

'*I know. You also picked up that American accent when you studied in California.*'
'*The thing is, Tom—*' Haverkort leaned forward and lowered his voice '*—nobody trusts anybody. Most of all, they don't trust you.*'
'*Do you trust me, Casp?*'
Haverkort hesitated. '*We're all in unknown territory here. We're defying habits we learned in the cradle. It's huge. But we know that however big it is for us, it's bigger for your country, Tom. Britain and America, you're family.*'
'*I don't know that the Americans think so.*'
'*They sent us a cop. Downing Street doesn't trust the military on this.*'
'*I didn't say that.*'
'*Give it to me straight, Tom. What did he tell you, the prime minister?*'
'*He said that the law is the law, and America is not above it. We are not attacking America, but we cannot allow these soldiers to avoid international justice.*'
'*And if America attacks us? Will you fight?*'
De Peyer grinned. '*If standing in the way is fighting,*' he said, '*I'll stand in the way.*'

'You've got some nerve, peddling that stuff over here,' said Lloyd.

'You peddle your stuff over there.'

'I ain't peddling no stuff.'

'Not you personally.'

'Your book stinks.'

'That's what they told me in New York.'

The bus driver announced that they were arriving at T's Corner grocery store, Oak Hall.

'My stop,' said Kellas.

'Listen, I got something to say to you,' said Lloyd. 'America is the greatest country in the world, that's ever been, and we don't need some British guy coming here with his bullshit novels, trying to teach us about justice. I mean, sweet Jesus, it's like the whole world is on our case right now, attacking us, and dissing us, and making us out like we're baby-killers. Well, I've got a message for the world: butt out, and watch out, 'cause we're coming back. We done Afghanistan, and now we're going to do Iraq, and we'll do whatever else it takes to stop all the terrorists and the motherfucking outlaws, alone if necessary. We're coming back.'

A cheer, a whoop and an 'Amen' came from other seats in the bus.

'It's only a novel,' said Kellas. 'A made-up story.'

'Why would you make up a story like that unless you thought it was true?'

The bus stopped and the doors opened. Kellas stood and Lloyd got up to let him out. 'To make money,' said Kellas.

'That's weak, brother. You got no right. You don't know us. You don't know this country and you ought to leave what you don't know and you don't understand well alone.'

'Isn't it the American way?'

'Bullshit! You can't be anti-American in the American way.'

Kellas nodded slowly and said goodbye.

'Yeah, take care, man. Take it easy. Someone picking you up?'

Kellas walked down the aisle of the bus, thanked the driver and walked down the steps into the storm. He reached the partial shelter of the roof over a set of petrol pumps when he heard a shout behind him. He looked round. Lloyd was standing in the doorway of the bus, waving the envelope containing his manuscript. He lifted it at Kellas and shook it, then threw it towards him. It fell short and landed on the wet asphalt. A sheaf of pages slipped out. Wind and water fought for control. After a few flips airward, the rain brought the paper down and the envelope and pages lay there, soaking. The bus doors closed and the bus drove off. Kellas picked up the envelope and the stray pages and pushed them into the slot of a trash can by the pumps. For a moment, anger hammered against the bounds of his body, and he struck the lid of the trash can with both fists. Then he walked into the grocery store, bright and deserted, apart from a single server on duty. It was five-thirty a.m. His wrist ached. He went up to the counter.

'Hi,' said the server. 'How are you today?' She was a young girl, small and slight, with large eyes and her hair in widely spaced cornrows. She looked barely sixteen.

'Regular coffee,' said Kellas.

'Small, medium or—'

'Small.'

The girl fetched him a paper cup and a lid. Her movements were precise and slow. 'You just come in on the bus from Salisbury? Was it snowing up there?'

'Further north it was.' Kellas's hand closed over the top of the cup.

'You must've outrun the cold front, then, 'cause they say it's heading on down our way, going to be here any time. They said on Weather Channel first the wind'd get up, then the rain'd come in, and once the storm was all wild and busy, the rain'd turn to snow, and we'd have a good inch by time the sun comes up. Only I'm not so sure, 'cause—'

'Jesus, can you stop prattling on about the fucking weather?' said Kellas. He opened his mouth to continue, then stopped. The girl's eyes had widened. Kellas looked down. 'I'm sorry,' he said.

'You don't have no cause to be shouting at me like that.'

'You're right, I'm sorry. Really.'

'I was only making conversation.'

'I know. I don't know what came over me. That is, I do know what came over me, but anyway, I apologise.'

'I've got a panic button right under the counter, and I can have the cops on your ass in sixty seconds. You want me to do that?'

'No. I'm – how much for the coffee?'

'Dollar ten.'

Kellas found two dollars in his pocket and gave it to her and told her to keep the change. She thanked him.

'What's your name?' said Kellas.

'Renee.'

'My name's Adam. I want you to believe that when I say I'm sorry, I mean it, it's not just . . . '

'It's OK.'

'How old are you, if you don't mind me asking?'

'Eighteen.' She was wary now.

'Am I keeping you from your work?'

'You're the only customer.'

'I should be getting on,' said Kellas, half-turning round. Instead he moved closer to Renee. 'Last time I lost my temper with someone your age was about a year ago. I yelled at him and I shoved him, with my hand, like that, pretty hard.'

'Maybe you should think about getting some of that anger management therapy.'

'Maybe. He did something that pissed me off but we didn't speak each other's language, not a single word.'

Renee had stretched her arms out on the counter in front of her and was leaning on them, arching her back. 'How come he didn't speak English?' she said.

'He spoke another language, probably two.'

Renee yawned and kicked one of her heels back. Kellas knew he should stop. 'I would never have shoved him if he hadn't had a gun. That made it OK. I could tell myself I was doing something dangerous.'

'What kind of a gun did he have?'

'An AK.'

'Pretty heavy.'

'You know what that is?'

'Oh, sure I know.'

Kellas went to fill the cup with coffee from the filter jug, emptied four sachets of sugar into it and went back to the counter. He stood with his back to it, leaning against it, drinking the coffee and watching the windows, which trembled in the wind. Every few moments a sound came from the glass as if someone had thrown a handful of gravel on it. Renee was working over some surfaces with a cloth.

'Where was that place you were at?' said Renee.

'Afghanistan.'

Renee stuck out her lower lip and nodded, moving her cloth from side to side over a clean shelf. 'That's a long way from here.'

'You could get there in a day.'

'D'you see any of those Taliban?'

'Only dead ones.'

'You a soldier?'

'No.'

'Some kind of bounty hunter?'

'No!' Kellas laughed.

Renee smiled. 'Why not? There's guys over there worth millions just for their heads. Dead or alive, it says on the poster. My boyfriend was like "I ain't joining the army" but somebody was to pay his fare out there and give him an Uzi and a pick-up, he'd go after them by himself.'

'I was a reporter.'

'OK. So no killing for you. You're a peaceful individual. A non-combatant.'

Kellas frowned. The counter was crowded with motoring atlases, cigarette lighters, drums labelled *Sea Salt Peanuts*, five-cent candies and stickers reading 'Virginia is for lovers'. The strong light in the store was taken up by thousands of yellow and red labels printed on plastic packaging.

'I used to think that. Now I'm not sure,' he said. 'If you stand by while somebody else kills some strangers in the distance, are you in on the killing yourself? What's the charge, aiding and abetting? I don't know where the law of Virginia or Afghanistan stands on that. I thought we were only *talking* about killing, and then one of us went and did it.' Kellas paused and looked at Renee. She was standing with her hands behind her back, leaning against a wall behind the counter, staring at nothing with her head slightly bowed.

'So maybe I helped out,' he said. 'Killing a couple of Taliban.'

'You should get in touch with the FBI,' said Renee. 'You might be in for a bounty for that.'

'Do you think?'

'I guess they'd need to see some sort of proof. Like an ear, maybe, or one each of their fingers.'

They stopped talking. Kellas became aware that if it wasn't for the faint sound of Bing Crosby singing *Rudolph The Red-Nosed Reindeer* on the PA, the store would be in complete silence.

He put the half-finished cup of coffee down and asked the way to Chincoteague. 'That's Chincoteague Road right there outside, between us and Pizza Hut,' said Renee. She nodded. 'Just follow it all the way, across the causeway, and that's Main Street, Chincoteague.'

Kellas thanked her and walked out of the store into the storm. After a few paces he stopped and considered going back to tell Renee that it had started to snow, but even the short distance he had travelled was hard-won ground, and he went on.

10

The wind was as strong as before, but the temperature had gone down steeply, and lush, sticky flakes of snow were hurtling darkly across the lamplight. Pale half-moons of a feathery texture at the edge of the road suggested it would settle. Looking further ahead, Kellas could see a strip of snow consolidating down the centre of the highway.

His left hand gripped the two halves of his jacket together at his throat. The bandage provided a little extra warmth but this was cancelled out by the chilling effect of snow melting on the skin of the hand and his face. The pain in his wrist was fading, numbed by the cold, perhaps. That was a good thing. Of most concern was the speed with which his jacket and trousers were absorbing moisture. Once all his clothes were saturated, which would be soon, he would begin to lose body heat rapidly. It could not be a good sign that the snow was falling thickly enough for the lower layer to melt and continue soaking his jacket, while a middle layer formed a transition, and an outer layer began to stick and accumulate on the jacket breast.

Ahead the snow was unbalding the asphalt swiftly. There were houses. Shelter to seek if it got rough, which, most likely now, it would. A phrase appeared in his head: once you experience unambiguous symptoms of hypothermia, it is already too late. Yet had he heard it, or read it, or made it up in that moment? It wouldn't do to ramble. No meandering, mental or pedestrian. Concentrate.

'Concentrate,' he said into the wind.

Lengthen your stride. Rapid march. Forward. On. Imagine you

are carrying someone sicker than you, someone you care for. Someone you care for more than you care for yourself. On with the loved one, on to safety. Think thoughts with ends and destinations. Think of making a case to the woman you've crossed the ocean to see. Don't think of the case itself, only of making it. Bombard her with words. One will get through. On now. Although certainly ten miles was a hell of a way to walk in a snowstorm. Two and a half hours at a fair pace on the flat. He was not dressed for this weather. It was not so much the thought of dying as the thought of embarrassing his father which might force him to knock on strange doors and seek help. Scot Found Dead On American Road. Father Critiques Footwear, Lack Of Coat. But he did not want to knock on those strange doors. The whole countryside was armed to the teeth, jaundiced at the very rumour of bums and footpads. He needed to keep moving. It would warm him up.

It would be sunrise in an hour, he supposed, already the middle of the morning in Dumfries. The post would have been delivered. It was Tuesday. It was due. One of the children would have found the letter, perhaps, the strange small communication sealed with a second stamp, fluttering through the slot onto the rug in the hall, along with the weight and bright colours of the junk mail, carried further by the tiny extra puff of air as the heavier letters struck the floor. Kellas couldn't unsend it, however much he longed to. Perhaps Fergus would have found it. The boy would have been intrigued and taken it to his mother. Five of them around the breakfast table, snatching, pouring, drinking and squabbling. Sophie would have opened it, curious, but with foreboding. M'Gurgan would have noticed the hand-scrawled address on an Ikea receipt, looked at Sophie's face, and wondered whether his wife was being stalked; whether she was having an affair. What she knew about him that he didn't know she knew. Sophie would have dropped the letter, put her hands to her mouth and rushed out of the room, weeping. No, that was a film. What would she really have done? Read it carefully, trying not to show what she was thinking, although

M'Gurgan would have seen. She would have folded the piece of paper very small, running her nails along the folds, and closed her fist around it, and she would have looked at M'Gurgan without saying anything, and he would have known that she had received information prejudicial to his good character in that home. Perhaps there would have been a moistness in her eyes, and certainly by this time Angela and Carrie would have realised that something was wrong. At the same moment, Angela would have said: 'What's wrong, Mum?' and Carrie would have said 'What does it say, Mum?' And Sophie would have said 'Nothing', and chased them out to school. M'Gurgan, sitting at the table, would have heard the front door close and Sophie striding back down the hall with her shoes hitting the floor hard and he would have got to his feet, ready for the fight. A possibility: they'd been worried about their friend Kellas. M'Gurgan might have recognised the handwriting and thought that it was a suicide note. What a good man, to care so much! And how much harder then to find out that Kellas had not killed himself, but had betrayed him, and betrayed Sophie, the ordinary woman who got things done. They would be fighting now, in the day of the east. By the evening Kellas would have blown his friends' family to fragments.

Kellas slipped and tumbled into a patch of snow. He jumped up and brushed the snow off his jacket and trousers in a frenzy, as if it was a mass of poisonous insects. Light dazzled him and he put his right hand over his eyes. A vehicle had stopped a few yards away. It was pointed in the direction of Chincoteague. After a few moments, it rolled forward till the open driver's window was level with Kellas. It was a pick-up truck with lines of ten year's antiquity. A man in his fifties or sixties, white-haired, in an old ski jacket, looked at Kellas over his elbow.

'Where are you going?' asked the man.

'Chincoteague.'

'You drunk?'

'No.'

'Are you high?'

'No.'

'Is there some medication you should be high on, and you skipped your dose?'

'No.'

'Get in. Quietly. The baby's sleeping.' Kellas walked round to the passenger side, climbed in and closed the door. A single seat ran the width of the cab, in the American style, and in the middle, between Kellas and the driver, was a sturdy white carry cot, with a baby's puckered face poking out of folds of wool.

'Thank you,' said Kellas quietly. 'I'm soaking. It's good to be out of the snow.' He tilted the vents with his finger and felt hot air blow onto him. 'Do you mind?'

'Where are you heading?'

Kellas named the street.

The man watched the road ahead for a while. In the cone of the lights the snow seemed to part and show the way at the same time, like the crowd around a body when the police arrive.

'Are they expecting you there?' asked the man.

'Expecting me?' repeated Kellas. He looked down at the baby. It was more tightly asleep than anything he had ever seen. Two small fists a-curl. It was unreprieved darkness outside, and the truck hammered forward, towards the island, with an old man at the wheel and a baby asleep beside him.

'She's six months old,' said the driver. He glanced at Kellas and turned back to the road. 'She's not yours.'

Kellas didn't reply, unsure whether he'd misheard, or whether the driver had said something so strange that it would signify Kellas's departure from one life and his entry into another, more real and secret. He looked at the old man. He was tall, as far as Kellas could tell; he would be well over six foot standing. He didn't appear to be carrying much fat under the ski jacket, which was unzipped. Underneath he wore a checked shirt and a white vest. He had a long, narrow face with a mark under his left eye, hidden from Kellas while he watched the road. His hair was cropped closely at the sides.

Had it not been thicker and looser on top, he would have looked military. Two long, sharp lines, like cuts, ran down the sides of his face, from cheekbone to jaw. There was a generic quality to his handsomeness, as if, when younger, he had begun to will himself into having a particular set of features at sixty, drawing for models on the likes of police chiefs, presidents and generals as portrayed on American TV specials, and it was difficult for Kellas to identify what it was about him that took him beyond performance and gave him gravity. It was, Kellas realised, that he seemed to have no tension in him, neither the fake forms of bad actors demonstrating weight-iness of purpose, nor the wound-up tautness of anxious western men and women of affairs who fretted, who exercised too much without having anything real to do with the strength they gained, ending up in the course of a day unconsciously tightening their muscles, ready to leap at and strangle the monster of their disaffection, which never appeared. This man was brooding over something, something that in a way Kellas dared not guess involved him, but he wasn't brooding with his body.

The man turned his face to look at Kellas. He had grey eyes. Under the left eye the mark, Kellas saw now, was a tattooed tear. 'My name is Bastian,' he said. 'Do you recognise it?'

Kellas shook his head, and began to introduce himself, but Bastian interrupted. 'I know your name,' he said. 'You're Adam Kellas.'

The tear was so out of place, seemed such a ridiculous mistake, that at first Kellas found it impossible to focus on what Bastian was saying. He wanted to ask about the tear, and couldn't. Gradually the strangenesss of Bastian recognising him and asking whether he was expected asserted themselves over the oddness of the tattoo. The real and secret life was, after all, beginning, now, when Kellas was filthy and exhausted; the information that the baby was not his was an act of joining of things so dizzying that Kellas involuntarily pushed his hands through his hair. The baby gurgled.

'My side of things is not as strange as it might appear, I should tell you,' said Bastian. 'What's strange isn't that I should happen to pick you up. I dropped Astrid off at the hunt site a few minutes ago. She makes an early start on hunt days. And I couldn't leave Naomi alone in the house. Went to the store for milk, and Renee was chewing her braids and swivelling from side to side, and I asked her what she'd done, and she said she'd directed a funny-looking guy in nothing but a light jacket down the road to Chincoteague, ten miles with the snow coming down, and only after he'd gone did she realise he'd come in on the bus and he didn't have a car. She was trying to work out whether to call police or ambulance and I said since I was going that way I'd see what was up. I thought there was something familiar about your face but it was only when you got in the car that I recognised you.'

'Have we met?'

'"Someone should have tipped Paris McIntyre off that he was about to be arrested, for he had many friends in the police who owed him favours, yet when the time came, each of them found their own way to forget that he had ever existed." Your picture was on the jacket. When Astrid came back from Afghanistan, she told me about you. She said that you'd written books. I tracked *The Maintenance of Fury* down on the Internet. Took a long time. I liked it. I have a good memory for first lines, and I liked that one. Echoes of Kafka and Tolstoy.'

'I don't need the fact I've been travelling for more than twenty-four hours as an excuse,' said Kellas slowly. 'I feel very awake now. But I could write hundreds of first lines to books and still not know how to begin asking all the things I want to ask.'

'Try picking the first question that comes into your head.'

'Why did you have a tear tattooed on your face?'

The snow had slackened and a watery blue was lightening the eastern horizon.

'Up ahead's the causeway that takes me and Naomi to Chincoteague,' said Bastian. 'I can take you across to the island, to our home. I will do that, gladly, and you'll be very welcome, and you'll see Astrid, which I guess is why you're here. Or, if you ask me to, I'll just as gladly drive you to Baltimore or DC, right now. Think about it. Of the two ways, my advice to you would be: go back. Don't come to the island. Think about that while I answer your question.'

'OK,' said Kellas.

'It was after I dropped out of college. I used to have a small-holding in the hills near San Francisco. I raised marijuana there, supplied the local musicians. It brought in a little cash and I read and wrote and collected books. I spent a lot of time in the woods, smoking and listening to the trees and the water. One year, I guess it would have been '68, this guy turned up and stayed. He was a little younger than me. He might have been dodging the draft, I don't remember.'

The car went over a bump. Some roadkill, presumably, a rabbit or large bird.

'He wore a fringed buckskin jacket and jeans and had a beard he thought made him look like Anton Chekhov, although to me he looked more like General Custer. He didn't bother me at first but after a while I noticed that wherever I was, and whatever I was doing, he was there, doing it too. I'd go into the library to read and he'd come along, take out a book and start reading. He'd go to bed when I went. If I went for a walk, he'd tag along. He wouldn't help out with the plants unless I took the lead. His name was Edwin. For a while I thought he was a narc. Then I thought he was a puppy. But it was something else. He wouldn't do, and he wouldn't learn; each time he followed me he did it so that he could watch himself. He was his own spectator. He was amazed at the quaintness of his own life. It was as if the actual him was in some other space, sitting on some soft chair, shovelling popcorn into his mouth, watching and commentating while the material Edwin experimented with living. I'd light a joint, and he'd come up and wait till I handed it to him, and he'd say: "I am going to get so stoned today." It would have made more sense to me if I'd heard him say "*They* are going to get so stoned today." He'd be twitchy in the woods. It wasn't in his nature just to *be* there. He had to be telling himself, and me, that we were there, and that it was a good thing, a great thing.'

Between the men, Naomi slept. She threw a couple of punches in the air, moved her head and blew a bubble. Kellas tried to listen to what Bastian was saying. He had a yearning to see Astrid and a cowardly yearning for delay. He felt as he had felt when the deafening motors of the lizard-coloured transport plane had changed their note on the descent to Faizabad, and he had longed to land and step out into Afghanistan, and at the same time feared the end of the clarity of journeying.

'One day in winter I got up early, had some coffee alone in the kitchen, and went out to see the sun come up,' said Bastian. 'Right then, Edwin was next to me, coffee in hand. And he started his commentating about how beautiful it was, and how he felt at one with the world, how he pitied the office workers and their bourgeois routines. It had a power on me, his incantation, I began to feel that the sun had been designed, made and marketed, and that I was buying it just by standing there and watching it and listening to Edwin. And Edwin said wasn't it a great life we had, and I said I supposed it was, even though him saying it made me doubt it. Edwin asked what I was going to do in the future and I said I didn't know, maybe the same as whatever I was doing now. And Edwin nodded and said he felt exactly the same way. He said: "If I ever come down off this hill and get a straight job in the land of white bread and adding machines, Bastian, will you please come and find me and shoot me?" I looked at him, and I thought about it. I thought about it seriously. I was sure he'd get that job and I believed in that moment that it was a real possible future for me to kill him as he'd asked. I saw myself walking into his office in some small-town real estate firm and him rising to greet me, with his tie tight in the folds of his neck, and saying "Hey Bastian! Long time, no see!" And me drilling him with twelve-gauge. But then I thought about myself and my own weakness. I could kill the future Edwin, but I didn't want to, I wasn't a killer, and what about me? I'd been afflicted by his shadow so easily. I needed to get back into the world, but I needed to change myself. I needed something to stop the world from swallowing me up.

'That day I went and got the tear tattooed. A tattoo on your cheek is hard to hide. It sets you apart. I didn't trust myself to avoid law school or advertising or journalism – sorry, Mr Kellas—'

'It's OK,' said Kellas.

'I didn't trust myself. And I didn't want to ask somebody to kill me, like Edwin. So the tear was my safeguard. Not to destroy me, only to fence parts of the world off, put it out of bounds. No country club for me. No golf club for me. No brokerage house for me.' He laughed a single, short laugh. 'Not in the Sixties, anyway. So that's what the tear is, it's to ward against possible weakness.'

'It could also be—'

'An excuse for failure, I know. But I'm not one. That same day I had the tear done, I threw Edwin out of the house and dug up the marijuana. A few weeks later I was in New York, looking for teaching work, writing short stories, trying to earn a wage. I owe the tattoo a lot. It put me back in the world by setting a limit on how worldly I could become.'

'I know what you mean,' said Kellas.

'And now. Now . . . ' Bastian lightly rocked Naomi's cot. After a second of silence he glanced at Kellas. 'Now I think it's better that those who have weaknesses are constrained, or constrain themselves, by means of quiet but tangible barriers like this.' He touched the tear. 'Like deliberately moving to a place where their weaknesses are outlawed. Or by . . . ' he sighed, a deep inhalation followed by an equally full breathing out ' . . . submitting to the rule of a warden. The flaw in barriers like that is, of course, that they're so easily breached. A pair of sunglasses and the tattoo's hidden. A causeway and a car—'

Naomi woke up and began to cry. They had reached the water

and the causeway. Bastian pulled over to the side of the road, lifted her out of the cot and held her against his shoulder. He murmured soothing words to her and jigged her softly up and down and the bawling eased. It was light outside. The sky was clearing, although the sun wasn't yet up.

'Are you Astrid's father?' asked Kellas.

'No. Did you think I was?'

'To begin with, yes. She said that they lived together.'

'Jack Walsh died in summer. He was a good friend of mine. Listen, I have to get Naomi home. I can drop you at T's Corner, pick you up later and drive you to Baltimore or DC, or you can come home with us. I have to ask you to decide. Keeping in mind that I recommend very strongly that you do not come to the island.'

'I'll be welcome if I come, but you think I'd be better to leave?'

'That's right.'

'I don't understand. Why shouldn't I come?'

'That concerns a third party who is not here to speak for herself.'

'But she invited me. She sent me an email.'

Bastian looked carefully at Kellas. His head was tilted slightly to one side. He was stroking Naomi's back.

'Did it say "I want to see you now. I want you to come to me . . . " Yes? I can see from your face now that you get it. It's too bad. You might have known better. Those emails are flying around all the time. Did you really think it was genuine? When did it come in? Because she sent out messages to everyone yesterday apologising.'

'Are you sure?' said Kellas.

'As far as I know, the virus sent that email out to everyone in her address book.'

Kellas rubbed his forehead with his fingertips. The news was bad, grievously bad. Yet in some last-ditch redoubt of nothing-to-lose synapses he thought: she had my email address in her list.

'So you're saying I've travelled here from London on the strength of a few words fabricated by a piece of malicious software?' he said. 'Astrid didn't contact me at all.'

'It looks that way. I'm sorry.'

Kellas nodded while he thought. 'I always liked that word of yours, "dumb",' he said. 'It means "stupid" and "ignorant" at the same time.'

'Don't be hard on yourself. You haven't done a bad thing, yet.'

'You don't think I should come to the island.'

'That's right.'

'You can't tell me why.'

'I'm not going to do that. But now you know you weren't invited.'

'Has Astrid ever said to you, "I don't want to see Adam Kellas again?"'

Bastian blinked. 'There are four people involved here,' he said. 'One of them being you.'

'Has she ever said it, or anything like it, about me?'

'No.'

'I'd like to see Astrid,' said Kellas. He blinked. He was light-headed and his wrist ached. 'I've travelled a long way. Whatever the situation between the three of you, I'd like to see her, and if there's room for me, to stay tonight.'

'There is room,' said Bastian. He handed Naomi to Kellas, who took her warm, soft weight under her arms. He cupped his right hand under her bottom and put his left hand on her back and let her lie back against his left shoulder, feeling her springy arms hook onto it. Kellas moved her up and down but it didn't stop her crying, only made intervals of silence.

Bastian drove onto the causeway, which ran for several miles through an expanse of khaki reed beds and creeks. The island lay on the eastern horizon and the sun was coming up behind it, making the coarse short reeds glow bronze. The view to the north was partly obstructed by a succession of painted, cabin-sized signs, advertising food and lodging for tourists on Chincoteague.

While they drove, Bastian told him that Astrid had become preg-nant before she left for Afghanistan, in September, before, in fact, the Twin Towers came down. It came from a one-night affair; the father was an Australian scientist on a short visit to the Nasa facility opposite Chincoteague who'd since gone back to Melbourne. Yeah, Melbourne. They weren't in touch. The house had belonged to Bastian since the Seventies, when he'd bought it with the proceeds of a book deal he'd done with the government. It was too big for one. It was a family-sized house. Jack and Astrid and the other Walshes would visit all the time and after Jack retired he and Astrid moved in.

'After Jack's wife killed herself, and his son went away to the north-west, Jack and Astrid looked out for each other, and I looked out for them. The suicide made Jack very hard. He made a cult of hardness. Reticence and obstinacy was all there was. He wasn't cranky, he wasn't even grouchy, but he hated a conversation. Anything that he could answer "Yes" to was a waste of time as far as he was concerned. He liked to stop you talking by saying "No". If you got a "Maybe" out of him, you were doing well. Astrid could get him to talk, I think, but then she was away a lot of the time. So now Jack's gone, and I'm looking after Astrid, and helping take care of the kid. You all right there? We'll be home in ten minutes.'

'Does Astrid need looking after?'

Bastian didn't answer at once. He kept looking straight ahead while they crossed a humped swing bridge over the last deep channel before the island itself. 'I don't speak for Astrid,' he said.

They turned left off the bridge and drove for about a mile along a street of shops, hotels and restaurants. It was narrow for America, a small shoreline town main street with a cinema and a petrol station and a sculpture of a horse. The buildings were two-storey affairs of brick or clapboard. A dozen old trees, winter-bare, opened out above the roof line. Green Christmas garlands, wreaths and scarlet bows were strung between wooden telegraph poles. Some of the houses had verandas enclosed by wooden latticework arches but nothing looked as old as a town on Virginia's east coast must be. Kellas asked about storms.

'Storms, fire, floods, we've had them all. The snow'll be gone by

209

noon, though,' said Bastian. 'There now, honey, soon be home now.' He stroked the screaming Naomi's cheek with the second joint of his index finger. 'She's hungry. You must be, too.'

They took a right onto a wider street. Maddox Boulevard, the street sign read. They passed an old whitewashed garage with a larger-than-life carving of a fisherman in yellow oilskins at the door. A sign on the wall read 'Island Decoy's', with two Canada geese in flight fixed alongside. They were heading east again, towards the Atlantic, and the sun ahead of them looked as if it might tip out of the sky and come bowling down the street. Here the houses were smaller and lower, the souvenir shops and motels bigger and louder. There were cycle rentals, a Chinese restaurant, drive-through banks and a shack called His & Her Seafood And Bait Shop. Bastian had been right about the weather. Although the grass verges were still dotted with clumps of snow, the roads and gardens and parking lots were already melted clear. The neck of a fibreglass giraffe in a pocket amusement park, and the ears of an African elephant, glistened where the sun caught the wetness. The park's palm trees were shrinkwrapped for the close season. After another mile the road crossed a further stretch of reeds and creeks. They reached a roundabout. Bastian took a left off it by a Family Dollar store and turned right at a church like a factory unit, with gothic arch windows cut in the vinyl siding in the gable ends and a thin white fibreglass spire fixed on top. Here the houses were larger and lay in groves of tall pine trees. Bastian turned off onto a potholed road covered in a layer of red-brown pine needles. The trees cast strips of shadow across the road. On the right, through the trees and beyond the houses, Kellas could see more reeds, water, and the green line of a second island.

'That's Assateague Island,' said Bastian. 'On the far side of that's the ocean. And this is where we live. I'm sorry Astrid couldn't welcome you herself.'

The house was closely encircled by a stand of forty-foot pines, with slender trunks and high crowns of bright green. It was a two-storey building, counting the rooms under the roof as an upper storey, with walls faced in lengths of unpainted, treated wood and a screened-in veranda projecting from the front. A stone extension had been added, with a chimney. A pile of logs lay under sacking at one end. The house sat on raised foundations and a short flight of wooden steps led up to the front door. The roof was streaked with snow, melting in the sun. An old bicycle with rusting chopper handlebars and white walled tyres stood leaned up against the wall by the door.

Bastian took Naomi from Kellas – she had stopped crying – and they walked over the patches of snow and the thick covering of fallen needles to the door. It was not locked. Water pattered from the trees around them and trickled in the drainpipes. In the porch Kellas recognised Astrid's pointed boots, carelessly left, one upright, the other on its side. He followed Bastian, took his own boots off when Bastian removed his in the porch, and found himself sitting at the table in the kitchen, which smelled of toast and coffee from an earlier breakfast.

'I have to change and feed Naomi,' said Bastian. 'I won't be going to pick Astrid up for a few hours yet. You don't have any luggage, right? I guess we can fix you up with a change of clothes. You'll be sleeping upstairs. Take a shower, if you like, or you can fix yourself some breakfast – coffee's there, fridge is full.'

'You're very kind,' said Kellas. 'I'll rest and wash later.'

It was warm in the house. He hung his jacket on the back of a chair, rolled up his sleeves, and set the coffeemaker going. He melted some butter in a frying pan and broke a couple of eggs in, with a few rashers of bacon. He offered to fry for Bastian but Bastian said he had already eaten. The two men worked without speaking, Kellas frying and Bastian changing Naomi's nappy and using gadgets to sterilise her bottles and heat her milk. Inside the fridge Kellas had checked, while he got the food, for items distinctively Astrid, but how could he tell? A packet of raisin bagels? Spring onions? Chipotle sauce? The kitchen was neat and clean. Along a tiled ledge under the uncurtained window, which looked out of the back towards a wooden shed and a pear tree, were bleached gleanings from the foreshore, shells, the bobbled, spherical integument of a sea urchin, a green crabshell and the long delicate skull of a bird. There was information on the fridge door: a scrap of paper with 'Call doctor' written on, fixed with a leaping salmon fridge magnet, a table of hunting areas and dates, and a grainy black-and-white photograph of a stone tablet with letters carved on it in two different alphabets; the upper alphabet looked like Greek.

Kellas set down his plate and coffee and began to eat. Bastian was feeding Naomi from a bottle and Kellas watched her, trying to find Astrid in her chubby head and new eyes. The sounds in the kitchen were Naomi's gurgles, Bastian murmuring words of endearment, Kellas's cutlery on the plate and the hum of the extractor fan he'd switched on over the hob. He felt more cheated of immediate reunion with Astrid, more indignant that there were not more signs of her life in the house for him to read, than he felt anxious about Naomi or Bastian, even though he hadn't expected to find either of them here. There was a docility in Bastian's manliness. If it came to it, Kellas couldn't imagine him fighting for Astrid. Naomi was more complicated. Of the two interpretations of Astrid going to Afghanistan while pregnant, the reckless and the defiant, Kellas liked both. He was moved by the thought of having slept with Astrid while Naomi was growing inside her. He didn't want her to be careworn and cradlebound, but the child gave Kellas more time, must slow Astrid down enough for Kellas to walk alongside her for longer. The implicit offer of stepfatherhood lay in his chase and he could surely coo as sweetly as the big old man on the far side of the kitchen table, who was poking his nose into Naomi's giggling face and getting it repeatedly clapped between the pink stars of her hands.

There was, still, the question of money.

'What's the inscription in the photo on the fridge?' asked Kellas.

'It's a tablet from the second century before Christ. An edict of King Ashoka, carved in Greek and Aramaic. It was found in Kandahar and put in the archaeological museum in Kabul until the civil war in Afghanistan in the Nineties. It disappeared.'

'Did Astrid put the picture up?'

'I put it up. Before she went out there, I asked her to see if she could find out anything about where it had gotten to. I leave it up there, hoping she'll write something, because although she never got to the bottom of it, she did the interviews. You know how it is. People who aren't reporters always think they have some idea that'll make a great article. Do you read Greek?'

'No,' said Kellas. 'I didn't know there were people speaking Greek living in Kandahar two thousand years ago.'

'Oh, yeah. After Alexander the Great. There were big Greek settlements in Afghanistan. That was where Aristotle met the Buddha. Not literally, I mean that's where Greek philosophy met Buddhism. That's what the inscription is about. It was the Greeks who first gave Buddha a face and a body, his corporeal image. Every Buddha statue comes from the Greeks of Afghanistan and India.' Bastian gave his short laugh. 'I recognise that expression on your face. You're thinking that time is going the wrong way, aren't you? That ancient Kandahar had Plato and the Dharma, modern Kandahar has Jehovah slugging it out with Allah, the Old Testament versus the Caliphate. You want to play, pumpkin? You want to go fishing with Bastian?' Bastian, who had been holding Naomi on his knee, lifted her up in the air and had a short discussion with her about tides and lures. He set her down again and jiggled her. 'When I moved east from California, that was what I was going to write about. I became fascinated by the notion – for which there is nothing except circumstantial evidence – that Jesus and the disciples were Buddhists without the name, that a Greek Buddhist from somewhere between Kabul and Peshawar made the journey to the Greeks of Palestine and taught the young Jesus self-denial, non-violence, the virtues of poverty, chastity and humility.'

'A novel?'

'Yes.'

'And the hero was to be that ancient Greek Buddhist?'

'Yes.'

Kellas felt the vertigo of the millennia and the lust of the billions for the revelation of hidden truths. 'That could have been . . . '

'I almost finished it,' said Bastian. 'Then I sold it to a government agency. They won't let it see the light of day for a long time. The act of corporate stupidity they committed by buying it was more embarrassing than anything in the text.' He looked down at the floor and stroked Naomi's head softly. 'I'd like to tell you what happened. I can see you're curious. It's an act of atonement to tell it.'

'Go ahead,' said Kellas.

'My life would have been different if I'd been British or French,' said Bastian, 'where London and Paris are the centre of everything. But I began to feel, after I moved to New York, that I was trying to stay upright on a steep slope that had Washington at the bottom.' What tugged at Bastian was the notion of service, not to be one who served, but to be in the polis where others did. He was a free thinker. 'I don't mean to brag,' he said to Kellas, 'but I was on a different plane from the hippies and the anti-war crowd, the anti-government radicals, the amateur American terrorists.' Anti-government, as Bastian saw it, defined itself by what it opposed. Bastian was lured by the notion of a city of eternal government that existed just beyond the Washington of four-year electoral cycles and drum-and-cymbals battles over money, war and race. At the time, he was ashamed of the visions that took him suddenly on his walks through the Village, of men in white shirts and black ties, gathered on green grass among white buildings reading through stacks of figures typed on crisp white paper, not to serve a cause or party but for the virtue of service itself; that the rituals were pleasing, and honourable, and good. He was ashamed; his girlfriend was a feminist activist, his friends were leather-panted musicians, campus warriors and civil rights fighters. It was to guard against the temptations of offices, shirts and ties that he'd put the permanent tear on his face. He was ashamed, until he reasoned that his conceptual Washington was more subversive than his friends'. They wanted to change it; he only anticipated its eventual disappearance into another age. The Washington that lured him was a Washington as it might be seen thousands of years hence, mysterious, coded, costumed, like ancient, imperial China seen from now, far enough away for its specifics to be invisible and the beauty of repeating patterns to emerge. Its achievements, virtues and cruelties, in so far as they would be remembered, wouldn't impress or horrify, only amuse. With this in his head, in 1975, Bastian moved to DC.

He found it tough to get a salaried job with the tattoo, but his experience and a few published short stories eventually got him a post as a roving creative writing tutor in some of the city's tougher neighbourhoods. He met Jack Walsh through a charity working with the homeless. Astrid's father sat on the board of trustees. He invited Bastian to dinner at the Walsh home in McLean, a western suburb of Washington, over the line in Virginia. Kellas worked out that Astrid would have been about eight at the time, and Bastian thirty-three. Kellas lost concentration for a few sentences. Men and women around a table, hair curling over the men's ears, big ties and big collars. Abundant eye shadow. A serious child in the doorway comes to say goodnight. All the faces turn. A man with a tear tattooed on his face. She remembers him.

'I knew that the main industry in McLean was the CIA. The front gate is right there, across the highway, in the trees. So I wondered if any of the students would be from the agency, or married into it.' Kellas frowned and apologised and asked Bastian to back up. Bastian repeated what he'd just said; he had got on well with the Walshes and their set in McLean, which was middle class enough, but not such a sought-after place as now. The tattoo, in this case, was just what they wanted – a badge of Bohemia on someone who was not dangerous, stoned or out to fling Society in their faces. They didn't want to embrace the counter-culture, but they wanted to shake its hand, be able to say they had it as an acquaintance. A white man with a tattoo on his face was less of a commitment than making the acquaintance of somebody black. The consequence was that Bastian got a gig taking a creative writing class in McLean, one evening a week, alongside others teaching conversational French and basket-weaving to bored and confined burghers.

There were about twenty-five regulars, mostly women. In the first class, Bastian read extracts from his own work in progress, about the Greek Buddhist from Kandahar who travelled to ancient Palestine, and encouraged the students to criticise it. Over subsequent weeks there was a rotation. Each week, a pair of students would read out their efforts, talk about the other's writing, then be subject to questions and comments from the floor. At the end of the ninth class, one of the students lingered to talk to Bastian while he was packing up. His name was Crowpucker. He was younger than Bastian, barely thirty, and pale, with pouchy cheeks. Crowpucker told Bastian that it was his turn to read-and-be-read the following week, and that he would, to his regret, have to quit the class, since the nature of his work for the government made it impossible for the material concerned to be made public.

'I can imagine the kind of work you do,' said Bastian to Crowpucker. 'But it doesn't have anything to do with what we're doing here. You're dealing, I guess, with secret government information during your working hours. Here, this is about you writing fiction and poetry in your spare time. You can keep those things separate. Nobody, least of all me, wants you to come in here and read classified material.'

Crowpucker smiled, shook his head, shifted his feet and looked around. 'Listen,' he said. 'D'you want to talk about this over a beer?'

They went to a Chinese restaurant and talked for several hours. Crowpucker said that he didn't want to be a novelist, a screenwriter or a poet; what he had was an interest in the imagination. He picked up on what Bastian had said: 'I can imagine the kind of work you do.' Perhaps Bastian could. There were techniques a government agency was interested in examining. Crowpucker and a group of other like-minded young administrators had backing to find specialists in these techniques. It was not a question of making things up. There would be no fabrication of facts. Rather it was the space between the facts, the assembly of the facts into a recognisable shape, and the direction the shape was pointed, that was the concern. It was a matter, in the end, of national security. Too much important information was being wasted because it was being passed to those with the power to use it in a fashion that was shapeless, untidy, confusing. Or dull! Dullness could also harm the national interest.

'A few months later, I signed up,' Bastian said to Kellas. 'It sounds odd, but I wasn't thinking about spies and the Cold War. I was thinking about a great hermetic bureaucracy, a secret city of servants in white shirts tending something eternal and arcane. It seemed I was to be a visitor in the cloisters of a silent order. When I went in I saw water coolers and ugly carpet tiles and heard squabbles about who'd booked which conference room, but by that time I was curious to see who was going to benefit from my two hundred and fifty dollars a week. I was surprised to get through the security clearance so easily. It turned out I could be cleared at a very low level. Same as the cleaners who vacuumed the low-security offices at night. I didn't have a record. I hadn't dodged the draft because I'd never been called up. I was surprised to see the word "Program" on the contract. It seemed over-pompous. But there I was one morning, driving to Virginia, past the gatehouses, and sitting down with the students of the CIA's first Creative Writing Program.'

There were only eight students, all men. Like Crowpucker, they were young, with soft hands and pale, office-bound complexions. Their faces beamed with optimism.

'And I don't mean hope,' Bastian said to Kellas. '"Hope" implies that you reckon there's a chance things might work out, and a chance they might not. These guys had an expectation of triumph. It was a sure thing. I could never figure out whether the triumph was to be theirs, or the agency's, or America's, or humanity's. I'm not sure they saw a difference.' They introduced themselves and Bastian outlined the way his classes usually worked.

'Sir,' said one of them, 'do you think it's always true that history is written by the victors? Couldn't losers write history instead, if they wrote it really, really well?'

Before Bastian could speak, the students began arguing among themselves.

'They went on for a long time,' Bastian told Kellas. 'I sat there and listened. By the time they quietened down, I knew I was the wrong man in the wrong place, and I wouldn't be coming back. What they were arguing about was events that hadn't yet happened, as if they were certain to happen, as if they already had happened. I kept hearing phrases like "When the Soviet Union invades Iran", "When the communists take over Italy", "When Moscow makes its move for Iceland", "When we start getting arms to the Muslims of Central Asia." If I'd been more paranoid, if these men had been older, I might have thought they knew what they were talking about. That they knew these events were coming, might even, who knows, trigger them. It was the CIA. But not these guys. They laughed too much. It was the strangest thing: they were serious and not serious at the same time. They were sincere when they talked about what would happen in the future; they honestly believed these real countries and peoples would experience these events. But there were no people among these peoples. The countries they spoke about were shapes on a map, with certain numerical qualities. It was a simple world of deviants, conformists and masses.'

When he could get a word in, Bastian said that perhaps there'd been a misunderstanding. Crowpucker apologised and recalled the meeting in the Chinese restaurant. What this was about, he said, was learning how to harness a writer's imagination in the service of intelligence.

Bastian said it was true that imagination could be applied to guess what individuals might be thinking, what they might be like, and how they might act. But it worked best when the individual was a fictional composite character, based on experience of other, real people. It couldn't be applied to nations or peoples, except in fantasy literature, or pulp fiction.

The students looked disappointed. They took notes. Bastian felt that he would not have to quit after all; they'd sack him and keep auditioning teachers until they found one who would teach them exactly what they had already decided they were going to learn.

Crowpucker wanted a debate. Surely, he said, there were three kinds of imagination. There was making something or somebody up that didn't exist at all. There was imagining how real people were going to act in the future. And then there was the third kind, where you imagined what you or your organisation, or your country, might be capable of, and then you went and did it. Wasn't the ideal when you were able to combine them all, imagination and action? Like the founding fathers. They had imagined a non-existent country, a democratic America, they had imagined how the British and the American settlers would treat the idea, and they had imagined a course of action they could take that would make the fantasy real.

Bastian told Crowpucker that he was confusing philosophy and practical planning with literature. Novels and plays weren't there to show people what to be, or predict what they would do. They showed what human beings are.

'That's a problem literature has to deal with,' said Crowpucker. 'The lack of a moral framework. The lack of templates for heroic and patriotic action. I could give you examples of what there should be. Tolstoy, for one. And you. Your work.' Crowpucker urged Bastian to admit that his novel about the Buddhist Jesus was more than an entertainment, a lyric, or a narrative of characters. It was a sermon of sorts, wasn't it? A lesson? A pattern for how humans should behave? Not one that he, Crowpucker, cared for, but he admired the intention.

'He was clever,' Bastian told Kellas. 'They were all clever, well-read wiseasses. He had me. No writer likes to be accused of having written a sermon—'

'No,' said Kellas.

'—but I couldn't deny that there was truth in what he said. I'd been working on that book for so long, and still I hadn't buried the thought that kicked it off, when I was sulking in the mountains, that I really wanted it to be that Jesus was a Buddhist Jew. That even if he hadn't been, he should have been, and I could make it so and tweak the believers my way.' Bastian struggled for an answer. He had noticed already that Crowpucker was holding a sheaf of double-spaced typed pages, and asked whether he'd brought the work he couldn't read to the class in McLean, and whether he'd care to read it now, to give Bastian and the others a better idea of what he meant.

Crowpucker was glad to read his work out loud. He explained first that the subject of his report was an actual country, and everything in it was based on actual, raw intelligence, but that, for Bastian's sake, he would refer to the country as country A. The story, or report, as Crowpucker called it, described the life of a boy, Abdullah, living in town K in country A, whose father was a successful exporter of carpets, a devout Muslim, and a member of a group of businessmen trying to persuade the king to step down in favour of an elected parliament. The young boy loved his father and was full of hope for the future of his country. Then, one day, with the help of money and arms from Moscow, the riff-raff of the bazaar and a bunch of misguided liberal intellectuals, the communists staged a coup and took power. The boy's parents were arrested, his carpet business was collectivised and the mosque placed under strict supervision by atheists. Instead of Koranic classes, the boy was forced to endure Marxist indoctrination. Years went past; repression increased, the boy's parents were executed, any stirrings of democracy and entrepreneurship were crushed. Islam was treated as a vulgar superstition. At sixteen, the boy fled town K and joined a band of rebel fighters in the mountains. Out-numbered and out-gunned, they fought for freedom. Their struggle hung in the balance. Moscow was helping the communists – but who was helping them? In their caves in the mountains, they dreamed of a powerful land on the other side of the world. Why did America not help them? They fought with their stolen rifles for freedom, democracy, capitalism and God. Where was the USA? The story ended with young Abdullah surrounded by communists, running out of ammunition, and dying with the word 'Freedom' on his lips.

With the applause came the end of the class. They were to reconvene in a week's time and Bastian was working out the best way to bail when, a couple of days later, he was visited at home by three serious-looking men in suits and ties. They said they worked for the government, and said they'd like to have a talk. They sat down in Bastian's living room, declining coffee. They were cold and angry. Later it occurred to Bastian that they wanted to frighten him.

They introduced themselves as Jim, Steve and Don.

'Do you know what Congressional oversight is, Bastian?' asked Jim. He took a copy of Bastian's CIA contract out of his pocket and held it up in Bastian's face. 'This is your name here, and your signature, right? Have you any idea what kind of a shitstorm goes down now when it comes out that the CIA has been running a covert program without Congressional authorisation?'

'A creative writing program,' said Bastian.

'Shut up, will you?' said Jim. The conversation went on for several hours, and recurred for many hours more over the months that followed. The classes were terminated. From hints and asides Bastian deduced that Crowpucker and the other seven writers had been acting beyond their authority, competence or duties; that they were all junior intelligence analysts. They were suspended. Over time Bastian learned that he wasn't in trouble, and that the severe demeanour of his interrogators was not to render him a pliable witness but to intimidate him into signing various waivers and confidentiality clauses.

'They were afraid,' Bastian told Kellas. 'They despised Crowpucker and his friends, I think, but they were less interested in punishing them than – you know the routine. The cover-up. It was that inter-lude of administrative contrition, after Vietnam and Watergate but before Reagan. The eye of Scrutiny briefly opened. They wanted to take everything that had been talked about in the two hours of that class and bury it as if it had never happened. Including the novel.'

'They wanted to buy your book?'

'They wanted to take it. I had to make them pay for it. In the end, they did pay. They paid me a lot and I signed everything they wanted me to sign. I don't imagine they could have forced me if I'd refused. I took legal advice. I could have brushed them aside. But I took their money because I'd already lost interest in the book. I didn't believe in it. I wanted it to disappear. I wanted it to be unwritten. I wanted to take the words and turn them back into whatever they were before they were words. In that one way, Crowpucker was right. I wasn't writing to entertain. I was trying to write something to live by. I thought: should I write words to live by if I do not live that life?'

'What happened to Crowpucker and the rest?' asked Kellas.

Bastian nodded slowly. 'That was twenty-five years ago,' he said. 'They started too early and the CIA was the wrong environment for them. There was too much reality there. They're in their fifties now, in their prime. They're still around and from what I can see they're in demand. They get a lot of patronage. In the last few months I've seen their names on the Op-Ed pages all the time. Writing their stories.'

Bastian took Kellas upstairs to a bedroom in the eaves, with a shower room off it. He gave him a towel and left him. The room was warm and full of light from the risen sun. The floor and slanted ceiling were of unpainted, thickly varnished wood that creaked when Kellas walked across it. Kellas took off his shoes and clothes and removed the bandage. A thin, fragile scab had formed over the cut. He showered and dried himself. The scab held. He took a small package out of the pocket of his jacket, lay down on the sheet, pulled the quilt over his body and closed his eyes. He started to count the hours of sleep he'd had since leaving the Cunnerys' house. As soon as he began to count, he fell asleep.

11

Kellas woke up and opened his eyes. Astrid was sitting on the bed, looking at him.

'Hi,' she said.

'Hi,' said Kellas. She had more blood and rawness in her than he remembered. 'It's strange to see you again.'

'It's more strange for me,' said Astrid. 'What are you doing here?' Her voice was not as warm as Kellas wanted. She was sitting on the very edge of the bed, with her legs in jeans crossed away from him, her hands clasped on her lap, her shoulders turned slightly so that she could see his head on the pillow.

'You sent me an email,' said Kellas.

'Come. On!' said Astrid, gritting her teeth and marking each word with a hard poke of her middle finger onto Kellas's thigh under the quilt. 'You knew it was a fake. That virus sent the same email out to everyone in my address book, and they're not here. Didn't you get the message I sent telling everybody, as if it wasn't obvious?'

'I haven't checked since I got the first message,' said Kellas. He sat up and reached out his hand towards Astrid. She looked at it and kept her hands clasped together. She shook her head and bowed her shoulders. 'What did you think was going to happen?' she said. 'I didn't return your calls, your letters, your emails. Did you think "She's crazy about me, that's why she doesn't ever reply"? Was that your logic?'

Kellas began to talk about thinking things are going to happen, and how foolish it was, when Astrid interrupted. 'You can't stay.

You mustn't stay and you shouldn't be here. You were out of your mind to think I'd want you to come, whatever it says in a dumb email. Don't look at me like that. It's not fair.'

'I was out of my mind. But now I'm here.'

'Bastian said he found you in the snow in just a suit and shirt, without even a bag?' Astrid laughed. She stopped quickly, and became serious and worried, yet in the two seconds of her laughter Kellas's spirit stretched. He realised he had gone to sleep with something clenched in his fist, and he remembered what it was. He handed it to Astrid.

'Here,' he said. 'I never gave you back those batteries.'

Astrid looked down at her hand as it closed around the batteries and she said: 'Why are you doing this?'

'There are things I need to talk to you about,' said Kellas.

'There's no need here,' said Astrid, getting up. 'There's no need between us. We did what we did and we went our separate ways. Don't try to make some phoney bond because we slept together once, because you have whatever feelings you think you have for me, or because of anything else.'

'I've been thinking about what happened at Bagram.'

'You're too conceited. You want to make somebody else's tragedy your own because your own mistakes aren't grand enough to be tragedies.' She shrugged. 'Did you think we were going to have a hug and a cry about it and release our suppressed emotions? I don't do that. I don't suppress and I don't release. I do remember. If you think you helped get those men killed, well, you probably did. I probably did. I'm not going to let you use that as a reason to hang out in my house when you shouldn't be here.'

'Is it your house? Or Bastian's?'

'It's not any of your business. Those were Taliban drivers, you know.' She opened the door. 'I have to clean a deer.' She left and he heard her going downstairs.

Kellas got out of bed. One of the occupants of the house had put clean clothes on a rush-seated chair in the corner; a pair of jeans, a yellow T-shirt and a thick, roll-necked oatmeal sweater. On top of them was a clear plastic bag containing a toothbrush, toothpaste, a disposable razor and a tube of shaving cream. Kellas's own clothes lay where he'd left them, on an old chest of drawers made from slabs of pine an inch thick. Next to his clothes there was a wooden decoy, carved and painted to imitate a swimming teal. By the bed was a table with a lamp and two books. There was a picture on the wall above the bed. Kellas guessed it had been taken in the late 1960s. It was an over-exposed colour photograph in a plain black metal frame. Standing in the background, on a lawn close to a fruit tree, was a handsome woman in loose summer trousers and a short-sleeved white blouse, holding her head to one side and squinting a little into the light, smiling and sticking the end of her right hand into her pocket self-consciously, while her left hand hung awkwardly loose. She looked like Astrid; her jaw was wider. Halfway between the woman and the camera was a young girl with a pony-tail, in a mauve polyester T-shirt with a flower motif, dark slacks and bare feet. Kellas recognised the girl as Astrid. Her image was slightly blurred because she was moving. She seemed to be running towards the camera, while her arm was stretched out behind her, her hand trailing towards the woman who must be her mother. There was an ambiguity to the motion implicit in the picture. It appeared that, just before the photographer pressed the shutter, Astrid had let go her mother's hand and run towards the photographer, leaving all three of them isolated. Yet even though Astrid had run away from her mother, she had left her hand stretched out towards her, a gesture of empathy and invitation. It was as if she had been reluctant to be together with her mother at rest, yet would run with her. I shall not stand with you but I shall move with you, if you will move with me.

Kellas went to the window, which projected out from the roof. It looked down into the back garden. He could see the pale belly of a headless deer hanging from a metal frame by its two front legs. Next to the frame Astrid had set up a folding table. On it was a saw, a cleaver, a butcher's knife, a roll of kitchen paper, a small, steaming basin of water, and the deer's head on a plate. It was not a large animal. There was a larger tub on the ground underneath the carcass. Astrid, wearing a stained white apron and holding a small knife between her teeth, was fiddling with a tube in a blood-stained opening she had cut around the deer's anus. She was tying a knot in it.

Kellas quickly showered, shaved, cleaned his teeth and put on the borrowed clothes. He wore his own old socks and, after hesitating, put on the jeans over his bare skin, rinsed his underpants in the basin, wrung them out and hung them over the shower curtain rail. He went downstairs. There was a smell of frying meat and the sounds of Bastian talking to Naomi while he opened and closed doors and deployed utensils. In the hallway, between Bastian in the kitchen and Astrid in the garden, Kellas was superfluous. His only reason to be there was to disrupt something that was working beautifully. He put his head round the kitchen door. Bastian looked up from the stove and Kellas asked if he could help. Bastian said no, he was in good time for a late lunch or an early dinner.

'If you'd like to join us,' he said.

Kellas said he would like to. Bastian lifted Naomi out of her high chair, handed her to Kellas and told him to take her outside to see her mother. Kellas did as he was asked.

Astrid had cut the deer open and gutted it. The beast's innards glistened in white membranes in the bucket under the carcass. She was halfway through skinning it. Kellas watched while she broke the delicate legs of the deer like sticks, cut between skin and bone around the joints with the small knife, and tugged the hide off. Naomi uttered a syllable and Astrid looked round. She greeted Kellas and her daughter. 'Hi, honey!' she said. She looped the deerskin over the corner of the metal frame. Her hands and wrists were bloody. She came over and rubbed her nose against Naomi's, holding her arms away, then went into the house. The head of the deer had its eyes open and they had a queer brightness to them still. Its tongue hung out of the side of its mouth. Astrid had placed it facing the frame so that it appeared to be regarding its own red, flayed body. Its eyes seemed to gaze on its corpse with the same lovely stupidity it had turned to the sun falling on the melting traces of snow in the woods not long before.

Kellas heard raised voices from the house. He couldn't make out the words. He heard what sounded like Astrid interrupting Bastian. Bastian came out of the house, took Naomi from Kellas and returned inside. Astrid came back out a few minutes later and began fishing around in the bucket of guts.

'Usually I'd clean the deer out there in the woods,' she said. 'Less weight to drag back and less chance of spoiling. Happened I made the kill close to the road, though. Bastian came up and gave me a hand. I thought, I can be home in half an hour, do it there. Now I've gone and got myself all mixed up. I got blood all over the hide, should have just left it on to hang.' Astrid took two bloody dark lumps out of the bucket, trimmed them with the knife, and put them in a bowl. She moved them around with the blade, flipped them over, lifted the bowl to her nose, and sniffed.

'Is that liver?' said Kellas, going closer to look in the bowl.

'The liver, and the heart,' said Astrid. 'You check on them to see they aren't diseased. If it looks as though you've got a sick deer, you can send the organs off to the county veterinarian, and he'll give you a new tag. Which means he'll let you kill another one. They're good to eat, too.'

Kellas offered to help and Astrid shook her head. She'd clean up and hang the deer in the larder. She rinsed her hands in the warm water and dried them off. 'Naomi's beautiful, don't you think so?' she said.

'Yes, of course.'

'I love my girl very much. She's all there is now. I don't want you holding her. I don't know you well enough to let you get to know her. So don't pick her up again.'

'I won't,' said Kellas. His voice wavered and he looked down at the ground.

Astrid began taking the deer carcass down and Kellas went back to the kitchen, where Bastian had laid the table. By the time Astrid came back indoors, Bastian had put Naomi to sleep in her nursery.

'Did you feed her?' asked Astrid.

'Uh-huh,' said Bastian.

'I'll go and check on her.'

'You don't need to.'

Astrid sat down. She and Bastian talked about Naomi's next doctor's appointment and the need to get the chimney cleaned. Bastian set a jug of water on the table, served the food and placed his hands palms down on the table on either side of his plate. Astrid did likewise and Kellas followed. Bastian said: 'Adam, Astrid and I, Bastian, declare our humility and gratitude that we may eat and drink well, and in kind company, in the blind glory of the world, in the short space granted to us between the unknown before our beginnings, and the unknown beyond our ends. Please, eat.' Bastian had made venison steaks with a juniper sauce, from the last deer Astrid had killed.

'White tail, from Assateague,' said Bastian. 'You can only hunt white tail there two days a year.'

'Tastes fantastic,' said Kellas. 'I had venison in London – what is today? Tuesday? – on Sunday night. There weren't any hunters at that table, I don't believe, I imagine the meat there came from Waitrose. That's a fancy supermarket, grocery store, in England.'

'Sunday night,' said Bastian. 'So you left when?'

'Yesterday morning. A few hours after I got what I thought was the email from Astrid.' Kellas looked down at the food on his plate. The words were less sticky today. He liked Bastian and the stillness of his brooding encouraged the notion that stories told to him were stories safely kept and wisely used. It did not seem to matter what Astrid heard him say. 'It was a bad evening. I lost control.'

'Sometimes when people say that, they mean that they lost control, and sometimes they mean that they decided to switch control off,' said Bastian.

'I lost it,' said Kellas. 'I saw my closest friend cheating on his wife in front of my eyes, and her not realising. An ex-girlfriend was abusing me. One of the guests was a sociopathic, misogynist, fascist photographer. And the host was a left-wing journalist who idealises any country which opposes your country without ever putting himself and his friends through the inconvenience of living there. It was all too much together. I smashed their crockery and glassware and turned the table over and threw a bust of Lenin through their front window.'

'I always thought the best thing when you don't like somebody is to avoid their hospitality,' said Bastian.

'Wait,' said Astrid. 'You threw a bust of Lenin through this guy's front window? Then what did you do?'

'I ran away. I went to a hotel. That was where I picked up your email. Bastian's right. I wish I hadn't gone. I accepted Liam's invitation because I like his wife, because my friends were going to be there, because Liam published articles of mine and, I suppose, if it came to the barricades and hard times, we'd be on the same side. He lived in Nicaragua under the Sandinistas when Reagan was giving them gyp.'

'So he did live in one of his idealised countries,' said Bastian.

Astrid was looking at Kellas and smiling as she had when they talked on the scraggly lawn in front of the compound in Jabal os Saraj. 'You just ran away from all the mayhem you'd caused, read an email and jumped on a plane,' she said.

'The message came at a particular time. I felt free. I felt untethered,' said Kellas. It was as he'd hoped. While he told his story it was passing into history. Crazy old Kellas! Remember him? A character, a hellraiser. 'I had the offer of a big advance from a publisher for my next book and I'd just given up my job. I flew to New York first class. When I got there yesterday I found out that the publisher had been taken over and they weren't going to publish it.'

Astrid laughed. 'First class! So let me see: you've lost your friends, lost your job, you've got no money, and the love letter you were following turned out to be fake? It's all going pretty well for you right now.'

Kellas laughed with her. Her eyes were focused on him again, with the intensity that required him to return her attention and to feel desired.

'I'm sorry,' said Astrid, 'but I am going to have to take this man for a walk.'

'You had the intention of minding Naomi while I went over to the Axiters',' said Bastian.

'I've changed my intention.'

'Seemed like a good intention to me.'

'Are you counting the times I change my intention?'

'You haven't done it for a long time.'

'It's happening now.'

'I see that it is,' said Bastian. 'When will you . . . ' he stopped. 'It's your choice.' He bent his head slightly.

'When will we be back? I don't know.'

The bending of Bastian's head as Astrid asserted her wants cleaved Kellas. He had seen it before, when a man yields to a woman he loves in her going with another man. He had been both men; had never noticed the gesture in himself, but had surely made it, involuntarily, the gesture of male deferral in the herd. He was ashamed and savagely proud to be the victor. The two, shame and pride, nestled together, mirroring in adjacent chambers of his heart.

Astrid came in wearing her too-big black anorak, the coat she'd worn in Afghanistan. She held out an army surplus parka for Kellas. 'Here,' she said. 'Let's go. Bastian, see you later.'

'Take care, sweetheart,' said Bastian, raising his voice as Astrid went down the hall towards the front door. The intensity with which

Bastian pronounced the three words moved Kellas, as if they were a code that signified a book of instructions she must carry out in order to stay alive. While he put on the parka, he asked Bastian if he wanted help with the clearing up.

'No,' said Bastian. 'Just bring her back safely.'

Kellas followed Astrid out towards the road. She'd already begun walking in the direction Kellas and Bastian had driven that morning. He caught up with her and they walked without speaking for a minute. Their footfalls were softened by pine needles. It was four o'clock and the sun was already low in the west. The last traces of snow had vanished and the air was milder. It smelled of moist earth.

Kellas asked about Bastian's grace before the meal. Astrid glanced at him and smiled, then recited the same words. She explained that Bastian didn't believe in God, but believed the flaws and limits of man required him to have some way of filling the needs that religion otherwise supplied. These were hope, gratitude, humility, restraint, confession and atonement. He'd found such a way for himself, and it came out in his graces, his conversations and his counsel.

'What does he mean by "blind glory"?' asked Kellas.

'The blind glory of the world – he means that we witness how beautiful and rich the world is, we see its glory, and it's right that we should; but we have to understand that the world doesn't see any glory in us.'

'Has he written this down?'

'He wrote most of a book once, a long time ago. A novel. But there was a weird deal when he sold it—'

'He told me.'

'And now he's turned against writing down what he believes. It has to be alive, he says, and it can only be alive and true when it isn't written down, when it doesn't even exist as a set of words. He thinks that to write down a credo is when it goes wrong. It becomes fixed and dangerous. Every word is like a nail hammering a living thing to a fixed place.'

'It's a secret doctrine.'

'Not in any way. Bastian doesn't like secrets. He'll tell you what he believes. But he'll say that the describing of the belief is not the belief. He'll describe it a different way each time. Overlapping, but different. And you'll get a good idea, even though it won't be the very thing itself. He'll tell you that his ideal is for it to be impossible to distinguish what he does from what he believes.'

'You sound like his disciple.'

Astrid laughed and linked her arm in his. 'I'm not his disciple and he's not trying to make converts or recruit followers. He's a wise man trying to live out a good life.'

'Have you slept with him?'

'Yeah, a long time ago. I would have been about twenty-three, I guess, and he was in his late forties. Not since then, since those few times.'

'I'm jealous.'

'Ah, because now I'm so old!' They reached the church and Astrid led Kellas past it, across the forecourt of the Family Dollar store and onto the road leading back downtown. He could feel the warmth of Astrid's arms through the anorak. He and Astrid were almost exactly the same height, the two of them in their boots, both with long legs, and they walked easily in step.

'I remembered him from when I was little,' said Astrid. 'He was a good friend to my father. He was loyal to him, even though when I was growing up Bastian spent a lot of time travelling. He was always moving, all over the world, and reading wherever he went. There was always this conveyor of parcels of books moving, a line of parcels on their way out to him and a line of parcels on their way back. Then I was the one who travelled. I lived in New York for a while. I studied there. That's where I met Bastian again. We met for coffee and went back to my apartment. It seemed—'

'I don't want to hear any more.'

'—the right thing to do. That's it, there isn't any more.'

'You must have made a handsome couple.'

'I don't know that it's such a great idea to be jealous of people's past lives.'

'Is he still in love with you?'

Astrid didn't answer. She kicked a pine cone into the scruffy, leaf-less shrubs at the side of the road. They were passing across the marsh. The setting sun ran across the reeds and a gust of wind pushed through them like fingers through golden fur.

'I think he is,' said Kellas.

They were walking inside a solid white line that had been painted on either side of the road, giving a yard's width of walking and cycling room. Every so often an SUV or a pick-up truck would drive past. Most had tinted windows, making their occupants invisible. There were buildings ahead on the far side of the reed beds but the traffic didn't alter the impression that Astrid and Kellas were the only live humans abroad in the twilight.

'It must be hard here with one car between the two of you,' said Kellas.

'I have a push bike,' said Astrid absently. She looked at him. 'What you mean is, what do Bastian and I do for money? That's what you were asking, wasn't it? Bastian was smart and lucky. He inherited money from his parents and he got the money for his book from you-know-who, and he put it in real estate. He gets rent off a couple of properties.'

'Do you still write articles?'

'Where would I find the time? I have a daughter.'

'Bastian helps you.'

'She takes all the time I have, and I don't mind. I never wanted to have a baby but now, you know, it's so wonderful.' Astrid spoke half-absently; she was looking at something on the far side of the road. 'See that building there? It's a hotel. That two-storey wooden building at the edge of the creek. Shall we get a room?'

They crossed the road and the unpaved parking lot of a restaurant. At the back of the lot was a gap in a low wooden fence. They went through and came to the hotel, which stood under pines as tall as those around Astrid and Bastian's house. Two sheds and a Coke machine stood in front and the hotel car park was empty. A pair of black squirrels darted around the roots of one of the trees.

'Ask for a room upstairs,' said Astrid. 'Ask for an efficiency.' She walked to a set of steps that rose to the upper floor at the near end of the building, away from the main entrance.

'Where are you going?'

Astrid grinned, and put her finger to her lips. 'See you up there. Say I'm your girlfriend!'

Kellas put ninety dollars on his card for a night in an efficiency, although he didn't know what an efficiency was.

'Two of us,' he told the manager, a gaunt, trouble-girt woman with a bandaged foot. 'My girlfriend will be along later.'

'You've got the place to yourselves,' she said. 'I got duck hunters coming in tomorrow but that's it till the weekend. You need anything, I'm at home. It's the house on the far side of the parking lot. You have a good night, now.'

The hotel stood on piles sunk into the marsh. It projected out into the reeds, its lower floor a few feet above black, almost liquid mud. There was a single row of rooms on each floor, entered through sliding glass doors that looked out over the marsh. Between the doors and the drop to the mud was a terrace and a balustrade, made of the same solid, unpainted, greying lengths of wood. A T-shaped jetty ran out from the hotel to the edge of a little creek, about forty yards away. As Kellas climbed the open stairwell in the centre of the hotel, he saw a line of Canada geese swim up the creek past the jetty. The sun had gone down and a half moon was up over the road. Astrid was waiting for him in one of the heavy wooden garden chairs, sheathed in cracked paint the colour of rust, that stood outside each room. She was lying almost horizontal in the chair, with her feet up on the balustrade and the end of a draw-string from her anorak in her mouth. Her anorak was open. She was wearing jeans and a white vest and a dark blue sweater under the coat.

She slipped her feet down to the floor and twisted round. The restraints on Kellas's happiness sprang apart. Astrid leaned forward to kiss him. They kissed for a long time.

He took the room key out of his pocket. They were outside that room.

'Lucky guess,' said Astrid.

'I'll bet.' Kellas was unlocking the door and sliding it open. 'Is this where Naomi was made?'

'Maybe.'

'You know the manager here.'

'It's a small town. You know everybody and everybody knows you. She and I don't see eye to eye.'

An efficiency was a suite of three rooms, one with a cooker, a fridge, a table and a sofa, one the bathroom, the other the bedroom. There was a TV in each room. The walls were hung with prints of ducks and geese in flight, and a painting of a red-and-white striped lighthouse, executed on a piece of driftwood. Kellas took Astrid's hand and tried to tug her towards the bedroom but she flopped down at the sofa and sat there, grinning up at him. Kellas shook his head in wonder. There was a place for him on this island. Three generations in one big house. He would be the bulge in the middle, until, perhaps, the base of the pyramid broadened with additional Kellas-Astridlings. It would be tough with Bastian but he would win him over. Flatter him – or better, honour him – by accepting him as a teacher. And he would follow Astrid on the hunt.

Astrid reached into her pocket, took out a fifty-dollar bill and handed it to Kellas. He didn't understand.

'There's a gas station on Maddox,' she said. 'You go back to the road and turn left, keep going the way we were walking. You'll see it on your left. We need some booze.'

'Are you coming?'

'They're assholes in there.'

Kellas looked down at the bill. He had it stretched out like a miniature map. He was reading the number '50' over and over again.

'That'll get you five bottles of red wine,' said Astrid.

'Five?'

'We're not going to drink it all tonight!' said Astrid, reaching out her foot and kicking him lightly in the shin.

Kellas went and bought five bottles of Californian red wine. The woman behind the counter did not seem like an arsehole. She was polite and did not ask if he was having a party. He bought some bags of nachos and jars of dip and lugged the goods back to the room in two carrier bags. He wanted to drink with Astrid, but the weight of the bags and the clinking of the bottles as he climbed the stairs bent his spirit.

It was dark. A row of lamps lit the terrace, one outside each room, and Kellas could see light spilling out through the glass doors of the room they had rented. On the far side of the marsh, beyond the trees, the beam of a lighthouse swept the wainscot of the world. Astrid was sitting on the sofa where he had left her, watching the Cartoon Network and turning a chrome-plated corkscrew over in her hands. There were two plastic tumblers on the table. Astrid got up, kissed him on the mouth, stroked his side and began opening one of the bottles while Kellas took the others out of the bag and put them in a line on the table. He asked if she minded him switching off the TV and she shook her head. She handed him a full glass of wine, clicked glasses, welcomed him to Chincoteague, and took a swallow. They sat down with the bottle on the floor between their feet.

'Can I stay with you?' asked Kellas.

'How would you live?'

'I have to call my old editors. They don't take people back easily but they might take me for the war. They spent a lot of money to train me.'

'The new war.'

'Yes, the new war. What else can I do? I'm in debt, badly in debt. I'm not much of a hunter. Perhaps you'll teach me.'

'I hunt by myself.'

Kellas ran his hand over Astrid's shoulder. 'I want to see your skin again. I love your skin,' he said.

'Love!'

'That was quite a jump you made out of that helicopter, for a pregnant lady. Must have been six feet.'

'No way was it six feet! It didn't hurt. It was a ride for the kid.'

'So you left later.'

'Much later.'

'When?'

'June.'

'Naomi was born in Afghanistan?'

'Happens every day.'

'And now you're glad to see me.'

'I don't recall telling you that.' Astrid hid her grin behind her glass. She'd taken off her boots. She brought her knees up to her chest and put her feet onto the sofa in front of her.

'Do you remember that day, when you jumped out?'

'Sure. I remember us all screaming at the guy who wouldn't let our car leave the guesthouse until we'd given him ten bucks.'

'I remember you turning up at the guesthouse just when the helicopter came in to land.'

'I remember you screaming "We'll kill you!"'

'Yeah.' Kellas blushed and looked into his wine.

'I thought it was funny, you saying "We'll kill you." Not "I'll kill you." You were issuing him with a death sentence on behalf of the whole group.'

'I don't think he was worried,' said Kellas, laughing.

'No,' said Astrid. She was laughing too. 'It was that healed-up bullet wound in his cheek, from where he'd been shot right through the face and survived. That's what made me think he wasn't worried about your death threat. And then we gave him his money and got into the helicopter and you said "Next stop, the bar, Hotel Tajikistan."'

238

'Was I really screaming?' said Kellas. 'Not shouting? Was that why you left? Me having one of my fits?'

'You'll work it out,' said Astrid, draining her glass and refilling them both. 'I'd rather be judged by what I do than what I say I do.'

'I was glad to see you. I asked after you all over Kabul and Mazar-i-Sharif. Nobody knew where you were. Until I met an MSF woman at the Intercontinental who said she'd seen you in Bamiyan, I was beginning to think you were dead or gone home. You vanished after we killed those guys in the truck.'

'We didn't kill them. That's your vanity again.' The expression in Astrid's eyes was so intense, and made Kellas feel so much a part of the world, that for a moment he experienced an ecstatic sense of discovery, as if he had found that a thing he had always known of and always wanted had, in fact, belonged to him all along, and all he had lacked was the words with which to claim it. 'We didn't kill them,' said Astrid again. 'We had a hand in it, that's all, a small part. Did you write about it for your paper?'

'No.'

'Why not?'

'I was ashamed. I didn't want people to think badly of me. Besides, how could I make it true? If I'd told the whole story, it would have had no place in a newspaper. I would have had to write about why I behaved the way I did. I would've had to write that I was influenced by love.'

'Don't say that!'

'Why not?'

'I knew you were taking it too seriously. I knew you were going to try and use it as a blood bond between us.'

'How could I not take it seriously when two men burn to death in front of me?'

'I know what happened. I know I did wrong. I'm carrying it with me. But it's my burden, Adam, not *ours*. What you care about most isn't those two guys dying. What you care about is that it happened while the two of us were there after we'd spent the night together and you figure the worse that happened, the closer it made us.'

'No. It wasn't like that.'

'I know you lied to me when you said you wanted to fuck me. I know you wanted something more from me. You wanted the love-thing. Everybody wants that. Everybody thinks everybody has it, so everybody wants to have it. Reckon they're entitled. Everybody wants love so badly that whatever they get, love is what they call it. It's the new religion. Love is God.'

'You're not right about the truck,' said Kellas doggedly. 'It mattered to me.'

'What did you do about it?'

'I went looking for the families of the drivers.' He had to repeat it for Astrid, who didn't understand at first. When he said it a second time she leaned forward and kissed him on the forehead. She went to open another bottle of wine. Kellas got up and went to the bedroom with his glass. He propped up the pillows at the head of the bed and sat down with his back against them. After a moment Astrid came through with the second bottle and sat down beside him. Kellas put his arm around her and she leaned her head against him while he told her about the weeks he had spent without her in Afghanistan, after Bagram. He could see the two of them reflected in the drab green square of the switched-off TV on the chest of drawers at the end of the bed. Once, while he was talking, he saw Astrid look up at him, when she didn't realise he could see.

After a time Astrid slipped out of Kellas's arm and sat up. They had opened the third bottle of wine.

'Take off your jeans,' said Kellas.

Astrid rolled off the bed, unbuckled her belt and pulled off her jeans. Kellas took off his jeans and socks. Astrid laughed when she saw he wasn't wearing any underpants. Like in a porn film, she said, as she sat down beside him.

'I did lie to you,' said Kellas. 'I was in love with you then. I'm in love with you now. That's why I came.'

'When I met you in Afghanistan, you talked as if you didn't believe one person could ever know another,' said Astrid. 'When we were heading up to the Italian hospital, you sounded like a man denying the possibility of love. You can see why I'm surprised at you turning up out of nowhere now, saying you love me. Back then you sounded like a man who'd been hurt and disappointed, and learned something. Now you sound like a teenager. The man seemed like someone I could trust. I'm not sure about this new guy.'

'I was wrong,' said Kellas. 'I'd forgotten there were other ways to know someone apart from watching, touching and listening.'

'Sure. You can just invent them. Is that what you're doing now? Inventing me?'

'Of course not.'

'Making a nice story out of me?'

'No!'

'There's a third person here, Adam,' Astrid said. 'There's some weird amalgam of what you imagine I am and what you imagine you are lying in the bed between us, and you're too interested in that creature. We can't be that. Besides, I told you. I like to be with you, in most ways, except that way. That love-way, whatever it is.' Astrid drew up her knees and folded her arms across her chest. She pressed herself more closely against Kellas. 'My mother was obsessed with the idea that she couldn't be close enough to me, or that I should be closer to her. She wanted to be alone but she wanted to be alone with some other identity, a twin, a shadow, a reflection. A satellite. That was her idea. She told me once that her soul was too big to fit inside one person. She said she had a fat soul.'

Kellas laughed.

'Yeah, it was funny. She was funny. But she was scary, too. The thing she wanted to make us closer – sometimes it was love and sometimes it was death. A couple of times she tried to kill herself while I was there. Once she chugged down a bunch of pills when I was in the bath and she was standing by the washstand. Another time she cut her wrists in the kitchen. We were talking across the table while she was chopping carrots and she just looked at me and ran the knife over her wrist. It was heavy and sharp and the weight of it cut into her without her needing to press much. I was twelve then. I often wondered about the phrase that suicide was a cry for help. When I was a kid I used to think it meant it was a summons to children to go help their mothers kill themselves. She always wanted to involve me in her activities. A mother–daughter thing. She got confused, I think. Death or love, it was the same. They both seemed like refuges and it seemed natural to her to have me with her in them.'

'Involve you in her activities? Like death.'

'I know it sounds crazy. I didn't want to go with her!'

'No.'

'I can move towards something, but I don't want to get there. I don't want to get stuck. It feels too much like dying.'

'It's OK, Astrid.'

'But that's where I grew up, you know? A family with one member who was always just about to leave, just about to go to a place she shouldn't go, and where I shouldn't follow her. It was like living in a house with an extra door. There's the front door, and the door onto the yard, and the door to the attic, and there's the door that leads to dying. And none of the doors are ever locked.' She looked at Kellas. 'I never wanted to die, Adam. And my Dad didn't, either, he just went quietly in his sleep; and my brother, he doesn't want to die. But if you grow up in a house like that, with an extra door to dying – it's your home. That's what seems familiar.'

They lay there in silence, listening to each other's breathing.

Kellas kissed her and whispered: 'Would you believe me if I said that touching you there ever so gently, as gently as that, while I look into your eyes, made me happier than anything?'

'Maybe. Do it some more and I'll be sure.'

A small part of Kellas wondered if it would be better not to have sex with Astrid now, when they were both tipsy, in the aftersound of her memories. That, if he refrained, it might prove something. But he wanted to, and so did she, and they did. Pleasures were not excused from evolution. No human pleasure would have survived that didn't promise comfort far beyond its own consummation.

12

Behind the hangover when Kellas woke up there was a fear that for a few moments he kept at a distance, unnamed. When he opened his eyes he saw the fan hanging from the ceiling. It floated there, somewhat darker than the dark, like a giant asterisk. Kellas picked up a glass of water standing on the shelf by the bed. He drained it and felt better but his heart was still kicking against his ribs, like a man having a fit in a cell too small for him to lie down in. Astrid was not beside him. She was not in the room. He should get up and look for her, but he didn't want to. He was afraid. He heard sounds from the other side of the bedroom door. Wood scraping against wood, and a creaking. He should go and see what it was, but he didn't want to. Reluctantly he switched on the bedside light. He counted the empty bottles in the room. There were three, and another empty next door. Kellas was sure he hadn't drunk more than one and a half. Astrid's boots were still on the floor. She was close.

He was as prey as anyone to the fears that crowd in on men and women in the small hours of the morning, yet there was a sharp-edged, granite weight to the thought that was forming in his head now. The mind drew patterns from isolated circumstances, coincidences and suspicions. This pattern was heavy. It was real. He could blink and take deep breaths and make the bedside lamp come on but the fear persisted.

Astrid was an alcoholic.

Hard as he rejected it, hard as he tried to persuade himself that the darkness was to blame, the pattern insisted on its reality. That

Astrid was an alcoholic who was trying hard, for herself and because she was a mother, not to be an alcoholic any more. Who lived on an island and had, as Bastian tried to tell him, submitted herself to the rule of a warden because of her weaknesses. That was his word. An island, come to think of it, with a limited number of bars and liquor outlets, from where it would be easy to get yourself barred, across the board, voluntarily or otherwise. Assholes. An island, for that matter, with no public transport, but where Astrid didn't have a car and didn't drive. Why would she do that unless her licence had been taken away?

The recovering alcoholic's fear of the binge. Had there been binges? What a fine idea it must have seemed when Astrid missed her period after 9/11 and found she was pregnant. To cover the great story of her generation for her magazine, and at the same time to protect her unborn child from her mother's temptations, in a Muslim country, where alcohol was forbidden. A place in which, as Astrid had told him, her affliction did not flourish. She flew into Dushanbe and checked into the Hotel Tajikistan. She'd binged there. That was her state when he'd met her in Faizabad, throwing up into the gorge: hung over. Of course there was booze in Afghanistan, a hardcore drunk with dollars could easily find what they needed, but Astrid was fighting it, and the child inside her was an ally of her will. She'd left Kellas twice. What did that have to do with alcohol? Nothing, nothing at all. Except that the first time, after crossing the Anjoman pass, had been when she realised he was carrying a litre of whisky, and the second, in the helicopter, when he had said to her 'Next stop, the bar, Hotel Tajikistan.' And she had stayed in Afghanistan.

Kellas got up, put on his clothes and switched on the main light. Standing in the ordinary brightness the pattern seemed less heavy and inevitable. Ridiculous man! Astrid liked a drink. One of the reasons the alcoholic theory was absurd was that it would make him, Kellas, the enemy, a serpent. Not winning her from Bastian for himself. Stealing her from Bastian and Naomi and delivering her to the sauce. Even more topsy-turvily, the cold, hostile Astrid who had greeted him when he arrived would be the good Astrid, and the laughing, affectionate Astrid of the past few hours would be the weak, beaten, greedy one. No, that would not be reasonable. It would be the same as imagining that in all Astrid's yearning, the hunting of the deer and sexual ecstasy, the pursuit of knowledge in humankind's wild places and of the mystery in the darkness, the kernel of her desires, was a glass of diluted ethanol.

He went into the sitting room. The curtain was drawn across the glass on the terrace side. All the lights were on and the room was chilly. The fourth empty bottle was where they had left it. The fifth bottle wasn't there. The snacks he had bought sat unopened in their bright packaging on the table. It was midnight. He'd slept for many hours. He opened the door of the bathroom, afraid and hoping. Astrid wasn't there. He heard the curtain flapping and came out of the bathroom. It was the wind; the sliding door must be wide open. Kellas went over and jerked the curtain aside.

Astrid was sitting on the balustrade with her back to the marsh, her bare feet just grazing the terrace as she swayed lightly. Her head was hanging forward. He couldn't see her face, only the top of her head. Her left arm hung down limp, as if dislocated. Her right hand clutched a plastic tumbler which she had put down on the parapet of the balustrade but which had toppled onto its side. Judging by the small dark spot that had sunk into the wood at the lip of the tumbler, it had been almost empty. The fifth bottle, which was empty, stood between the chairs.

Kellas stood in the doorway, watching her. If he spoke, she might wake up suddenly and fall. He could hear the rough sound of her breathing. She listed, inhaled sharply, belched and muttered something. Kellas took two steps forward and put his hands firmly on her shoulders. Astrid's head shot up and he was looking into her face and seeing that his fear was true.

She was both alive and dead. There was a crusty tidemark of black wine remnants running across her lips and her nose and eyes were red. There was a bruise on her left cheekbone. She was awake yet operating in the secondary consciousness of someone who'd become habituated to huge infusions of alcohol. Kellas had seen them, the forms of men and women who came up to him in pubs at eight in the evening, when they had been drinking since morning. At first they seemed sober, merely grey and red and thoughtful in their speech, until he realised they were repeating the same sentences over and over, and all that was left of them was motor function and senses enough to communicate their simple needs to bar staff and cab drivers. Really they were three-quarters dead and Kellas had always been chilled by the gradual awareness that he was talking to the container of a familiar human being when the human was not present. The cold, lizardish emptiness of the eyes was not easy to forget even once the human returned and now he was looking into Astrid's eyes and they were like that. He had told the woman through these eyes that he loved her and the eyes were watching him now but the woman was not there.

Astrid tossed her head hard to the left and Kellas tried to pull her off the balustrade but she struggled and called him a fucking asshole.

'Come on, honey,' said Kellas. 'A little time vomiting under observation, and a lot of water.' He would find it hard not to remember the reptile stare and the slackness of her jaw.

'Get me off this fucking island, asshole. Where's Naomi? I love my girl. Get off me!' Astrid kicked Kellas hard in the stomach and he fell back winded. His head reminded him how much he had drunk.

'Hey, I never showed you the pictures of Naomi,' said Astrid, with sinister clarity. Kellas was taking deep breaths. Astrid dug in her jeans with her left hand and with her right hand lifted up the tumbler. She looked into it and raised it to her mouth, tipping it vertically and hanging her head back, her other hand still squirming inside her pocket. Kellas saw that she was about to lose her balance, lunged forward to stop her and almost toppled over the balustrade after she did. Astrid fell without a word or a cry and the impact of her body in the marshwater spattered Kellas's face with cold wet filth. The sound triggered an alarm of goose-honks and panicked feathers beating air.

Kellas ran to the stairs and down to the jetty. The din of geese smothered any sound Astrid might be making. Shouting her name, Kellas crouched down at the edge of the jetty, swivelled round, placed his hands flat on the decking, and with a vault as soft as he could make it jumped into the reeds.

His feet were clasped in cold black pap and he sank till the water came to just over his knees. There was no firmness underfoot, only the tightening of the yield of the lower mud to the point where he could lift the foot without the other penetrating much deeper. He realised that he should have taken off his boots. He kept shouting for Astrid as he stepped forward. He could not hear her over the noise of the geese and the splash and suck of his own progress. The lights of the hotel were screened from the marsh by the projecting terraces; they destroyed Kellas's night vision without illuminating the reeds where Astrid had fallen.

The cacophony of the geese began to diminish and in front of him Kellas heard an evil sound, as if somebody was vomiting underwater. He tried to break from wading to a canter and fell forward into the water and, a foot beneath it, the black mire. For an instant the mud's dead, passionless softness held his face in its gummy bite. He struggled to his knees and stood again and in two more steps reached Astrid. She was prone, keeping her head out of the water with her arms held stiff, like a woman doing press-ups. Her shoulders shook with the effort and her face was dark and dripping, as if she had only just managed to raise herself up out of the mud. She coughed, whimpered, her back flexed in a spasm and as she retched her elbows gave way and she went down. Kellas squatted, braced, clamped his arms around Astrid's chest under her armpits and heaved her up. He hadn't the strength or leverage to get her on her feet so he pulled back and kneeled down at the same time till the two of them were together, on their knees in the mud, the water up to their waists.

'Get your hands off me,' said Astrid.

'No,' said Kellas, hugging her more tightly. He felt her body stiffen and gag and she retched. A fluid stream of vomit splashed into the water.

'Get off! Get OFF!' shouted Astrid, her voice rising to a scream, almost a bark. She twisted in Kellas's embrace, struck him with her elbows and threw her head back, cracking him hard on the bridge of his nose. She broke free and managed to stand and began to wade in the direction of the creek. Kellas pulled off his boots and went after her. His nose warmed and filled and he felt blood oozing over his upper lip. He wiped it off with his sodden sleeve and began to shiver. The cold was testing him now. Astrid fell and got up but she had a start on him. He yelled at her to come back and she answered with a shriek in which there could have been a word, not one he recognised.

When he reached her, they fought. She struck him with her knees and elbows and the flat of her hand and he wanted to hit her back but couldn't get a good swing at her. He tried to grasp her, tie off her flying arms with his and start to drag her back to the jetty. While they fought, and Kellas rose to Astrid's level of fury, hoping it'd help him overmatch her, in the darkness, in the smell of blood and mud and vomit, and while his hysteria spiralled till the crashing of the water and the blaring goose-brass was overcome by a man and woman's screams of fucking sons of cunting whoring bitches, Kellas could see the lights of the cars passing on the road less than two hundred yards away, following their tunnels of light, which did not reach to the two fools fighting over nothing in a dark, freezing marsh.

Astrid tired first and went limp. She began to weep. Kellas held her still for a little while, then led her slowly, sobbing and shivering, to the jetty, which was close. She pulled herself up onto the decking, with his help, and sat with her legs dangling over the side. By the time Kellas was out of the water and standing over her, she had her head thrown back and was howling Mom, and that she was sorry.

'Your mom's gone,' said Kellas. 'You're mom now. Get up, you can't stay here.' But Astrid stopped crying and lay down on the jetty with her eyes closed and would not move.

It had only been a few weeks since the pre-Iraq hostile environment course and Kellas hadn't had time to forget the proper way to carry an injured comrade to safety. Of all the skills they had been taught, this had seemed the least useful. He would drag a photographer a few yards behind a wall by their collar, if it came to it. Now he was squatting and hoisting Astrid over his back and carrying her along the jetty rather than have her choke and die alone in the cold while he went for help.

He carried her through the lobby, kicking the doors open as he went, down the steps and across the parking lot, the gravel biting his bare feet. A light was on in the hotel manager's house. An old wooden toboggan hung with white ice skates was planted upright in front of the house by way of Christmas decoration. Kellas let Astrid slip off his back as far as to let the ground take some of the weight and banged on the manager's door. Astrid moaned and coughed and Kellas ran his hand over his face to clear what crusted blood and mud he could. The door opened and the manager stood in front of them unblinkingly, wearing a synthetic fleece over a pair of pyjamas.

'Astrid Walsh,' she said. 'Godammit, honey! What is it about my hotel? I thought you were a good girl now. Oh, God!' She was taking off her slippers and putting on boots. 'How much you let her drink?'

'I reckon she had three and a half bottles.'

'Of what?'

'Wine!'

'Wine ain't so bad. But you, sir, have got no reason to be proud of yourself . . . Damn right! Jesus Christ, you been in the creek? There's easier ways of catching duck than chasing them with your bare hands in the phrags after midnight. And bare feet, dear Lord. Hold on there. Don't think you're coming in.' She began going and coming back. She brought them each a blanket, and galoshes, then a large tumbler of something and a bucket.

'Make her drink this, and throw up in the bucket,' she said. 'I'm getting the car ready.' She backed her car up closer to the house and began spreading newspapers over the seats.

'You're very kind,' said Kellas. 'I'm sorry for this.'

'Any damage to the room comes off your card,' said the manager. 'For the rest, you can answer to Bastian. Oh, Astrid Walsh, I saw you with your daughter in Parks Market on Saturday and I thought, those two're going to be OK.'

'Sleep,' said Astrid. 'I want Naomi.'

'It's two of the toughest, fullest-timest jobs in the world, being a mother and being a drunk,' said the manager. 'I know plenty have tried holding the both of them down at once and it's pulling day shift and night shift, one after the other.'

Astrid mumbled a set of disconnected abusive syllables and Kellas tried to get her to drink. She gulped down a few swallows, trembled and leaned forward. Kellas got the bucket under her and vomit splashed into it with force enough to spray back over the rim.

'That's the way, honey,' said the manager. 'Come on, sir! You were enough of a gentleman to cheer her on when she was putting the drink in, you can give her a bit more of a boost when she's trying to get it out.'

'Drink some more, Astrid,' said Kellas, holding the glass up to her mouth. 'It's better to be as sick as you can.'

Astrid sipped some more of the liquid, spat it out, and looked at Kellas. A thread of saliva spooled from the corner of her mouth, which hung open. She was covered in drying mud and puke and her hair looked like a bittern's nest. Her eyes were dull and tarnished, her skin was waxy and she moved clumsily, like a puppet hanging from a single string.

'Naomi,' she whispered.

The manager was standing watching them with her hands on her hips. The doors of her car stood open.

'Are you sure that's the same girl you wanted so bad last night?' said the manager. 'Are you sure? Maybe they got switched.' She laughed. 'That's what you're thinking, ain't it? Took your pretty girl away while you were sleeping and left you with some crazy shrew lady from the swamp.'

'Give me a break,' said Kellas.

'You've had your breaks,' said the manager. 'Get in, the two of you.' She put Kellas and Astrid in the back of the car, Astrid with the bucket on her lap, Kellas instructed to keep her on target if need be. They drove off. Kellas's hangover was now in place and the smell of sick from Astrid's bucket made him fear that he might have to add to it. He looked at Astrid and looked away. He didn't see Astrid in this one. What he'd thought was her was a costume over a husk of a woman. Bastian! Sly, wanting this to happen, the self-made monk. And where had the other Astrid gone? She'd seemed so real. He remembered her so well, and yet it turned out that she did not exist. He'd been in love with her. He still was in love with her, and he could never find a woman to love in the broken sot on the seat next to him. It was hopeless. He'd never entered into Astrid and had never left himself.

'You need that bucket?' said the manager, who'd been checking him in the mirror.

'No. I'm fine.'

They arrived at the house and the manager left them standing a few yards from the door. Kellas thanked her and the manager bade them look after themselves and not to come back to her hotel and drove away. As they walked towards the door, lights came on and the door opened. Bastian had been listening out for a car. He reached into the border between the darkness and the light spilling out of the door and took Astrid from Kellas, easily and lightly, and began to lead her away. As Kellas followed inside, he heard Bastian murmur to Astrid that Naomi was sleeping and Astrid saying, with a rising, petulant note which nonetheless contained a note of submission, that she wanted to see her. Bastian looked over his shoulder and asked Kellas to shut the door.

'Don't you want to know what happened?' asked Kellas.

'If you tell me now, will it get you or Astrid cleaned up quicker?'

'Where are you taking her?'

'To get her cleaned up.'

'I'll do it.'

'You need to take care of yourself first.'

Kellas went after them. He followed them to a bathroom and watched Bastian lead Astrid in by the hand and sit her down on the closed seat of the toilet. She slumped and her head fell forward.

'How much did she have?' asked Bastian, starting to take off Astrid's clothes.

'Three and a half bottles of Merlot.'

'And you?'

'One and a half. Why didn't you tell me?'

'Why didn't I tell you what?'

'That she was an alcoholic.'

'I don't care for that word.'

'Fastidious, aren't you? If you'd told me, this wouldn't have happened.'

'You mean you would have left straight away, like you were asked to?'

'I didn't say that.' Kellas saw Astrid stripped of her underwear in front of him till she sat there, thin, white and naked in bright light, her hands clasped between her thighs, her vertebrae sticking out of her hunched spine like the buds on a twig in winter. Her filthy clothes were piled on the glossy white floor tiles. 'Should you be doing this? You're not her father. You're not her partner.'

Bastian turned on the shower. 'I offered you the choice to come or go before you crossed the causeway,' he said. 'And Astrid told you that you had to leave.' He took Astrid's wrist. The casual way that the knuckles of his big weathered old hands touched and pressed into Astrid's upper inner thighs as he pulled out her hand caused Kellas's heart to begin to thud and the anger begin to rise in him.

'I should be doing that,' he said, as Astrid stood up and tottered towards the shower, led by Bastian. Bastian was wearing a baggy old sweater over a pair of striped pyjamas.

'Go upstairs and get yourself cleaned up,' said Bastian. 'Think it over. Come on, sweetheart. Put your head under it.' The water hit Astrid's head behind the half-closed shower curtain. Bastian unhooked a bottle of shower gel from the rail and flipped it open with his thumb. Kellas couldn't see what he was doing with his other hand through the curtain. He saw a beast in the mirror and it was himself.

'Not a fucking alcoholic!' yelled Astrid through the steam and water.

'I'm coming back down,' Kellas said, and went upstairs to the room where he had slept the previous day. He took off his clothes, made a bundle of them and put them by the door. He showered and watched the dissolved swamp mud and flecks of dried blood spin into the drains. The water flowed through his matted hair for minutes before it ran clear, and he put shampoo on. His headache had settled to a clear, simple pain. He drank a glass of water and put on a black towelling dressing gown he found hanging on the back of the shower room door. He gathered up the dirty clothes, added the shirt he had left London in, and went downstairs. The bathroom where he had left Astrid and Bastian was empty, the light switched off. Kellas listened. There was no sound in the house. He went to the kitchen; it was dark. A digital clock on the stove read one-forty-five.

Still carrying the clothes, Kellas padded down the hallway in his bare feet. The bare, varnished floorboards yielded and creaked. He opened doors and felt for light switches. He found Bastian's library, a broad room on two levels, lined with bookshelves from floor to ceiling. It had a window seat and leather armchairs, with patches worn pale, by an open fireplace. A single live ember glowed in the ashes on the grate. There was no desk. A laptop lay charging on a rug. He found Astrid's study, with framed A4 photographs of refugees in Kosovo on the walls, piles of magazines and open notebooks that looked as if they were being transcribed onto the computer. In the clutter on her desk he saw the electric blue of an uncut, unpolished lump of lapis lazuli. He found the utility room and saw Astrid's clothes in a laundry basket on top of the washing machine.

He went back upstairs and found the room where Astrid and Bastian were sleeping. It was at the far end of the hallway from his room. The door was not completely shut. Kellas pushed it open and when his eyes had adjusted to the darkness he saw a double bed with two figures under a quilt. He moved closer and stopped to listen. He could hear them breathing. He couldn't tell how close they were to each other. Why did it matter? He was leaving. He would leave now, if he had shoes.

He found the switch and pressed it. Astrid whimpered, rolled over and pulled the quilt over her head. Bastian sat upright, blinking. Now that the light was on, Kellas could see that there had been space between them. Bastian was wearing his pyjamas.

'I was looking for the washing machine,' Kellas said. 'I couldn't find it.'

'It can wait until tomorrow,' said Bastian, rubbing his eyes.

'Astrid said you didn't sleep together.'

'We don't.'

'You shouldn't take advantage of her.'

'She needs to be watched.' Bastian yawned. 'There's still a lot of alcohol in her body.'

'I should be sleeping with her, and not you.'

Bastian's eyes widened a little and he looked at Kellas, awake now. 'Seems to me you wrote my friend and roommate off tonight as an alcoholic.'

'You're not denying that's what she is?'

Bastian swung his legs out of bed and went past Kellas, nodding at him to follow. Kellas went after him to the utility room and they put the dirty clothes in the washing machine and switched it on.

'I'm going back to bed,' said Bastian. 'If I were you, I'd do likewise.'

'I'm not tired. I was asleep most of the evening.'

Bastian regarded Kellas. 'I know it's tough for you,' he said. 'It's tough when someone isn't the way you imagined. It's a powerful temptation to believe that the deficiency lies in the object of your plans, and not in you.'

'You're full of wiseassness tonight.'

'Having you as a guest in this house is hard merit to acquire.' Bastian clenched his fist, held it up to his face and turned it in the light, as if appraising an antique. 'I used to use this,' he said. 'I had two of them, and I used to use them both. That's not a threat. I don't use them any more.'

'Try me.'

'No. With a man like you here, I remember what I used them for, and how I used them.' He looked at Kellas. 'I really think you should go to bed. Otherwise, sooner or later, Naomi will wake up, and I'll get up to look after her, and we'll see each other again.' Bastian turned his back and went out. Kellas put his hands in the pockets of the dressing gown and leaned his back against the machine. He was a little sleepy. His eyes hurt now as well as his head. If he went to bed, he would wake up after an hour. Locked into a cold, heavy suit of fear, the suit they fitted you with for the nights after you had lost everything, your hope of love, your hope of good work, your money and your friends. Your dignity and decency. No matter what Kellas did now, it could never be said that Kellas had been decent in the face of his host's merciless charity. Men started out looking for love, and ended up looking for dignity.

He wandered out of the utility room towards Astrid's study. He would not try to sleep, but waking was no comfort in the rural small hours. He was shaking inside, almost trembling, like in the aftermath of some angry, meaningless altercation with a stranger in the street. Like the aftermath of the Cunnerys'. He was unsure

256

what day it had been. He could make himself sure, he could work it out, but he would rather it was on no particular day. He'd been in that state, with the jitters, when he came out of there and wrote to Sophie M'Gurgan. He pressed his eyes shut and bared his teeth. He opened his eyes and began to look through old numbers of *DC Monthly* for Astrid's articles. He found several and took them to the kitchen. He sat down at the table and read through Astrid's reports from Afghanistan. There were four; each, except for the last, was some five thousand words long. One was about the women of the Panjshir valley, all they had endured and lost during the wars against the Soviets and the Taliban. Another was from inside an American unit hunting for Osama bin Laden in the southern mountains. The third was about an Afghan soldier, a Dari-speaking Tajik from the north, who had travelled to the Pashtun realm of Kandahar for the first time in his life as the Taliban retreated, and then returned to his home village, where his uncle had taken up opium cultivation.

Kellas heard Naomi crying. Bastian brought her into the kitchen and made her up some formula and fed her. Neither man spoke. Kellas read Astrid's fourth story, a short sketch at the beginning of the magazine about the experience of giving birth in an Afghan maternity hospital, where 'everything was fine, except for the swaddling' and how hard it had been afterwards to get the documents to prove that Naomi was her own, American, baby. Nothing was said but some kind of companion was implicit in the last, and perhaps the third article. There was reference to 'a friend'.

Bastian took Naomi away and returned, alone. He filled a glass from the tap and put it down at the far end of the table from where Kellas was sitting. He sat down, took a drink of water, folded his arms and looked at Kellas.

'I was reading Astrid's articles from Afghanistan,' said Kellas.

Bastian nodded. 'Uh-huh.'

'They're great. The last one, about getting Naomi home, it was pretty funny. I guess she could have written a lot more.'

'She could have. Taking Naomi out of Afghanistan was nothing compared to getting her into the country. She was launched home by the helpful side of American bureaucracy but when she landed it happened that she got caught by the suspicious side. Then social services got involved. There were calls to Nasa, blood tests, affidavits FedExed from Australia. By the time they believed it was her baby, they'd come across Astrid's other files. Two DUIs, damaging property, discharging a firearm in public.'

'Did she hurt anyone?'

'It was ten years ago. She emptied a gun into a guy's car, outside a bar, to stop him following her. There wasn't anyone in the car when she did it. He'd been hassling her all night. She never went to jail, but social services didn't like it. The righteous superstitions of the enlightened. They knew her mother. They whispered about bad blood. It was a hard summer, what with bringing back Naomi, and Jack dying. And from the day she came back from Kabul until tonight, she's stayed on the wagon.'

'You're trying to make me feel bad.'

'Do you feel bad?'

'Of course I feel bad. I know that if I hadn't come here, your commune would still be ticking along.'

'I don't like to call Astrid an alcoholic because it sounds too much like the end of the story.'

'Isn't it supposed to be the beginning of—'

'I know what AA says,' interrupted Bastian, his voice raised. 'I can't stop you calling her an alcoholic. I'm not going to tell you that I've never seen her this way. I'll tell you some more. She's never said she drinks too much. The only way she recognises what she does is how she tries to stop herself doing it. She's never gone to a meeting, stood up and said: "I am an alcoholic." If you tell her she's drunk, she'll tell you to go to hell. Three and a half bottles of wine, now, in December '02, that's a drink. Two, three years ago, it would've been her mid-morning lemonade.'

The reptile eyes. 'When you see her that way, even once . . . I know how weak it makes me sound,' said Kellas. 'But I have seen her now, and the alcoholic, it's the real her.'

'Look out of the window,' said Bastian. 'Do you think the darkness is day, pretending to be night? Is the day just darkness with light hiding it? How can you tell? Astrid was a drunk tonight, but she wasn't this morning, and she won't be tomorrow. They'll start out calling her an alcoholic, and they'll try to cure her of that. It doesn't stop there. They'll diagnose all her weaknesses, they'll put a medical term on everything that makes her human, and they won't be happy till they've cured her of the disease of being Astrid Walsh.'

Kellas nodded and looked down at the table. He bit his lip.

'I'm disappointed in you,' said Bastian. 'You have to make your own lover before you can know her. Everybody does that. What else are you going to do? But you've got to leave space for the real woman to grow inside. Otherwise you'll end up alone.'

'Like you.'

'Three people share this house.'

Kellas stood up, rinsed off his plate and glass and put them on the drying rack next to the sink. He asked Bastian for his glass and Bastian passed it to him and Kellas rinsed it.

'You're not bad-looking,' said Bastian. 'But you're not so perfect that a woman would want you just to play with.'

'What's your point?'

'It turns out Astrid's not what you wanted. What about what she wanted?'

'I'm no use to her.'

'This has happened to you before,' said Bastian. 'You're some kind of -aholic. They'd give it a name, too, and try to cure you, if they could.'

Kellas turned round and stood with his hands behind his back, leaning against the counter. 'No,' he said. 'I gave it plenty of space and time with my ex-wife, and with my Czech girlfriend, and with a woman I was – with an English girlfriend.'

'I thought there'd be more.'

Kellas laughed, sat down and ran his fingers through his hair. He sighed and held his hands out open towards Bastian. 'What do you want?' he said. 'Details of my schoolboy crush?'

'Was it a schoolboy crush?'

'No,' said Kellas, licking his lips and frowning. 'I've always thought of it as love. Something total, a real sickness, which left me changed. I never felt that way again until. Yes. But that was twenty years ago.'

'OK. You dated while you were at school, and that was the end of it.'

'No, we never went out. I was too shy to speak to her. I moped after her from a distance for a year, I worshipped her, I wrote her poems. I was amazed at the power she had over me.' She had taken hold of the world when he was there and shaken it till all its folds snapped and shone like a flag in the wind. 'But after a year I went to university and she stayed behind.'

'You never saw her again.'

Kellas found himself blinking rapidly as he faced Bastian down. 'I didn't say that. She contacted me out of the blue twelve years ago, after she saw my name over an article. We went for a drink and she came home with me. We didn't sleep together. She looked the same, and the talking was good, but she no longer had those powers to shake the world. She looked exactly the same, yet she'd become ordinary. She took a cab home. That was the end of the story.' He shrugged. 'When I say the end of the story, I mean the end of that story, the love story. I still see her, often, but I don't have those feelings for her now. She married a friend of mine, Pat M'Gurgan, the writer I talked about yesterday.'

'What's her name?'

'I don't see why it matters to you.'

'Tell me.'

'Sophie.'

'You're jealous of your friend because he married your old sweet-heart.'

'I'm jealous of my friend for finding a way to stay with a woman he doesn't love any more.'

13

Kellas got up at dawn and found clothes and shoes where Bastian had told him to forage. The shoes were Bastian's, an old pair of sneakers, a size too large, but with a pair of thick socks and the laces pulled tight, he could walk in them. He took everything out of his wallet and spread the bills out on top of the chest of drawers to dry. He wrapped himself in an oil-stained grey-and-black checked overcoat, put the mobile in his pocket, still switched off, and left the house before anyone else was up. He walked to the main road and crossed the causeway to Assateague as the clear sky gained light. The wind touching his cheek was almost warm. Kellas followed the road into the pines of the outer island, passed a set of empty tollbooths marking the edge of the wildlife refuge, and took the way signed to the beach.

He had to be the first man out. As the road curved he saw a deer up ahead, a dappled animal not three feet high. It turned its head towards him, tensed its thigh muscles, and dived off the road, its hooves clicking on the blacktop, then splashing through the pools on either side. The sun caught the white plumage of a trio of egrets loitering in the crook of a pine branch and herons had spaced themselves out along the margins of the waterland, like the weathered piles of a vanished causeway. The trees ended and the road ran straight east towards the dunes. In the open water to the south were the camouflaged cubes of hunters' hides. There was a sound in the distance like a commuter train approaching. Kellas looked to the north and saw a white cloud rising, shifting, curling and sharpening. It was thousands of white birds, flying and braying at once: snow geese. The lightening of the air was not only from the sun rising but from the flattening of the land as he approached the ocean. Here at the continent's eastern edge the light was cold and pearly, promising great wonders, in its own time, for the patient among the species. In the lee of the dunes was a visitors' centre with a tall flagpole. There was wind enough to make the Stars and Stripes twitch, rise, sag and twitch again. Kellas reached the dunes and tramped over them and down onto the beach.

It was a plain, clean beach of fine pale sand. The breakers rose waist-high, smashed and hissed, and a flock of birds with walnut-sized bodies raced in and out, as fast as spiders, to scour the raked-up sand for protein as each wave advanced and retreated. The sea roared with the same great raw throat, always drinking and never swallowing, that Kellas had grown up with. He had spent evenings on the beach closest to his home in Duncairn in the year before he left, at the time when the last light was going down yellow over the city and the first star rose over the forest further down the coast. He'd sat on the sand, digging his hands into it and feeling that he was becoming a poet and a lover, when he was neither. Like Pat M'Gurgan, Kellas believed that the light belonged to him, but Kellas had wanted to be loved for understanding it, not for sharing it.

Talking to Bastian the night before, he had still made the sixteen-year-old Sophie 'the girl', and the married Sophie, Sophie. It was easier to think of them as two people, the one he had imagined, adored and kept his distance from, and the one he knew, his clever hard-working friend, who'd never been supposed to hear him blurt that she was one of those ordinary women who got things done. It was an odd thing to have said. She was not ordinary. She was the fixed place that the ever-drowning staff of her radio station clung to amid their solipsistic woes and squabbles, she'd raised a son, made two stepdaughters think of her as their mother, and moored M'Gurgan in the semblance of a haven for the last twelve years. The word 'ordinary' was an after-echo of the word that had jumped into Kellas's head in 1990, when Sophie had sought him out and they had met for a single evening.

He'd been surprised at her courage and recklessness in contacting him after so much time had passed, when she knew nothing about him except his bad poems to her, his loitering near her house in the hope of seeing her outside school, his obscure novel and a few articles she'd read. Her claim was that it was curiosity. In the night and day before they met, at a bar in Clerkenwell, a conveyor of possibilities revolved around Kellas. That a great mercy had been shown to him, a second chance. That she would have changed out of recognition, become fat or drug-raddled. That they would make love that night. That she'd lose her nerve and not come. That he might call her and cancel. That, whether he was seventeen or twenty-six, he still desired a sixteen-year-old.

He was late. As he approached the bar, he saw her coming towards him in the distance. Nothing obvious about her had changed that he could see, her features, her expression, the way she moved. Yet when they were close, he saw that something in her, an obscure quality he had once yearned to have by him, was no longer there. They talked all evening and nothing harsh was said on either side and Kellas managed not to pronounce the word 'ordinary', but she could tell that he was disappointed, and she was hurt, and the more hurt and disappointed she was, the more affectionate she tried to be. Towards the end Kellas was trying to keep talking while he thought wild, enraged thoughts about how the Sophie who should have been there had been murdered by this Sophie. They stood at Kellas's door, and when Sophie realised that Kellas did not even want to kiss her, she said: 'Well. This hasn't worked out, has it?' And she left him there. He watched her walking away and told himself he should run after her, as if to see whether his body would act on its own; as if his legs might find the will his heart lacked. But he didn't move until she was out of sight.

On the beach, Kellas walked along the edge of the tideline, the hard-packed wet sand. There were shells, fine scallop half-lids, black ones and white ones. After walking for a mile he saw that a soldier's helmet had been washed up and partly buried in the sand.

He went closer. If it had been painted once, the paint had worn off to reveal the material underneath. It did not seem to be made of the usual synthetic composite. It was metal, like bronze, with a light reddish sheen in the brown of it. How had it floated and not sunk? It was slightly oval in shape, dented on top, as if whoever wore it had been struck a violent blow over the head. The form was a flattened hemisphere, with a raised line around the rim. It resembled the helmets Soviet troops had once worn, and which Kellas had seen Russians and Chechens wearing in Grozny. Perhaps some cohort of new American foederati had been on exercise here, Azerbaijani marines, or Ethiopian sailors.

He put the toe of Bastian's sneaker against the helmet. With the first touch he apprehended that it was not metal after all. He pressed a little harder and pushed to flip the helmet over. His guts were pinched by a spasm of fear and he took a brisk step back, baring his teeth. Occupying the helmet, and fused to it, was the remains of an arthropod, a jointed beast eight inches long, like a headless scorpion, with ten or twelve jointed legs and a demon's tail. The vision that came to Kellas's mind in the instant was of a wounded soldier's head becoming stuck to the material of his helmet with his own blood, and some battlefield scavenger creeping out and feeding off it from the inside, till the head was entirely consumed. The vision only lasted a second, but it was long enough to shake Kellas, and even after he saw what the helmet and its owner really were, the vision stayed with him.

This creature had been coming to these shores for longer than humans, and would be here when the humans were gone. Unless, that is, the evolutionary tendencies of human beings merged towards that of the horseshoe crab, and the two creatures became one. Why not? Humankind had been provided with an excellent protection for its mind in the form of a skull, yet had found the protection inadequate, and had designed extra, thicker, larger outer skulls, helmets of steel and Kevlar. In time, humanity might learn the advantage of larger helmets, covering more and more of the body and being worn continuously, until they realised in full the lesson of the horseshoe crab, that to survive for hundreds of millions of years it was better to live permanently inside a thick, all-encompassing helmet, seeing but not being seen, feeling safe.

Good for the species, if not, evidently, for all its individual members. Kellas could see now that this part of the beach had dead horseshoe crabs scattered across it, some buried in the sand, others overturned or broken into pieces. It looked like the Kuwaiti desert in 1991 after the mass surrenders of the Iraqi army, when they had dumped their helmets after their weapons were collected and they were led away. Under the gathering darkness of the day, as the oil wells burned, Kellas had picked one up as a souvenir, thinking he might drill holes in it and use it as a flower basket, knowing that this was something he would never do and that he wanted to leave it out in his flat to impress girls. He was twenty-seven. When he took it home he did leave it out, hanging it from a nail in his living room, and found that visitors treated it with revulsion, assuming he had taken it from the corpse of a dead soldier. He told them the truth, but they didn't believe him, and eventually he took it down and threw it away.

When they had driven through Saudi and Egyptian lines and through the US Marine positions and were heading towards Kuwait City, Kellas and his companions passed groups of Iraqi soldiers in green fatigues who had surrendered and whose wrists had been tightly bound behind their backs with plastic handcuffs. The Americans had ordered them to march south and they had done so, without water, not sure where they were going. Kellas and the reporter he was driving with had stopped to speak to one man who was walking by himself, handcuffed, exhausted, thin and unshaven, his head lolling at an angle as if somebody had accidentally broken it off and put it back, hoping nobody would notice. He didn't speak English. They had given him water and driven on and only afterwards did it occur to them: why had they not cut through the plastic of the cuffs and freed his hands? He was unarmed and alone and they could have given him a bottle of water to carry with him. Kellas realised that this was what the soldier had been saying, the Arabic phrase he kept repeating and which Kellas could not understand, when even the possibility of using sign language was denied: 'Free my hands.'

Kellas took the mobile phone out of his pocket, switched it on and sat down on a bleached fragment of tree trunk. He placed the phone on the sand a short distance away and waited. The phone began to chirrup with the messages he had been sent over the preceding three days. It went on for several minutes. When the phone became quiet Kellas picked it up and dialled the number of his old newspaper. He talked to different editors for half an hour, then waited for them to call him back. They couldn't give him his old job; couldn't give him any job. All they could do was offer him a short contract to cover the invasion of Iraq, which they anticipated would be in the spring. Kellas agreed, with conditions, and after balking and consulting, they accepted.

Kellas switched the phone off and put it away. He walked back. Others had begun to arrive at the beach. A woman walked a red setter and two anglers had pulled plastic handcarts close to the water's edge and were setting up rods in the sand. Kellas crossed the dunes and returned to the road. After walking a mile he saw Astrid riding towards him on her bicycle. She cycled up and stopped with one foot on the ground and one foot on the pedals. They greeted each other. Kellas took his hands out of his pockets, then put them back.

Astrid was pale and had blue patches under her eyes. Otherwise she was restored. The breeze gusted and blew her hair into her eyes and she shook it clear. She had returned from the netherworld where the souls of the dead drunk reside in the hours of their stupor. In the darkness of the marsh it had seemed certain to Kellas that the alcoholic crust of this woman was the actual Astrid, and that what he thought he loved was, like his memory of the sixteen-year-old Sophie, a spirit of his own callow summoning, never more than lightly present in Astrid. Now, in the morning, seeing her in front of him, proud and nervous, it was difficult to see her alcoholism as anything other than a recurring wound which would open and bleed unpredictably, but just as surely heal again. That the Astrid he had loved was real, yet not a fully able human; if any were fully able. Even though he had failed her terribly, a feeling of lightness came over him. The terms had changed. It was no longer a question of whether he was looking at an alcoholic disguised as Astrid, or Astrid carrying a drinker's scars. Now the question could only be who Kellas was – the Kellas who had been repelled by the drunken Astrid, or the Kellas who could barely see the marks that the drinking had made in the sober woman of Wednesday; or a Kellas who understood that both Astrid and himself were to be perceived not as the beasts and beauties of this or that moment, but as the long, twisting shapes they carved in time as they flowed through it.

'A friend of ours is driving over to Baltimore later,' said Astrid. 'He can drop you off at the airport. There's a flight to London tonight. Bastian looked it up on the Internet.'

Kellas nodded. He asked Astrid how she felt.

'Hung over.'

'Do you remember?'

Astrid looked down and fidgeted with her nails. She met Kellas's eyes for a moment and turned quickly away, looking out to the left and the right as if she were facing a panel of interrogators. She said, in a voice so quiet he could hardly hear it: 'A partridge fallen among chickens.' She stepped off the bicycle and let it crash onto the road and Kellas put his arms around her. He felt a tear fall from her face into the collar of his coat and trickle down his back. She stepped away and wiped her eyes.

'I spoke to *The Citizen*,' said Kellas. 'They're taking me back for the war.'

Astrid smiled, still a little teary-eyed. 'So now you've got a stake in it happening.'

'I guess,' said Kellas. He hadn't thought of it that way. 'It's settled, isn't it? Whatever they say.'

'It's strange how we all know that, and yet we don't do anything about it when they tell us they haven't made up their minds.' Astrid stuck her hands in her pockets, hunched her shoulders and traced an arc on the road with her foot. 'What's going to happen, do you think?'

'I've no idea,' said Kellas. 'But I'm trying not to be dependent on the outcome.' He told Astrid that *The Citizen* had agreed to send him on an intensive Arabic course when he got back to London. He'd take a house in Baghdad after the invasion, once things had quietened down. Somewhere close to the river. He would live as an exile, not trying to be Iraqi, not trying to live uncomfortably, far from it. He would be Adam Kellas there. He would deepen his knowledge of the language and the arts and recipes of the place. At first he'd make a living by writing a weekly column, then, after a year, when British readers had lost interest in Iraq, he'd write a book and try to find work in Baghdad University as a teacher. Perhaps they would be able to make use of him. He would get up early, sleep in the afternoon and listen to the stories of old men in coffee shops in the evening. Where an entire quarter of middle-class Scottish atheists might cause offence, a single one resident in their midst would give him the shield of eccentricity. Maybe he'd get to be a messenger – no more, not an advocate, not an emissary or inter-mediary, only a messenger – between the world he was born into and the world where he lived.

'What are you going to do for women?' asked Astrid.

'I'll get by.'

'Your plan stinks. You can say it but you won't get to live it.'

'You don't understand,' said Kellas patiently. 'I'm getting away from that, from the misimagining. I'm going to get away from the idealising and the demonising. I'm not going to live like them and

I'm not going to change. I'm going to be there as the man that I am.'

'Your not-idealising's just another kind of idealising,' said Astrid. 'You think you're getting past the fantasies of our crusaders and the apocalypses of our doom-mongers, that you've got real. Well, I'll tell you this for free, if you reckon we've misimagined Iraq, it's nothing to how Iraq misimagines us.'

'But that's exactly why I'm going to live in Baghdad. After the invasion.'

Astrid shook her head. She glanced at Kellas from under her fringe, drew in breath and opened her mouth to speak, then changed her mind. With her mouth still held slightly open, she turned sunwards to consider, and the light lit up her face.

'Where are you starting from?' she asked.

'Kuwait.'

'Hm.'

'They're pretty strict about booze there.'

'Uh-huh.'

'We're not friends, are we?' said Kellas.

'Never had a friend like you, anyway.'

'Or lovers.'

'Not as would come out ahead in a crash test.'

'We're not looking for each other. I was looking for you but unfortunately I found you.'

'I wasn't asking to be found.'

'So I guess we're over.'

'Paths cross,' said Astrid.

'Leaving it to chance.'

'Yeah. But it could happen that I bend my path a little.'

Kellas raised his eyebrows. 'What about Naomi?' he said.

'It would have been worse for me if my mother hadn't been around when I was a kid,' said Astrid. 'But I might have been better off if she'd spent more time away. The sadness built up in her when she stayed in one place. I could feel it building up in her and her wanting everyone around her to share the load.'

'And Bastian?'

'He knows better than to think he can hold me close by being good to me. He knows I'll come back.'

A passing car heading for the beach hooted at Astrid and she waved. 'Come on, we should go back to the house,' she said. 'Mount up.'

The two of them managed to perch on the saddle. Astrid pedalled and Kellas held on as best he could. It was uncomfortable and they wobbled fiercely as they traversed a cycle path that led through the woods back to the causeway. Several times Kellas yelled out as Astrid almost lost control and he felt himself slipping. By the time they reached the causeway, it was easier, and as they coasted down off the causeway's camber, Astrid whooped and Kellas laughed. When they reached the flat, Astrid set to pedalling again and Kellas looked down to watch the shadow they were casting. It was a wide creature. It must have had a fat soul. But for a few seconds their shadow did look like two people merged into one, a single being racing across the reeds.

14

Kellas flew into Heathrow the next morning before first light and took the Tube to Bow. He showered, put on clean clothes and made coffee. The skimmed milk he had bought on Sunday was still drinkable and the flat had not had time to acquire the odour of neglect. Just before he went out, the landline phone rang. He looked at it, hesitated, and left without answering. It was the middle of rush hour when he took the Tube west, standing with his back hard against the door and his neck bent close enough to the right cheek of an office worker to count each individual grain of powder on the small mole on her jaw. He tried to switch to the Northern Line at Moorgate but there was a suicide under a train at Angel and the system was snarled. He went up to the street. The pavements and crossings teemed with black coats and hungry strides, springing through the drizzle to the morning log-on. He bought a copy of *The Citizen* and boarded the 205 bus. He climbed to the upper deck and found a seat next to a woman hunched over a tiny book with leather covers and small print in an unfamiliar alphabet. She was moving her lips silently as she read, and rocking backwards and forwards. The windows were steamed up. Some of the passengers cleared circles in the condensation with their hands and some did not, but looked through the windows anyway, as if the diffused grey-blue light alone was narrative enough.

Kellas went through the sports pages first. He liked to read the placings in obscure sports he would never see or take part in; canoeing, shinty, women's cricket. The fact that so many people could devote so much time, effort and passion to competing according to an arbitrary set of rules gave hope to the unbelievers. Then the obituaries, the letters, the columnists and the news. Three-quarters of the US military's women met the criteria for eating disorders. Michael Caine had persuaded the producers to release the film version of *The Quiet American*, after they held back for fear it would look unpatriotic after 9/11. The White House scorned the United Nations for saying the Iraqis were cooperating with their inspectors. Several hundred British officers were going to Qatar to take part in an American wargame, but the Ministry of Defence said it had nothing to do with Iraq. Forty-seven per cent of Britons said Saddam Hussein should be removed by force, and forty-seven per cent of Britons said he shouldn't be. A Sky Movies critic was quoted as saying after a preview that the director of *The Two Towers,* the second instalment of *The Lord of the Rings*, 'captures some of the most ferocious battle scenes ever put on film and puts his camera right in among the blood and guts'.

The bus crested Angel, descended Pentonville Road and negotiated the cones and temporary concrete dividers around King's Cross. Only twenty years earlier people of Kellas's age had wondered whether, should they get as far as the twenty-first century, it would be to write by the light of rags torn from the bodies of the dead, on scavenged paper, with precious pens, leaving crumbs of their own petrifying flesh across the page to be brushed away. Instead the lights had only become brighter, and the diversions more wonderful. The invasion he'd agreed to take part in had been scripted for an audience that knew as much about orcs and Sauron as it did about Iraqis and Saddam; yet for his own country, it was more. Everywhere this morning he saw new tokens of public wealth breaking through, a new European rail terminal emerging at St Pancras, a new hospital in a skyscraper rising above Euston, the cranes circling the old Wembley Stadium in preparation for its demolition and the construction of a new one at a sumptuous price. As his train left the city, one of the new, faster trains which would replace it shimmered past, like an emissary from the year 2000, which, although it was now in the past, Kellas still nostalgically thought of as the future. An unnecessary war where the only victims were volunteers or foreigners was the last luxury of a society that could not accept it had more money than it knew how to console itself with. It was an attempt to buy seriousness with other people's blood; to taste the words of high tragedy in your mouth, and savour your own doom and hubris, yet skip aside at the last minute and let a spear-carrier take the knife your flaws had summoned for you.

Kellas was impatient for it to begin.

His train pushed north like a scraper stripping the rainclouds off the wet render of the Midlands. The low-lying fields were flooded and the bellies of the livestock were splashed with dirt. One town merged into another, pylons daintily hitched their cables up out of the mire, no green field went unlooked on by a window; it spoke of the narrowness of the island. Kellas dozed. North of Preston the land began to be yanked and folded and the hills rose over the train, yellow and bare. They passed backpackers on the platform at Oxenholme. Closer to the track were pines and gorse and stone dykes and the motorway shadowing the trains through the Pennines. At Carlisle Kellas changed to a local train in a plum-and-custard livery which hummed more quickly than he remembered or wanted through the green flatlands around the Solway Firth, crossed the border and delivered him, in the middle of the afternoon, to Dumfries.

He crossed the footbridge, came out of the station and turned left down the Lockerbie road. There was a stillness over the heavy red-stone terraces and bungalows, a blindness to their dark windows, which was, he knew, because almost all their residents were working or at school or watching afternoon TV but which he could not help sensing as a waiting for his arrival, like the stillness of the corridor and the waiting room leading to the place in which some final account would be delivered to him.

Kellas approached the scruffy hedge around the M'Gurgans' patch of front garden. He unlatched the waist-high gate of hooped iron rods. His hand was shaking. The gate opened with the rusty two-note mew he knew and he took the three paces to the door. He put his finger on the doorbell, the white plastic button in the black plastic box he was used to ringing carelessly, and looked to his right. A souvenir from a holiday long ago was sitting on the inside windowsill, between the window and the Venetian blinds: a painted red wooden fish with a hole running through the middle. For as long as he'd been coming to this house the fish had sat there, for no better reason than that nobody had felt inclined to move it. It was hard for Kellas to force himself to remember that he had already interfered with the course of the five people in this household. He had committed his deed, and whether he rang the bell or not, it couldn't be undone.

He pressed the button. He heard the inner door opening, the echo of the stiff handle in the tiled space of the porch, and then M'Gurgan was looking at him. From M'Gurgan's hesitation, the quick flick of his eyes up and down from Kellas's shoes back to his face, Kellas knew that the letter had arrived and that its contents had been discussed.

The two men stood regarding each other in silence.

'I'm sorry,' said Kellas.

'Your agent said you were in America,' said M'Gurgan.

'I got back this morning.'

M'Gurgan turned and nodded his head for Kellas to follow. His silence rang of earlier fighting. He led the way to the kitchen. Past him Kellas could make out Sophie at the kitchen table, looking to see who it was. Her eyes were red. When she saw it was Kellas she folded her arms across her chest, looking straight ahead, and tipped her chair back on two legs. On the table were two mobiles, a dozen balls of scrunched-up paper tissues and the box they came from, a neat pile of the morning papers, which had not been read, a bottle of champagne and Kellas's letter.

'We got back this morning ourselves,' said M'Gurgan.

'Lots of mail waiting for us,' said Sophie, not looking at either man. 'Mostly junk mail but not all of it.' Her voice was scratchy and it wavered.

Kellas stood in the doorway. It seemed presumptuous to sit, or to take off his coat. M'Gurgan couldn't sit down either. He stood by the sink, nervously clenching his hands and stretching his fingers, looking from Kellas to Sophie.

Kellas walked over and put his right hand on Sophie's shoulder.

'I'm sorry,' he said. 'I'm sorry for what I did on Sunday and I'm sorry I wrote that letter.'

'What use is sorry to me?' said Sophie, looking up at him, her eyes beginning to glisten. 'Tell me. I don't even know which one of you I'm supposed to be angry with.' She grabbed another tissue. 'This one for shagging around, or this one for telling me about it? For fuck's sake, get your hand off me and sit down. And take off your coat.' Kellas did as he was told. He sat with a chair between him and Sophie. She turned to look at him. 'Five hours ago I was sitting on a plane, worrying about you, wondering where you'd gone and what had happened to your mind. Why did you send me that letter? How did you think it was going to help me? How did you think it was going to help him? He's your friend, isn't he? I mean—' Sophie sniffed, wiped her eyes and nose, and curled her hand around the tissue '—I know the answers, but I want to hear what you have to say. Come on.' She smiled and the tears came again. 'Come on.'

Kellas bit his lips, considering.

'Come on.' Sophie raised her voice. 'Tell me!'

'Malice,' said Kellas. 'I was jealous of Pat and his book.'

Sophie and M'Gurgan shouted 'Oh!' and turned their heads away at the same time. Sophie said he was a terrible liar and M'Gurgan laughed exactly the laugh Kellas had heard an old Jewish man who survived an atrocity laugh when he was describing a particularly absurd passage of murder.

'I was jealous of Pat getting off with Lucy,' said Kellas.

'You're on surer ground with that but still way off,' said M'Gurgan, reaching inside the fridge and taking out a two-thirds full bottle of white wine. He set down three glasses and filled them as he talked.

Sophie watched him. 'What're you doing? He's still the honoured guest, is he?'

'Every year, Adam, you've brought some woman of all-surpassing, God-help-me gorgeousness to our door—' said M'Gurgan.

'Have I?'

'—and you see me, for one time in my life, attracting the interest of a girl—'

'You *cunt*,' said Sophie. Kellas had not heard her swear like this before.

'—I don't see it stirring the waters of your jealousy like that.' M'Gurgan began rummaging in the fridge.

'You should be a fuck of a lot angrier with him,' said Sophie. 'You're not putting out cheese?'

'What was it, then?' said Kellas, grabbing a glass of wine and taking a gulp.

'Sophie,' said M'Gurgan, nodding at his wife but continuing to look at Kellas. He sat down so as to sit opposite to, and equidistant from, both of them, and took a glass. He cut himself a piece of cheese. 'You still fancy her.' He drank and gobbled the cheese. 'You never got over it.'

'Jesus,' said Sophie, putting her hands down flat on the table and knocking her forehead on them, 'you don't—'

'Listen,' said Kellas, raising his voice to interrupt Sophie. She widened her eyes and mouth and looked at him, a sarcastic mime of surprise.

'Listen,' said Kellas again. 'I didn't come here to apologise. I am sorry, and I wish I'd never written that letter, but it's true what you say, my sorry's no use to you. I came to say, Sophie, that I've known Pat since we were boys, and I'm sure in my heart that whatever he did with that one girl that one night, the only woman he loves, and will always love, is you.' He finished, glad that he had said it without pausing or backtracking or digressing. Sophie's expression had gone from fake to real surprise. Kellas turned to M'Gurgan for the required affirmation. Bastian had shown him how it was possible to invent new para-religious rituals and the advantage was that, like real believers, unbelievers did not have to believe in the truth behind the words; they simply had to believe in the words.

M'Gurgan lifted his glass, looked into it, swirled what was left, swallowed it, put it down on the table hard and leaned back in his chair. Kellas began to sweat. Several days earlier he had expanded for M'Gurgan and Sophie the parameters for the amount of destruction one man might wreak in a domestic setting. Yet how could M'Gurgan let go the chance for exculpation Kellas had offered him? On Tuesday morning, walking through the snow towards Chincoteague, Kellas had imagined his letter destroying this family, and he had thought that, by imagining it, an incantation was cast preventing the realisation of the exact thing he had imagined.

'"Sure in your heart",' said M'Gurgan. 'Are you able to make your heart work like that? I've always found mine to be an inaccurate instrument.' He thumped his chest with his fist. 'You're lucky to have a reliable heart. It's all mine can do to keep beating. As for measuring love, I'd be better with a pair of callipers, or a ruler, or a set of scales. I'm going to need a second opinion, I'm afraid. Get me a brain scan or an x-ray, stick a colonoscope up my arse, purge me and give me a barium meal.' He poured himself more wine. 'Biopsy me. Swab me. Sample me. Transplant your heart into me and I'll give you mine. But you'll need to watch out 'cause my heart's a liar. It's a poet's heart and poets are liars. You know the Egyptians used to pray to their hearts before they died, because they didn't trust them not to lie to the gods about them. "O heart," they used to say. "Do not betray me."'

He was going to go on, but Kellas interrupted him and Sophie started to speak over him and Kellas yielded.

'I don't know how the two of you ever became friends,' she said. 'You both like the sound of your own voice too much.' She spoke to Kellas. 'You don't listen to what he says because you're too busy worrying about what you're going to say next.' To M'Gurgan: 'And you switch Adam on and have him going quietly like a radio in the background until it's time for you to talk again. I've seen it. And now I've heard you both saying the other one wants me, when the fact is neither of you does. Adam's not interested in me, Pat. He hates me for not being the sixteen-year-old girl he never had the bottle to speak to—'

'That's not true,' said Kellas.

'—and he's jealous of you because he knows all his imaginary women are going to turn into plain, ordinary women like me, and he believes you've found some poet's alchemy for loving me for ever for my beautiful inner self. That's why he wrote his nasty letter. See, he doesn't say that's not true. Well, Adam, he hasn't. You see, if he loved me,' she put one elbow on the table and leaned towards Kellas, 'he wouldn't have put his cock inside a girl not much older than his daughters while I was in the same house. Would he?'

'All this talk about love is making me nauseous,' said M'Gurgan, getting up. 'Have we got any bread?'

'There's some Ryvita in the breadbin,' said Sophie.

Kellas had an urge to leave, to run away. It was not his house. M'Gurgan put the crispbread down on the table on a plate with more cheese and started opening another bottle of wine. Sophie took a piece of Ryvita, broke it in half, broke a corner off one half and put it in her mouth.

'I wonder if she got anything out of it,' she said. 'Your cute Lucy. You're not a great lover.'

'Have I got worse?' said M'Gurgan, laughing his atrocity laugh again.

'More perfunctory, I'd say.'

'For God's sake, after twelve years, I know what your clitoris tastes like.'

'You know what bacon tastes like too and that doesn't stop you stuffing it down your fat neck.'

'I should go,' said Kellas, getting up.

M'Gurgan reached out a hand, pushed him back into his seat,

and addressed Sophie. 'Do you want me to leave you? Because I don't want to.'

'You wouldn't survive,' said Sophie. 'I remember the state you were in when I found you. There were creatures living in your bed sores.'

'You didn't answer the question.'

'I don't want you cocking around!'

'Do you want me to admire you? I admire you. Do you want me to praise you? I praise you. Do you want to travel with me? I want to travel with you. Do you want to share my bed? I want to share your bed. Do you want to share my life? I want to share your life. Does that not add up to enough for you?'

'You never put me in your book.'

'It finishes before you found me.'

'I don't want to be who you both think I am!' shouted Sophie. Her face coloured. 'How do you think it feels for a woman when a poet starts getting pragmatic with her? I don't want to be who I am. I don't want to be so real. I want to be, for one moment, the woman he imagined I was.' She stabbed her thumb in Kellas's direction.

They heard the front door opening and Angela came into the kitchen in her school uniform. Everyone stood up and Kellas had time to glimpse the anxiety on her face before Sophie squeezed her in a tight hug. After her release Angela was attentively kissed by Kellas and her father.

'Holy Moly,' said Angela. 'You'll never let me go on holiday by myself if you're all over me like that when you've only been away a few days.'

'Where's your sister?' said Sophie.

'No idea. What was all the shouting?' She was examining the faces, the glasses, the stances. The three adults sat down and said it was nothing and urged Angela to join them.

Angela's eyes narrowed. 'You two have been having a row, and he's involved somehow.' Nodding Kellas's way. 'Sitting around boozing in the middle of the afternoon and blaming each other for something.' She shook her head. 'Nobody's innocent here. You're all guilty 'cause you're old.'

Angela went upstairs. Kellas, Sophie and M'Gurgan each knew that the first impulse of necessary denial was not 'I'm not guilty' but 'I'm not old', and the consciousness of this stunned them. A sense of solidarity flew through them.

'I never said this before,' said Kellas to Sophie, 'but I always thought it was strange that you went looking for me and then for Pat in the same year.'

'Shows you which one she preferred,' muttered M'Gurgan.

'I sometimes wondered if finding him wasn't why you came to me. I gave you his address,' said Kellas. He helped himself to more wine and a biscuit and some cheese.

'If what you're saying is that I was as much an idealistic fool as you were, you're right,' said Sophie. 'You're wise now you've come back from America, are you? What was that about? The woman you met in Afghanistan?'

'Astrid.'

Sophie asked him how it had gone.

'It turned out that she had a baby. It turned out that she has a drink problem. And it turns out that I was ready to walk away from her as soon as I found out.'

M'Gurgan and Sophie laughed, then apologised, and looked contrite.

'Did you?' said Sophie.

'No,' said Kellas. 'I didn't.'

'That doesn't sound like you.'

'We're going to meet again. But it won't be for a drink.'

Fergus came in with a boy his age and size. They were carrying shopping bags. Fergus greeted his parents and said: 'Is it OK if me and Jack make dinner?'

'I don't know if you're helping me as much as you might think by de-skilling me now,' said Sophie. 'Have you got enough for everyone? There'll be . . . seven of us, I suppose.'

'Aye,' said Fergus. 'Turkey escalopes en croute with a cranberry jus.'

'Call that a meal?' said M'Gurgan. 'Hey, Jack, easy with that.' Fergus's friend had pulled an eight-inch stainless steel blade out from inside his blazer.

'It's my chef's knife,' he said. 'I got it for my birthday. It's a Sabatier.'

The three adults watched in silence while the boys tied white aprons around each other and set to work, swaggering and at ease with their tools, like young butchers.

'Take your tie off, Fergus,' said Sophie.

'I spoke to Liam yesterday,' said M'Gurgan. 'He called. He thought you might be in touch.' He glanced at Sophie and turned back to Kellas. 'You haven't spoken to him since you got back? He's going to cash that cheque. You did a lot of damage. But the thing with Tara was a false alarm. I'd say Liam's forgiven you. More than forgiven. He thinks you did a brave thing. He said to tell you that he understood what you were trying to do.'

'The fucking bastard.'

'Adam, the boys.'

'People like Liam aren't exposed to sincere passions very often,' said M'Gurgan. 'Particularly from a nice middle class fellow like yourself. He's . . . honoured. He's really happy that you've made him feel like one of the victims. He said: "At first I was angry, and then I realised my anger was the same as the anger experienced by an Afghan or an Iraqi whose house was bombed for no reason, and I understood what Adam was trying to tell me." He's going to write a piece about it.'

'What a fuck he is. Who does he think he is, understanding me? If I go back and burn his house down, kill him and rape his wife and daughter, will he understand that?'

'Adam! Stop that!'

'Yeah,' said M'Gurgan. 'About Margot. That's not such jolly news. She is not going to forgive you. She's sure about that. She doesn't want to see you again. The way she looks at it is that war never gave you a commission to act in its name in her house. She said you were a fraud.'

'She used that word?'

'She said that you had no right or cause to try to pass yourself off as one of war's destroying angels. She said it was a kind of blasphemy.'

'Did she really say that? Blasphemy?'

'She was very harsh, Adam. Do you want me to go on?' Kellas nodded. 'She said that when somebody drops a bomb, it doesn't make any difference whether they're doing it to destroy your home, or to show you what it's like to have your home destroyed. All there is is the bomb.'

'If she thinks that was destruction . . . '

'I'm only telling you what she said. She said you'd been infected. You'd caught something, maybe in the wars, maybe earlier. And whatever it is, this infection, according to Margot, the symptom is this great longing for silence. Which is strange for someone who puts words together for a living. But somehow, she said, you got infected with this loathing for dissent and persuasion. You can't bear it that people have to use these clumsy instruments to open each other up. Somewhere along the line, Margot reckons, maybe when you were writing one of your passionate despatches about how terrible it all was, you fell in love with it, the destruction, because of the silence that comes afterwards. It seemed to you that force is truth, because it's final and afterwards there's only silence.'

'You recorded Margot's speech, did you, and memorised it?'

'You didn't have to hear it.'

Kellas looked towards Sophie. The boys were making a purposeful clatter with knives and bowls and chopping boards. 'Were you there when Margot was saying this?' he asked.

Sophie leaned towards him and lowered her voice so that Fergus and Jack couldn't hear. 'I remember the first time you sent me a poem. I saw you the next day and I couldn't understand why you would write that, work so hard to write such passionate lines, and then still not speak to me. Now I understand, of course, that it wasn't about me.'

'Not right at all,' croaked Kellas. His mouth had dried out and he rinsed it with wine. They were all a little tipsy now. He noticed that Jack and Fergus had provided themselves with glasses from which they occasionally refreshed themselves as they prepared the food.

'To finish what I was saying,' said M'Gurgan, 'Margot wanted to tell you that she does have the negatives for the photographs you smashed, but the prints themselves, which you destroyed, were unique. Apparently that's the way it is in fine art photography. She made those prints herself and she can't reproduce the same conditions twice.'

'Did she mention the Sistine Chapel?'

'She compared it to something closer to home. She said to imagine if she deleted the file where you'd saved one of your books. How would you feel, she said, if she did that and then told you not to worry because you still had the story and the characters in your head, and you could just write it out again? She's bigger than I knew in that world. Those prints were worth ten thousand pounds each, and she wants you to pay her that money. A bite out of your big advance.'

Kellas grinned and shook his head. 'Something beautiful happened,' he said. 'France and America came together to save Europe and America from going to war.' He told Sophie and M'Gurgan about Karpaty Knox, and his intentions for Arabic and Iraq. He added a new embellishment that had just occurred to him. He would sell his flat in London, pay off his debts, and buy a couple of flats in Baghdad immediately after the invasion, when prices were low and foreign currency was in demand. His friends listened. As Kellas came to the end of what he had to say, he felt the pain in his belly of having done an irredeemable wrong. The thought of not being forgiven till death by a woman he liked began to ache, and it would linger.

Jack appeared at Kellas's shoulder with a plate of bruschetti, which he placed on the table with an eerie casualness, as if the M'Gurgans' kitchen was a hectic gastropub where he served dozens of such platters through crowds each night.

'Thanks,' said Kellas.

'They grow up fast,' said M'Gurgan, helping himself to a piece.

'Dad, you owe Jack twenty pounds for the groceries,' said Fergus.

'How?' said M'Gurgan sharply, getting up. 'I left you and your sisters with sixty quid.'

'Angela took twenty.'

'What for? Keep your eye on that onion while you're cutting it.'

'I don't know.'

M'Gurgan stalked off and yelling commenced on the stairs. Sophie stood up and moved to the chair next to Kellas's and put her face close to his, speaking quietly, almost in a whisper.

'Any other time I'd be concerned about you going to Iraq,' she said. 'I don't care now. I've got troubles of my own. This could be it. I could leave him. I should. I love the kids but I don't want to be kept prisoner by them. Our single friends come here and they sit in the kitchen, like you, and they watch it all as if it's a zoo. And I'm not sure which side of the bars I'm on.'

'I have too much freedom for any animal,' said Kellas. 'I hope you don't split up.'

'You have to say that, of course,' said Sophie. 'If it happens, you'll visit him, and you won't visit me.'

'It's not just about my conscience. I really do hope you stay together.'

'I don't want your hope. I need something more concrete. I don't want to sit here like some sailor's sweetheart while he's roaring around the world with a hot book and a mid-life libido. What can you tell me? Was this a one-off? Has he been shagging around for years?'

The truth was that Kellas didn't know. He suspected that M'Gurgan had been and would continue to do so. He looked Sophie in the eye. 'No,' he said. She looked away. She wanted to believe him.

'Maybe we'll talk it out,' said Sophie.

'How long would that take?'

'About forty more years, I think.'

'Is that what it is? Is it time, then?' said Kellas. A pulse of excitement beat in him. 'Is that the language I need to be learning? Not Arabic?'

'Time's hard to learn. It takes so long,' said Sophie. She smiled without rancour for the first time that evening. 'This Iraq venture of yours. It is about money, isn't it? It's not some kind of bullshit atonement exercise?'

'I hope you'll all come out to visit me in Baghdad once I'm settled there,' said Kellas. 'Maybe next autumn, when it's cooler, or the spring of '04. I might be able to get a place with a pool. I don't know if they still have houses with colonnades and courtyards. I'd like that. With a fountain in the middle. Shade is everything. Good shade, running water, and a good library. And patience. Don't look at me like that! Don't think I couldn't learn Arabic and patience together. Don't think I couldn't give Baghdad forty years.'

Sophie shook her head. 'You've never even been there. You don't know what it's like.'

'Here's the difference,' said Kellas. 'My imaginary Baghdad doesn't require anything of the Iraqis, only of me.'

'It requires that they don't kill you.'

'I should be making a move,' said Kellas. Fergus and Jack stopped chopping, glanced round, looked at each other, then resumed their work.

'Stay,' said Sophie.

'To be punished or to be forgiven?'

'For God's sake!' said Sophie, putting her hands on his shoulders and shaking him. 'Just to *be* here!'

Angela came in, followed by M'Gurgan. They were shouting at each other, and Sophie joined in. The matter was that, if it was a choice between the two, M'Gurgan would rather Angela had bought drugs than a tattoo, but a tattoo was what she'd bought; M'Gurgan's anger was intensified because the tattoo was in such an intimate place that Angela refused to show him what she'd got for his money.

Carrie put her head round the door, looked at the three people arguing and the two boys hacking away with their knives, winked at Kellas and went upstairs. Kellas smiled at her but she'd already gone. She looked like her mother. The thin black line all round her eyes and the pale lips. But then Sophie was not Carrie's mother, was she? The words flowed out of the mouths of M'Gurgan and Angela and Sophie. Tomorrow they would not remember the truth of all that spiky eloquence. They would not remember even in a couple of hours. Kellas stood up. Something would remain, a contour without meaning by itself, but it would not be by itself. A river was to be known by its course, not by tasting each drop which flowed past as you walked its banks. After checking with the boys, Kellas began with great care to lay the table for dinner.

March 2003

15

The silver Tahoe carrying Rafael, Zac and Yehia stopped up ahead. Three of the doors opened at once and the men got out and walked slowly back towards Kellas and Astrid's Mitsubishi. Rafael's eyes were narrowed against the light and his head was bent forward. He wanted to confer about where they should go next and he had many other things on his mind. He spent hours during the day and night on his Thuraya, conferring with his colleagues around the theatre and in America. He didn't sleep much.

Their two cars had stopped just short of a viaduct, which led over a wadi and, so far as they could tell, on towards Basra. The road was a straight, well-made line of tarmacadam, black against the granular weed-sown churn of the desert. There were no other vehicles on the road. There were no people or buildings and there was no wind or sound. Kellas switched off the engine and he and Astrid got out. The five of them stood close together, facing inwards, each of them turning again and again to search the horizon for any movement or smoke, except for Yehia, who searched the faces of the other four. Kellas felt the heat of the sun on his back. He'd taken off his flak. He was the only one still wearing his helmet. To the south, from where they had come, he saw two Marine gunships, far enough away that their rotors couldn't be heard and only just recognisable by their ashy outlines, scorched flakes blown out of a distant fire. After a few seconds they moved out of sight.

Yehia and Zac smoked. Rafael was afraid that Basra would fall and he would miss it. Kellas wanted to be there, too, to see the British tanks trundle squeaking down the main street, the commanders grinning under their black berets, teeth bright in sunburned faces, with the crowds ten deep and cheering, flowers bouncing off the tank armour, the girls in their spring dresses scrambling up onto the turrets to kiss the soldiers and the man in the white suit proclaiming liberty. It was easy to imagine because it was not really imagining, but remembering; and not even remembering something he had seen, but remembering newsreel clips of British tanks liberating Europe in 1944, except for the man in the white suit, who was from *Casablanca*. The girls didn't wear spring dresses here, or kiss strangers; and where would they get flowers?

Astrid had a map. She pointed to where she thought they were. Basra was only twenty miles away.

Rafael shifted his weight from foot to foot, spun the Thuraya in his hand, with its aerial up, like a baton, and invoked shit. 'I don't know. I can see this on the front page of the *Post* tomorrow,' he said. 'I need the fucking dateline.'

'This is a beautiful road,' said Kellas. 'It leads straight to Basra. There are fifty thousand British and American troops back there who want to take Basra. And yet we're the only people on this road.'

'It sounds to me like it's over,' said Zac. 'If you believe the BBC, the American armour's halfway to Baghdad already.'

'They only crossed the start line the night before last,' said Kellas.

'Let's get closer to Basra,' said Astrid. 'We'll take it carefully. Do it like this, move, stop, surveill, move.'

'Carrying two hundred litres of fuel in a sports-utility vehicle in these parts can never be careful,' said Kellas. They stopped talking, looked, listened and fidgeted.

'Hear that?' said Kellas.

'Yeah, sounds like a skylark, doesn't it?'

'We shouldn't be able to hear a sound like that in the space between two armies. It's a bad sign.'

'Ah, if the Iraqis were going to put up a fight, they'd have done it by now.'

'At this moment, they're the ones I'm less concerned about,' said Kellas. 'Didn't you notice what that Marine told us an hour ago? A bit of a problem around Zubair, he said.'

'That's Zubair.'

'He also talked about "free-fire zones".'

They all looked up. The sky was clear and silent, apart from the larksong.

'We've got the orange panels on the vehicles,' said Rafael, a little sulky now.

'What is this, the new Ghost Dance?' said Kellas, and laughed. 'Bullets bounce off?' His voice was high and he thought he sounded as if he was afraid. He was, and wished it didn't bother him that the others might think it. He asked Yehia, who shrugged. He would go where Zac and Rafael went. They were paying him and he was the only interpreter.

'Well, all those in favour of driving on,' said Rafael. Everyone except Kellas raised their hands.

'I could go with them, and you could drive back,' said Astrid to Kellas.

Kellas watched her looking at him, with the apparent indifference which, he had learned, did not mean that she did not care, rather that she gave great weight to the responsibility of others for their own fortune.

'I'd rather you stuck with me, of course,' she said.

Since she'd joined him in Kuwait a few days earlier, he had found himself starting to cherish his ignorance of her inner nature. Yet it seemed so unlikely that he had learned patience. It seemed unlikely that he had learned to apprehend time, rather than the events and words of which time was made. He believed what Astrid had told him once, that you could not change, except by becoming more like you really are. Had he learned to see people and countries in time, or had it always been in him to do so? He unclipped the helmet strap, took it off, and ran his fingers through his hair. In the past, in situations like this, he had sometimes found himself the boldest one. Those times it had been the ones with children and dear partners who'd been more cautious. This group had five children, two wives and a partner between them. Yehia alone had a wife and three children in Beirut. Their recklessness was a sign of the scale and lavish allure of this enterprise.

'Four to one,' he said. He struck his helmet with his knuckles three times and put it back on. 'It's fine. Let's go. There, we brought democracy to Iraq, and it didn't hurt at all.'

As they dispersed to their cars, Kellas called out that it was his and Astrid's turn to drive in front. Kellas drove the Mitsubishi up onto the viaduct and in the mirror he saw the Tahoe pull in behind. Astrid was looking straight ahead. She felt he was watching her and smiled at him.

'Did we bully you?' she said.

'Say something more fine,' said Kellas. 'I want to hear something that matters. I want to hear an old story. I hate the emptiness of this road. Are the hairs on the back of your neck sticking up?'

'I like it when they do that. Usually it's going into the woods at night that gives me that feeling. Do you know the story of Artemis and Actaeon?'

Astrid began to tell the story. Kellas put his hand in hers, and listened to the tale of how the goddess turned a huntsman who angered her into a stag, and how he was killed by his own dogs. After a while, in the silence of the desert, he felt his consciousness dividing; he was still Adam Kellas at the wheel of the car, watching the road ahead, and at the same time he was another, estranged version of himself, watching Kellas and Astrid as they drove. They looked peaceful and thoughtful, half-kind, half hungry, the sort of fortunate people in whom hope and defeat are still in balance – although you cannot tell, of course, in a moment's watching. Perhaps they were dreaming a little. Gradually the watcher drew back, until Kellas and Astrid could no longer be distinguished as individuals; they were two dark, generic figures in the car. The watcher continued to extend his distance. The two cars became smaller and smaller, shrinking into the landscape, and seemed to move more and more slowly, until in the black-and-white glow of his reticulated screen the watcher saw nothing but two dark spots, crawling like lice through the desert along the empty road.